Stephen Lucius Gwynn

Highways and Byways in Donegal and Antrim

Stephen Lucius Gwynn

Highways and Byways in Donegal and Antrim

ISBN/EAN: 9783744791458

Printed in Europe, USA, Canada, Australia, Japan

Cover: Foto ©Andreas Hilbeck / pixelio.de

More available books at **www.hansebooks.com**

The Church.

Highways and Byways
in Donegal and Antrim

BY
STEPHEN GWYNN
WITH ILLUSTRATIONS BY
HUGH THOMSON

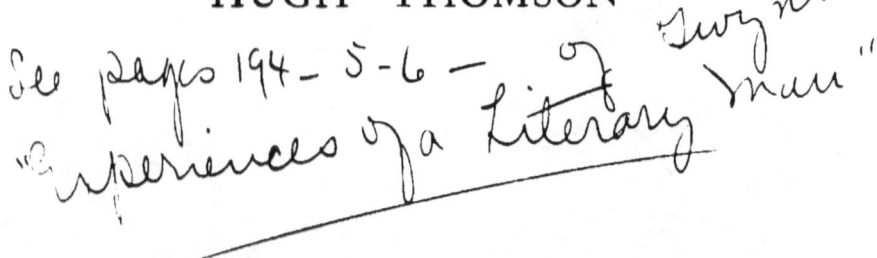

London
MACMILLAN AND CO., Limited
NEW YORK : THE MACMILLAN COMPANY
1899

PREFACE

I HAVE laid myself under so many debts in this task of compilation that it is impossible to make complete acknowledgment : yet I cannot omit some mention of Dr. MacDevitt's excellent volume *The Donegal Highlands*. For the history I have consulted chiefly the *Dictionary of National Biography*, Hill's *Macdonnells of Antrim* and of course O'Curry's edition of the *Annals of the Four Masters*. I owe a more personal debt to my friend who is known as Moira O'Neill for her permission to reprint two charming lyrics, and acknowledgments on the same account are due to the editors of the *Spectator* and *Blackwood's Magazine*. But chiefly I have to thank Mr. John Cooke, editor of Murray's *Hand-book to Ireland*, first for the assistance afforded to me by that excellent work, and secondly for his great kindness in revising the proof sheets of this book. To my many friends in the North I owe a gratitude which goes back to days long before I ever troubled them about things that I was writing ; and I entreat their indulgence for stories maimed in the telling, and for whatever else I may seem to have written amiss in these pages which treat of a country not to be separated from my remembrance of them.

STEPHEN GWYNN.

CONTENTS

LIST OF ILLUSTRATIONS

Ireland, oh, Ireland ! centre of my longings,
  Country of my fathers, home of my heart,
Overseas you call me, " *Why an exile from me?*
  Wherefore sea-severed, long leagues apart ? "

As the shining salmon, homeless in the sea-depths,
  Hears the river call him, scents out the land,
Leaps and rejoices in the meeting of the waters,
  Breasts weir and torrent, nests him in the sand ;

Lives there and loves ; yet with the year's returning,
  Rusting in his river, pines for the sea ;
Sweeps down again to the ripple of the tideway,
  Roamer of the ocean, vagabond and free.

Wanderer am I, like the salmon of thy rivers ;
  London is my ocean, murmurous and deep,
Tossing and vast ; yet through the roar of London
  Reaches me thy summons, calls me in sleep.

Pearly are the skies in the country of my fathers,
  Purple are thy mountains, home of my heart :
Mother of my yearning, love of all my longings,
  Keep me in remembrance, long leagues apart.

HIGHWAYS AND BYWAYS

DONEGAL AND ANTRIM

CHAPTER I

THE country of which I have to write is the coast and coastward parts of Ireland from Donegal Bay to Larne Harbour ;
and the line which I have to trace will take you from the
wildest corners of the west, where Irish is still the language
even of trade, business, and the schools, into the very neighbourhood of prosperous, commercial, up-to-date Belfast. Yet
even at Larne, with all its kirk-going associations and its
memories of outlawed Covenanters, you will still be conscious
of the Celtic fringe ; and even in Donegal and the Rosses you
will meet not only civility—that has never been to seek in
Ireland—but growing evidence of modern comfort and civilisation. And everywhere, whether the folk about you be Celt or
Saxon—though you will scarcely find either unmixed—always
you will be among the same brown and purple mountains,
always in sight and seldom out of hearing of the sea, always
you will be crossing swift, peaty streams and rivers, every
one of them the home of trout and salmon, and harbouring no

B 2

coarser fish : always there will be, on the one hand, the home
of snipe, grouse and woodcock, and the haunt of cormorant
and seagull on the other : in short, you will be in the ideal
country for a holiday, always somewhere between the heather
and the sea.

It is a country for the most part remote, lonely, and stormbeaten ; in many districts so wild and barren that to this day no
industry of man (even in places where the land hunger makes
the main fact of existence) has attempted to reclaim it.   But,
inhospitable though it looks, welcome is ready enough where
there are human faces ; and desolate as the place seems, it is
not so in reality.   You may stand where the road winds over
the shoulder of Errigal, and look back and forward for twenty
miles, and never see a house ; yet ten miles off, on the stony
sea coast of the Rosses, cottages cluster like the suburb of a
great town.   And stormbeaten though the land is, the fiercest
winds there blow fresh and soft from off the Atlantic : they
have no cruel edge to them.   Bleak it may seem to a stranger
—a wilderness among lands : but, wilderness or not, it is a
country much beloved, a country to which men return from
over seas gladly, and where many hearts in America, New
Zealand, and Australia still hold fast to their rocky anchorage.

For strangers, of course, it will never have this irresistible
magic : yet those who come there need not be afraid of going
home shocked and haunted by the nakedness of the land.
Donegal can never be a thriving county, but it may cease to be
clouded by the shadow of famine ; and it is in the meantime
no worthless appanage of the Empire.   While human beings in
these islands increase and multiply as they are doing, every
year will give an added value to these lonely regions which
become the breathing spaces and playgrounds of our laborious
race.   And for a playground, I do not believe, that as things
stand, there is a better to be had in Great Britain or the Continent, for the ordinary man with the ordinary purse, who seeks
his pleasure most willingly in some form of open air exertion.

A Lavery.

Till a few years ago, the country was difficult of access, and ill found with places to stay in ; but now railways bring you into the heart of it, roads are plenty, inns are always available and decent, while there is a considerable sprinkling of really good hotels.

For the other charm of travel, that depends not on the mere beauty of glen, moor, and mountain side, river, lake, and sea, but is woven from a web of clinging memories and traditions, this country cannot vie with a land like Devon and Cornwall, where every town and harbour evokes the richest historic associations. It is impossible for me not to envy Mr. Norway, of whose *Highways and Byways in Devon and Cornwall* I am a humble imitator. The birthplace of Arthur and all the other legendary sites that cluster in Cornwall awaken endless memories of beauty in every mind ; in Devon the names of Drake, Hawkins and Grenville are like trumpet-calls to the imagination. Donegal and Antrim are counties certainly not devoid of legend and history, but it is a history cherished only in the vague popular tradition of a defeated race, and a legend lore which has never been wrought into famous poetry. Patrick and Columba are great saints, yet the English-speaking world knows and cares little for them—scarcely troubles to distinguish truth from legend in their histories. The O'Neills and O'Donnells were great warriors, but even in Ireland Red Hugh and Owen Roe are ill remembered, and at best they lack the nimbus of victory. Ireland has never had her Bannockburn to reconcile her to many Flodden Fields. Yet it was in the mountains of the north that the Gael made his fiercest and longest stand against the conquerors, and the name of Tyrconnell was dreaded long after the Armada had battered its last remnants to pieces on these northward jutting shores, and to this day, in sign that the conquest was never crushing, Donegal is the only part of Ireland, they say, where those who "have the Irish" will own to their knowledge if a stranger questions them. At least there is this in my favour when I try to string together

some of the old legends, some of the old histories ; that there is
little fear in writing for English readers, or indeed for Irish either,
of appearing to recite needlessly what is already familiar.

What has to be done then is to endeavour to stimulate a
desire to go to this playground of northern Ireland and to
furnish out some sort of running comment by the way. But
the best comment really is what any civil-spoken friendly
traveller can collect for himself. This book is planned on the
assumption that the tourist wants to make a tour. For my own
part I had far sooner pitch my tent at one, two, or three of the
places by the way where one can fish, play golf, boat, or climb
mountains according to one's inclination, and above all, where
one can make friends. For there are two things in this part of
Ireland that never disappoint—the scenery and the people.

Innumerable pleasant talks, by the roadside or in the fields,
with carmen or with boatmen are among the best things to
look back on in one's memories of holiday making there.
Everywhere the people are friendly and willing to talk. But
there is one point which every Irishman writing a book for
Englishmen in his country would wish to impress, and that is
to beg that tourists will not spoil the country side by indiscrim-
inate generosity. Killarney with its swarming beggars is an
awful example. Even on the Antrim Coast small boys pursue
the car or bicycle, clamouring for pennies, and expect, on the
beaten line of travel, to be paid for telling you the way. In
Donegal happily none of these things exist. If you go into a
cottage and ask for a drink of milk, it is often hard to get payment accepted ; and to propose payment for what is freely
offered is,—just as it should be—taken for an offence. If the
tourist finds money burn in his pocket at the sight of much
poverty, he can always consult the clergy of either church at
any village and learn where help is needed, but bare feet and
even tattered clothing are no mark of destitution in many parts
where boots are chiefly worn on high days and festivals as a
somewhat cumbersome mark of respectability. Any one who

talks to the people will find them for the most part very cheer-
ful company, old and young, and for the student of queer forms
of speech their talk is delightful merely for the dialect. Everywhere in Ulster they speak a kind of lowland Scotch. I have
heard it said that in the old times when you addressed a person
in Donegal who had only the Irish he would answer you, "I have
no Scotch." But there are many curious words and turns of
phrase peculiar to them, and the Antrim talk, scholars tell one,
retains more than any dialect in the kingdom phrases that
were current in Elizabethan English but are now obsolete.
This dialect you will only meet in the more settled parts, for it
is a relic of the "plantation." In Glen Columbkill or Gweedore
the men will speak to you in a deliberate stately English almost
like the speech of foreigners ; sometimes indeed with a strong
foreign accent, the accent of the Gael; for English is to them an
acquired language, not the speech of their first years.

In addition to the national peculiarities of their speech is the
almost invariable liking of Irish peasants for a certain
picturesqueness in diction. Sometimes this results in a real
choice of the word which any artist in style would commend :
sometimes in an equally delightful perversion. "Are there any
fish in the pool to-day ? " you would say to the old Keeper on the
Lackagh river. " Fish is it ? It's fair polluted with them." The
choicest example I ever heard related to a turnip cutter which
had been working stiff and was handed over to the local
mechanic who explained his operation upon it. "You see,
your reverence, she was a wee thing proud in the pitch, but I
hae alleviated her bottom." That meant that the knife had
been cutting too perpendicularly, but he had eased the slope of
the cutter.

Another instance was the phrase used by a man relating the
outrageous conduct of a mother, who, being incensed with her
son had pursued him with a spade.

"An' it was telling the boy he got awa' : if she'd caught him
she wad hae persevered on him."

Both these, of course, are misuses of words, though the word as used bears an odd relation to the right meaning. "Persevere," for instance, is used as a kind of verb superlative. But for what may be called legitimate examples of Ulster speech, and also of Ulster ways of thought, I refer my reader to the following collection which has been jotted down for me by one long familiar with the people.

The first four belong to an Antrim man—an old ploughman and farm steward.

Speaking of a field overgrown with rushes, he said, "It'll be a quare tragedy gettin' them rushes out o' thon field."

Of barn doors gnawn away near the ground·by rats, he remarked, "Th'are quare ventilation for vermin under them doores."

His description of a paddock in early spring was, "It's just fit for an outsport for them young beasts."

In answer to the objection that it was bare of herbage, he replied, "It's not for what they wud get off it, but they'll just peruse over it" (pronounced "per*eu*se").

There is a regular idiom in this admission made by a young man about to marry : "A'm no that rough o' cash." It recurs in this sentence: "There's them that wudna' see me at a dis-short for a pound or twa." A variant on this idiom would be "wudna' see me disshorted."

A Donegal man's description of a well-to-do house, whose prosperity was in kind though not in coin, was : "They're short o' cash maybe, but there wud be aye a roughness aboot the hoose, meal and potatoes and the like."

Some of their phrases are epigrammatic in their brevity. A daughter petitioned on behalf of her father : "Wud yer honer do something for a poor ould man that can nayther work nor want" (want = do without)—and she summarised his needs, outside and inside, by saying, "He's just needin' whativer your honer's plased to give him, back or belly."

A married woman's reply when asked her name was,

"A'm Mc'Adoo by my feyther, but A'm Gallagher by my man."

Another who counted herself as we ll "fathered and hus banded" as Portia, observed, " It's the hoighth o' dacency my childer's come of on a' sides "

She was franker than an old man who declined to boast of his pedigree. " My people, it's from Strabane they come ; an' A'm not goin' for to brag till yer honer, but their cara'kter was just noble, that's what it was."

A grumbling old woman, asked whether her daughter was not attentive to her, replied, " Ay, she's kind eneuch by lumps ; she's lumpy, Sally is " (the metaphor is from carelessly made stirabout).

Harvesters from West Donegal apologised for their imperfect English by saying, "It's the Irish we speak among wursel's, but we hae eneuch Scotch to speak till yer honer."

A R. C. native of Gartan expressed "liberal spirit of church-manship" (the water in the hollow of a stone on the altar in Columbkille chapel, used with prayer, is sought as a cure for many ailments) : "There's many comes here for the watter, Scotch and Irish ; an' for a' that A see, a Scotch prayer goes as far as an Irish prayer." Here "Scotch " stands for Protestant ; " Irish " for Roman Catholic.

An old man tells how he has walked all night with his wife, to see his daughter in hospital. " My wumman an' me, we niver stretched side a' nicht, we wur thinkin' that long to see the cutty."

Vote by ballot for representatives in Parliament first came into effect at the bye-election for the City of Derry in 1872.

A few days after (November, 1872), on my way to Derry, I heard the following conversation between a Derry pig-jobber and some small farmers who were going into Derry with pigs to sell.

1st Farmer (to pig-jobber) : " Now sir, you're one that knows, an' we're just ignorant men, an' we'd like that you'd tell us

about this Derry election that they're talkin' aboot, for we
dinna richtly understand this ballot."

P.-J.: "Oh, I'll tell you all about it. You just go in, and
they hand you a paper with the candidates' names, and you go
into a booth and make your mark against the one you vote for,
and that's the whole of it."

2nd Farmer: "Well now, A wud just like you'd tell me if
this is the way o' it. A have a vote maybe, and we'll say this
gentleman" (pointing to man on right) "axes me for it, an'
maybe A promise it till him. An' then *that* gentleman, we'll
say" (pointing to man on left), "he's the other candidate, and
he axes me for it, an' maybe A promise it till him too. An'
maybe A vote for the wan, or maybe A vote for the tither, or

maybe A vote for nayther o' them. An' nobody kens what way A voted."

P.-J. : "That's just it ; that's just the way it is."

(Chorus of Small Farmers, with fervour) : " Agh, that's dacency, so it is."

3rd Farmer (following up the success scored by No. 2) : " Well, now, if it wudn't be troublin' ye too much, maybe ye'd tell us this. We'll say A promised my vote till this gentleman " (to right), "an' A tuk money maybe frae him ; an' then, we'll say, A promised it to *that* gentleman " (on left), "an' A tuk money maybe from him ; an' then A gang intil the booth, an' maybe putt my **X** " (pronounce Ax) "to this man's name, or maybe A put it till that man's name, or maybe A dinna put **X** till ayther of them, an' A've tuk their money frae the baith o' them. Is that the way it is ? "

P.-J. : "Ay, that's just the way."

(Chorus as before, with redoubled fervour, rising into enthusiasm) : " Agh, that's dacency, that's just the hoight o' dacency, that's what it is."

There is a delightful idiom as well as an odd shot at a medical term in this remark made by the daughter of a sick woman to a visitor.

D. : "The ould wumman's far through ; A'm thinkin' she'll not be long troublesome to me."

V. : "And what is it that's ailin' her ? "

D. : " Just the brown cats " [*bronchitis*].

Medical details were often wonderful. An invalid goes insane ; her friends explain : " You see, yer honer, she had aye a narvish wun' that wrought her [a nervous wind that worked her] ; an' it just wrought up an' up to it got till her heed " (*gh* guttural).

There is a capital story of a parson introducing his newly married wife to a parishioner, who remarks : " Ay, A was just thinkin' that was yer missis, when A seen ye comin' up the hill hookit wi' a strange wumman."

The parishioner proceeded to criticise the lady's personal appearance. After she had gone on, the parson remained.

"Well, yer reverence, it's yersel' was aisy content wi' a wife," said the parishioner.

His Reverence : " What makes you say so ? "

Parishioner : " A'm just meanin' this : she's as or'nary luckin' a wumman as iver A set eyes on."

The same parishioner described the effect of her criticism on the parson to a third person : —

" He sat, an' he lauched, an' he better lauched, till ye cud hae tied him wi' a strae."

Sometimes dialect leads to confusion, as in this dialogue :—

Visitor : " I hear the new rector is a very clever man."

Rustic : " Cliver? not him ; he is just a small, wee man. But he's a gran' preacher." (Cliver, in Donegal, means stout and comely.)

Here is a description of a preacher's impressive manner :—

" He just pits his twa hands thegither, an' he looks over them down on the congregation as if they were the dirt under his feet."

The following Scriptural illustration of *faith* was overheard in the waiting-room of a country railway station, where sundry country folk (Presbyterians) were waiting for a train :—

1st Farmer (black coated and stiff cravated) *:* " Ou ay, man, faeth's a wunderfull thing. There's quare examples o' faeth in the Scraptures. The grandest example maybe is Jonah."

2nd Farmer : " Is it Jonah ? A don't richtly mind aboot him. Maybe ye'd just axplain till us how it was."

1st F. (didactically) *:* " Well, the way o' it was just this. Jonah was sent for to prache till the men o' Ninnyvay, an' he went aboord o' a ship, an' a storm come on them, an' the sailors they throwed him overboord : an' a big whale swallowed him down, an' he was three days an' three nichts in its bally ; an' after three days it throwed him up on the dry lan'. An' what did Jonah do ? He just went on till Ninnyvay, just the way·

he was, an' he prached till a' the great men that was in that big fine city. Think o' that; an' him that had been three days an' three nichts in the whale's bally, so yez may judge the condashion his clothes was in. Oh man, Jonah had great faeth."

2nd Farmer, and all the audience: " Ay, that was great faeth, so it was."

This is how an elderly young maiden accounted for her single state : --

" Ye see, mem, the way o' it was this. Them that wad hae me, A wadna hae ; an' them that A wad hae, wadna hae me."

I keep the prettiest for the last. A poor woman's answer to a charitable lady, who asked whether she was a widow, was—

" 'Deed, mem, A'm the worst soort o' a wudda; A'm an ould maid."

It is just as well to warn the tourist not to take quite literally all that is told him. Cardrivers particularly and people of the class that comes most into touch with the English travellers have observed that the Saxon is for the most part willing to believe anything that is told him in Ireland : the more palpably ridiculous the better ; and they get a good deal of amusement to themselves out of circulating the wildest statements.

One lady, whom a friend of mine met, began to talk to him of the north of Ireland, which she said was a delightful country in the early summer, but that it usually became insupportable to a stranger as soon as the shamrocks came into flower. This was naturally quite news to my friend and he inquired further. It appeared that she had been driving somewhere in the neighbourhood of Lifford and was struck by the universal prevalence of a most intolerable stench. After a while she made bold to mention it, but her driver promptly told her, " Sure, ma'am, that's just the shamrocks coming into flower." My friend recognised at once that this had happened when the flax was being steeped and dried on the fields, a process which used to make a good

deal of Donegal and Derry unsavoury enough, but it was no use
for him to explain ; the lady had her explanation given her on
the spot by a native and she bore a grudge against the shamrocks
that nothing could obliterate.   The flax crop is nearly a thing
of the past now, and nobody who goes to Donegal in August
will find this particular kind of shamrock fragrant on the breeze.

Another tourist was driving along Donegal Bay and from
both shores along the whole length of it columns of smoke
went up from the piles of wrack that was burning to make kelp.
He inquired naturally enough what the smoke was.   "Sure, sir,"
said the driver, "them's the stills working " "And do the police
never interfere?" asked the horrified Saxon.   "Oh ! sir," said
the driver with the utmost gravity, " it wouldn't be telling them
boys if the polis saw them."   The tourist said no more but
was eloquent when he got back to his native land on the in-
competence of a constabulary that could not see smoke that
was visible every mile or so over ten leagues of coast.

Folklore of course abounds, but it is not easy to come by :
the peasantry are shy of telling stories about the good folk and
others, because they believe themselves and see that you do
not.   The botanist will find Donegal at least, a happy hunting
ground ; the oddest things grow in the oddest places.   On the
face of Slieve League, the huge cliff that looks out straight
towards America, maidenhair fern grows freely, and in the
savage Poisoned Glen under Errigal, the wildest of all these
wild places, an enterprising land commissioner discovered the
Killarney fern, a plant so delicate that it is hard to keep even
in a specially arranged fernery.   But these are matters for
specialists whom I do not profess to enlighten or direct.

The object of study which will attract most people in
Donegal is that of social conditions.   Here you have to begin
with, in many of the wildest parts from Inishowen to the
Rosses, a population living in houses set closely together upon
a soil manifestly incapable of supporting them, yet willing to
pay exorbitant prices for the right to occupy these holdings.

For the men of the families it is merely a home, not a place of subsistence—a sort of roosting-place for the winters. In the springtime they till their tiny patches of soil, set in among rock and heather, often too small and stony for a plough to work in : when summer comes, away they go many of them to Scotland, and in the harvest time there is a general exodus to England while the women get in whatever scanty produce there may be at home. St. John's Eve is the signal for this migration : that is the day on which they like to enter on an engagement ; and about June 18th the quays in Dublin are a strange sight with these wild-looking folk crowding to their boat. It is a strange economic problem that is presented by these habitations on a land apparently unfit for anything but a sheep-run, yet where men will not be deterred from living. This has been permanently the case : but within the last twenty years has come the great change since England turned Ireland into a laboratory for political experiment, and you may study in Donegal the attempts to fix an economic rental for land that in other countries would probably find no occupants. You may see also, what is more encouraging, the results produced by many essays in paternal legislation. The "congested districts board" has been so busy in the west of Donegal that it has generated an adjective : there is a "congested" bridge over the Gweebarra river, "congested" roads carry you over much of the country, and you may meet "congested" fish being hawked all the way from the Bloody Foreland down into Cavan.

Donegal used to be expensive to travel in, except for a very strong walker, as inns are far apart and posting costs nearly a shilling a mile ; but the cycle solves that difficulty. Antrim is fully organised for tourist traffic, and a long car or van runs daily in summer from Portrush to Larne by which you may travel if you are weary of the machine. But the coast road there is so good that you will have less temptation to laziness : and in Donegal, though one would not pick it out as a cyclist's

Geese for English Markets.

C

Paradise, yet the roads along the coast are on the whole very fair and in parts excellent. Inland they vary from passable to traversable. But everywhere the country is hilly, distances are reckoned by Irish miles, and for the ordinary mortal twenty miles, especially with a knapsack, is quite enough for a day's stage, if you are to come in fit and fresh and willing to look about you at your destination. It is in short a country where bicycling is a means rather than an end in itself. For my own part I would sooner go through it on a car, taking walks wherever it suited me : but your machine will save you—if you travel alone—nearly a pound a day, which is a consideration, and will be the means of conveying you to places where some of the best links in existence are readily available to golfers, and to the only country in Great Britain, so far as my knowledge goes, where fishing worth having is to be had for the asking or even without that ceremony.

Assuming then that you want to go round the coast of Donegal and Antrim, why go from Ballyshannon to Larne rather than from Larne to Ballyshannon ? The excellent reason which I discovered by bitter experience between Gweedore and Glenties, is that six days in the week in that country the wind blows from the west and oftenest from the south-west. Therefore, for whatever distance you make your tours, go from west to east. That is the first main point, the guiding principle. As to details, my experience points to the fact that if you ride your bicycle to Euston and label it, it will arrive safely enough, but if you pack it in a case or take any trouble of that sort you will probably have to disinter the fragments. So long as a bicycle has a will of its own and can swerve and hit people in the legs, it makes itself respected : when it is reduced to the condition of helpless luggage, porters, who hate bicycles, take advantage of it. The Irish railways are very moderate in their charge for bicycle tickets and in many cases have a special arrangement of slings in the vans for carrying them, an excellent institution,

Secondly, as to your outfit. Of course you will take a Glad stone bag or portmanteau—the smaller the better—which can be sent by rail or mail car from point to point. But the facilities for doing this in the west of Donegal are not great, and it is desirable to have the means of carrying what will keep you going for three or four days. That means a knapsack as well as the bag between one's knees. I found the two no great encumbrance on a ride of over thirty miles. But I was exceedingly glad to accept a good offer, and for two days following to get them taken on by car by a traveller who had the same destination. This piece of luck would probably fall into the way of any one in the tourist season who has the taste for scraping acquaintance with fellow guests in the various stages of his travel, and even failing that, your landlord can generally find out if there is any car going in the desired direction and arrange on your behalf.

Thirdly, as to kit. If you sleep in pyjamas it simplifies matters as, in the event of coming in drenched—the case arises in Ireland—you can put them on and present, if not a decent, at least a clad appearance. I prefer to travel with a spare suit of flannels. Ladies will no doubt find instructions in one of their own journals. But both to ladies and mere men I would say, " Remember that you have a lot of walking to do." An old servant, whose sayings were treasured in the family for which he did such work as he saw fit to do, used to declare that the best way to get up a mountain was to " keep sitting down constant." My opinion is that the way to bicycle in Donegal is to keep getting off constant. Most of the hills can be ridden—unless with a headwind : but it seems to me pleasanter to walk them especially as the fatigue that comes from bicycling is the most disagreeable sort of severe fatigue which one can experience. Walking and rowing distribute the exertion over the entire body : cycling concentrates it on a few muscles and it is far easier in consequence to overdo the thing. Therefore be prepared to walk. Bring cycling shoes if you like and use them for slippers in the

evening, but have at least one pair of some good stout foot-gear
for use on a bad day or a hilly road.   Fourthly, do not cycle in
a cap, as it gets wet through and lets the rain down the back of
your neck.   A soft hat is the best thing both for fishing and
cycling.   Lastly, if you take a macintosh at all take a
strong one.   The flimsy things are no good in heavy rain and
they give the same disagreeable kind of heat as a heavy cape.
For my own part, I should always take a good long waterproof
coat for lake fishing, when it is necessary to keep dry as one is
not walking, but this is not for the bicycle. I should send it by
post or rail to whatever place I meant to fish, and on the machine get as wet as heaven chose to make me, knowing that I had
a change of clothes in my knapsack, to put on at whatever place
I happened to stay.   For the cycle a repairing outfit is of
course indispensable, though happily thorns are scarce along
the coast roads.   Rods can be carried on the machine con-
veniently enough.

Golfing gear can be sent by public conveyance everywhere
except from Port Salon to Rosapenna, and that is only a short
distance.   But for further remarks upon fishing and golfing the
reader is referred to the chapters devoted to these subjects.
As a general remark, however, this is the place to say that a
tourist who does not care to go in seriously for fishing, but is
tempted by a good-looking day to try for brown trout (which
require no license), may as a rule easily borrow a rod and net
from the hotel proprietor or gillie.   It is well to bring a fly
book along to meet such occasions : two or three sound casts
or a couple of dozen flies suffice.

CHAPTER II

YOUR best way to Donegal from London or elsewhere is to go first to Enniskillen. That is about fifteen hours from Euston. Sleep in Enniskillen—where I may as well say that I found the Royal Hotel comfortable, and the sort of place where service appears to be an inheritance and waiters—not German—grow into confidential advisers. Any time after June 1st a steamer leaves Enniskillen which will take you down the twenty-three miles of Lough Erne, threading its way through the innumerable islets. It leaves at 10 o'clock all days except Saturdays, when it starts at 12 : and it takes about 2½ hours to do the journey. I cannot speak at first hand of this trip, having reached Enniskillen just before June 1st, but to judge from the glimpses of the lough got from the train, all that is reported of its beauty may be implicitly believed. You will reach Castle Caldwell at the western end of the lake about half past twelve and a train will take you on to Ballyshannon, or if you are energetic you can send on your things and ride the six miles yourself: or again you can get out at Belleek, where the narrow winding end of the lake plunges over a fall and definitely becomes a river.

If so you should notice the pottery works, where is made the well-known Belleek ware, whose curious and admirable quality should some day find an artist to turn them to really decorative purpose. Cross the river at Belleek and follow this famous

piece of fishing water down the four miles of its course to
Ballyshannon.   There was a time when that river made
the southern boundary of Tyrconnell, and every ford between
Belleek and Assaroe has seen its battle.   But you probably do
not know exactly what Tyrconnell was, so while you are steaming
down Lough Erne it will be a good moment to take a view of
the State of Ulster as it was before the English set their
ineffaceable stamp upon it.

As you steam down Lough Erne, all the country to the right
lying northward of you is Tyrone.   Tir Eoghan—the province
of Owen—was once a great principality, which stretched its frontier from the west of Lough Erne across Lough Neagh to the
shores of the Channel by Belfast.   In the days when Ireland
had a fate of her own Tyrone was the country of the O'Neill.
Centuries after Strongbow—centuries after the Norman invaders
had become "more Irish than the Irish themselves," Tyrone
was still undisputed to chiefs of the Gael.   Then came a
period of nominal vassalage when the O'Neill was also Earl of
Tyrone, a noble created by the English crown : and, while the
Tudors ruled, the chief of Irish chieftains wavered between
his two dignities, until finally in the wavering both were lost and
the fall of Hugh O'Neill, the last and greatest Earl of Tyrone,
cleared the way for the Plantation of Ulster.   It may simplify
matters if I attempt the briefest and most summary sketch of
the history of the latest subdued among Irish provinces.

Three great clans bore rule in Ulster.   In the east were
the Macdonnells of Antrim, Lords of the Isles, with a foot on
each side of the narrow sea that we call the Moyle.   Their
sway at its height stretched from Larne to the Bann and
inwards to Antrim and Coleraine.   In the north-west was the
lordship of Tyrconnell, which answers roughly to the county
of Donegal, though many a time the O'Donnells, its rulers,
overstepped their bounds into Sligo : while on the other hand
Inishowen, the peninsula between Lough Swilly and Lough
Foyle, was disputed to them by the O'Neills.   Between the

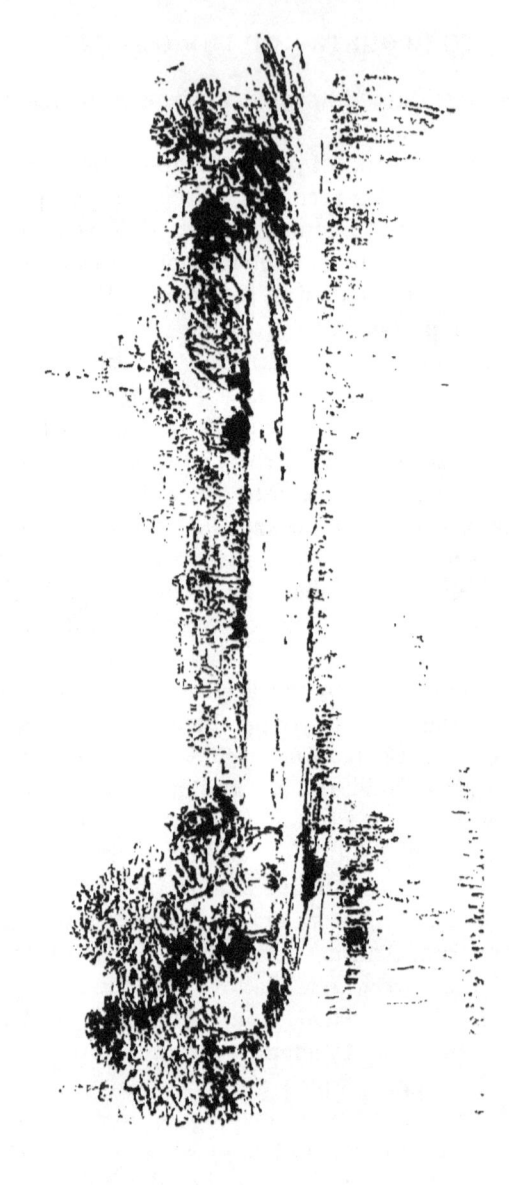

two lay Tyrone, stretching its power down to the very confines
of the English pale at Dundalk. But the divisions were there
long before England was a coherent nation. Niall of the
Nine Hostages was King of Ireland from 379 to 405, and his
eight sons cut themselves out principalities all over Ireland.
The Hy-Niall, or sons of Neill, soon divided into a northern and
southern branch; and of the four sons who came north the
two greatest were Eoghan and Conall, who because he was
fostered on Gulbane mountain—now Benbulben—was called
Conall Gulban. Conall made his home on Donegal Bay,
and Eoghan upon the Inishowen hills, and from them
descended the Kinel Conall and Kinel Eoghan, who ruled in
Tyrconnell and Tyrone. Patrick in his first missionary
journey, about 450 A.D., found and baptised Conall in his
palace on the north bank of Erne; and thence he made his
way to the Grianan of Aileach, where Eoghan held his fortress
perched on the heights that lie between Derry and Lough
Swilly. Time went on, and the descendants of Niall fought
either as foes or as allies. Together in the ninth century
they drove out the Danes who attempted landings on Lough
Foyle; but oftener the Kinel Eoghan found the Kinel Conall
driving their cattle or in their turn repelling a raid. About
950, the leaders of the two great clans adopted the practice of
calling themselves the O'Neill and the O'Donnell. This use of
surnames was soon rendered universal by a law of Brian Boru
passed in 965, that every family should take a surname from
some distinguished ancestor; and so from that day begins the
era of the Macs and Os. Sons of Donnell, sons of Niall,
sons of Brian, and the rest.

By this time Ireland was no longer only the land of the
Irish. Danes had a strong footing there, and before long
intestine sedition called in adventurers from Wales—for
Strongbow and his people were Norman-Welsh. But neither
Dane nor Norman found holding-ground in Tyrone or
Tyrconnell, nor yet on the Antrim sea-board, except in the

castle of Carrickfergus. But to the south gradually the
pale was settled and ringed about with fortresses. Tyrone's
country lying midway was wasted in return for wastings now
and then, and by the reign of Henry VII. Con Bocagh (or the
Lame) thought well to make his peace and accepted the title
of Earl of Tyrone, disowning that of the O'Neill, and recog-
nising Henry as his lord paramount. But in Tyrconnell there
was as yet no thought of submission : and the Macdonnells
made themselves strong on the eastern sea-board, bringing in
"redshanks," as the Scotch mercenaries were called. Nor did
the submission of Con Bocagh bring lasting peace to Tyrone.
Con's son Shane an Diomas—John the Proud—denied that
his father had any right to recognise a lordship over Tyrone,
for Tyrone, he said, belonged not to Con but to the Kinel
Owen, and the business of the O'Neill was to lead and rule his
nation, not to give away their birthright. So Shane led the
O'Neill faction in battle, north, south, east and west, and when
Elizabeth's deputies offered him the Earldom of Tyrone, he
declined to treat except as power with power. "Ulster is
mine," he said ; "by the sword I won it ; and by the sword I
will keep it."

But to keep Ulster, Shane had not the English only to
reckon with. That was his weakness and their strength. One
may say that Shane marked a turning point. He was a greater
man in Ulster than any that had been before him since the
English came to Ireland ; and he departed from the traditions
of the past in extending his ambitions beyond those of his
forefathers. He aimed at an Irish monarchy, and before him,
since the last Ard-Ri—King of Ireland, though only in name-
there had only been chieftains. The history of the English in
Ireland is the history of a strong, well-organised monarchy
contending with a welter of principalities. On the side of the
Irish was a country very difficult for campaigning and a nation
of excellent and numerous fighters. On the side of the English
was superior equipment, a navy, and a settled policy. The

struggle was protracted, but it could only end one way. Ireland was eaten slowly, but it was bound to be eaten so long as the sea was a wall of defence to England, but a highway of approach to any point in Ireland. Ulster was eaten last ; the toughest and the least tempting morsel. Up till the reign of Elizabeth there was no serious attempt at general conquest of it : and when the conquest was undertaken it was begun and carried out by the help of the Irish ; empire came of division. Shane O'Neill after defying the English successfully till Sir Henry Sidney said that "this man" could burn if he liked "up to the gates of Dublin and go away unfought," had enemies on each flank ; he had tried to crush the Macdonnells in Antrim and the English had applauded him for doing it : he had tried to crush the O'Donnells in Tyrconnell, and the English befriended the O'Donnells, or rather swore to befriend them. So when at last Shane the Proud was defeated with great slaughter by Hugh Roe O'Donnell at Letterkenny, he found himself ringed about with enemies and could only choose which of them he should flee to. He chose the Macdonnells, and they, partly in revenge and partly as the most assured passport to English favour, made a short end of him and left Ulster without a head.

The whole principle of succession in Ireland was that loose and ill-defined half-hereditary system which one finds every where among martial and semi-barbarous tribes. The chief was theoretically elected by the clan from the princely family : and while he lived his tanist or successor was theoretically recognised : but practically when it came to elections the strong hand decided. Hence there was never a clan but had in it some dependent prince who either was plotting his way to chieftainship and ready at all times to clear rivals from the path by any means, or else was aggrieved at having been passed over. Further, the urraghts or vassals of the ruling clan were often of doubtful loyalty. If the O'Donnell was strong in Donegal, the O'Dogherty of Inishowen was his trusty

supporter ; if the O'Donnell was weak, who so likely to lift his
cows or raid his crops as the O'Dogherty ?   The one tie which
seemed to hold in spite of everything was that of fosterage.
Every son of a chief was put out to be reared in the household of
some other chief ; thus Shane O'Neill was bred among the
O'Donnellys, Red Hugh among the MacSwineys of Doe on Sheephaven. Other O'Neills might turn upon Shane, other O'Donnells
might make war upon Red Hugh, but the O'Donnellys would
stand by Shane, and the MacSwineys by Red Hugh, while a man
of the tribe had food to eat or blood to shed.   This was an element of strength for the chieftain : but every chief's rival had fosterers too, and between loyalty to their fosterers and loyalty to the
head of their clan, they would no more hesitate than did the
McDevitts when Cahir O'Dogherty sought help from the English
against Red Hugh.   Treason to their country was an offence
they hardly conceived of ; their duty to the fosterer was plain.

Thus there was on the one side the settled inexorable policy
of the English Court pursued with men and money, by fair
means or foul : on the other side a medley of chiefs, hating the
English certainly, but often hating each other far worse.   The
real struggle came first in the days of Shane O'Neill, when
Ulster was subjugated to a single will ; and the English, as I
have said, were helpless against Shane in open battle : they could
only do their best to raise hostility against him.   The second
crisis in the days when the Earl of Tyrone, also an O'Neill
but the son of a brother whom Shane had murdered, leagued
himself with Red Hugh O'Donnell, and these two chiefs at last
held loyally together till the day of their final defeat in Kinsale.
Then, and not till then, was there a real conquest of Ulster in
the last year of Elizabeth : but that conquest would have been
impossible had not Sir Henry Docwra known how to detach
from the O'Donnells, Neil Garv, Red Hugh's cousin, a defeated
aspirant to the O'Donnellship who made himself master in
Tyrconnell while Red Hugh was risking everything on a luck-
less throw in the South.   But the history of these different

episodes I shall have to tell more in detail at the scene of some of the deciding battles.

Most of the shores of Lough Erne were under the O'Donnell influence in the great days of Tyrconnell. Enniskillen and Fermanagh were the country of the Maguire who stood loyally by Red Hugh. North by Pettigo Sir Owen O'Gallagher was lord, and he was the marshal of the O'Donnells. South-west of the Lake the MacClancy's country stretched towards Lough Melvin, on which a few Spaniards under Captain Cuellar held out in a castle after their shipwreck in a vessel of the Armada. The river Erne was the frontier of the O'Donnell's own country, and across it ran the highway from Connaught into Tyrconnell, passing through Bundoran and Ballyshannon. All the north of Donegal from the Rosses to Fanad was held by the three divisions of the MacSwineys. Inishowen was the country of the O'Dohertys, and to this day they say you cannot beat a bush in Inishowen without starting an O'Doherty.

The other highway into Tyrconnell led by Lifford across the fords of the Mourne and Finn ; thence there was a road through Barnesmore Gap to Donegal, which is now followed by a line of rail. Another led by Raphoe to the fords of the Swilly near Letterkenny. It must be remembered that bridges did not exist in this country in the days of Elizabeth ; but except for roads and bridges there is probably no great change in the face of Tyrconnell from Red Hugh's day to ours. It was not a fully civilised country in the days when it had a history ; it is not over-civilised now. Indeed in the business of looking up the local traditions, a certain malapropism has often come into my mind. A gentleman proposed to enlighten the town of Ramelton upon the history of its surroundings, and his lecture on " Irish Antiquities " was duly advertised. One day in the street an old woman who kept a stall on fair days came up to him. "So, your Reverence, you're going to give us a lecture on Irish iniquities. Faith, and there's plenty of them any way."

But it would be a great mistake to suppose that these ancient and warlike tribes were merely nations of savages like the Zulus and Afridis. They had analogies with such races in that they existed mainly for war, that they had no settled hereditary succession, and only in a limited sense any security for private property. But the O'Donnells were devout Christians, founders of monasteries, and many of their chiefs retired to make an edifying end in some of the O'Donnell foundations. They were patrons, too, of literature and learning. Not only did they, after the fashion of all Irish chiefs, maintain bards, but there flourished under their guidance a great school of historians. One of the O'Donnells was himself a writer. Manus, the father of Calvagh, a contemporary of Con Bocagh, first Earl of Tyrone, and of the great Shane O'Neill, built a fortress at Lifford, a frontier castle on the highway between Tyrone and Tyrconnell ; built it and lived in it in spite of the O'Neills and their warriors ; and it was not an easy thing to do. But it was in this "gap of danger " that he spent long years in composing the Life of Saint Columba, the great saint of Tyrconnell, by birth, like himself of the blood of Conall Gulban. Above all, however, the greatest of the Irish chronicles was composed under the auspices of the O'Donnells in their own abbey of Donegal. " The Annals of the Four Masters " is a chronicle of events in the history of Ireland, year by year from the year of the world 2242 (B.C. 1762) to A.D. 1616. Its compilation occupied the time from June 22nd 1632 to August 10th 1636.

The work has a pathetic interest, for it was written to give a full history of Erin in days when men clearly felt that the history of Erin was a closed book. Since those days a new Ireland of mixed race has arisen ; but the old Gaelic-speaking Ireland was finally crushed and subdued in the last days of Elizabeth ; the symbol of its extinction was the flight of the Earls, the inauguration of the new order was the Plantation of Ulster, the greatest and most oppressive measure of spoliation of which England has ever been guilty. There was a final spasm, a terrible death throe, in 1641, when England was

divided against itself, and here and there throughout the country
the Celts rose against the men who held lands that had been
forcibly taken from the older race a generation before ; but it
was little more than a jacquerie ; not even the genius of Owen
Roe O'Neill could weld the heterogeneous forces into a whole.
Ulster was still almost capable of united action ; but Owen's
death came before he could accomplish anything of moment,
and it left the people defenceless. The Four Masters, had
they lived a century later, would have had to add to their story
only two rebellions, the second weaker than the first ; for not
even after James II. had tried to foster that Celtic spirit which
his predecessors had so zealously beaten down, and had given
to the man charged with the task the title which of all others
seemed fittest to awaken memories—the Earldom of Tyrconnell
—not even so could Ireland with strong backing from France
make even a creditable stand against a divided England. The
war under Charles and Cromwell was made honourable by the
figure of Owen Roe, as that under James and William was by
the heroism of Sarsfield ; but the real history of Celtic Ireland
and its long resistance to England had terminated before the
Four Masters sat down to write : and the history of the New
Ireland did not begin till Swift wrote the first page of it in the
Drapier Letters.

As the *Annals* make the source from which almost all the historical information in this book is derived, it may be as well to give
some account here of the work and its writers. It was compiled
by four scholars, of whom three were O'Clerys and belonged to
a family in which historical scholarship was a hereditary profession. The fourth, Ferfeasa O'Mulconry, was a Connaught
man, also an " ollave " or accredited student. The book was
written at the request of Fergal O'Gara, Lord of Coolavin in
Sligo ; the O'Donnells would have been the natural patrons of
such a work done in the Abbey of their foundation, but by 1630
there was no representation of the O'Donnells in Tyrconnel.
The Four Masters set about their task with a full sense of its

importance ; they collected all available annals, they put at the forefront of their book a list of the works to which they had access, and the text was verified and countersigned by the Abbot of the monastery. The narrative varies in character greatly according to the source from which it is taken : but speaking generally, the first part up to 1208 A.D. is a bald statement of facts—or what they took for facts—with their dates assigned : from that onwards there is a good deal of vivid detail, and in many cases, especially in the narratives of battles, one finds the curious inflated style of bardic literature with its reduplications of phrase, which I need not here illustrate, as numerous quotations from passages of this kind have to be given later on.

The chief of the four was Teague na-tsliebhe O'Clery (Teague O'Clery of the Mountain), and it is worth while to give a few details about him, for the reader of Irish history is apt to overlook the fact that there were other people besides warriors in Ireland. The O'Clerys were a tribe whom the de Burgos drove out of Connaught when they settled there and became Bourkes. The O'Clery sept scattered ; after a while an O'Clery came into Tyrconnel and settled there. O'Donnell's hereditary ollave of historical studies (ollave means something like Master of Arts and implies a title bestowed on proof of competence) was without a son ; so he gave his daughter to O'Clery on condition that their son should be bred an annalist. The O'Donnells gave them lands in Kilbarron near Ballyshannon, and they built a castle there which stands for you to see. Teague O'Clery was born in 1575, became a lay brother of the Franciscan order and entered the Irish convent at Louvain under the name of Brother Michael. The Warden of this convent, MacWard, was engaged on a book of Lives of the saints, and he sent O'Clery to Ireland to collect materials—which were afterwards used by Colgan, a native of Inishowen, who took up MacWard's work. O'Clery besides the *Annals* wrote also two other books of which copies exist ; one in his own hand at Brussels ; the other in Dublin, written by Cucogry or Peregrine O'Clery, who was chief of the O'Clery sept. The original copy of the *Annals* is in the Royal Irish Academy; it was purchased by the famous antiquary Petrie.

Cucogry O'Clery was a peaceable scholar who owned certain lands in Boylagh, as was reported before an inquisition taken at Lifford in 1632 ; but " being a mere Irishman and not of English or British descent " he was dispossessed and the lands became forfeited to the king. He had, however, other possessions for which the English had no covetous desire, and his will exists bequeathing "the property most dear to me that I ever possessed in this world, namely my books, to my two sons Dermot and John." The Ulster confiscations have never been justified : but an attempt is often made to represent them as a banishment of predatory savages to make way for civilised men. The case of this patient scholar and scribe, stripped of his land for being an Irishman, is worthy to be remembered by those who wonder at the slowness of the Irish to be won over by an occasional grant in aid of some light railway or curing station for fish, and may stand for a typical instance of the process by which the Catholic Irish were converted into a nation of Helots—a status from which they are only gradually and painfully emerging.

Donegal.

CHAPTER III

BALLYSHANNON, standing on the ford of the Erne, was the
O'Donnells' frontier town and a place of some mark in history.
Many expeditions went out through it into Sligo, many
droves of lifted cattle were driven through it back to Donegal.
But the greatest event in its history was in the days of Red
Hugh O'Donnell.

In July 1597 Lord Burgh was making war upon Hugh O'Neill,
or the great Earl of Tyrone, and he sent orders to Sir
Conyers Clifford, Governor of Connaught, to attack Red Hugh.
Accordingly a great army—twenty-two standards of foot and ten
standards of cavalry—marched up Sligo and fought their way
across the ford Ath-cul-Uain, about half a mile below Belleek.
But in the crossing Murrough O'Brien, Lord Inchiquin (collateral
ancestor of the present Baron), was hit in the armpit, between

D

the plates of his armour, by a ball, and fell into the river. The monks of Assaroe found his body and interred it; but the Franciscan friars of Donegal insisted that the O'Briens were always buried in their houses, and appealed to have the body lifted and interred with them, which was done by Red Hugh's order; so great was the contention for the bones of a descendant of Brian Boru. Clifford having crossed the Erne marched down the right bank to Assaroe, and on the same day a ship from Galway bringing ordnance for his support put into Inis-saimer, or Fish Island. The troops then took up a position on Mullaghnashee (the hill on which the parish church stands) and planted their guns there. Probably one of the Four Masters saw the scene, so eloquent is his description.

" On Monday, Tuesday and Wednesday they continued to fire, shooting at the castle with heavy loud-sounding fiery balls from the loud-roaring shot-vomiting guns of that heavy and huge ordnance which they planted opposite the fortress. They sent large parties of their choicest soldiers to the castle with wall-razing engines and with thick and strong iron armour about their bodies and bright shining helmets on their heads with a bright 'testudo' of round broad hard iron shields around them to protect them from the shot of their enemies. The resolute attack they made upon the fortress, however, was of no avail to them; and it had been better for them that they had not come this journey against it; for from the castle were poured down upon them showers of brilliant fire from well-planted straight-aimed guns and from costly muskets and some rough-headed rocks and massive solid stones and beams and blocks of timber which were kept on the battlements of the fortress in readiness to be hurled down; so that the coverings of the razing party were of no shelter or protection to them and great numbers of them were destroyed, and others who were severely wounded became so exhausted that they delayed not to be further slaughtered, and turning their backs to their enemies they were routed to the camp."

Meanwhile the levy of O'Donnell's urraghts, or vassal chiefs, was coming in ; Maguire from Fermanagh ; O'Rourke from Brefny ; and the Governor of Connaught's army was hard put to it between O'Donnell's sorties and the attacks from without. Moreover all the fords now were held from Lough Erne to the sea. But starving men will risk much, and the army was starving ; so it was decided to attempt the " rough turbulent cold streamed ford over the brink of Assaroe called Casan na-g Curadh "—(the Path of the Heroes) and they advanced unperceived to this. Many of the horses, many of the women and many of the wounded or those weakened by hunger, were swept over the fall ; but the strong men got across. O'Donnell, full of anger that his prize should escape, pursued him, and there was a running fight from the Erne to Carbery ; but the governor got safe away. He was less lucky the next time he met Red Hugh in fight.

Of the castle there is now no trace, but as you cross the bridge over the Erne you will see the " path of the heroes " below you. Turn to the left and come to the side of Assaroe; an ugly ford it must be to cross in swollen water, and indeed not easy even on a day when the river sparkles and the sandhills are yellow in the sun between you and the blue Atlantic. It would tempt one to a description, but a better man has done it.

On the bridge you should notice a tablet to the memory of one of the few poets who have yet been born to English-speaking Ireland. William Allingham was born at Ballyshannon in March 1824. The son of a bank manager, he was at first put into the counting-house, but left that for a place in the customs, which gave him more leisure for poetry, on which his heart was set. He corresponded with Leigh Hunt, Coventry Patmore, and became an intimate friend of Rossetti, whose letters to him have lately been edited by Dr. Birkbeck Hill. Dr. Hill tells a story of Allingham's youth, related to him by Mr. Arthur Hughes ; "how in remote Ballyshannon, where he was a clerk in the customs, in evening walks, he would hear the Irish girls at their cottage door singing old ballads, which he would pick

up. If they were broken or incomplete, he would add to or
finish them ; if they were improper, he would refine them. He
could not get them sung till he got the Dublin 'Catnach' of
that day to print them, on long strips of blue paper, like old
songs ; and if about the sea, with the old rough woodcut of a
ship on the top. He either gave them away or they were sold
in the neighbourhood. Then, in his evening walks, he had at
last the pleasure of hearing some of his own ballads sung at the
cottage doors by the crooning lasses, who were quite unaware
that it was the author who was passing by."

Here is Allingham's description of his birth-place. " The
little old town where I was born has a voice of its own, low,
solemn, persistent, humming through the air day and night,
summer and winter. Whenever I think of that town I seem to
hear the voice. The river which makes it rolls over rocky ledges
into the tide. Before spreads a great ocean in sunshine or storm ;
behind stretches a many-islanded lake. On the south runs a wavy
line of blue mountains ; and on the north, over green, rocky hills,
rise peaks of a more distant range. The trees hide in glens or
cluster near the river; grey rocks and boulders lie scattered about
the windy pastures. The sky arches wide over all, giving room to
multitudes of stars by night and long processions of clouds
blown from the sea, but also, in the childish memory where
these pictures live, to deeps of celestial blue in the endless days
of summer. An odd, out-of-the-way little town ours, on the
extreme western verge of Europe ; our next neighbours, sunset
way, being citizens of the great new republic, which indeed to
our imagination seemed little, if at all, farther off than England
in the opposite direction."

But Allingham has celebrated his native town in a far more
haunting medium than this graceful prose. I may be pardoned
for reprinting what is too little known.

THE WINDING BANKS OF ERNE; OR, THE EMIGRANT'S
ADIEU TO BALLYSHANNY.

Adieu to Ballyshanny ! where I was bred and born ;
Go where I may, I'll think of you, as sure as night and morn ;
The kindly spot, the friendly town, where every one is known,
And not a face in all the place but partly seems my own ;
There's not a house or window, there's not a field or hill,
But East or West, in foreign lands, I'll recollect them still.
I leave my warm heart with you, tho' my back I'm forced to turn,
So adieu to Ballyshanny and the winding banks of Erne !

No more on pleasant evenings we'll saunter down the Mall,
When the trout is rising to the fly, the salmon to the fall.
The boat comes straining on her net, and heavily she creeps,
Cast off, cast off—she feels the oars, and to her berth she sweeps ;
Now fore and aft keep hauling, and gathering up the dew,
Till a silver wave of salmon rolls in among the crew.
Then they may sit, with pipes a-lit, and many a joke and yarn :—
Adieu to Ballyshanny and the winding banks of Erne !

The music of the waterfall, the mirror of the tide
When all the green-hilled harbour is full from side to side,
From Portnasun to Bulliebawns, and round the Abbey Bay,
From rocky Inis Saimer to Coolgarnit sand-hills grey ;
While far upon the southern line, to guard it like a wall,
The Leitrim mountains clothed in blue gaze calmly over all,
And watch the ship sail up or down, the red flag at her stern :—
Adieu to these, adieu to all the winding banks of Erne !

Farewell to you, Kildoney lads, and them that pull an oar,
A lug-sail set, or haul a net, from the point to Mullaghmore ;
From Killeybegs to bold Slieve League, that ocean-mountain steep,
Six hundred yards in air aloft, six hundred in the deep ;
From Dooran to the Fairy Bridge and round by Tullen strand,
Level and long, and white with waves, where gull and curlew stand ;
Head out to sea when on your lee the breakers you discern ! —
Adieu to all the billowy coast and winding banks of Erne !

Farewell Coolmore—Bundoran ! and your summer crowds that run
From inland homes to see with joy th' Atlantic setting sun ;
To breathe the buoyant salted air, and sport among the waves ;
To gather shells on sandy beach and tempt the gloomy caves ;
To watch the flowing, ebbing tide, the boats, the crabs, the fish ;
Young men and maids to meet and smile, and form a tender wish :
The sick and old in search of health, for all things have their turn
And I must quit my native shore and the winding banks of Erne !

Farewell to every white cascade from the harbour to Belleek,
And every pool where fins may rest, and ivy-shaded creek ;
The sloping fields, the lofty rocks, where ash and holly grow,
The one split yew-tree gazing on the curving flood below ;
The lough that winds through islands under Turaw mountain green ;
And Castle Caldwell's stretching woods, with tranquil bays between ;
And Breesie Hill, and many a pond among the heath and fern ;—
For I must say adieu—adieu to the winding banks of Erne !

The thrush will call through Camlin groves the live-long summer day ;
The waters run by mossy cliff, and banks with wild-flowers gay ;
The girls will bring their work and sing beneath a twisted thorn :
Or stray with sweethearts down the path among the growing corn ;
Along the river-side they go, where I have often been,—
O never shall I see again the days that I have seen !
A thousand chances are to one I never may return,—
Adieu to Ballyshanny and the winding banks of Erne !

Adieu to evening dances, where merry neighbours meet,
And the fiddle says to boys and girls, " Get up and shake your feet ! "
To *shanachus* and wise old talk of Erin's days gone by—
Who trenched the rath on such a hill, and where the bones may lie
Of saint, or king, or warrior chief, with tales of fairy power,
And tender ditties sweetly sung to pass the twilight hour.
The mournful song of exile is now for me to learn—
Adieu, my dear companions on the winding banks of Erne !

Now measure from the commons down to each end of the Purt,
Round the Abbey, Moy and Knather,—I wish no one any hurt ;
The Main Street, Back Street, College Lane, the Mall, and Portnasun,
If any foes of mine are there, I pardon every one.

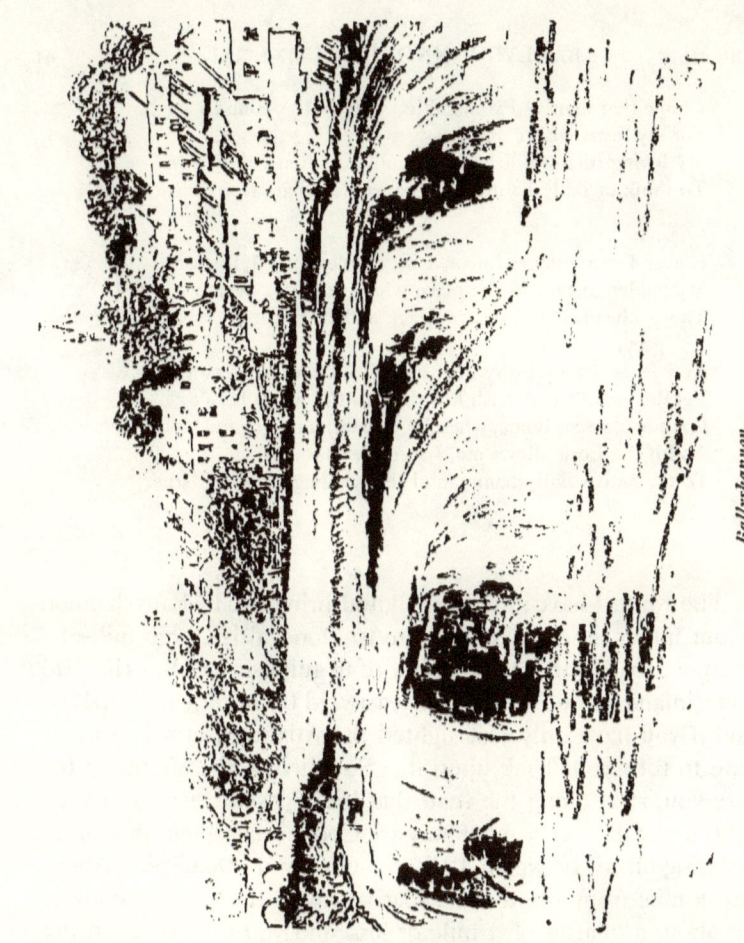

Ballyshannon.

I hope that man and womankind will do the same by me ;
For my heart is sore and heavy at voyaging the sea.
My loving friends I'll bear in mind and often fondly turn
To think of Ballyshanny and the winding banks of Erne !

If ever I'm a moneyed man, I mean, please God, to cast
My golden anchor in the place where youthful years were past ;
Though heads that now are black and brown must meanwhile gather
    grey,
New faces rise by every hearth, and old ones drop away,—
Yet dearer still that Irish hill than all the world beside ;
It's home, sweet home, where'er I roam, through lands and waters wide.
And if the Lord allows me, I surely will return
To my native Ballyshanny, and the winding banks of Erne.

The route I have indicated should bring you to Ballyshannon
about lunch time.   From there to Donegal is eleven miles by
the post road with a telegraph wire to guide you.   But the road
runs inland to cut across the eastward trend of Donegal Bay,
and if you have only just sighted the Atlantic you will scarcely
care to turn your back upon it.   So with all the afternoon before you, start along the road that leads past Assaroe and keep
by the coast.   Ask your way to Coolmore, which is a little
watering-place between Ballyshannon and Donegal.   About
half a mile from the town a road turns to the left.   Follow it
for about a quarter of a mile or less and you will come on the
ruins of the old Abbey of Ballyshannon—only a few walls.
About three miles further down the river stands Kilbarron
Castle, the home of the O'Clerys who furnished three out of the
Four Masters : also a fragmentary ruin nowadays.   Turn back
to the Coolmore Road—which, I must own, though not too hilly,
presents a very uneven surface—and you will have as you go
along a series of admirable views seaward : the Sligo coast on
your left, and in front of you the northern coast of Donegal
Bay ending in the gigantic mass of Slieve League.   Avoid two

roads to the left, which lead nowhere, and after about four miles
you come to a sharp downward hill, and at the bottom is a path
leading on to a mile of exquisite strand all trending in the direction of Donegal.   If the tide is not full in, get your bicycle
down on the sand and spin along the water's edge with nothing
but blue sea between you and America.   Unfortunately like all
good things this strand has got an end, a projecting point—it extends no further than you can see—and about a quarter of a mile
on the near side of the point a road runs up from the strand to
Ballintra.   It is not a good road when you get to it; but to get it
you go through sand hills full of pink cranesbill and innumerable
blue and yellow pansies, and all the other delightful things that
grow on sandhills.   After about a mile it lapses into the ordinary
jog trot of roads.   Just about that point avoid one more road to
the left which leads you nowhere—and you have three miles
easy going to Ballintra.   Then you strike the main road—
and excellent it is—with telegraph posts to see you safe all the
way to Donegal.   What is more you travel through a well-
wooded country rich with lush grass, showing prosperity in
its well-kept hedges; altogether as prosperous-looking a district
as you would see in Ireland.   Decidedly the O'Donnells knew
what they were doing when they settled at Donegal.   No part
in the English Pale looks richer or trimmer, yet here you are in
purely Celtic Ireland.   Something perhaps must be allowed for
the magic of May on a sunny morning when every hawthorn
bush was dashed with white and made the air heavy with deli-
cious scent, and all the trees were decked out in the first fresh-
ness of verdure, or, lovelier still, in a gold that was not yet
changed to green.   Donegal town comes at last with a surprise
on you as you round a shoulder of hill and come in sudden view
of the pool and quay with the old town clustered about it.
You ride past the quay and up into the Diamond, and there you
will find excellent quarters at the Arran Arms, a hotel kept by a
retired officer.   The day I got there the Diamond was full of
people and of carts and cars tilted on their end; I counted over

fifty of these vehicles. It was the big hiring fair. Boys and girls engage themselves to employers from the 27th of May to the 20th of November, and there is another hiring fair then for the winter-season. A good stout workman will get up to £7 or £8 in addition to his board for either period : a girl from £5 to £4. There was a large crowd, many of them true peasants of the Gaelic type—though I heard no Irish spoken—wearing big black slouch hats, almost a certain sign in these parts of a Catholic and Nationalist—the older men with grave close-shaven high cheek-boned faces—wearing only a short side whisker close clipped. On the fringes of the crowd were booths in rows selling crockery and hardware and—the invariable delicacy of Irish fairs - *dilsk* or *dulse*—a sweet-tasting seaweed spreading all about it a strong whiff of the sea.

The dialogues that one overheard were curious. There would be a knot of men—ten or a dozen—pressing close round two who stood face to face—the hirer and the hired. Most of the talking was done by the onlookers. They exhorted the boy. "Speak up now, don't be dumb with him. Get the best price you can : why wouldn't you ? Say what's the least you'll take. But speak up !" Then there would be a colloquy. The hirer apparently had made conditions that work should be done even when his back was turned. The boy began after a long silence. "When I go to it, I know work as well as any man. And the work will be done just as well as you would do it, let you be there or not. I know well Mr. — that you do be away many days—I know you, though may be you don't know me "—and so on. Then a pause. Then a bystander suggests a compromise, "Say seven pounds ten now. Come now, Johnny, you won't break my word." And he slaps his hand in the hirer's hand and tries to get the hired to do the same, but nothing comes of it. Then there is another notion—for all the onlookers are feverishly anxious to see a bargain concluded—and they take the pair by the shoulders—" Come, now, go away the pair of you and talk it out by yourselves, we don't want to hear

what you're saying; it's none of our business." Then the two
go off a little way and there is immediate comment. " He's
asking eight pound "—" He offered seven, and five shillings."
" Ay, but he's wanting eight." " There was bigger boys in the
fair took less nor eight. Och it's not the size that's the thing;

Cattle Drover.

it's the spirit." " Them McGrortys was all decent fellows:" "Ay,
and he's a stout chap; no great size on him but he's strong made."
And so on, discussing the boy's points as if he were a horse for a
minute or two, but by the end of that time a crowd has again
gathered round the pair and the talkers drift in to make part of it.

But unless you come on May 27 you won't see a hiring fair
in Donegal, and what will strike you at once will be a glimpse
of the castle with its mullioned windows beautiful even in ruin.
The river skirts its walls on the farther side though no
ship of any tonnage could ever have come up so far. But a
little way below the present quay are the ruins of the famous
Franciscan abbey under whose auspices the Four Masters lived
and wrote, and it has a regular landing-place. Close by it,
embedded in the mud, may be seen the fluke of an immense
anchor which according to local tradition was left there by a
French vessel in 1798, which called in—presumably to inquire
after Humbert's expedition—but beat a hasty retreat. Little
is left of the Abbey except a few arches, but happily the castle
remains for a monument of the O'Donnell power; though
unhappily that magnificent piece of Jacobean architecture
cannot be credited to Irish workmen. The great carved mantel-
piece of stone preserved in the banqueting hall bears the arms
of the Brookes, and reminds one only of confiscation, for in 1610
the castle was granted to Sir Basil Brooke. The architecture
of the building, shattered as it is, may well put to shame
anything of more modern date in the county. But of the
exterior semblance of the Abbey—in which Tudor work has
been added to the more ancient keep with its solid walls several
feet in thickness—and of its picturesqueness I need not speak,
as an illustration is far more convincing. Of its history I may
say something.

As far back as we know, Donegal—Dun-na-gal, the fort of the
foreigners—was the seat of the O'Donnells. Hugh O'Donnell
and his wife Fingalla, a lady of the O'Brien house of Thomond,
completed in 1474 the Franciscan monastery which Nuala
O'Donnell, another pious lady, had already founded. In the
days when Red Hugh was a captive, his father, Hugh O'Donnell
the conqueror of Shane O'Neill, was worn out and feeble, and an
English force in 1593 seized an island in the harbour, occupied
the Abbey and pillaged the country. It was just at this time

that Red Hugh, still a mere boy, reached Ballyshannon, half
dead from the exposure in his terrible flight over the Wicklow
hills escaping from Dublin Castle.   But hearing of this insult
he mustered his friends who had come to greet him and they
marched on Donegal and quickly put the invaders to rout.
His father resigned the O'Donnellship in his favour, but Red
Hugh lived rather on his frontiers and beyond them than in the

Donegal Castle.

ancestral stronghold.   Soon he and O'Neill were in alliance
levying fierce war on the English, and at Ballinabuie in 1598
they inflicted on the English one of the heaviest defeats that
nation ever sustained in Ireland.   By 1600 they were masters
of all Ulster and Connaught.   A landing had been made at
Derry by Sir Henry Docwra, but the little force was closely
cooped within its intrenchments by a force of O'Donnells,

under Red Hugh's cousin and brother-in-law, Nial Garv (the Fierce), a famous soldier. But now came the fatal weakness. Nial, older than Hugh, counted himself wronged in being passed over for the O'Donnellship, and Docwra tempted him with recognition not only as O'Donnell but as Earl of Tyrconnell. Nial yielded, and, while Red Hugh was ravaging Clare, his general in the north went over to the English, and by Docwra's own admission changed the whole aspect of affairs. Nial made a sudden descent on the fortress at Lifford which opened the way through Barnesmore into the heart of Tyrconnell; and in spite of Red Hugh's efforts could not be dislodged. Later on Red Hugh was again called off southward by the war, and Nial struck at the very heart of the principality which he coveted.

This is how the Four Masters tell the story of the year 1601.

"After this news reached O'Donnell that Nial Garv, the son of Con, Son of Calvagh, with his English and Irish, had come from the east across Bearnas and encamped at Donegal in the east of Tir Hugh. When O'Donnell received the news that the English had arrived at that place he felt grieved for the misfortune of the monastery, that the English should occupy it and inhabit it instead of the sons of Life and the Culdees whose rightful property it was then; and he could not forbear from going to try if he could relieve them. He left the farmers and the betaghs of Tirconnell with their flocks and herds through Lower Connaught, with some of his soldiers to protect them against attack from the harbours and against the kernes and foreign tribes, and he himself proceeded with the greater part of his army across the rivers Sligo, Duff, Drowes and Erne northward and pitched his camp in strong position exactly at Carraig, which is upwards of 2,000 paces from Donegal where Nial Garv and his English were stationed. As for O'Donnell he ordered great numbers of his forces to blockade the monastery in turns by day and night, so as to prevent the English from coming outside its wall to destroy anything in the country. Neither did the armies pass their time by any means happily and pleasantly, for killing and destroying, conflict and shooting, were carried on by each party against the other. The English were reduced to great straits and distress by the long siege in which they were kept by O'Donnell's people ; and some of them used to desert to O'Donnell's camp in twos or threes in consequence of the distress and straits they were in from the want of a proper ration of food. Thus they passed the time till the end of September when God willed to take revenge and satisfaction of the English for the profanation and abuse which they had offered to the churches and apartments of the psalm-singing ecclesiastics of the monastery of Donegal and the monastery of Magherabeg in which they were quartered and encamped. The vengeance which God wreaked upon them was this, however it came to pass: fire fell among the powder which had been put in the monastery of Donegal for carrying on the war; so that the boarded apartments and all the stone and wooden buildings of the entire monastery were burned. As soon as the spies and sentinels whom O'Donnell had posted to spy and watch the English perceived the brown-red mass of flames, and the dense cloud of vapour and smoke that rose upon the monastery, they began to discharge their leaden bullets and their fiery flashes in order that O'Donnell might immediately come to them to attack the English, for they thought it would occasion too long a delay to send him messengers. The signal was not slowly responded to by O'Donnell and his army, for they vehemently and rapidly advanced with their utmost speed in troops and squadrons to where their people were at the monastery. Bloody and furious was the attack they made upon the English and their own friends and kinsmen who were there. It was difficult and almost impossible for O'Donnell's people to withstand the fire of the soldiers who were in the monastery and the castle of Donegal and in a ship which was in the harbour opposite to them ; yet, however, O'Donnell's people had the better of it, although many of them were cut off. Con Og, the brother of Nial Garv, fell with three hundred others in that slaughter.

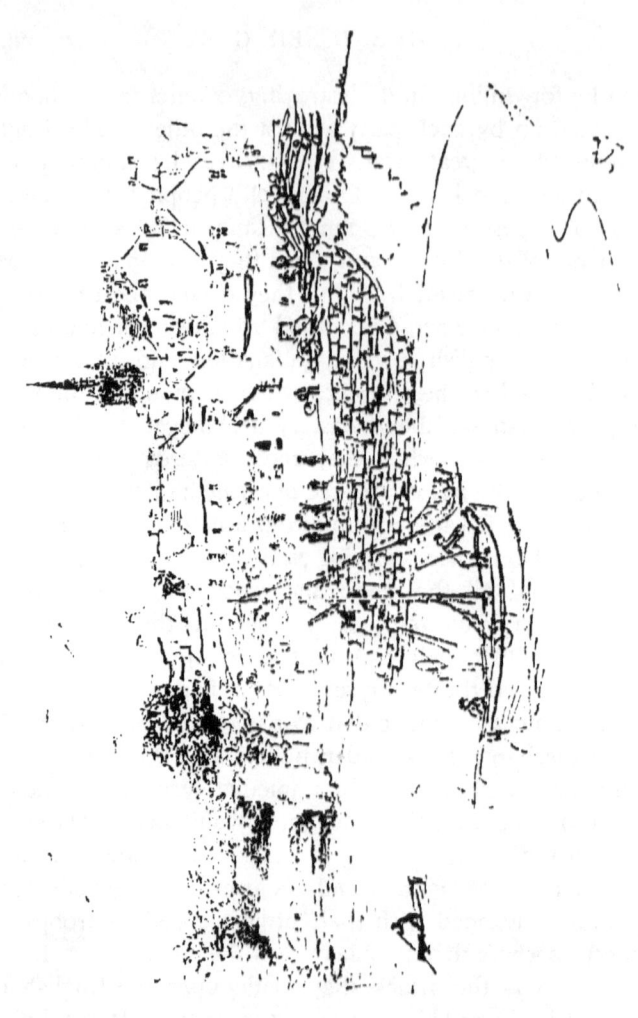

E

" As soon as Nial Garv perceived the great jeopardy in which his people and the English were he passed unnoticed westwards along the margin of the harbour to Magherabeg where a great number of the English were ; and he took them to the relief of the other party ; and the crew of the ship kept up a fire in defiance of them until they had passed inside the central walls of the monastery. When O'Donnell observed the great strength of the place in which they were and the great force that had come to the relief of the English he ordered his soldiers to withdraw from the conflict and to return back, for he did not deem it meet that they should be cut off in an unequal contest."

All this happened on Michaelmas Day. O'Donnell maintained the blockade by land till the end of October when news reached him that a Spanish fleet had arrived in Kinsale, and instantly abandoning his own country to the invaders—whom he looked to deal with later on—he marched to effect his junction with the Earl of Tyrone, and with him to meet the Spanish forces and attack the English. The result was, by bad generalship, ruinous defeat. Red Hugh left Ireland for Spain to plead for more help, never to return ; he died there by poison. A pacification, false and hollow, succeeded ; Rory O'Donnell, his brother, was recognised and created Earl of Tyrconnell ; but after four years he and Tyrone found themselves surrounded with intrigues, and in despair fled with all their belongings. Their property was declared forfeit and Donegal was among the *spolia opima* of the confiscation. The unhappy Nial Garv, who more than any man had contributed to this consummation, proffered his claims, and in full settlement of them was sent to rot till he died in the Tower of London. So ends the history of Donegal as the seat of a Celtic Princedom.

Killybegs.

CHAPTER IV

YOUR next day from Donegal should take you to Killybegs for lunch and Carrick for dinner. From Donegal to Killybegs it is fourteen Irish miles—say eighteen English—along what is called in Donegal a level road; that is a road free from hills in going up which a humane driver would dismount from his car. As to being level the nature of the country forbids it. You have the sea on your left hand, generally close under you, and fine views across Donegal Bay, but candour compels me to state that I did the stage by railway; knowing that for a good while to come I had to rely on my own exertions. In any case you will send your luggage by rail to Killybegs, and thence by mailcar to Carrick ; that involves despatching them early in the morning. At Killybegs I recommend Rogers' Hotel, which is clean and comfortable ; but it is better to get on to Carrick. An alternative is to make your way on the first day to Donegal in time to catch a 7.20 train, and sleep that night at Killybegs, and have only the ten miles' ride to Carrick next day. But it is a pity to be hurried in Donegal, as the castle is really worth seeing, and there is a charming walk down by the river, with seats along it, on the side opposite the town.

Killybegs is not a place with an exciting past ; but it may be a place with a future. It has the best harbour on the West of Ireland, and there is talk of arranging to make it a place of call for steamers bound to America ; in that case Killybegs will grow rich and prosperous. Its harbour has always given it some touch with the outside world. In 1598 a vessel put in there with ambassadors from Spain, and Red Hugh O'Donnell and Tyrone interviewed them in the port. But ten years earlier, Spanish vessels in a very different trim had put into Killybegs in their stress.

When the great Armada was staggering homewards on its terrible journey this shore was the scene of many disasters. Medina's instructions to his fleet were to run well northwards and then far to the west of the dangerous Irish coast, but heavy weather met them, and ship after ship failed to weather the jutting shore of Connaught, and was driven to cast anchor. In nearly every case the tackle proved too weak to hold them against such a sea ; the cables parted, and they went ashore, where the unhappy crews, if they succeeded in landing, were stripped or slain by the natives, and such of them as the Irish spared were hanged by the English. This was in the days when Sir John Perrott had brought the country into something more approaching a willing loyalty to the British crown. Ten years later, in the days of Red Hugh, any Spaniard who landed on

the coast of Tyrconnell would have met a very different
reception; but Ireland had not yet been driven to hold that
her best friends were the enemies of England. Three great
ships went ashore on Streedagh Strand between Sligo and
Bundoran. Another, the *Rata*, under Don Alonzo de Leyva,
broke loose from her anchors and ran ashore ; but her crew
were hospitably sheltered by O'Rourke. of Brefny, till they
embarked again upon another vessel, the *San Martin*, which
had been able to hold out in the offing. They met the *Girona*,
and *Duquesa Sta. Anna*, and made their escape northwards,
the wind being still westerly ; but the three were obliged to
put into Killybegs when the ships again foundered, but the
crews—2,000 in number—got ashore with their arms. Here
they obtained fresh stores, and a welcome from MacSwiney of
Banaght, lord of this country ; and having managed to patch
up two of their vessels they again put to sea, abandoning the
San Martin. The *Duquesa Sta. Anna*, however, had no better
fortune ; she ran upon the rocks in Glennagaveny Bay, west of
Inishowen Head. De Leyva, escaping from her, made his way
to the *Girona*, which lay at anchor in Mulroy or Sheephaven.
After a week's labour upon her to make her seaworthy, he and
the remnant of three crews, stood out to make the coast of
Scotland, where there was some chance of friendship ; but,
hugging the Antrim coast, near the Giant's Causeway, ran on a
rock and perished. Sorley Boy Macdonell, Lord of Dunluce,
came to the rescue, but recovered only five of the crew. certain
butts of wine, and three pieces of cannon, which he mounted
on his castle and refused to give up. Another wreck occurred
at a neighbouring point, and eleven of this second crew found
shelter with Sorley Boy, who eventually despatched them over
to Scotland.

Another ship of the first class, *La Trinidad Valencera*, went
on shore in the O'Doherty's country of Inishowen. A large
number of the crew succeeded in landing, and were tolerably

treated by the natives. Matters soon changed for the worse. As soon as the news reached Dublin that the Western coast was being strewn with wreckage and plunder, Fitzwilliam, the Lord Deputy, posted off in haste to the scene, gathering what treasure he could, and making a short end of all Spaniards. Having seen the whole length of Streedagh Strand littered with twelve or thirteen hundred dead corpses, shattered timbers, boats, cordage, and huge masts, he reached Ballyshannon. Thence taking with him the O'Donnell, Red Hugh's father, bound to acquiescence at this time, for his eldest son was a kidnapped prisoner in Dublin Castle, he made a peregrination through Tyrconnell and seized upon the survivors from the *Trinidad Valencera*, all of whom were put to death.

Two other vessels—one, it is said, a treasure-ship—went ashore on the coast of Donegal in the Rosses. One treasure-ship lies, to this day, in the sand off Mullaghderg, and various expeditions have been made to recover her spoils; but a few brass guns, brought in a century ago, are all that has been won back from the sea. As lately as the spring of 1895, the *Harbour Lights* steamer stayed for a fortnight on the spot trying to disinter treasures, but went away empty-handed. The other wreck lies about two miles to the south in Castleford Bay, inside the Island of Aran. In 1853 the coastguards at Rutland Island tried their luck on this vessel, and fetched up the great anchor which lies outside the United Services Institution in Parliament Street.

The tale of losses, then, as I count it, on the Donegal and Antrim coast is this. The *San Martin*, abandoned as a wreck in Killybegs Harbour; two nameless vessels lost off the Rosses, the *Duquesa Sta. Anna* and *La Trinidad Valencera* wrecked on the Inishowen headlands; and the *Girona* and another near Sorley Boy's Castle of Dunluce.

Any one interested in the matter should read Mr. Froude's *Spanish Story of the Armada* and also a booklet by Mr. Hugh

Allingham, M.R.I.A. (published by Elliot Stock in 1897) called *Captain Cuellar's Adventures in Connacht and Ulster*, which contains, among other interesting things, Professor Crawford's translation of Cuellar's narrative. This was one of the documents given to the world by Captain Duro, of the Spanish navy, in 1884. It is a letter, written by Captain Cuellar, who commanded a galleon of twenty-four guns in the Armada, and describes his adventures from the time when he was wrecked—not in his galleon but in a large ship—on the Streedagh Strand, up to his escape into the Low Countries.

He was one of about 300 who got on shore and were all maltreated and stripped absolutely naked. However, he managed to get clear away with his life, and was advised to hold northward for the O'Rourke's country. His only means of communication was in Latin, and it sounds strange enough to read that among these " savages," as he calls them, he not infrequently found one who spoke it. A wound in his leg proved his salvation, for of a company of about twenty collected in O'Rourke's house, Cuellar was the only one who could not make his way to the coast when word came that a ship was lying there. This vessel, he says, set sail in two days, was wrecked again, and all her crew drowned or killed on landing by the English ; but whether on the Donegal or Connaught coasts I do not know.

Cuellar, having fallen behind the others and lost his way, met a Latin-speaking priest, who directed him to MacClancy's Castle, on Lough Melvin, and after some difficulty he got there and found ten other Spaniards, but contrived to obtain special favour by telling fortunes to the ladies of the castle, who, it would appear, also understood the Latin tongue.

Cuellar stayed for three months with MacClancy, a refractory chief living in a difficult country, and he has left a curious description of native manners and customs.

"The wife of my master was very beautiful in the extreme and showed me much kindness. One day we were sitting in the sun with some of her female friends and relatives, and they asked me about Spanish matters, and of other parts, and in the end it came to be suggested that I should examine their hands and tell them their fortunes. Giving thanks to God that it had not gone even worse with me than to be gipsy among the savages, I began to look at the hands of each, and to say to them a hundred thousand absurdities, which pleased them so much that there was no other Spaniard better than I, or that was in greater favour with them. . . .

"The custom of these savages is to live as the brute beasts among the mountains, which are very rugged in that part of Ireland, where we lost ourselves. They live in huts made of straw. The men are all large-bodied and of handsome features and limbs, and as active as the roe-deer. They do not eat oftener than once a day, and this is at night; and that which they usually eat is butter with oaten bread. They drink sour milk, for they have no other drink; they don't drink water, although it is the best in the world. On feast-days they eat some flesh half-cooked, without bread or salt, as that is their custom. They clothe themselves, according to their habit, with tight trousers and short loose coats of very coarse goats' hair. They cover themselves with blankets and wear their hair down to their eyes. They are great walkers and inured to toil. They carry on perpetual war with the English, who here keep garrison for the Queen, from whom they defend themselves, and do not let them enter their territory, which is subject to inundation and marshy. That district extends for more than forty leagues in length and breadth. The chief inclination of these people is to be robbers, and to plunder each other; so that no day passes without a call to arms among them. For, the people in one village becoming aware that in another there are cattle, or other effects, they immediately come armed in the night, and attack and kill one another; and the English from the garrisons, getting to know who had taken and robbed most cattle, then come down upon them and carry away the plunder. They

have, therefore, no other remedy but to withdraw themselves
to the mountains, with their women and cattle, for they possess
no other property, nor more movables nor clothing. They
sleep upon the ground, on rushes, newly cut, and full of water
and ice.

"The most of the women are very beautiful, but badly dressed.
They do not wear more than a chemise, and a blanket, with
which they cover themselves, and a linen cloth, much doubled,
over the head, and tied in front. They are great workers and
housekeepers, after their fashion. These people call themselves
Christians. Mass is said among them, and regulated according
to the orders of the Church of Rome. The great majority of
their churches, monasteries, and hermitages, have been demolished by the English, who are in garrison, and of those
natives who have joined them, and are as bad as they. In
short, in this kingdom there is neither justice nor right, and
every one does what he pleases."

This is of course the description of a poor, outlying district.
In Donegal Abbey at this time there were "forty priests' vest-
ments with all their belongings; many of them were of cloth
of gold and silver, some of them interwoven and wrought with
gold ornaments; all the rest were of silk. We had, moreover,
sixteen large chalices all but two of them gilt."

Cuellar's stay with MacClancy seemed likely to come to an
end, when Fitzwilliam came down, hanging all Spaniards, and
punishing their harbourers; MacClancy decided that he, as a
chief who paid no Queen's rent, must fly; but Cuellar undertook to remain with the other Spaniards and hold the castle
on Lough Melvin which is still there. Fitzwilliam came to the
lough side with a large force but failed to make the Spaniards
surrender, and was driven away by a heavy fall of snow.
Cuellar's reputation now stood so high that MacClancy was
unwilling to let him go; so he escaped secretly and made his
way east, travelling for twenty days through the mountains of
Donegal and Derry till he got to Dunluce, where he heard of

Alonzo de Leyva's wreck. Finally he got off in a ship with twelve others, from some point in O'Cane's country—that is the east shore of Lough Foyle—and they ran to Shetland ; whence after six months' anxiety the Duke of Parma contrived to have them brought by a merchantman to Dunkirk, where the Dutch treacherously lay in wait for them, and this shore also Cuellar reached on some timbers of wreckage.

Glen Columbkille.

CHAPTER V

THE road from Killybegs to Carrick is one you cannot well miss, for telegraph wires will guide you the whole way. Very little of it is really level, but it is fairly divided between up-hill and down. I rode it on a Sunday, and for my sins had to carry my baggage, as Carrick, like London, has no Sunday delivery of letters; extremes meet. Also I had driving rain and a head wind and soft roads; and under these conditions I was almost an hour and three-quarters on the way. Of the landscape I can say nothing, except that at first you are by the sea, then you turn inland, and wind your way over very wild mountain; but the

shapes of everything were lost in what we in Ireland call a
Scotch mist, though we all know Scotland has no monopoly of
the article. About the seventh mile you begin to go down a
long hill, and at the bottom of that hill is a bridge; on the other
side is a sharp rise, and from the top of that you see the village of
Kilcar, with a church and chapel down in a valley to the left.
Here you may leave the telegraph posts and turn to the right for
about a mile, when you will meet the posts again climbing the
hill from Kilcar, and they will take you over the wildest of all these
wild hills into Carrick; but on the slope you may turn to the
left on a new road which will take you over a gentler gradient.
Along this part of the way one had little cause to regret that
the view was blotted out. I never saw anywhere so many wild
flowers as among these marshy meadows. Somewhere on the
other side of the hill leading down to Kilcar I had noticed the
finest patch I ever saw of the beautiful white bogbean growing in
a swamp to the right of the road. Bog-cotton was everywhere
through the heather, of course. But this hill-side about Kilcar
was simply flooded with bluebells : growing, not in the shelter
of trees or hedges—for trees and hedges there are none on these
wild moors : but the ocean winds which sweep the heads off whatever resists them deal gently with the soft bluebells and let them
carpet the open meadows to the colour of an Italian sky. Sometimes in the same field with them one saw in rushy places a radiant mass of marsh marigolds, shining like the sun ; by the ditches
were quantities of pale pink cuckoo-flower, and everywhere in
masses some small white umbelliferous blossom. But the most
beautiful thing of all was to see here and there the young fronds
of the King fern—*Osmunda regalis*—shooting up straight and
strong, not yet come to near their full height and dignity, but
wonderful in the glow of golden olive and brown.

When you crest the hill, the village with its Roman
Catholic chapel lies directly below you : you cross the Glen
River by a bridge, come up the little street, and at the head you
will see a low, comfortable-looking house with trim white

verandah ; that is the Glen Columbkille Hotel—built in 1869 by a gentleman who has rivalled in this district the good work done by Lord George Hill at Gweedore.

Slieve League from Carrick.

As I remarked before, there is a great deal to be said for staying at one place instead of attempting perpetual motion; and if you adopt the usual British formula of a compromise, there

is no better place to stay in for a week than Carrick. Dunfanaghy is the only place I know with rival attractions in the
way of scenery, and the hotel at Carrick is decidedly the better.
You could spend your week there sight-seeing and never go over
the same ground twice. Besides, it is an excellent spot for
fishing. Brown trout fishing is free to all guests on two rivers
and three lakes, all quite within easy distance of the hotel.
Salmon and sea-trout fishing is free also, provided you take out
your licence in the hotel. This arrangement will suit admirably
on the route I propose, as it is the first fishing hotel you
come to and the licence taken there will be available at any
other river in the county. You are allowed to keep your fish,
and with luck you should get plenty. But the essential thing
for you to do is to see Slieve League and Glen Columbkille ;
Malin-beg, the caves at Muckross and so forth are minor
attractions. The chief centre of the new fishing industries
developed by the Congested Districts Board is at Teelin Harbour, where the Glen River flows into the sea, and Carrick is one
of the two markets for the homespuns whose production has
been so energetically developed of late years. But of these
matters I shall speak elsewhere in some detail. Scenery is the
business of the moment. To see Slieve League is possible by
the use of a boat, a pony, or your legs : not by a bicycle. I
recommend a boat for all this cliff scenery, time and weather
permitting : there is said to be a cave of extraordinary dimensions
in the Slieve League cliff. But I must describe the thing as I
saw it from on foot.

Leaving the hotel, one walks down a road which follows the
swift and rocky course of the Glen River seawards for about two
miles ; then a track turns off to the right up which ponies can
carry a lady almost to the very top. A few hundred yards
further on a road branches away also to the right, towards
what simply appears to be a very high mountain with a sharply
serrated ridge defined against the sky. The other side of that
mountain is a precipitous cliff varying from 1,000 to 2,000 feet,

Coming down Slieve League.

and part of the serrated ridge is the One Man's Path. All
the water you can see from here is the estuary winding down to
Teelin Harbour, and beyond that the mouth of Donegal Bay
with the Sligo mountains showing blue on the far side. The
road goes on for a considerable way and turns into a path up
which a donkey can travel; I made the journey in company
with a man who was going up to cut turf. Here in Glen
Columbkille parish they get their firing free, but they have to go
a far way for it in some cases. A few of the more fortunate can
cut on their own farms : my companion had to ascend at least
a thousand feet before he reached his own particular bog; yet
there are plenty less lucky than he, for they have not all donkeys
to carry the sods. He was a fisherman by trade and belonged to
the crew of a yawl, one of the row-boats which go out to fish for
cod, ling, and mackerel off this rocky coast. They never go far
from Teelin, as it is the only safe place to run to. Most of the
fish caught in this way is sold to cadgers or travelling hawkers ;
the Congested Districts Board make no objection to this trade
provided the price given is at least sixpence a dozen above what
they give at their curing station. For instance, if the Board's
price is 5s. a dozen for ling, the men who deal with them must
not sell ling to the cadgers under 5s. 6d. a dozen. My friend
seemed to envy the more fortunate crews of smacks who take to the
nets and go round to Galway Bay or Downings Bay in Sheephaven; but he had "an old father and mother that had no other
son but him," and they objected to these protracted and risky
cruises. On every smack is a crew of eight ; six Irish, and
with them two Scotchmen, who are regularly retained by the
Board at a fixed wage to teach the others how and where to
shoot their nets and how to mend and keep them. It is a
school of technical education and one sorely needed, for the
Irish have never at any time used the sea for peace or war : and
the men seem to take to it. I saw a gang of a dozen tramping in
from Malinmore and Glen Columbkille to a day's net mending,
after which they must tramp back the eight Irish miles : for

there is no place in Malinmore or Glen where a smack can find
refuge, and even row-boats, if there be any ground-swell, are hard
set to it to get in without a shattering.   These details, I con-
fess, seemed to me more interesting than scenery, and when my
acquaintance broke off to show me a slab called the Giant's Grave
with some old wives' story attached to it, I headed him off antiquities.   But when one reached the cliff edge and saw the sea
a thousand feet below and the Connaught coast stretching
away in its interminable line, one felt there was something to be
said for scenery.   Carrigans Head is below on the left, where
stands one of the old signal towers, which communicates with
Malin-beg, that with Glen Head, and so on.   From this brow the
grassy path runs level for a bit along the cliff edge till you come
to the side of Bunglass—a sort of horse-shoe bend or bight in
the three miles of cliff, and from this you see Slieve League in
all its glory.   About a thousand feet below you is the blue
water, bright green round the rock base, and breaking upon what
seems to be smooth fine sand, but really consists of water-worn
pebbles big as your two fists.   About a thousand feet higher
than you stand rises the cliff on the far side of the bay, and its
seaward front shows a singular variety, red and yellow in streaks,
beside the greys and browns, for Slieve League is not granite.
But the extraordinary beauty of the scene was given by a sight
which must be common at that point.   It was blowing half a
gale, the bay was full of spindrift, and the sun striking on
this made a rainbow right below us, arched against sea and cliff.
I never realised what intensity of colour was before.

From this point you begin a really stiff climb, following the
edge of the cliff in its upward winding.   The stiffest of the
actual climb is over when you get to the One Man's Path.
Here the cliff top is literally a narrow edge of stone about two
feet across, mounting very steep for about fifteen yards.   It
must be done on hands and knees.   On your right inland is
a very steep slope running down towards a tarn ; on the seaward side is practically a straight drop, but only over a heathery

F

slope. It is my opinion that if you fell off the One Man's
Path on the landside you would roll down with little damage,
and that if you fell off on the seaward side you would be able
to stop yourself by clinging to the heather. My guide—for I
took the gentleman with the ass as a guide—was of a very
different opinion ; and there is no doubt that although the
cliffs here are not absolutely plumb—as they are at Glen
Head and Horn Head—you could toboggan down them with
every certainty of a speedy run to the bottom. But the One
Man's Path is nothing to be afraid of. Your guide, if you
have one, will industriously try to frighten you, and then flatter
you when you have got across. All I can say for mine is that
he was genuinely afraid, for he declined to carry my macintosh over the place, on the ground that his boots were bad ;
and I had to wear it, which gave me an insight into the difficulties of cliff work for ladies. The path can be circumvented
on the inner side, and with a strong wind may be an ugly spot
enough to cross. Oddly enough, the day I was there some
eddy of wind protected it from blasts, though a little further
up one could hardly stand.

Further on a little, one sees the Chimneys—some not very
interesting pinnacles of rock—half-way down the cliff, but the
view from the top is wonderful. The whole of Donegal Bay
and the Sligo coast is spread out to the south and south-west ;
inland are the mountains from Lough Erne to the Glen Beagh
range, and north-east you see Glen Bay and Glen Head, and
the coast away up by Ardara and Glenties. West and north-
west stretches the limitless Atlantic. On a bright sunny day,
with wind about one, that place gives the sense of immense
space more strongly than I ever experienced it before. On a
ship you have sea all about you—perhaps nothing but sea—
but you are not looking straight over ocean and land at once
from a height of two thousand feet.

Coming back is an easy affair. You will see the pony track
in the valley below you, and it will take you back to the road ;

A Guide to Slieve League.

an hour's very fast walking brings you to the hotel. The whole
thing should take an active man four or five hours. Tourists
should be careful to believe what they are told about the
dangers of Slieve League when it is capped with mist. Under
these conditions a guide is indispensable. Any one who wishes
to walk back across the mountain will find it rough work, and
possibly dangerous, even on a clear day, to people who do not
understand bogs. In a short cut which I took I saw several very
nasty-looking places. The mountain is full of hares, which add
a charm of wild life to it, and everywhere one is haunted by
the pretty little snow buntings, a bird strange to English eyes.

Having seen Slieve League, it is your next duty to see Glen
Columbkille and Glen Head, perhaps the only piece of coast
scenery that can hold its own for grandeur with the famous
cliff. Now there are three ways of doing this. Either you
may continue to stay at Carrick and make a day's excursion of
it : that means in all about fifteen miles to ride and a walk of,
say, three hours. Or, secondly, you may go to Glen and put up at
the inn there, which is a very clean little public-house, the sort
of thing which is common in England but rare and deserving
of every encouragement in Ireland. Or, thirdly, you may
take the Glen on your way to Glenties or Ardara, which means
a ride of twenty-eight or twenty-two miles, in addition to the
three hours of sight-seeing, involving a climb of 1000 feet. My
advice, on the whole, is to stay at Carrick, and that is the plan I
adopted ; although, in spite of excellent intentions and much
industry, I can scarcely be said to have seen Glen Head. Perhaps I may, for once, recount my day. I started then from
Carrick with rain threatening and the usual headwind ; pushed
the machine nearly all the way for a matter of two miles up a
road—which on a calm dry day could easily be ridden—following
the course of the Owen Wee River. Then I came to a bridge,
at the far side of which a road went up to the right. This I
avoided, and kept straight on past many cottages with dogs
that necessitated an occasional stone, while on my left the river

wound through boggy flats.   After about a mile, a road turned
to the left, crossing the river by a wooden bridge, but this led
up Slieve League, so I went on over the crest of the hill and
came to Lough Auva which was being lashed by the westerly
wind.   Here I stopped and fished the lough from the bank
for an hour or so ; if you care to know the bag, it consisted of
two trout of which the larger might have weighed so much
as one ounce : they are both growing bigger and wiser as I
write.   An old watcher who hailed me to see my pass for the
fishing spoke of the river below as the Yellow River, from
which I infer that Owen Wee is really Owen Buidhe   Owen
simply means "river" and "buidhe" is "yellow."   This old
gentleman comforted me with the assurance that it was only
two miles to Malinmore, and that I would go down "like
thundher."   I did not make so much noise as thunder, and
I was much below the pace of lightning, but still I had a downward slope, and after a while met a view of the sea and Rathlin
O'Byrn Island ; when I got to the village of Malinmore the
road turned sharp to the right past a coastguard station, and I
had the wind nearly behind me and sailed along so cheerfully
that I forgot to look out for the Druidic remains on my left.
Lest you should do so, I will quote Mr. Cooke's description of
them.   Cloghanmore is an oval enclosure internally measuring
forty-eight by thirty-six feet.   At the west end are two double
chambers roofed with enormous flags, and traces of others
adjoining.   Two cells exist in the wall on opposite sides near
the entrance.   The enclosing wall is modern.   On the opposite
side of the road are two standing stones seven feet high and
a fine cromlech.   Six more cromlechs (almost *trop de luxe*)
"are to be seen while passing through the village and another
as we turn north towards Glen."

But whether I forgot the Druids or no, there was no forgetting
Glen Head ; suddenly the road turned and there it rose before
me—a huge cliff shrouded in mist at top, with a leaden sea
breaking round the base of it, and two great rocks standing up

at an angle as if slices had been cut off the cliff and fallen apart. It was impressive to the point of startling one. The bicycle ran easily—though not smoothly—down the hill, and I noticed two or three boats drawn up in the cleft between two great rocks which serves Glen Columbkille as an apology for a harbour : a truly terrible coast it is, and there are not many of us who would like to have a son engaged in fishing there. Down the road you spin and here for the first time since I entered the county from the South, I saw what is familiar all the way to Horn Head—seaweed used for manure. The valley is closed to seaward by a curiously bare ridge of sand-hills, and as one gets a little further in towards the village one sees sand piled on the roadside and on the lee side of every ditch. That is caused by the drift in from the beach. I ran through the town and up to the little inn I have spoken of near the chapel ; there I left my bicycle and asked the landlord to find me some one who would show the antiquities of the Glen. For this Glen, wild as it is, in perhaps the most inaccessible part of Ireland, whether by land or sea, was the peculiar sanctuary of Ireland's greatest missionary, Saint Columbkille " the dove of the Churches," who founded numberless monasteries in Ireland before he went to Iona, and set to evangelising the barbarous Scots and Britons.

English people when they hear this suppose that it is some sort of joke ; but the historic fact remains that, from the beginning of the sixth century to the end of the eighth, Ireland was the University of Europe just as Greece was in the late days of the Roman Republic. *Si monumentum quæris, circumspice.* John Gillespie, who showed me over the place, will no doubt do the same for you if you ask him ; he is lame, but to judge from my experience can tire out most walkers on our mountains. He will show you first the nearest of twelve " crosses " which are set within a range of three miles in the Glen. These crosses are erect stone slabs graved with Celtic designs—which an illustration can best make familiar. Some of them are greatly

weather-worn, some scarcely distinguishable, but all are treated
with veneration.   As we went up the Glen I marvelled more than
ever at the flowers; bluebells everywhere—I saw even some white

Stone Cross, Columbkille.

ones; marsh marigolds : orchises bright purple or pale and livid ;
white pignuts; a few surviving primroses, and a few early flag
irises ; I saw even one foxglove that day—May 29 · but it was at
Carrick.   There were all the vetches from the tiny yellow ladies'

finger to the taller purple kinds ; a handsome purple thornless thistle ; bog cotton, of course, and the fragrant bog myrtle on boggy heather slopes, and a queer little fleshy pink flower, almost like a great lichen in its leaf, whose name I have forgot.   In the ditches were purple bog violets with their picturesque mottled leaf ; and above all, by the little river which runs up the Glen—as also by the Carrick River—quantities of Osmunda growing already to a lordly height.   It reaches six or seven feet. The valley is full of a swamp, a great place for snipe, Gillespie told me : a great place also for otters, which abound in this region both in sea and rivers.   In the grey stony face of Craig Beevna which overhangs the valley, badgers abound, and there are foxes on the hills.   Of this wild life I saw no trace, but there were numerous birds of the bunting order which were strange to me, and I could not put names to them.   Altogether it should be a good camping ground for a naturalist.

One of the most interesting things in the Glen—more interesting even than the crosses or Columbkille's ruined chapel on the hillside—is a cave in the cemetery of the Protestant church which was discovered by chance by men digging a grave not long ago.   It is an artificial underground passage leading between two underground rooms.   The roof is constructed of immense transverse slabs of stone.   A precisely similar cave is found in a field at Ardrummon on Lough Swilly, and is always said to have been one door of a passage communicating with Killydonnell Abbey, a mile or so away.   No doubt they were built as places of refuge.   But perhaps still more interesting are the old remains of huts, roofed in likewise with huge stones, somewhat on the plan of cromlechs.   These buildings a little way up the valley on the left occur in a regular group.   One of these, alas ! is, by a utilitarian generation, converted into a pigstye.   One has a fern growing in luxuriant grace across its doorway.   What they were for—what species of hermits lived in them—whether St. Columba's mysterious sect of the Culdees or others, is matter for con jecture.   My guide set them down as pagan.

The day was misty, as I have said, but Gillespie observed that I might never be there again, so up the head he took me to the Sturrell or Spire point. After a stiffish climb we came to the cliff brow. On the way up my companion discoursed of many things, the praise of the Congested Districts Board chiefly. What they have done for the fisheries was not news to me. He was of opinion, also, that the homespun industry was a real source of profit to the peasants, and if this last year was not as bad as the early eighties, that was thanks to a potato spraying system that the Board had introduced. The Irish Industries Association, too, had done good work; had helped homespinning, distributed looms, and started lace-making. But what hurt them was the American tariff, for America had once, it seems, been a good market.

Discussing these things, we got to the brow of the cliff. Eight hundred feet sheer below, one could see through the mist a sort of ghost of the surf—a very impressive sight. Just by us was the ruin of an old signal tower. Gillespie had known an old man who remembered having wrought at it in the days of Napoleonic war. It was just off here, near Malin Head, that Sir John Warren sighted Bompart's invading squadron in 1798, on board of which was Wolfe Tone. But that story has to be told when we get to Rathmullen, as the story of Columba must be when we get to his birthplace at Gartan.

We plunged along the cliff front in the driving mist, and ultimately struck a road leading out to the Sturrell itself, which is a high conical piece of rock, with a limitless drop below it. At this point the youths of that side of the Glen are in the habit of climbing down the cliff face in search of strayed sheep. From the Sturrell there should be a view of the Rosses and Aranmore, far away north ; but this day we could not even see Tormore, the island a couple of miles out, famous as a wonderful gathering of sea-birds in the breeding season, ill reputed for a recent fatal boating accident. Having seen we came down, passing Columbkille's holy well, which is not a place where cure

are wrought, but merely a religious centre where folk go for
penance and add their tribute to a great cairn of stones. As
we were there and were tasting the water, I thoughtlessly asked
Gillespie if he had ever seen Doon well. "Once," he said with
a curious intonation ; and I knew instantly, what I might have
guessed, that he must have been taken there in hopes of a cure.
Unhappily his crutch has no right to be in the group of which
you will find a drawing further on. He hurt his knee at
"hurling," or hockey-playing, from a blow of the hard wooden
ball, and is very lame indeed. To that circumstance, no doubt,
he owes an exceptional taste for education. I was surprised to
find how interested he was over the fact that Lord Leighton
had stayed in Malinmore a few years back ; and indeed there
were few things that did not seem to interest him, for he had
the temper that makes of so many Irishmen either scholars
or wanderers, though living in this out-of-the-world place.

Cashel, the village in the valley, is, however, in the stream of
affairs compared with the townland of Beevna, where Columbkille's chapel stands. It is separated from the rest of the glen
by the river and the marsh, over which runs a causeway, and
constantly in winter, and sometimes even in summer, tide covers
this ; thus, the folk of Beevna who have no boats, have no way of
communicating with society at all, except by a journey over the
top of Sturrell or Craig Beevna and round by the head of the
Glen. Altogether I felt that I had learnt much from my day,
though the dense mist prevented sight-seeing, and we concluded
with a dissertation on the theory of rundal, which was illustrated
by reference to one or two plots in the Glen. It appears that
in Kilcar, three miles from Carrick, there is a whole townland
where the farms have never been "squared," and the land is
still held in rundal ; for an explanation of the term you must
see the chapter on Gweedore.

I had tea—very good—at the little public, took my machine,
wheeled it laboriously up a mile or so of hill ; found a level of
a mile at top, then a generous descent of about four miles, the

whole of which to the hotel may be coasted, and it is barely
needful to pedal again even once.   This is all very well when
the road is dry and clean, but whizzing down among stones and
on a muddy surface I was thankful to escape a sideslip.   I ran
also into a flock of sheep—but gently ; and there is always the
losing hazard of a pig or a cow.   That is why coasting is hardly
safe in Donegal : the reader may take the warning.

CHAPTER VI

FROM Carrick, if you have done Glen Columbkille, the next stage should be Glenties, twenty Irish miles, unless you are fishing, in which case it is well worth while to stop at Ardara, six miles short of Glenties, and on the coast near the mouth of the Ownea river. O'Donnell's hotel in Glenties I found very comfortable, and the little town makes a pleasant stage on the way northwards.

The road from Carrick follows the course of the Glen river north, then crosses by a bridge and turns to the east, then north again; but it is so lonely a moor that even the map supplied at Carrick hotel—an example of cartography not much more trustworthy than a West African Boundary Commissioner's—cannot mislead you. For about six miles the road rises slowly, and on a dry day, especially with wind behind, it could all be ridden. Then it turns straight to the left, up a long straight mile, perfectly hopeless to ride. Beyond that is a drop to a valley, where a road comes in from Glen, and then it goes up again like the side of a house, and when you get to the top you meet the only C.T.C. warning post known to me in Ireland. This is Glen Gesh hill, at the head of a valley which runs down to Ardara, and is probably the steepest piece of roadway in use for any considerable wheeled traffic in these islands. It is very carefully engineered, and a part of it can be ridden, but the beginning and end of it nobody but an idiot would attempt. An

accident would be deplorable.   If a couple of English tourists
broke their necks on Errigal or Slieve League it would make a

From the Bridge at Glenties.

capital advertisement for the country ; but a road mischance is
different.   Englishmen seem to like their cliffs dangerous and

their roads safe.   From the bottom of the hill is a slope of four
miles into Ardara, most of which can be coasted.   There are
probably beautiful views along the whole road ; but I travelled
it very tired and heavy-laden on a dismal day with a nor'-wester
driving sleety rain at me on the last day of May, and glad I was
to see a great fire in the inn at Ardara.

Ardara is the centre of the hand-weaving industry which has
always existed in Western Donegal, but has been recently
developed by the Congested Districts Board and the Irish Industries Association, founded by Lady Aberdeen.   Many efforts
have been made to popularise in England their stuffs and also
the hand-knitted things of which Glenties is a great market.
But they will probably continue to be produced chiefly for local
use, and long may they continue ; as it is, you will see everywhere poor men wearing stuff admirable in colour and pattern,
which costs them no more than the cheap and nasty products of
Manchester factories.   The industry, for local purposes, is an
old one ; from time immemorial Donegal women have spun the
wool of their own sheep, and Donegal weavers have woven.
But up till quite recent times, the wool was left in its natural
colour and the product was a grey frieze, which you may still
see occasionally, especially in Inishowen.   I can well remember
old Lord George Hill's picturesque figure, which was never clad
in anything else.   Some twenty years back, however, Mrs.
Ernest Hart started at Derrybeg near Gweedore an institution for
teaching the peasants to use dyes ready to their hand ; heather,
lichen and the rest.   Since then skilled supervision has improved
the spinning and weaving ; better looms have been introduced,
and a standard set to the workmen : and the few—or many—
who choose to dress themselves in Donegal homespuns will
find them very pleasant to look at, and comfortable and service-
able to wear.   They are to be seen in the shops in any of
these western towns and in the hotels at Carrick and Gweedore.
But it may be as well to quote an account of the industry given
by Mr. T. W. Rolleston, who was secretary of the Irish In-

dustries Association till that body ceased its years of volunteer
work, and left what it had begun to be fostered by the Congested
Districts Board.

"If one could take a bird's-eye view of this country, at an early
hour in the morning, on the last day of any month, he could
not fail to notice the number of persons, single or in groups,
men and women, who are moving along these roads from every
direction towards Ardara. Each wayfarer carries on his or her
back a large and heavy bundle wrapped in a white cloth, and
slung in a rope generally made of twisted rushes. Some of these
travellers have risen in the middle of the night, and have, perhaps, walked these wild roads for hours under a storm of sleet
or snow. When they arrive in Ardara the nature of their business is soon made clear. The white bundles contain each a big
roll of homespun cloth, and they are bringing them to the
Depot of the Congested Districts Board to be examined by the
Inspector. Inside the Depot a scene of great activity is in progress. The tired peasant slings the big roll off his back, and
straightens himself with relief as he gives in his name, and lays
the cloth on a counter. Here two assistants take charge of it,
and begin rapidly to unroll it for examination. The man's
name, and the name of the townland where he lives, are entered
on a label, which is attached to the piece of cloth. A duplicate
label is handed to the owner, which he must produce when he
comes to take his cloth away for sale in the Fair next morning.
On the other side of the room there runs another long counter,
before which the Inspector stands, carefully scrutinizing the
cloth which is drawn slowly along the counter before him. He
is on the look out for faults, such as unevenness of width, or bars
and streaks caused by irregularity in weaving. If the cloth is
of good and uniform quality throughout, he places upon one
corner of it a stamp composed of the letters C.D.B. (Congested
Districts Board). The stamp carries with it a small award
paid by the Board to the maker of the cloth.

"The number of webs examined at each monthly inspection

varies according to the season. When work is going on in the fields, weaving is largely suspended. In the winter season, the number sometimes exceeds one hundred—fifty, sixty, and seventy are usual returns. Each web will be worth, on an average, say £5 at first cost. It will be seen that the interest dealt with, although purely and solely a cottage industry carried on in the homes of the people, is one of considerable extent, and it is one of vital importance to the inhabitants of this wild, remote, and barren region.

"The morning after the inspection, the first day of every month, the rolls of cloth are handed back to the owners, and if they have not been stamped, the nature of the faults and the proper remedy for them, which are recorded in the Inspection-book, are pointed out. Patterns of new and saleable designs are also distributed to all who desire them. Then the Fair begins. The rolls of cloth are laid down on the footway, on both sides of the road ; a great deal is brought in which was not finished in time for inspection : buyers are present from the neighbouring towns of Donegal, Killybegs, and Glenties, and there are several in Ardara itself. There is the usual bargaining and haggling ; and Ardara, thronged with the mountain-folk, becomes for a time a Gaelic-speaking town. In two or three hours everything is disposed of, and generally at good prices ; for now that certain defects in workmanship have been overcome, this beautiful and unique fabric, stained with the soft, unfading colours produced by the people from common plants and mosses, is in great demand.

" Of the native dyes, those principally used are 'crotal' and heather. Crotal is the Gaelic name for the grey lichen that grows on granite and certain other rocks in boggy districts. Boiled down with the wool it yields a dye, varying, according to the quantity used, from a pale buff to a very dark red brown. Heather gives a bright yellow. Peat soot is used for a brownish yellow dye, and the roots of the blackberry give a beautiful rich brown. Indigo and madder, which, of course, are bought in the shops, are also much used. These colours are often combined to form other shades, and a pretty, variegated effect is obtained by a cunning admixture of little spots of pale red or blue in the weft of a brown or fawn-coloured piece. A shade called "silver gray" is produced by using a white warp with a weft of natural black wool. These webs are made from the fine Shetland-like wool of a breed of sheep which are found towards the extremity of the peninsula, about Malinmore. The other sheep of the district are mostly the black-faced Scotch sheep—hardy little animals, with curly horns, which roam at will over the mountains, and pick up a living like their owners, with much difficulty and hardship. As a rule, the owner of the raw material is not also the weaver. He clips his sheep; his wife and daughters card and spin the wool, and the yarn is then handed over to the weaver, who returns it in cloth, and who is usually simply a peasant artizan, working for hire; though there are, of course, cases where a sheepowner is a weaver as well, or when a weaver will buy wool to make cloth for himself.

"The work of the Irish Industries Association in this region has been guided by Ruskin's golden maxim : " Ascertain what the people have been in the habit of doing, and encourage them to do *that* better : cherish, above all things, local associations and hereditary skill."

The Bridge at Dungloe.

CHAPTER VII

FROM Ardara or Glenties a choice of routes is open. The easiest way upon the whole is to hug the coast and make for Dungloe, about sixteen Irish miles to the north of Glenties. And a wild road you will have to travel over the treeless mountain side, seeing, if you meet with such a day as I did, nothing but a shifting panorama of brown crests and grey mists, with here and there a dim glimpse of the Atlantic, till you reach the neighbourhood of Dungloe itself and its cluster of neighbouring lakes. Now, there are sundry good motives for taking this line. First, Dungloe is a good fishing centre; its lakes abound with brown and white trout, though for some reason the salmon seldom come into them. Secondly, the whole coast off the

Rosses—which is a general name for the district between Dungloe and Gweedore— is scattered in the most curious way with
a multiplicity of islands, big and little, ranging from Aran down-
wards, and in fine weather must be exceedingly picturesque.
Thirdly, just here are brought into conspicuous juxtaposition a
monument of legislative failure and a living evidence of successful help given by the Government. Just inside of Aran lies
Burton Port ; and just off Burton Port is Rutland Island, where
in 1785, under the Duke of Rutland's Viceroyalty forty thousand pounds was expended in making quays for the herring fishery, a military station, and general emporium for this part of the
country. The sand and storm had their will of this enterprise ;
but Burton Port looks a more thriving concern, and likely to
defy rough weather. Six or seven years ago fishing on any
large scale was practically unknown here : what was the use of
men's risking their lives to take a haul of herring and mackerel
when all they could do with them would be to spread the
rotting fish on their fields for manure? However the parish
priest harangued his parishioners on the duty of catching these
fish and curing them ; but that was a new idea to Donegal
peasants and new ideas are not welcome. Harangues failing,
he got a boat and nets and tried the game on his own account
to set an example, but was not successful in spite of the
apostolic precedents. However one of his flock, a man who had
been in America and seen things done, tried the experiment also
and made a big haul, then a second and a third, and by that time
the neighbourhood was encouraged. Then came in the Government and advanced money to buy boats and nets, established a
curing station and brought men over from Scotland to teach the
process. What is the result? Last year there was paid down
on the quay upwards of £12,000 for the take of fish to almost
a hundred boats. Local tradesmen in Dungloe cured, one 3,000
another 4,000 barrels. Women do the curing and can earn, I
was told, about fourteen shillings a week at it not working excess
in hours ; and it must be remembered that in the agricultural

parts of the country nine shillings a week is the highest wages
paid to a labourer in regular work.   Besides all this, a cooperage
has been set up at the port, giving more employment; a big
London merchant is establishing a curing station of his own on
one of the little islands ; and net-making, if not boat-building,
should follow in process of time.   If you ride down to the port—
it is about four miles from Dungloe by a picturesque road along
the coast,—you will be surprised to see how prosperous the
little place looks with its row of neat coastguard houses and other
quite comfortable stone buildings and such a fashionable shop-
window as twenty years ago would scarcely have been found in
the whole west of the country.

On your way, too, you will pass the beginnings of another
industry.   The red granite of Donegal is accounted the best in
the three kingdoms for colour and closeness of grain ; but
hitherto the cost of transport has prevented all attempts to give
it a commercial value.   Now, however, a company has secured
quarrying rights on what is practically a small mountain of it on
the right of the road when you cross the little river.

There you can see the stone in all stages ; rough as it comes
from the rock, or squared into blocks as it goes into the market
and, in a couple of specimens, with its final polish on it.   A
short rail has been run across the road to the water about
a quarter of a mile off; thence the stone is taken in barges to an
island; across the islet is another rail to the port of call on
the seaward side, whence steamers take it to Liverpool,
Manchester, or wherever it may be needed for decorative work.
Donegal is not rich as yet, but if any one can make money out of
her stones, there is little fear of the material running out and
the enterprise deserves good wishes.

So much for Dungloe and Burton Port, which, small as they
are, are yet worth going to look at—thriving centres of commerce
where the whole business of life is transacted still in Irish.
Dungloe is also the most convenient stage between Glenties and
Gweedore, being an easy ride from either.   Yet upon the whole

I would advise the cyclist who does not shrink from a day of thirty miles to leave the coast at Glenties and strike inward up the line of the Gweebarra and cross the mountains till the streams begin to run east instead of west. For this wild coast, beautiful as it is, wearies the eye with its desolation, one craves the sight of trees: and so my advice is that you should make your next halting place in the excellent new hotel at Gartan Lough, whence the river Lennan finds its way into Lough Swilly. But for safety's sake it is desirable to write or wire from Glenties to the St. Columb's Hotel to know

The Mill at Dunglee.

if you can be taken in, for there are only eight bedrooms available; still if the worst came to the worst there is a decent inn close by at Churchhill, and it is only an easy ride of seven or eight miles from there into Kilmacrenan, where there is also fair accommodation.

It would be a great mistake to accept the dictum that Ireland is "an ugly picture set in a beautiful frame;" and quite apart from the beauty of the lake and river scenery at Gartan and Glen Veagh, there is the extraordinary historic interest of Columba's birthplace and the famous Rock of Doon.

Decide then to go to Gartan, whether from Glenties on the way
to Gweedore, or as an alternative from Gweedore on the way
to Dunfanaghy ; but I recommend the former.

For the stage that is to bring you to Gartan it is distinctly an
advantage to start from Glenties, as even the six level miles
from Ardara to Glenties make a perceptible addition to what
may be a trying, although a very beautiful, ride. Leaving
Glenties then, past the railway station, your road follows the
line of the railway for a matter of two miles, then the telegraph
posts turn straight up the hill to the left, and here you must get
off and walk, but once you top the hill you have a perfectly
delightful ride for seven miles along the Gweebarra estuary
and up to Doochary bridge. The road runs down an easy
gradient until you meet the Gweebarra, which is a long narrow
cleft in the land. If you follow that cleft it takes you straight
up the line of the Gweebarra river to Lough Barra, and straight
over the pass there to Glen Veagh, and thence straight down
the line of the Owen-Harrow river to the level of Sheephaven
and Mulroy. It is, in short, one end of the great pass that
divides the Donegal mountains from north-east to south-west.
After an hour or so of riding along this beautiful but lonely road,
you will come at last to Doochary bridge, where the tideway
ends. Cross the bridge to your left, and you will see your road
running up the north side of the valley. You can easily trace
your direction, for the road is a continuous ascent now of six or
seven miles, but the valley is well-wooded and the road is well-
engineered, so that, at least on a dry day with the wind behind
you, you will have nothing to complain of. When the Gweebarra has become a mere trickle and trees have disappeared,
you certainly have a stiff piece of work and a very wild country.
I went into a house here to ask for some soda bread, and found
three people in the cottage : an old man, and an old woman
and a young woman, not one of whom could understand English
—a very rare experience nowadays. But, although the hill is long
and steep, the surface of the road is very good, and on a fine

Doochary Bridge.

day the view of Lough Barra should repay you for much.   It
lies, a perfectly pure cold sheet of water, under Glendowan
mountain, with neither trees nor sedge about it, and one side
surrounded with the shelving bank of crisp white fresh-water
sand.   To the left of the lake the road runs on through a gorge
which reminded me of one of the gray Cumberland passes : on
the left were the precipitous slatey brows of some smaller hills,
and over the lower slopes a shepherd and his dog were working
some sheep—just a touch of life that threw into relief the wildness
of the scene.   On the right rose Glendowan, an easy climb,
which would certainly be rewarded by a magnificent view, for
at this point even from the road one can see almost to the
Atlantic and easily distinguish Slieve Tooey and the other great
hills near Glen Head.   But I was late and tired on that road,
and glad I was when I got to the watershed and after a short ride
on the level top saw underneath me the long straight cleft of
Glen Veagh with Mrs. Adair's castle looming large in the
evening.   My road turned to the right, skirting the mountain.
On the hill-side was the high fence, which encloses the whole
Adair property, and enclosed by that fence, on the southern
side of the Glen Beagh mountain, is the Derry Beagh district,
which causes the name of the Adair estate to be unhappily
familiar.

Lough Barra was the meeting place for one of the most
disastrous military expeditions ever sent into Donegal.   I doubt
if soldiers were ever despatched on a less congenial duty than
were the detachment who marched there on April 7th, 1861, to
protect the civil power in executing the Derry Beagh evictions.

In 1857 Mr. John George Adair, a wealthy gentleman of
Queen's County who had been taken with the beauty of Glen
Veagh, bought up the Gartan estates.   Mr. Adair was a friend
of so well known a Nationalist as Sir Charles Gavan Duffy, editor
of the famous *Nation* newspaper : he had stood for Parliament
as a tenant-right candidate and is admitted to have been a
kindly, well-meaning man.   Unfortunately he at once came into

collision with the Derry Beagh tenantry, as in August 1858 he
went to shoot a mountain over which the late landlord, a Mr.
Johnson, still claimed sporting rights. The tenants came out
in a body and turned him off: the result was a series of actions
and counter actions for assault, and various appeals. Mr. Adair
determined at all costs to make himself master in the country
side, the more so as several of the neighbouring gentry were

Aghla Mountain and Lough Finn.

openly sympathising with his tenants in the quarrel, and he
bought up altogether an estate of some ninety square miles.
At the same time he determined to give full trial to an experiment
then much talked of and stock the mountains with Scotch
sheep. Other landlords were doing the same, and the main
result so far was to strew the mountain side with dead mutton.

Accusations were freely brought against the tenants and presentments sent in by the grand jury, which raised a levy on the district for compensation, the sheep being rated at a handsome value. The result was a great embittering of the relations between landlord and tenant, which was particularly acute on the Glen Veagh estate. The unfortunate tenants saw their goods distrained to pay for sheep which, in many instances, at all events, had died of exposure to the weather. The magistrates sitting at Church Hill passed a unanimous resolution to the effect that the losses which Mr. Adair charged on malice were due to natural causes. By this time there was a very strong feeling in the countryside that Mr. Adair with all his money and all his beneficent intentions was rapidly turning a peaceable neighbourhood into a hornets' nest. Nothing, however, would convince him but that the people were banded together to do him injury. As he was calling at Gartan Rectory one day, an outhouse took fire, and though the Rector was conspicuous for his sympathy with the tenants, Mr. Adair would have it that an attempt had been made to burn the Rectory and him in it. Finally on November the 13th his manager was found dead on Derry Beagh mountain: no evidence was forthcoming. Mr. Adair determined, under the guidance of a strong sense of duty, to make a great example of this pestilent community. Accordingly in the spring of the year he served ejectment notices on every tenant in Derry Beagh. Matters were serious now and every effort was used to stop so dreadful a measure as to exile a community of several hundred souls not only from their homes but in many cases from their only available means of livelihood. But Mr. Adair was inflexible. The sub-sheriff of the county demanded an escort of 200 police and troops as well. The soldiers were sent down from Dublin, taking tents with them, as if for a campaign: and the rendezvous was fixed at Lough Barra for April 7th. On April 8th the whole force moved on to its work, and a matter of three days was spent in the task of dragging men and women out of their cabins and levelling the poor dwellings with the ground. The evicted tenants hung about the ruins like ghosts and spent the night, many of them, on the hillside. Happily, however, the affair was so flagrant as to excite wide notice, and from Australia came the most effectual relief. The Government of Victoria was induced to offer free passages to all who cared to emigrate, and the great body of the expelled did so.

Such are the plain facts of the transaction, which is narrated with angry eloquence in Mr. A. M. Sullivan's *New Ireland.* A debate was raised in the House of Commons by Mr. Vincent Scully, who demanded that Mr Adair should be withdrawn from the commission of the peace ; certainly no man had done more to disturb the country. If it were not a tragedy it would be a comedy to contemplate this gentleman, abounding with sympathy for the Irish tenants, coming down with full pockets and excellent schemes to make the felicity of this desolate region ; then at the end of three years, as a result of his efforts, determining to punish the crime of one man by a sentence of exile upon hundreds of innocent persons, most of them helpless women and children. And the sadly humorous part of it was that Mr. Adair probably believed honestly that he was following the dictates of conscience in carrying out this appalling severity, which is so plainly accounted for by the most merciless of all feelings, wounded self-esteem turned into violent self-assertion.

These, however, are " old, unhappy, far-off things ; " and you will not have time to think much about them going down the hill from above Glen Beagh towards Gartan. I fancy that a good cyclist could run for about five miles here with his feet off the pedals, but for my own part the pace was too much for me, and there is one very ugly sharp turn over a little wooden bridge, so I give my warning. But a great deal of the road can be coasted with most perfect safety, and it continues to fall till you get to the level of the lake, which lies, broad, peaceful, and island-studded, between its sloping shores. A beautiful private demesne runs all along the south side of the lake, admirably timbered, and, on a

June evening when I reached it, it was indeed a sight to see. All along the road, inside a wall, was a high hedge of hawthorn, then in full bloom and thickly interspersed with laburnums in the most glorious rain of gold that I have ever beheld. Rabbits lobbed in and out of the hedges, and the whole scene was inexpressibly grateful to one's eyes after a week on the west coast, where trees practically do not exist and the eye gets weary of the grandeurs of cliff and ocean. You ride along this pleasant road until you reach a police barrack, then turn to the left, cross a bridge over the river Lennan where it flows out of Gartan Lake, ride on three or four hundred yards further, and even if you do not see the house, for it is thickly sheltered in trees, you cannot miss a gateway where the name of the St. Columb's Hotel is written up. Go up the avenue and you will find a pleasant welcome, and what is to all intents and purposes a very well-appointed private house.

Lough Finn.

Gartan Lough.

CHAPTER VIII

WHAT is now the hotel at Gartan was originally the Glebe House in the days when Church of Ireland clergy had larger incomes and larger dwellings than now fall to their share. It stands with its grounds on a neck of land projecting into the lower lake, and should be an ideal place to fish from. All about it is pleasant wooding, which follows the course of the Lennan down to Rathmelton, and I would advise any one who is not in a hurry, to stay a day or two, and fish either lake or river; the river for salmon, the lake for trout. But in any case it is a good place to stay in, for all about you are venerable memories. Here at Gartan in 521 A.D. Columba was born.

Tyrconnell had its share of holy men in the days when Ireland had its name of the Isle of Saints—that is, in the four

centuries after the coming of St. Patrick, when the land fell into
such a habit of restful peace that the Danish sea rovers found
its sea boundary easy prey.   But the special saint of Tyrconnell
was the greatest of all Irish saints after Patrick, St. Columba.
In about 450 A.D. Patrick, on his missionary journey, crossed
the Erne from Carbery in Sligo, where Cairbre, one of Niall's
sons, had received him roughly : but on the north bank, after
he had passed by Assaroe and ascended Mullaghnashee, he
found Conall Gulban sitting in council in the palace that the
fairies had built him.   Conall came to Patrick for his blessing,
but Patrick turned from him and laid his hand first on the head
of Conall's son Fergus.   " For," he said, " of his lineage will be
born a youth that is Columbkille."   Then after baptising Conall
and his household, Patrick went through Barnesmore Gap and
turned northwards, but when he was on the top of Cark mountain, overlooking the Swilly, at a ford of the river Deele, which
runs through Convoy, the axle of his chariot broke and when
mended broke again.   Then Patrick knew the sign and bade
his people not wonder, for the land north of that river had no
need of him ; for a son should be born there who should be
called " The Dove of the Churches " - Columbkille—who should
bless the land to the northward.   So he turned away eastward
and made his way to the Grianan on Aileach which looks upon
the Foyle and Lough Swilly, and there baptised Eoghan the
founder of the Kinel Eoghan, and first lord of Tyrone.

Columba was born in 521 and lived to 597.   He was son of
a chief Feidilmid, and grandson's grandson to Conall Gulban.
His mother was Ethne, who by divine monition, say the
chroniclers, went to Gartan for the birth.   His fosterers were
the O'Ferghails (Freels) who lived at Kilmacrenan, then known
as Doire Eithne (Ethne's Grove).   After he came to be a youth
he went to Strangford, where he studied under St. Finian.   In
those days Ireland was the great home of universities, an island
remote from the wars that ravaged Europe, honoured for its
scholars and resorted to by students from all lands.   Columba

was ordained and lived for a while in a monastery at Glasnevin
near Dublin; thence he returned to his own country and founded
his first monastery at Derry—the first of those many foundations which earned him his title Columbkille—they are too
many to enumerate here; those in Donegal are Kilmacrenan
—(that is Cill Macnenain—the church of the sons of Enain, who
married Columba's sister Mincholeth); Gartan; Glen Columbkille; Tory island; Raphoe, Temple Douglas between Gartan
and Letterkenny; and Ballymagroarty (Drumhome) where the
Cathach of Columba was kept.

But this Dove of the Churches was no dove in disposition,
and there were bitter feuds between him and Diarmaid the
Ardri or High King of Ireland.   A manslayer who sought
sanctuary with Columba was dragged away and killed by
Diarmaid's order, and in return for this Columba stirred up the
northern Clan na Niall—the folk descended like himself from
Niall of the Nine Hostages—and they defeated Diarmaid, head
of the southern Clan na Niall, at Cooldrevny.   Another quarrel
arose over a matter of literary right.   Columbkille was a great
scribe, and is said to have made 300 copies of the New Testa-
ment with his own hand.   He had copied also a Psalter from
a book of St. Finian's, and much store was set upon it, for this
became the famous Cathach.   St. Finian claimed the copy as
his own, the matter was referred to Diarmaid and Diarmaid
laid down the law that, as the calf went with the cow, so the
copy went with the book.   It is not certain whether this second
dispute was cause or consequence of the fight at Cooldrevny;
at all events Diarmaid's decision was disregarded, for the
Cathach remained an heirloom with the heads of Kinel Conaill.
The battle of Cooldrevny is always regarded as a youthful error
of St. Columba's, and is said to have occasioned him bitter
repentance.   But it was not the only one which he provoked.
The second also arose out of a quarrel with another saint—
Comgall of Bangor—who claimed jurisdiction over a church at
Rostorathair near Coolrath or Coleraine.   Columbkille was

supported by the northern Hy-Niall and Comgall by the
Dalriadan Clan Donnell—a branch of the Hy Niall lords of
Antrim and the Scotch isles.   The third battle was that of
Cul-fedha, in which the northern Hy Niall under Aedh (Hugh)
defeated the southern under Colman, son of Diarmaid.   A
saint so contentious was hardly a blessing to his country, and
there is no cause for wonder why in 562, after the first of these
battles, a synod sitting in Meath, under Diarmaid's influence,
excommunicated him.   Either for this cause or, as some say,
because another saint enjoined exile on him for a penance, he
left Ireland in 563 and went to Conall, King of Dalriada, who
welcomed his kinsmen—for both were descended from Niall of
the Nine Hostages—and gave him the island of Hy.   This isle—
better known under its Latin name of Iona—became the seat
of a great monastic foundation and a centre from which
Christianity and the arts of peace were taught to the still
barbarous Scots and Saxons.

Sometimes this great prince of the Church interfered in the
affairs of Ireland for war or peace : twice, as we have seen, he
stirred up battles, and in 573, when the Ard-ri held a great
national gathering to consider questions of moment, he accompanied the King of Dalriada.   One point for settlement was
the position of the Irish colony on the Scotch coast, and
Columba gave his opinion, which was accepted, that it should
be an independent State.   The other question was the status of
the order of bards, who went through the land demanding free
quarters for themselves and their following, and, if not entertained as they desired, revenged themselves by composing
scurrilous libels and songs.   The assembly was well minded
to abolish their order altogether : but Columba, as a friend of
learning, advised only that the number of bards should be
restricted, and some rules made for their conduct ; under these
limitations their ancient privileges were maintained.

In his latter days Columba was rather a Scotch than an
Irish saint, but his successors in the Abbacy of Iona were mostly

Irish and of the lineage of Niall. Such certainly was Adamnan, or Eunan, patron saint of Raphoe, ninth Abbot, who wrote the famous life of the founder, describing all his piety and personal graciousness.

The Cathach, however, was essentially an Irish relic. It was preserved by the O'Donnells, as Manus O'Donnell writes, for "the chief relic of Columbkille in the territory of Kinel Conall Gulban; and it is covered with silver under gold; and it is not lawful to open it; and if it be sent thrice, rightwise, around the army of the Kinell Conaill when they are going to battle, they will return safe with victory, and it is on the breast of a coarb or cleric who is to the best of his power free from mortal sin that the Cathach should be when brought round the army." From this custom it took its name—Cathach "The Battler."

The relic was officially kept by the MacRobhartaigh (MacGrorty) of Ballymagroarty. After the plantation of Ulster there was no one who could claim to represent the O'Donnells. But, about 1700, the Cathach was in the keeping of an O'Donnell whose career is typical of the fortunes of the old Celtic nobles. Daniel O'Donnell was born in 1666, and at the age of twenty-two held a commission under James II. After the Treaty of Limerick he was one of the thousands who went to recruit the Irish brigade, and fought in Germany, Italy, and the Low Countries; commanded the regiment of O'Donnell at Malplaquet, and in the siege operations that followed it, and finally earned his rank as brigadier-general. From that day to this it would be hard to count the O'Donnells who have risen to distinction in almost every service but the English.

Daniel O'Donnell guarded the Cathach carefully, but at last thought better to leave it in the custody of a Belgian monastery —probably the Irish convent at Louvain. He left instructions that it should be given up to whoever could prove himself to be the chief of the O'Donnells. There it remained till in this century an Irish abbot thought it should go back to Tyrconnell, and restored it to the O'Donnells of Newport, in

county Sligo; they in their turn entrusted it to the Royal
Irish Academy, where it is for all the world to see.

But at Gartan there are no memories of Columba's
diplomatisings and bickerings ; only memories of his sanctity.
They show you, on a slope that overlooks the upper lake
from the north, a great flagstone where his mother, the Princess
Ethne, made her bed when he was born ; the dints are in it yet
of her hands and knees. Ethne was too great a lady in her day
to have had so rough a couch ; but the stone is honoured in
tradition, and they say that whoever sleeps on it will never know
home-sickness. Many a man starting for America has tried the
remedy that was to keep him from the torment that people in
Ulster call "thinking long" ; but I doubt it has not helped
them. The place of real worship is the "station" of St.
Columba above the upper lake, Lough Akibbon. There at least
you must go : not that there is much to see ; a graveyard on
the hillside, carefully walled in, and a tiny chapel that could
never have held fifty people, roofless now, and its east window
that once showed ornament, blown in lately by a storm. But
the day I went there an old woman was on her knees before
the ruined altar, and when she had finished her devotions she
showed the "good stone"—from which she said Columbkille
gave out holy water. It had certainly been hollowed for some
sacred use, though likely enough Columba never saw it. But
the memory of his name was then as living as the faith that
brought this old woman to step aside on her day's errand to
kneel at the place he had hallowed. In the graveyard, they
told me, Protestants and Catholics alike were buried, where no
quarrellings disturb them. They sleep there quiet and whole
some on the green hillside, with the lovely lake below them.
In the very centre stands a new and conspicuous monument,
ugly enough indeed, but costly. Some one in Wilmington of
the United States erected it in memory of his father and
mother, natives of that parish. There you have the very spirit
of this country. Hard and stubborn as the soil is, ungrateful

to the tillers of it, it breeds a strong race; they go out over seas, and win to a prosperity impossible in their homes; but you shall scarcely hear of one but sends back constant remittances to the old people, and gray stones, brown moors and blue waters make a living image for ever in their hearts; and it pleases them, if they cannot be there to close the eyes of those they love, at least to erect some memorial that shall link their names to the home they have not forgotten.

On one day in the year—so I was told—there is a great station at this shrine—it is the 15th of August; and at least at the time my informant knew it, people gathered from all parts to have cures wrought. It was accounted on this day the most healing place in Donegal, and the good woman remembered well going there with her father for pains he had, and a deal of good it did him. But the great place of pilgrimage that heals all ailments all days, is the Well of Doon. If you go, go there reverently, and even if you have nothing to be healed of, as is likely enough after a week's touring in Donegal, you should go to this place of pilgrimage. I have seen myself, when I was a boy, pilgrims flocking there on crutches, and I have known of a man who came all the way from Glasgow, bringing with him his worldly possessions—an old mother and an old mattress, and carrying both of them, for the old woman could make no shift to walk. Her son got her by public conveyance as far as Rathmelton, but for the ten long Irish miles to Gartan he carried the two of them. First he would leave the old woman and go on with the mattress; then leave it by the road in sight, and go back for his mother, and so on. Whether he cured her or not we never heard, but surely he deserved a miracle. The piety of Cleobis and Bito, who drew their mother to the temple when the oxen died, was a small thing compared with his.

To Doon Well then I would have you go from Gartan, and the best way is to cross the bridge over the Lennan where it leaves Gartan Lough and follow the road for a matter of seven miles to Kilmacrenan. Nearly all the way the slope is with

you, and you can easily trace your line by following the river
which keeps you the pleasantest of company, sometimes on
your right, sometimes on your left.   The telegraph wires show
the way to Letterkenny, so you must take the first road that
diverges from them to the left.   Kilmacrenan itself is a pretty
little village with a tributary stream – the Lurgy   flowing through
it—and you can get lunch there.   Suppose you order it at one
of the two inns, you will have time to ride half a mile down
the Rathmelton road and see the ruins of an old Franciscan
Abbey that was built in the fifteenth century by the O'Donnells.
Little of it is standing now, but enough to measure the extent,
which was very considerable.   The tower, which was fairly complete, with pointed windows in the top stage of it, is more recent,
and under the tower is buried the most remarkable type of the
old Irish clergy of the Established Church that any living man
remembers.   Dr. Anthony Hastings was appointed by Trinity
College, Dublin, to Kilmacrenan, which was one of the old college livings which studded the whole of Ulster with huge barracks
of houses.   He was a relation of Warren Hastings and well
come of on the mother's side ; if you had met him on the roads,
so they say, you would have known him for a man of good
birth and breeding ; but when he spoke to you as he
certainly would have done—you would have heard a brogue
that even Irishmen marvelled at.   It was part of his unique
personality which has made him the subject of more stories in
that countryside than any man who has lived there in this
century.   Happily there still lives a gentleman, old, alas ! in
everything but mind, but most fit to preserve the traditions of
the wit and humorist, who was the delight of his boyhood.
Here is a story—one of many—that he told me of Dr.
Hastings—but I wish you could have heard it from himself.
One day when he was staying at Kilmacrenan he went down
to the church to see his host marry a couple.   There was
a great assemblage, and the Doctor came in looking very
grave in his surplice.   The bride and bridegroom took their

places confronting him, and the service began, when suddenly the Doctor stopped and said to the bridegroom, who had a name of being close-fisted, "There's a matter of money you know, that's due to me this day : have you it with you?" This was a fee of half a sovereign which Dr. Hastings never thought of exacting. The bridegroom was confounded. "Sure, your reverence, I never thought to bring it : I'll send it to your reverence the first thing." "Have you it with you?" said the Doctor. "No, your reverence." "Then," said Dr Hastings with a grave face, "not a one of you will I marry to day ;" and with that he shut the book and walked away towards the vestry. The bridegroom who had the neighbours all invited and the refreshments ready was in a terrible way and clamoured entreaties, but Dr. Hastings walked on regardless. Then, just as he reached the vestry door he turned round. "Well, now," he said, "if I forgive you and marry you to-day, will you promise me one thing?" "Anything, your reverence, anything in the world." "Will you mind now and take the money that's owing to me and buy a new dress for your wife?" The unfortunate man was only too glad to promise, but Dr. Hastings heaped threats upon him in case he should go back on his word, before he would go on with the service and marry them off. All this was done with the utmost gravity and seriousness, to the wild delight of my friend, who sat chuckling in his pew. But imagine a scene like that in the Church of Ireland to-day !

Kilmacrenan lies on the high road from Derry to Dunfanaghy, and in the old days was a necessary halting place for any one coming through from the great houses at Ards and Horn Head ; so it happened tolerably often that some stranger of the better class, having heard the fame of Dr. Hastings, would be in the church on a Sunday. It was always noticed that on these occasions the sermon rose above the usual level. One day a couple of mischievous lads staying at the Rectory thought it would be a fine joke to leave the rector without his sermon, and they well knew it resided in his coat-tail pocket.

Accordingly on the way to church they contrived to pick the pocket; but to their amazement the rector when he mounted the pulpit only showed a moment's hesitation and then launched into an excellent discourse. Coming out of church he shook his head at them. "Ah, ye young rascals, I know what ye were up to! But I tell you, boys; you forgot the bully in the other pocket." The "bully" was a second and superior article held in reserve for the chance of distinguished strangers.

One of the pickpockets was a son of the late Mr. Cæsar Otway, whose *Sketches in Ireland*, published some seventy years ago, contain a great deal that is amusing, but are not to be relied on for strict veracity. I give, therefore, with all reservation, one more story of Dr. Hastings, told by this authority, who was, at least, undoubtedly an intimate friend of the Doctor's. One fine summer morning Dr. Hastings heard a noise at his back door and observed one of his servants trying to keep out a man who was anxious to get into the house. This person had that air of something between the classes, which in those days and at that place, could belong only to a gauger. "Let me in," he begged, "or my life's lost, and hide me somewhere." While Dr. Hastings was parleying with him, up came the forerunners of a great crowd demanding the gauger. Hastings remonstrated, but the crowd said they wished him no harm, but the gauger they must have or they would pull the house down to get him. "Well," said the Doctor, "there's no way to stop you, but there must be fair play given. The man had ten minutes start of you when he got here; he must have the same law when he gets away." The pursuers consented, and the Doctor explained to the hunted man that if he could reach the Lennan, about half-a-mile off, and swim it he might get clear that way. Accordingly the crowd gathered, the Doctor stood on his doorstep watch in hand, and away went the gauger down the lawn, forded the Lurgy and was taking up the ridge that divides it from the Lennan, when just as he was reaching the crest the hunt was up and after him, and away they went. The gauger took the water but was spent with running and weighted with his clothes and so came near to drown; but the hillmen went in after him, pulled him out, rubbed him and dosed him heavily with the *poteen* it was his trade to discover. Then, tying a bandage over his eyes, they mounted him on a pony and took him over the hills to Glen Beagh; put him in a curragh and rowed him up and down the lake for some hours, and then stowed him in a dark cell on a little island. Here they kept him in the dark but well fed, for a matter of six weeks : then he was taken out, blindfolded again, marched for a day over the mountains, and finally left alone on a road near his home in Letterkenny.

The object of this was to keep the man from laying information at the assize. Under the existing revenue laws, any townland where a still was found working, fell under a heavy fine; and this gauger held evidence against several townlands, the fines amounting to a matter of £7,000. The assize passed, and with it the legal date for laying the information, and the gauger was restored to the bosom of his family.

Such is the tale as Cæsar Otway tells it on the authority of Dr. Hastings, and if it is not true I can only say that other wilder and queerer stories still are truly enough told of this queer, wild country. But you will have had lunch and be ready to start for Doon Well. Crossing the bridge over the Lurgy and proceeding along the high road to Dunfanaghy, you will first meet an old road that continues its course straight up the hill. This used to be the only way to Dunfanaghy, crossing the shoulder of the ridge above Lough Salt, which is the chief point, with its serrated top 1,500 feet high, in the range between Sheephaven and the Lennan valley. A delightful road it is to walk, but too hilly and rough for cyclists. On the south side of Lough Salt mountain lies Lough Kiel, a good fishing lake, in almost the wildest and

least-travelled district of the county. A servant in the house
where I was bred came from there, and she became a
tradition. Once she went off to a wedding and returned
jubilant. The bride was, like herself, a M'Gettigan and the
bridegroom was a M'Gettigan, and they each brought fifty
M'Gettigans to the wedding. And it was the grand wedding!
First they danced and then they sang, and then they fought.
Oh, it was the grand wedding! Another time there came a
tragedy. Her father was taken up for stilling and she shed floods
of tears to induce my father to go and get him out of gaol—sure
his reverence could do it if he liked. She had to console
herself by writing a lampoon in verse on the police-sergeant
who made the capture. Her talent for comic verse was a
delight and a surprise to us, but she always insisted that
the poet of the family was her sister, who only "had the
Irish," and used to come over and see her sometimes. I
remember asking what she wrote about, but only got a vague
answer "about the blue mountains and the heather and the
salmon in the rivers"—in short, the usual Celtic repertory.

On the other side of Lough Salt is a tarn of surprising depth
—240 feet—into which the cliff falls sheer from near the
summit, and this gives the mountain its name, Lough agus Alt,
the Lough and the Crag, of which Lough Salt is a corruption.
But for the present you have not to go up the Lough Salt road,
unless you are energetic—and indeed it is well worth your while,
for the view over Sheephaven to the west, and Mulroy and
Lough Swilly on the east, is among the finest in the county.
Moreover, the only time I was on top of Lough Salt an
eagle came and flapped round me, within twenty yards, as I lay
in the heather, the only one of these birds I ever saw in
Donegal. Supposing, however, that you leave Lough Salt
unvisited, you will proceed up the Dunfanaghy road for about
half a mile from Kilmacrenan, when you come at the top of a
sharp hill to some cottages and trees, and a road running to
the left. That is the road for you to take; and in one of these

cottages, when I went in to ask my way, I saw in the far corner three people eating their mid-day potatoes at a table, and near me on the floor, stretched out upon a clean truss of hay, a fine sow, looking the picture of luxurious contentment, and eight pink little piglings cuddled up together in a heap : the traditional Irish cottage equipment, but a thing very rarely to be seen in these days of sanitary inspections.

The road to Doon Well is one of those by-tracks where the cyclist has to remember that he is still a strange beast. Horses—not fiery, untamed steeds, but decent, quiet animals in the cart or plough—will still shy at him, and that has to be borne in mind, for one's own safety and other people's. After about two miles up and down hill over waste moorland, you will see on the left the Rock of Doon—a bold scarped hillock or bluff, standing conspicuously out from the rest, with a road, or rather a raised causeway, running across the bog to it. Follow that the best way you can ; there is generally a track made by barefoot traffic along the edge of it possible enough for the machine, and you will notice on your left a tossing series of heathery hills and hummocks. Then the road rises, and as you come to the top of the hill look back and you will see a ring-fence of mountains all about you—Lough Salt quite near at hand, then east of him the Knockalla range above Mulroy, all brown and purple with heather ; beyond them again—on the far side of Lough Swilly, which you cannot see—rise the Inishowen Mountains, Slieve Snacht (Snow Peak) the highest. Then set your face west again, and suddenly you round a corner of the Rock of Doon, and there in front of you, on a level green space, is something like a flight of strange birds—tall and leggy herons. That is the array of crutches, left there by the healed cripples, and they are all swathed about with the rags worn in sickness. Wind and rain and sun have wrought upon these unsightly objects till they are cleansed and bleached and softened into a conformity of tint with the grey stones

about them ; just so in the cliff faces you see streaks and lines of
a blotchy red or patches of a soft brown that is lichen.   When
you come near them, you will find that the whole space of
ground on which they stand is carpeted with a litter of rags
that have fallen   for nothing is taken away—and are quietly
perishing into dust on the ground.   Every little tuft of rushes
that grows there has its share of old linen or worsted knotted

Doon Rock and Well with the Votive Crutches.

into the rushes or strings of beads tied about them.   The
Well is in the centre of the greensward ; it is roughly roofed
over with stones, and beyond it is a bank and stream where pilgrims take off their shoes and wash their feet, for you must go
barefoot to the well.   There is a cottage close by, where the good
woman will tell you all you want to know.   If you have any
ailment, and will take the cure in good faith, you must wash

first, and go barefoot, then say five Our Fathers and five Hail
Marys and one Creed, and then drink, praying God speed you
in the errand you came on ; then you will say five more Our
Fathers and five more Hail Marys for the bottle of water you
should take away ; then one of each for Father Freel, the
priest that blessed the well, and one for Father Gallagher, the
under-priest, and one for the man that put the shelter to it,
that his soul may have profit of his good work.

What number of real cures there are I cannot say, but faith-
healing has a good chance with Irish peasants. And the well
is efficacious not for yourself only, but for others. An old
woman was praying by it the morning I was there, for the neighbours come all days, though the great concourse is on Sundays.
I passed her on the road going away, and wished her well quit
of her sickness. "Thanks be to God," she said, "there's
nothing the matter with me. It's my son that's in Scotland
writes to me that there's a deal of sickness on the people there,
and I came this length to say a prayer for them." No doubt
she had brought away a bottle of the holy water too, and would
send it to him for the many Donegal folk that are at work in
Scotland these times : for Scotland begins to take the place of
America. Whatever she was to do with it, she had walked a
good six miles for it that morning, and was starting back, cheery
enough. She probably would have been hard put to it to find
even the widow's mite ; but what she had, her prayers and her
toil, she gave freely, and in full assurance that they would profit
those for whom she gave them.

Such is the present sanctity of Doon Well, not less venerable
among its solitudes than the pomp and processions of Lourdes.
But legend and history also lend an interest to the spot. On
the south of the rock is a cave which gives entrance to Fairy-
land ; stories are told of rash mortals who watched here on
midsummer nights, and saw a great company of " the gentry,"
green jacketed and red capped, entering and sallying forth.
Many a woman of the countryside has believed that her dead

child never died at all, but was made prisoner by this strange
folk and lived with them, thoughtlessly happy, or perhaps for
popular fancy varied on this point—continually "thinking
long" and desiring to be back, but detained beyond hope of
rescue.

The historic associations have something also of this legendary vagueness. Here was the place where the O'Donnells
were proclaimed lords of Tyrconnell ; here was the stone of
inauguration where each chieftain was bound to stand before
his clan, with feet set in the footprints hewn into the stone
where the first chief of Tyrconnell had taken his station.
The ceremony was performed by the Coarb or successor of
Columbkille in the Abbey of Kilmacrenan ; and this succession
remained in the family of the O'Ferghails, or Freels, who
like Columbkille himself descended from Niall the Ardri.
To this family Father Freel belonged, who consecrated the
Well.

So much is certain. But no one knows what has become of
the inauguration stone, which, according to the Four Masters,
was kept in the abbey ; whether, as some say, it was stolen, or,
as others hold, it was broken up, as was the inauguration
stone of the O'Neills at Tullaghogue. Accounts differ also
as to the ritual of the ceremony. Giraldas Cambrensis, the
Welshman who accompanied King John to Ireland, has left
a wonderful story.

"The people of Tyrconnell, a country in the north of Ulster,
created their king after this manner. All being assembled on
a hill, a white heifer was brought before them, and he who was
chosen as king, approaching it, declared himself to be just such
another. Whereupon the cow was cut in pieces, boiled in
water, and a bath prepared for the new king of the broth, into
which he entered publicly, and at once bathed and fed. All
the people meantime standing round fed on the flesh and
supped up the broth. At this comely feast and ceremony it
was not proper that the king should use any cup or vessel, nay,

not so much as the hollow of his hand ; but stooping down his
mouth, he lapped like a beast on all sides of the bath of broth
in which he was immersed.   Having thus washed and supped
until he was weary, the whole ceremony of his inauguration
was ended, and he was completely instituted in his kingship of
Tyrconnell."

This is, of course, a traveller's tale of the wildest sort.
An Irish account gives what no doubt is the accurate
description.

"When the investiture took place at Kilmacrenan, the
O'Donnell was attended by O'Ferghail, successor to Columbkille, and O'Gallacher, his marshal, and surrounded by all the
estates of the country.   The Abbot O'Ferghail put a pure
white straight unknotted rod into his hand, and said : ' Receive,
sire, the auspicious ensign of your dignity, and remember to imi-
tate in your government the whiteness, straightness, and unknot-
tedness of this rod, to the end that no evil tongue may find cause
to asperse the candour of your actions with blackness, nor any
kind of corruption or tie of friendship be able to prevent your
justice.   Therefore in a lucky hour take the government of
the people, to exercise the power given you with freedom and
security.' "

The last O'Donnell here inaugurated with the full consent
of his tribe, was the famous Red Hugh, whose history I must
tell fully in another place.   After his death in 1602, his brother
Rory submitted to the English, abjured any claim to the
O'Donnellship, and was named Earl of Tyrconnell.   But Neil
Garv (the Fierce), Red Hugh's cousin, who had betrayed the
O'Donnell cause, and joined the English for a promise of the
lordship of Tyrconnell, was in actual possession of the country,
and when he learnt of Red Hugh's death caused himself to
be proclaimed at the Rock ; though a great part of the clan
looked up to Rory as their leader, and regarded Neil with
hatred as a traitor.

But it mattered little, for the English were determined that

there should be no more lords of Tyrconnell. Rory the Earl
was forced to fly with the Earl of Tyrone in 1607, his lands were
forfeited, and in 1609 Neil Garv, the last "O'Donnell," was arrested
on suspicion of complicity in the last outbreak that disturbed the
dreadful "peace" into which Mountjoy and Carew crushed
Ulster ; an outbreak which came to its inevitable ending at
this very Rock of Doon.

Sir Cahir O'Dogherty was chief of Inishowen, a district over
which Red Hugh claimed lordship.   On the death of Cahir's
father, Hugh seized the boy, and wished to cause Phelim
O'Dogherty, Cahir's uncle, to be proclaimed the O'Dogherty.
But Cahir's friends and fosterers, the McDevitts of Birt, near
Lough Swilly, appealed to Sir Henry Docwra, who held the new
built forts of Culmore and Derry : and Docwra established Cahir
as chief, and moreover bred the youth under his own eye in all
courtly and warlike exercises, for a staunch supporter of the
English.   Cahir fought for his allies, was knighted, and in 1607
was foreman of the jury that pronounced the fugitive Earls to
be traitors and their property forfeit.   What more could an
Irish noble do for the English ?   But Docwra was succeeded
by Sir Henry Paulet, who mistrusted Cahir, and after many
quarrels was rash enough to strike him.   The O'Dogherty
went back infuriated to his castle of Birt, which to this day
stands south of Inch Island, looking over Lough Swilly, and
there he plotted revenge with his fosterers the McDevitts—the
clan who, for his sake, had deserted Red Hugh and gone over
to the English.   In April, 1608, he marched out with a following largely consisting of McDevitts, marched over the base
of the Inishowen peninsula, took Culmore Fort on Lough
Foyle either by treachery or surprise, garrisoned it with his
own men, and advanced on Derry, which he sacked and burnt.
Sir Henry Paulet paid with his life for the insult.   Thence he
proceeded to Lifford, at the junction of the Finn and Foyle, but
failed to take it, and retreated into the fastness of Glen Veagh.

But Sir Arthur Chichester, the Lord-Deputy, sent out hotfoot after him, and on July 5th one of the divisions advanced by way of Kilmacrenan, and Sir Cahir made his stand by Doon Rock. He was a conspicuous figure, of remarkable height, and distinguished by a great Spanish hat with nodding plumes; so it is no wonder that a bullet in the first volley reached his brain. His head was cut off, for there was a thousand pounds set on it in Dublin Castle; and the story is, that the man who got it set out to travel alone with his burden, but slept the night under the roof of an O'Dogherty, who looked into the bundle, recognised the head, and determined at least to keep the profit in the clan. The original captor only reached Dublin in time to ascertain that the price had been paid some hours before. Whoever got the money, the head reached its destination; Sir Cahir's head was "set on a pole of the East Gate, called New Gate, and his body was quartered between Derry and Culmore." Phelim McDevitt, his chief supporter, was not long after betrayed to the English, who hanged him at Lifford. All this materially assisted the settlement of Ulster; indeed, it is probable that when Paulet laid his horsewhip on the Irish chief whom Docwra had knighted, he had a shrewd vision of confiscated lands in case of any outbreak. If so, the forecast was a good one, though it happened to benefit, not Paulet, but the Lord-Deputy, Sir Arthur Chichester, to whom the whole peninsula of Inishowen was assigned after Cahir's forfeiture. Such was the last incident of any note in that pacifying of Ireland, a process which is wholly forgotten by those who owe to it their estates, but which the descendants of those who were despoiled remember with a resentment perfectly unintelligible to the winners.

When leaving Doon Rock, you get back on the main road which you left for the Causeway, keep straight along to the left, and it will take you back to Gartan, but there is a hill on it too steep to ride down. You will sight Gartan lake before

there is any diverging road : and having seen that, if you take
to the left and go up towards Letterkenny, you will have yourself
to thank for a detour.   Your best way is to keep straight on,
avoiding a road which runs due for the lower lake, and in time
you will come to the upper end of Lough Akibbon, below
Columbkille's "station," and a road down the south side of the
lake will take you back to the hotel.

On the way to Gartan.

CHAPTER IX

From Gartan, should you wish to shorten your tour, there is an easy road of ten miles to Letterkenny, which is at present a railway terminus, though within three or four years the line will be carried through Kilmacrenan to Dunfanaghy, thence along the coast to Gweedore and finally to Burtonport. From Letterkenny you can get to Derry, and if you have had enough bicycling, train and steamer will take you from Derry to Buncrana and Portsalon on Lough Swilly, or to Moville on

Lough Foyle. If, again, you do not care to go round by
Gweedore and Dunfanaghy, you can cycle from Letterkenny to
Ramelton, which is six miles, and thence along the west shore
of Lough Swilly - a hilly but beautiful road - to the pretty town
of Rathmullen. At Letterkenny and Rathmullen there are
good inns, at Ramelton a poor one. Luggage can be sent from
Gartan as far as Ramelton by mail car, or to Rathmullen by
way of Derry.

I do not on the whole recommend this line of travel, because
to miss the great chain of mountains from Errigal to Muckish,
besides Horn Head, Sheephaven and Mulroy, is to miss perhaps
the very best things in Donegal : but it is a way of knocking
sixty miles off the tour, and it takes you through a pleasant
inland country full of historic associations. Nearly opposite
Rathmullen Lough Swilly divides ; one short arm running up
to Ramelton and becoming the estuary of the Lennan ; the
other longer one, with Letterkenny at the head of it, receives
the Swilly. There is no more beautiful view in Ireland, to my
thinking, than that which is before you for the last three miles
from Letterkenny to Ramelton. Lough Swilly, the Lake of
Shadows, lies before you, to all appearance wholly land-locked :
Dunree Head projects from the Inishowen shore, and the
course of the water swerves westward beyond Buncrana. You
cannot see the Atlantic, but only this great sheet of blue water
encompassed by mountains ; in the centre of them Slieve
Snacht of Inishowen the highest point of the peninsula rises
to a point, falling away on each side in beautiful curves.
To your right, a little east of it and nearer you, is the
mountain island of Inch ; behind it, opposite Rathmullen,
the Scalp ; on the west of the lough the Knockalla range,
serrated and fanciful in outline, runs north towards the sea.
There is no want of wooding in the landscape, and the white
houses of Buncrana and Rathmullen, seen in the far distance,
subdue the wildness into something perhaps more human and
lovable than the barren grandeur of Slieve League.

Here, too, history has been made; for all this country of
comparatively fertile land lay on the marches of Tyrone and
Tyrconnell. Lifford, ten miles from Letterkenny, where the
Finn and Mourne join to make the Foyle, was the frontier
fortress, and the stream of war often passed the boundaries.
In 1248 Godfrey O'Donnell was chief of the Kinel Conaill
and for the first time in that year English-speaking invaders
pierced the barriers of Tyrconnell. But they came as allies,
Maurice Fitzgerald crossed the ford of Ballyshannon to help
O'Donnell to drive out a rival pretender to the O'Donnellship.
In 1257 Fitzgerald returned, this time as a foe, but O'Donnell
crossed the Erne to encounter him and they met in the north
of Sligo. The chieftains fought Homerically, hand to hand,
and each gave the other a death wound, but victory rested with
O'Donnell's party. He was, however, too weak to pursue, and
was carried off the field to rest in safety in a crannog, or
artificial island stronghold, in the inaccessible Glen Veagh.
This seemed to be the chance for the O'Neills, who always
claimed lordship over Tyrconnell, and after a year word came
to Godfrey O'Donnell on his sick bed bidding him submit.
The old chief was dying but his spirit was strong in him. He
sent the summons to his gallowglasses and kerne, and he bade
carpenters make ready his coffin. In the coffin he made
them lay him and, using it as a litter, carry him at the head of
his forces against the O'Neill. They marched under this
strange leadership past Lough Akibbon, down the Lennan
valley and over the hills into Glen Swilly; and on the
Swilly the Kinel Owen were waiting for him. Tyrconnell
attacked, and after a bitter fight drove back the invaders. They
carried the chief, still living, along the Swilly into the street of
Conwall, where the old ruins of an abbey still may be seen,
a mile above Letterkenny; they laid him down in his bier on
the street; and here, say the Four Masters "his soul departed from the venom of the scars and wound which he had
received in the battle of Creadran. This was not death in

cowardice, but the death of a hero who had at all times triumphed over his enemies."

That was not the only struggle between the two great clans fought out on the Swilly shores. If you leave the Ramelton road at Ballymaleel, three miles from Letterkenny, and turn to the right, the road takes you along the eastern arm of the lough, and here you pass the places of several gentry, set among fine wooding on the south-west shore. The first of them, Oak Park, belongs to the Wray family, who date from the earliest forfeitures in Tyrconnell. John Wray, for his services against the Earls, received in 1603 1000 acres near Letterkenny, and his descendants are there yet ; though Castle Wray, the next place to Oak Park, is now in the hands of the Mansfield family, who were among the settlers in 1610 after the Flight of the Earls ; and Ards, the great and beautiful Wray estate, at Dunfanaghy, passed from its owners three generations ago. Next to Castle Wray is Castle Grove, then Ardrummon, another house of the Mansfields ; and next to that again Fort Stewart, an estate which is still held by the lineal representative of one of James I.'s baronets ; but the old mansion stood near the adjoining house of Shellfield. All these prosperous Protestant gentry represent the descendants of those who came in when the disaster at Kinsale and the final crash of 1607, left Ulster with neither an O'Neill nor an O'Donnell to resist the English. But there is trace of the older nobility and the older creed in the ruins of Killydonnell Abbey, close to Fort Stewart, which an O'Donnell founded in the sixteenth century for the Franciscan Brothers : (Killydonnell means the Church of the O'Donnells). In 1558 Hugh Boy O'Donnell (the Fair) died there in the odour of sanctity, as his father, Hugh Duv, (the Dark) had died in the Donegal Abbey. But in this very same year Calvagh O'Donnell, the redoubtable son of Manus, to whom the Earldom of Tyrconnell was offered for the first time, had attacked the still more redoubtable Shane O'Neill. Shane and Calvagh should have been friends, for their positions were very similar.

Each of their fathers, Con Bocagh O'Neil and Manus O'Donnell, had submitted so far as to accept the title of Earl from an English king, though Manus never received his patent of nobility, and each ruled by usurpation; Calvagh had imprisoned Manus, and claimed to be the O'Donnell; Shane had raised a faction against his elder brother (whom he accused of being no son of Con's) the Baron of Dungannon. Yet, for all this affinity, no love was lost between them, and in 1557 Shane mustered a great army to march into Tyrconnell, and pitched his camp at Carricklea, in the angle made by the junction of the Finn and Mourne. Calvagh O'Donnell, by his father's advice, planned a surprise, and so when Shane marched over the hill and encamped at Balleeghan (in the parish of Raymochy), on the eastern slope towards Lough Swilly, Calvagh sent two spies into his camp. They went safely by night from fire to fire till they came to "the great central fire which was at the entrance of the son of O'Neill's tent; and a huge torch thicker than a man's body was constantly flaming at a short distance from the fire, and sixty grim and redoubtable gallowglasses, with sharp keen axes, terrible and ready for action, and sixty stern and terrible Scots, with massive broad and heavy striking swords in their hands to strike and parry, were watching and guarding the son of O'Neill. When the time came for the troops to dine, and food was divided and distributed among them, the two spies whom we have mentioned stretched out their hands to the distributor like the rest; and that which fell to their share was a helmetful of meal and a suitable complement of butter. With this testimony of their adventure they returned to their own people, and upon their exhibition of it their entire narrative was believed."

The last touch is an odd one; but the whole description is so graphic that I have been tempted to quote it. Calvagh had with him only thirty horses and two companies of gallowglasses from MacSwiney Fanad—always the backbone of O'Donnell

forces—but he decided to attack at once. It was a very dark,
wet night, and the surprise was complete. They made straight
for Shane's tent, and he had only just time to flee by the
further end of it ; he got away almost alone and had to swim
three rivers before he reached safety. After a desperate
struggle the Kinel Conaill were left masters of the camp " in
which O'Neill and his army had passed the beginning of the
night in merriment and high spirits ; and they remained until
morning, drinking the wines of the party whom they had
defeated."

It was not till 1559 that Shane got his return blow home,
and it was a shrewd one. Caffar O'Donnell, son of Manus,
was at strife with Calvagh, and held out in the Crannog on
Lough Beagh, where Godfrey O'Donnell had lain sick and
ordered his coffin. Con, son of Calvagh, was besieging him
with all the force of Kinel Conaill. Word came to Shane
that his enemy, Calvagh, was at Killydonnell Abbey, taking
his ease, with only a few soldiers " besides women and poets."
Shane launched a sudden troop of horse round the head of
Lough Swilly, swooped upon Killydonnell and carried the
captives back into Tyrone. With all his ability he was a
barbarian. Calvagh's wife became his concubine, and Calvagh
himself was fettered so that he could neither lie down nor stand
up, and used with such barbarity that we read in *The Four
Masters* for 1561,

" Mary, the daughter of Calvagh, son of Manus, son of
Hugh Duv O'Donnell, and wife of O'Neill" (she was step-
daughter of Calvagh's wife whom Shane had taken), "died of
horror, loathing, grief, and deep anguish, in consequence of
the severity of the imprisonment inflicted on her father,
Calvagh, by O'Neill in her presence."

In that year the Earl of Sussex, after much vain negotiation,
invaded Tyrone, turned Armagh Cathedral into a fortress, and
harried the country. But Shane fell on his retreating army and
slew many, and negotiations began again, in the course of

which Sussex gave Shane's messenger a bribe to assassinate
his master. This also failed, and the victorious Shane now
invaded Tyrconnell and was *de facto* king of all Ulster. He
released Calvagh in this year on condition that Lifford should
be surrendered; but Calvagh failed to keep his word, and
Shane had to reduce the place. Sussex in 1562 marched
through the North unopposed and reinstated Calvagh; but
intestine feuds followed, and Shane, who had just defeated the
Macdonnells of the Antrim coast, came in upon his western
foe again at Ballyshannon. Calvagh went to plead his cause
at Dublin, and thence shipped across, a ragged, solitary figure,
to get an audience of Elizabeth. She sent him back in company
of Sir Henry Sidney, who finally restored him by the strong
hand in 1565. He died in the following year and was succeeded by his half-brother, Hugh, who, like himself, was for
the Crown and against the O'Neills. Hugh O'Donnell—not
long after knighted by Sir Henry Sidney—was the father of
Red Hugh; and if Elizabeth's servants in Ireland never had a
worse enemy than the son, certainly no man did the English a
better turn than Hugh O'Donnell when he avenged the Kinel
Conaill on Shane O'Neill for his many oppressions.

In 1567 Shane invaded Tyrconnell in great force. O'Donnell
assembled his hosting at Ardingary, just near the town of
Letterkenny. On May 8th Shane made a rapid advance upon
them, and crossed the estuary of the Swilly about two miles
below Letterkenny. O'Donnell was posted on the heights
overlooking the level ground which is now called the Thorn.
It should be said that owing to embankment and reclamations
the Swilly is no longer fordable anywhere so far down as
Ardingary, if fordable in the tideway at all. The whole battle
passed in the space enclosed between the Swilly and the
Ramelton road, bounded east by Oak Park, and west by
Letterkenny. There was a cavalry skirmish somewhere down
by the foreshore which delayed O'Neill's advance at a critical
moment, for the O'Donnell host was only assembling. While

it was going on, in came MacSwiney Doe, MacSwiney Banad, and MacSwiney Fanad, with the gallowglasses, four hundred in all, so that the whole force was trifling ; but O'Donnell addressed them upon the continued injuries that they had endured, and they declared that for his sake and for their wives and children they would face Shane's host. So they advanced, say the Four Masters—who of course are O'Donnell partisans—" in a regularly arrayed small body and in a venomous phalanx." It was not a day of strategy ; or if it was, the annalists give no hint of it. " The Kinel Owen were at length defeated by dint of slaughtering and fighting " that is probably about the truth of it ·" and they were forced to abandon the field of battle and retreat by the same road they came." But the tide was up now, and the ford did not offer " an approach to warmth after cold or to protection after violence," yet the O'Neills were glad enough to risk drowning with that fierce crowd at their back, and no man waited for his brother. Thirteen hundred of them were left there that day on the field or in the tide ; two grandsons of Shane's, Macdonnell Galloglagh, his constable, and many another man of the Clan Donnell ; O'Donnelly, Shane's own foster-brother, " and the person most faithful and most dear to him in existence," and many another O'Donnelly with him ; many of the Quins and many of the O'Hagans. " There were not many houses or families from Cairlinn (Carlingford Bay) to the River Finn and to the Foyle, that had not reason for weeping and cause for lamentation."

As for Shane himself, he escaped westward, guided by some O'Gallaghers, up the Swilly river, and crossed at a ford called Scariffhollis, about two miles west of Letterkenny, and made his way by lonely passes to Tyrone, whence, in an evil hour, he threw himself on the protection of the Antrim Macdonnells, and so met his fate at Cushendun.

So that upon the whole, what between Godfrey O'Donnell's march to victory in his coffin—borne on the heads of gallow-

glasses—Calvagh's raid on the camp at Raymochy, and Sir
Hugh's final overthrowing of Shane the Proud, it may be said
that the vale of the Swilly is full of glorious memories for the
Kinel Conaill. Yet it was in a bad day for the lords of Tyrconnell that Shane was driven to his ruin. Sir Henry
Sidney—Big Henry of the Beer, as the Irish called him
—feasted lovingly in Hugh's castle, and dubbed his host
knight, and bade him go on and prosper. Not twenty years
after that, Elizabeth's Viceroy, with Elizabeth's full sanction,

Cushendun and Mouth of Dun River.

was treacherously kidnapping Sir Hugh's eldest son on this
same Lake of the Shadows, to hold him fast in prison, even in
fetters, till he broke loose at the last. But for Sir Hugh's defeat
of Shane, it is possible that Elizabeth might have had no Viceroy
in Ireland in 1587. Sir Hugh's son was to show what Tyrone
and Tyrconnell, leagued together, could accomplish ; and had
Sir Hugh stood for Shane and not against him, history might
have been altered: there might have been no Flight of the
Earls, and no broad lands of the O'Donnells for division among

James's hungry settlers.   But Irish history is full of these
" if's."

There is a story, less matter-of-fact in nature, clinging to
Killydonnell. The church, besides its architectural beauty—of
which some remnants can be seen in the tracery of an east
window—owned a fine peal of bells. Marauders from the
Tyrone shore crossed the water and robbed the abbey, and
made a shift to carry off the bells with them. But a storm
rose, and the heavy cargo was fatal to these sacrilegious persons, for they all went to the bottom with the bells. And once
every seven years at midnight, if you are listening, the bell
may be heard tolling deep down under the waters of the
lough.

One more battle was fought in the vale of Swilly, which
seems indeed to have been the cockpit of Tyrconnell. It was
in that strange and confused war which began with the Irish
outbreak in 1640, and was finally put down by the hard hand
of Cromwell. In that war the Irish, divided as always against
themselves, yet were more or less held together by a great
general, Owen Roe O'Neill, of the house of Tyrone. After his
death in 1649, there was a hopeless break-up. His brother,
Black Hugh, the only man who could ever claim to have inflicted
a severe check on Cromwell, was passed over because of insur-
mountable jealousies : and by a senseless compromise the
command of the Ulster army was given to Heber M'Mahon,
Bishop of Clogher. The result was many defections of soldiers, who had no desire to serve under a " Bishop-General."
M'Mahon marched from Tyrone, where Owen Roe had left the
army in an impregnable position, into Tyrconnell, and Sir
Charles Coote followed him from Derry. Henry O'Neill,
another of Owen's brothers, begged of the Bishop not to
risk a general action; but M'Mahon taunted him with cowardice,
and the armies met at Scariffhollis Ford, where Shane had
escaped eighty-three years before. The Bishop ordered his

battle like a bishop, not a soldier. Henry Roe O'Neill was taken fighting desperately ; about 1,500 men fell. The Bishop escaped, only to be taken ten days after, and finally hanged and quartered in Enniskillen. Since that day no war has been levied north of the Swilly, if we except Mr. Balfour's famous campaign with the battering-ram against the tenants at Gweedore.

Glen Veagh.

CHAPTER X

FROM Gartan you have an easy and pleasant day's ride to
Gweedore. Take the road up the side of Lough Akibbon, and
you will continue thence over the hill east of it for about three
miles over moorland, till the road from Kilmacrenan comes in,
on your right. From this point to Glen Veagh is about two miles
of the most delightful surface that any heart could desire, running
down an easy slope, while in front of you rises Muckish, "The
Pig's Back," a huge turf-stack-shaped mountain, and it makes
the most distinctive feature of North Donegal scenery, for
Errigal only shows its contour from about Gweedore. But
here a warning is needed. After you have gone about a mile
down this slope, you will see the little-used road to Creeslough,
taking straight across the shoulder of Muckish ; yours turns
sharp to the left, and you will not see the turn till you are on

it ; and if you are riding fast, or have your feet up, it is ten to
one but you will go over a very ugly drop. So take the corner
with discretion, and continue, passing a little tarn on the right,
till you see a private road with an iron gate across it leading to
the left, and up this you may be bold to venture, for it is Mrs.
Adair's road to Glen Veagh castle.

Glen Veagh is a straight, narrow sheet of water about five
miles long ; and if one were to compare it with even the Upper
Lake at Killarney, it should hold its own. On the north is a
steep wall of grey cliff, of great height, 1,200 feet, over which
fall several streams of water in cascades ; the south shore is a
steep rising hill of the most luxuriant heather which reaches ten
feet in height ; the lower slopes are wooded with one of the few
patches surviving of the primitive forest. Here you have juniper
in quantities, and even a few trees of yew. Half-way up on this
side is the great castle, and a road runs right to the head of the
lake ; thence a rough track climbs the steep wall of hill to reach the
pass over the Glendowan mountain by Lough Barra. You should,
of course, ride up to the head of the lough, and you may even
have hopes—though keepers probably have crushed them—of
seeing an eagle, for Glen Veagh was one of their great breeding
places. They still appear occasionally in the county, and if only
two or three of the great proprietors—say Mrs. Adair, Sir James
Musgrave, and Mr. Stewart of Horn Head—would direct their
keepers to treat them as inviolable, these magnificent birds
would soon be back in reasonable plenty. The *crannog*, or
island built on piles, in which Godfrey O'Donnell lay sick before
they carried him in his coffin to meet the O'Neills near
Letterkenny, is, I believe, a largish island, with wooding on it,
which lies near the road before you reach the castle. Or
rather, I believe this to be the island referred to by the Four
Masters ; it has an underground dwelling, said to have been
used in "ould pagan times," and the scribes, knowing there
was an island fortress of some kind, may have called it a
crannog at random.

The Royal Irish.

As you come down the glen again from the castle, turn to
your left when you strike the road ; about a quarter of a mile
down a very sharp hill, you come to a bridge over the beautiful
Owen Carrow river, and by the bridge stands a police barrack—
fifteen miles from Gweedore—erected in the old days, when
Mr. Adair's life was a matter of anxiety to the Government.
From that day to this the barrack has been tenanted by three
or four strapping young men, well fed, well clad, and well paid,
each of them costing the country his £200 a year. I doubt if
there are twenty houses within a radius of five miles. Decidedly
if Ireland grows quieter, she will have to economise on constabulary. Crossing the bridge, you go up a hill; on your right
the Calabber, a mountain torrent scarcely big enough to be
called a river, dashes down ; and you can trace the gorge of the
Owen Carrow, making a line of trees through all that treeless
expanse of heather, on its way to Glen Lough ; out of which
it runs again on its short course of two miles, now called the
Lackagh, before it flows into the sands of Sheephaven, by
historic Doe Castle. Rosapenna is down there, but you have
to sleep at Gweedore and Dunfanaghy before you get to it.
The road rises steadily now for a full five miles, and for about
half of that distance you are following the valley of the Calabber.
Muckish, in all its huge bulk, is on your right, Dooish on your
left. Presently a bridge over the Calabber carries a road running northward to the sea; it passes to Falcarragh through
Muckish Gap, which separates the steep scarped gable end of
that mountain from Crocknalaragh.

Aghla-beg is another long ridge, but at each end rises a little
cone or mamelon, modelled like a woman's breast; and blocking
the valley to the north is the towering summit of Errigal, jagged
as a saw. That is the highest point in Donegal—2,466 feet.
Well will it be for you going up this valley if the wind blows
from the east ; if it sets from almost any other quarter, it will
come down in your teeth, and I defy you to drive a machine
against it. However, it is a beautiful road, and you can always

stop and turn to look at Mulroy spreading blue waters in the
distance, with the low ridge of Fanad beyond them. The road
winds up and up, and gradually you begin to see that the mass
of Errigal is cloven in two as if with a knife; the nearer peak
they call Wee Errigal, and between it and Aghla beg lies Lough
Altan, a desolate enough looking lake, from which a river runs
into the sea by Falcarragh. There are a few houses on the

Errigal Mountain, Gweedore.

slope of Aghla, but presently the shoulder of the hill hides
them, and as you reach the watershed you look north east over
Mulroy and south-east towards the great height of the western
Slieve Snaght whose other flank you saw coming from Glen
ties. Not a house is in sight. It is a wild place, and the
fantastic shape of Errigal, with its sheer precipice on the east
ward side, makes it almost threatening. However, it is a short

way back to civilisation. From the top of this pass the road lies downhill to Gweedore, a good six or seven miles. Pedal down it as fast as you like, and rounding to the west of Errigal you see far below you the beautiful Dunlewy valley, with fine plantations on the further side of Lough Nacung, under the hill's shelter—a strange contrast to all the savagery of the mountains. To your left the Poisoned Glen runs up into the Derryveagh mountains, a sinister-looking spot; it gets its bad name, they say, from a spurge that grows there. Now if the day is clear, and you feel energetic, you should leave your bicycle at the first wayside hut you come to, and climb Errigal; it only takes about an hour from where you are, and with clear air it gives you a map of Ireland from Inishowen Head to Sligo and even Galway.

From the shoulder of Errigal your road runs straight along past the conspicuous Roman Catholic church of Dunlewy and skirting the lower lake, till at last, where the Clady river flows out, you reach a prosperous looking homestead set among trees, and that is the Gweedore Hotel. From Gweedore there is no want of expeditions to be done. You may go up Errigal, or you may cross the river and strike out for the coast. Three miles off you reach Crolly Bridge over the Gweedore river, and further on at Mulladerg, on the coast, is the resting-place of one of the Armada's vessels. Spanish Rock it is called, and at different times within the last century brass guns and other relics have been found; and the vessel herself, or such part of her as remains, is deep bedded in sand; but I know a gentleman who has had his hand on her. It is long ago, over sixty years; but there came word to him then, when he was staying somewhere in the Rosses, that a strong east wind, helping a spring tide, had swept the sea out so far that the vessel could be seen. At the next tide he went down in a boat, and sure enough she was visible from stem to stern. One of the party, with a taste for carpentry, sawed a piece off and turned it in his lathe; the wood was Spanish chestnut. A coastguard got out some lifting-tackle—a crane rigged on two boats— and tried to lift a gun out, but the tackle broke, and before next tide a heavy storm got up, and no more was seen of her.

If you have come from Glenties by way of Dungloe, you will have seen that strange coast of the Rosses, with its swarm of petty islands. Going to Dunfanaghy by way of Bunbeg and the

The Rosses.

Bloody Foreland you will get a fair specimen of that kind of scenery, and except for anglers there is nothing to detain you long at Gweedore. The place, however, has a special interest, for there is no spot where any one man has done so much to redeem the reproach that rests on Irish landlordism. Lord George Hill, in 1838, purchased 23,000 acres of land in the parish of Tullaghobegly, which is a less euphonious name for

Gweedore. What the state of the country was may be gathered
from the following memorial, addressed in 1837 to the Lord
Lieutenant by Paddy M'Kye, the teacher in the national
school ; I take it and the subsequent notes from a pamphlet
entitled *Facts from Gweedore*, originally issued in 1846 by Lord
George. Paddy M'Kye's diction is very characteristic of the
schoolmaster—old style—whose type Carleton made immortal.

"To his Excellency the Lord Lieutenant of Ireland :—

"THE MEMORIAL OF PATRICK M'KYE

"MOST HUMBLY SHEWETH—

"That the parishioners of this parish of Tullaghobegly, in
the Barony of Kilmacrenan, are in the most needy, hungry,
and naked condition of any people that ever came within the
precincts of my knowledge, although I have travelled a part of
nine counties in Ireland, also a part of England and Scotland,
together with a part of British America. I have likewise per-
ambulated 2,253 miles through some of the United States, and
never witnessed the tenth part of such hunger, hardships, and
nakedness.

"Now, my Lord, if the causes which I now lay before your
Excellency were not of very extraordinary importance, I would
never presume that it should be laid before you.

"But I consider myself bound in duty to relieve distressed
and hungry fellow-men ; although I am sorry to state that my
charity cannot extend further than to explain to the rich
where hunger and hardships exist in almost the greatest degree
that nature can endure.

"And which I shall endeavour to explain in detail with all
the truth and accuracy in my power, and that without the least
exaggeration, as follows :—

"There is about 4,000 persons in this parish" [this is under-
stated, the population was 9,049 in 1841, the people were not

so easily counted as their furniture], "and all Catholics, and as
poor as I shall describe, having among them no more than

One cart.

No wheel car.

No coach or any other
vehicle.

One plough.

Sixteen harrows.

Eight saddles.

Two pillions.

Eleven hurdles.

Twenty shovels.

Thirty-two rakes.

Seven table forks.

Ninety-three chairs.

Two hundred and forty-
three stools.

Ten iron grapes.

No swine, hogs, or pigs.

Twenty-seven geese.

Three turkeys.

Two feather-beds.

Eight chaff-beds.

Two stables.

Six cowhouses.

One national school.

No other school.

One priest.

No other resident gentle-
men.

No bonnet.

No clock.

Three watches.

Eight brass candlesticks.

No looking-glasses, above
3*d.* in price.

No boots, no spurs.

No fruit trees.

No turnips.

No parsnips.

No carrots.

No clover,

Or any other garden vege-
tables, but potatoes and
cabbage; and not more
than ten square feet of
glass in windows in the
whole, with the exception
of the chapel, the school-
house, the priest's house,
Mr. Dombrain's house,
and the constabulary
barrack.

"None of their either married or unmarried women can afford
more than one shift, and the fewest number cannot afford any,
and more than half of both men and women cannot afford shoes
to their feet; nor can many of them afford a second bed, but
whole families of sons and daughters of mature age indiscrimi-

nately lying together with the parents, and all in the bare
buff.

"They have no means of harrowing their land but with
meadow rakes. Their farms are so small that from four to ten
farms can be harrowed in a day with one rake.

"Their beds are straw, green and dried rushes, or mountain
bent; their bed clothes are either coarse sheets or no sheets,
and ragged, filthy blankets.

"And more than all that I have mentioned, there is a general
prospect of starvation at the present prevailing among them,
and that originating from various causes; but the principal
cause is a rot or failure of seed in the last year's crop, together
with a scarcity of winter forage, in consequence of a long
continuation of storms since October last in this part of the
country.

"So that they, the people, were under the necessity of cutting
down their potatoes, and give them to the cattle to keep them
alive. All these circumstances connected together have brought
hunger to reign among them, in that degree that the generality
of the peasantry are on the small allowance of one meal a day,
and many families cannot afford more than one meal in two
days, and sometimes one meal in three days. Their children
crying and fainting with hunger, and their parents weeping,
being full of grief, hunger, debility, and dejection, with gloom-
ing aspect looking at their children likely to expire in the pains
of starvation.

"Also, in addition to all, their cattle and sheep are dying
with hunger, and their owner forced by hunger to eat the flesh
of such.

"'Tis reasonable to suppose that the use of such flesh will
raise some infectious disease among the people, and may very
reasonably be supposed that the people will die more numerous
than the cattle and sheep, if some immediate relief are not sent
to alleviate their hunger.

"Now, my Lord, it may perhaps seem inconsistent with truth

that all that I have said could possibly be true ; but to convince your noble Excellency of the truth of all that I have
said, I will venture to challenge the world to produce one
single person to contradict any part of my statement.

"Although I must acknowledge that if reference were made
to any of the landlords or landholders of the parish that they
would contradict it, as it is evident it would blast their honours
if it were known abroad that such a degree of want existed in
their estates among their tenantry. But this is how I make
my reference, and support the truth of all that I have said :
that is, if any unprejudiced gentleman should be sent here to
investigate strictly into the truth of it, I will, if called on, go
with him from house to house, where his eyes will fully convince
him, and where I can show him about one hundred and fifty
children bare naked, and was so during winter, and some hundreds only covered with filthy rags most disgustful to look to.
Also man and beast housed together, i.e., the families in one
end of the house and the cattle in the other end of the kitchen.

"Some houses having within its walls from one cwt. to thirty
cwts. of dung, others having from ten to fifteen tons weight of
dung, and only cleaned out once a year !

"I have also to add that the national school has greatly
decreased in number of scholars through hunger and extreme
poverty ; and the teacher of the said school, with a family of
nine persons, depending on a salary of £8 a year, without any
benefit from other sources. If I may hyperbolically speak, it
is an honour to the Board of Education !

"One remark before I conclude. I refer your noble Excellency for the authenticity of the above statement to the
Rev. ——, Parish Priest, and to Mr. ——, Chief Constable
stationed at Gweedore, and Mr. ——, Chief Officer of Coast
Guard in same district.

"Your most obedient and humble servant,
"PATRICK M'KYE."

I have quoted this singular document *in extenso* not only because Lord George vouches for its accuracy, but because it gives a clear picture of what must have existed in the backward parts of Ireland, everywhere that the population relied solely on the potato. A certain number of the features remain constant. Ploughs are still probably scarce because the land is so rocky and fields so small. Scythes are not used, but in those days even the sickle seems to have been absent. Bare feet are still common; and Donegal is one of the few places where a woman may yet be seen riding pillion behind her man. It is, however, an increasingly rare spectacle. But the whole condition of the peasantry is changed, as any one may see with a glance. Paddy M'Kye's list will be useful to any observer who thinks them wretched at present. Poor enough they are, Heaven knows! but Gweedore is a paradise to what Lord George Hill found it. It was even then a notoriously uncivilised district; to cross the border was accounted an adventure, and to visit a fair in it required an escort. For the change it would be wrong to give the credit wholly to external agencies. The Irish people have been busily improving themselves since the schoolmaster was abroad, and if neither Lord George nor any other benevolent individual had helped, the countryside would still be very different from its misery of fifty or sixty years back. Still, it is at least equally certain that the improvement would have come more slowly but for Lord George; it is by no means certain that without him it would have reached its present stage. Moreover, one of his early acts was to build a grain store at the port of Bunbeg, where the Clady river flows into the sea. The object of this was to put down the illicit whisky-making which was almost a necessity to the people. By the time they had taken their corn to the nearest market, they were almost obliged to take what they were offered rather than waste a journey of fifty miles; whereas distillation paid better and was conducted on the spot. There was, per contra, the risk of seizure, which meant heavy

Halfway down.

loss, to say nothing of the demoralisation caused by the abund-
ance of cheap and fiery spirit.   However, Lord George's grain
store did not work marvels in this way; but when the famine
came in 1846 and 1847, Government leased the building for
a food depot, and it was the means of keeping the population
in that remote country alive.

The first step, however, necessary to any improvement in the
way of living among the tenantry was the abolition of a system
of land tenure known as rundale.   This reform, it is only fair
to observe, was carried out not only by Lord George Hill—
perhaps the best landlord who has lived in that county—but
also by the third Lord Leitrim, who was, not less probably,
the worst.   Under the old pernicious system land was let, not
in compact blocks, but by shares in so many fields.   The
good-will, or tenant-right, was transmitted by gift, sale, or will,
and infinitely subdivided.   Lord George quotes an instance
where a field of half-an-acre had twenty-six holdings in it; and
of a man whose tiny farm existed in thirty-two separate pieces.
Houses were not built on the farms but in groups, for the
people are extraordinarily gregarious, and love to sit up by
night—for turf costs nothing—gossiping over the fire.   When
the new system was introduced and the dwellings separated,
one man complained he was a heavy loser, for now he had to
pay a servant girl to keep his wife company.   Further to com-
plicate this extraordinary tangle, there was the system of letting
or devising, or selling, not by the acre, but by a cow's grass.
Thus a man would leave his son " one cow's grass " in a certain
field, the extent of ground being fixed by its quality.   There
was a further subdivision into fourths of a cow's grass, each
known as one cow's foot : and even this was halved again into
the unit one cleet, which is half a " foot " and one-eighth of a
cow's grass.   The result of this joint tenure was that, in the
Irish phrase, " Everybody's business was nobody's business."
Nobody would manure for his neighbour's benefit: nobody
would sow turnips or clover, as his neighbour's sheep would

eat them; and agriculture was reduced to the most rudi-
mentary operations, complicated by endless disputes. The
rundale arrangement which dated, no doubt, back to the time
when all land was the common heritage of a sept or clan, ex-
tended itself even to animals. There is a story of a horse that
was owned jointly by three men on one of the islands, but
ultimately went dead lame because none of the three would
pay for shoeing more than one foot. Each kept his own foot
in order, but the fourth went unshod. If any man were rash
enough to reclaim a piece of bog land, he was allowed one
crop off it, and it was then divided among the tenants of the
townland in proportion to the rent that each paid.

Lord George, who came with a singular appeal to the people
—he spoke Irish—explained his project to an unwilling
audience with infinite patience. He proposed to resume all
the land, and redivide it, and relet, a committee of the tenants
assisting. How a settlement was reached, Heaven knows! but
it was reached; no man was dispossessed, no man was robbed
of his tenant-right, and a system of fencing was instituted.
Then premiums were offered for the best kept cottage, the
greatest amount of new fencing, the best field of turnips, and
so forth, till gradually new habits were implanted in the people.
But to this day the old craze for subdivision is the despair of
landlords. No other means of livelihood but the land is recognised, every man has a large family, and his one idea of pro-
viding for them is to divide up among them what land he has.
The result of this exclusive devotion to the land is to give a
fabulous value to tenant-right. And for the benefit of English
tourists who hear the clamour against rent, it is well to set down
a few facts bearing on the whole question.

The country, for instance, between Dunfanaghy and Gweedore
looks incapable of yielding any return for cultivation. It would
seem impossible that a man should find it profitable to pay anything for the privilege of farming it—any rent, that is. Moreover,
that impression is confirmed when one sees on the farms, now

unhappily too common, from which tenants have been evicted
for a refusal to pay rent, the fields after a year's neglect running
back into bog and rushes. Yet, as a matter of fact, this country
supports a large population—the men eking out the earnings
of their farms by a month or two's harvesting in England. It
will also be apparent that the population is much denser close
to the sea, though the land seems even more hopelessly barren
there, and is utterly devoid of shelter. But along the sea there
are great gleanings ; sea-wrack after storms, which is carted or
carried on to the fields for manure ; kelp, which used to be
burned in great quantities for the manufacture of iodine, though
this industry is nearly killed by new discoveries of a cheaper
method of procuring the stuff. Then there are the edible sea-
weeds ; sloak which everybody knows, and dilsk (or dulse), a
sweetish tasting weed which is dried and hawked round in
pennyworths with apples and oranges at inland fairs. Lastly,
there is the chance of fish, and the certainty of cockles,
mussels, and other shell-fish. All these things cost merely the
trouble of getting them. Further, the actual rent which has to
be paid for land is a trifle. It used to be said that Lord
George Hill's rent book had no pounds column ; actually in
1868 the highest rent paid by any individual was £6 ; some
were as low as 4s. The highest rental per acre was 5s. 6d., the
average from 2s. to 3s. Now it is obvious that the distress in
Donegal cannot arise from a tenant's having to pay 10s. on each
quarter day ; obvious also that if he got his ground rent free he
would not be much better off. The real obstacles are, first,
the enormous sums paid for tenant-right—amounting frequently
to £30 for the goodwill of a farm whose rental is £1 per
annum—in some instances rising to forty or fifty years' purchase
of the rent ; and secondly, the habit of subdivision which
makes it impossible to cultivate on a paying scale in a grazing
country. Each of these rentals, it must be remembered,
includes the right to turf-cutting and mountain pasture.

This is no place to go into an economic discussion. I will

add, however, a single set of facts.   Some years ago when the
Plan of Campaign was started in Donegal and there was an
organised stand against rent, a gentleman having a small
property near Falcarragh was obliged to get rid of his tenants.

A Vanishing Type.

The gross rental amounted to something under £30. The land
being left on his hands, his son offered to take it for a term of
years.   The son fenced it in, put stock on it, with an
emergency-man in charge, and by his own account found it
pay him well. He went into the Land Court and had a

judicial rent fixed, thus acquiring tenant-right. A year or two ago the parish priest came and offered him £400 for the tenant-right on behalf of the original occupiers, who were forthwith reinstated in their holdings.

But whether big or small the rent has never been easy to come by in Gweedore. In the old days, now unhappily almost forgotten—when one used to hear that if Lord George's horse broke down the tenants would gladly draw his car back the twenty miles to Ballyarr, on the Lennan, where he lived—things may have run smoother. But before he took the property rents were paid only as a sort of favour and collected only by stratagem. There is an amusing tale on record of a bailiff who swore that he would get the rent from a tailor who had never been known to pay rent, cess, or any other tax.

" Having heard that the tailor had engaged a horse to go to Dunfanaghy to buy potatoes, the bailiff took the opportunity and boldly went to his wife for the rent. She assured him there was not one shilling in the house. But the bailiff, not wishing to be put off, told her that was not true : her husband had sent him for it : and if two years' rent was not paid at once they would get none of the land that was dividing. ' And by the same token,' he said, ' the money is in the chest in his breeches pocket.' It was a lucky hit ; the wife never doubted, but ran to the chest, got out the breeches and gave the bailiff the two years' rent ; and off he went to the office. He had hardly paid it in when up came the tailor not able to speak for rage ; but when he got words, he wanted a warrant against the bailiff for robbery. The bailiff took no notice of him but coolly said to the agent, ' Och, yer honour, was not I the lucky man that happened for to say that it was in the breeches pocket.' "

I could sketch my memories of Lord George, whom I remember well, a very pattern of gentleness and courtesy, short, white-haired and white-bearded, always dressed in grey Gweedore frieze, as you may see his photograph shown in the

hotel : but a great writer has left his vivid picture of the man.
Carlyle came to Ireland in 1849 and on returning wrote a
journal which was published in 1883.   Not many people

An Irish Piper.

escaped the severity of that awful pen ; but Lord George
softened even Carlyle in his most dyspeptic humour.

Here is his first impression of the host who met him after

the drive from Letterkenny to Ballyarr. " Handsome, grave-
smiling man of fifty or more; thick grizzled hair; *elegant* club
nose, low cooing voice, military composure, and absence of
loquacity; a man you love at first sight." Next day Lord
George drove his guest to Gweedore, passing through
Kilmacrenan, over Owen Harrow Bridge, and so between
Dooish and Errigal. "I never drove, or walked, or rode, in
any region such a black, dismal twenty-two miles of road," is
Carlyle's comment. And indeed, if you are looking out for
high farming and the homes of an industrious and thriving
peasantry, that road is little fitted to please you. The plantations on Dunlewy lake rejoiced his soul, however, and here is
his sketch of the Gweedore inn, photographic as usual.
" Gweedore inn; two-storied, white, *human* house, with offices
in square behind, at the foot of hills, on the right near the
river; this is the only *quite* civilised-looking thing; we enter
there through gateway into the clean little sheltered court, and
there under the piazza at the back of the inn Forster waits for
us and is kindly received."

The purpose of the hotel was in those days more evident
than it is now. It was to make an oasis in what Carlyle called,
rightly enough, the "desolate savagery" round it; the farm
attached to it was to show what could be done with the same
sort of land as any one else had; it was to be a kind of standard
of *human* civilisation. Incidentally also it was no doubt
meant to make tourists a possible source of revenue, and
shame the other inns of the country into cleanliness and
comfort. All these things it has done to some extent, and
naturally the oasis is no longer so conspicuously an oasis.

It is no longer necessary to teach the folk of that country
that it is better to put harness on a pony than yoke him to a
harrow by the tail, which was their primitive method. But the
desolation and savagery were marked enough when Carlyle
went out to spy with keen unsparing vision upon the nakedness
of the land. He writes: "On the whole I had to repeat often

A Donegal Lass.

L

to Lord G. what I said yesterday, to which he could not refuse essential consent. It is the largest attempt at benevolence and beneficence on the *modern* system (the emancipation, all for liberty, abolition of capital punishment, roast goose at Christmas system) ever seen by me or like to be seen; alas, how can it prosper, except to the soul of the noble man himself who earnestly tries it and works at it, making himself a 'slave' to it these seventeen years?"

Go now and look at Bunbeg, which Carlyle saw, "a village perhaps of 300 or more, scattered distractedly among the crags," and judge between the man who denounced idleness, ignorance, slavish superstition, and the rest so eloquently, and the man who peaceably tried his philanthropic experiment. The store founded to supply articles, then not purchasable within twenty miles, found soon enough "the practical shopkeeper," who was still desiderated when Carlyle saw it; no minerals have been worked; but once the impulsion was given, work went on, and there was progress. Yet if Carlyle judged harshly here as elsewhere : worse than harshly, with arrogance; at least he knew a good man. Parting with Lord George a day or two later at Rathmullen he wrote :

"In all Ireland, lately in any other land, saw no such beautiful soul."

Before you leave Gweedore you should certainly run down to Bunbeg and Derrybeg, unless you take them on your way to Dunfanaghy.

From Gweedore to Bunbeg it is an easy four miles of fairly good road: on the left you have the Clady River, with its succession of delightful swirling streams and pools. The harbour of Bunbeg is singularly picturesque ; a little lake of salt water shut in by high rocks on all sides, and entered by the narrowest cleft that it would seem possible to get a good-sized vessel through. Over the harbourmaster's office you will trace Lord George Hill's hand in the inscription from Proverbs, set up there in Irish, "A just weight is a pleasure to the Lord,

but an unequal balance is an abomination in His sight.   I
asked a knot of men there to interpret it for me, and after some
confusion elicited the fact that they all spoke Irish, but none
of them could read the character.   The tongue survives everywhere in speech only, and most of the Gaelic tradition passes
exclusively from lip to lip.   By the way, you will need to ride

Bunbeg Quay.

warily as you go to the harbour, or you will be apt to find
yourself shot over the quayhead.   Plenty of the yawls which
the fishermen of these parts use lie by the quay, but no bigger
boats ; and the local opinion is that fishing in these waters
must be confined closely to the shore, for nothing except a
really large vessel can hope to ride out all weathers, and there
is a plentiful lack of shelter to run to.

Leaving Bunbeg, you take a road running eastward along the coast to Derrybeg, about two miles off; you will know when you get there by a very steep and rather tortuous hill, on which there is more than the usual chance of meeting a cow or donkey, owing to the presence of some cabins halfway down. At the hill's foot a small stream flows under a bridge, and in the tiny hollow of a gorge is Derrybeg chapel, unhappily too well known. In this hollow, when the penal laws existed, the people of the district assembled to hear mass in the open air; the spot itself was secure from observation, and sentries posted in the heather round easily guarded against a surprise of the priest. So when the penal laws were repealed, and Derrybeg grew rich enough to have a chapel—it is wonderful how much money the poorest parishes will contribute for this end—they were determined that the chapel should stand nowhere but in this spot of many memories. The chapel actually stands astride of the stream; and early in the eighties, on one Sunday a heavy flood came down, burst the culvert under the chapel, and instantly filling the building, drowned several of the worshippers. Worse, however, had to come. In February, 1889, the whole Gweedore district was in a state of suppressed rebellion. The Plan of Campaign had been preached, great evictions followed on the Olphert estate, and troops were sent down to keep the population under. They brought with them the famous battering-ram, which was used for knocking in the walls of cabins whose inmates refused to open to the officers of the law. If these things have to be done, it is well to take the simplest and most efficacious means of doing them; but the necessity was not an agreeable one, and the feelings of the peasantry were inflamed to the uttermost. Their leader was the priest, Father Macfadden, who in all negotiations with landlords acted as a spokesman for his flock; and to the influence which his office gave him among a people superstitious or religious in the highest degree, he added the natural ascendency of a strong character. The Government was anxious to arrest him, but the warrant did not admit of seizing him in his own house. On Sunday, February 2nd, however, Father Macfadden determined to celebrate mass, thinking probably that the authorities would not risk so unpopular a measure as his arrest in the chapel. Five hundred soldiers were at Gweedore. In the Derrybeg school-house, two hundred yards from the chapel, on the ground above the stream to the right, were eighty police under the county inspector. From the east of the chapel a private path leads uphill to the priest's house, and during service District-Inspector Martin was sent down with eight men, to take up a position on this path. Father Macfadden came out of the chapel, still wearing the robes in which he had officiated—not less sacrosanct in the eyes of his congregation than the very elements of the mass themselves. He was immediately arrested by Inspector Martin, and demanded to see the warrant; the congregation of peasants, at least a hundred of these wild Gweedore men, gathered round, and when the sergeant tried to force the priest up the hill, they broke out, tore stakes out of the palings, and attacked the police. The inspector was separated from his men, the sergeant with Father Macfadden was in front, and Mr. Martin managed for some time to keep the crowd at bay with his sword. He shouted to his men to fire, but they were already at hand-grips. Much has been made of the fact that Mr. Martin left his revolver behind, "for fear he should be tempted to use it." It would have been a wiser prudence to bring down an overwhelming force. The whole thing passed so quickly that there was no time for word to go up to the force at the school-house. Mr. Martin, turning for a moment, was struck down from behind. Stones were flying, and Father Macfadden's sister opened the door hurriedly to let him in, and was herself shut out, to see the unfortunate inspector being battered to death by an infuriated mob, who beat his skull literally into a pulp. The crowd drew back from the body when their priest shouted to them from an open window, but the work was done.

Much blame has, and rightly, been attached to Father Macfadden, who could by an instant acceptance of the warrant and a word to his people to keep quiet, have prevented the whole thing. He was prosecuted for murder, but naturally acquitted. There was, indeed, no sort of premeditation; the weapons were improvised—they were paling stakes not black-thorns—and no reasonable man would suppose that either priest or people contemplated such a bloody tragedy. But enough blame can hardly be laid upon the authorities, who, with the means at hand to render resistance impossible, neglected to use it, entirely ignoring not only the fierce temper of a wild people goaded on by a struggle for their homes, but also their literal and ingenuous horror at what they held to be a profanation. This folly cost a brave man his life, came near to cost another —for one of the sergeants was beaten almost to death— and two men a long imprisonment. The crime, terrible as it was, had no motives of private malignity ; and the wildest of these slayers would neither have robbed a man nor harmed a woman, if they had met them alone and unprotected in the soli-tudes of their hills. Two murders in Donegal— this one and that of Lord Leitrim —have had a wide-spread notoriety. Yet from ordinary crime the people are singularly free, and the worse forms of the agrarian horrors—cattle-houghing and maiming of helpless women and children have never dishonoured the county.

On the Shore at Dunfanaghy.

CHAPTER XI

FROM Gweedore your next stage is to Dunfanaghy. If you like you may make a détour northward, so as to skirt the Bloody Foreland and join the main road at Falcarragh; but I do not recommend this route, for, so far as my recollection serves, the finest view in these parts is that of Errigal, as it rises like a pyramid with its top snowy white from the powdery rock that covers it; and as you ride eastward you see the edge of the pyramid turned toward you, so sharply defined for a matter of two thousand feet that it looks as if at any point you could sit astride of it. The road continues to skirt on its right the same great range you had to the north of you, coming up from Glen Beagh. The distance is about seventeen miles, and of the character of the road I cannot say much, as I only know it from driving some years back.

Dunfanaghy you will find to be a clean little town, on perhaps

the most beautiful of these loughs or arms of ocean that
indent the whole northern coast of Donegal. If you look at the
map you will see that Lough Swilly forms the base of a rough
equilateral triangle, whose corners lie in Letterkenny, Dunaff
Head, and Horn Head ; the whole space enclosed is a
chequered network of land and water.   Sheephaven lies broad
and open to the sea, between Horn Head and the Rossgull
promontory, which is capped by the peak of Ganiamore.   One
arm of the bay runs up past Dunfanaghy, making the square
bulk of Horn Head all but an island.   Another arm runs
straight inland; and as you look up it from the bay the huge
gable-end of Muckish seems to fill the whole view.   The bay is
everywhere shallow and sandy, and never anywhere have I seen
such bright contrasts of colour.   The sand is almost orange,
and the great banks of it, dazzling in the sunlight, can be traced
shading away into a salmon pink, where the blue water lips
them.   Here certainly you will be wise to stop a day, for Horn
Head is not a thing to pass without seeing it.   If the weather be
fine I should advise a boat ; the cliffs, rising a sheer 600 feet,
look their best from the water, and the myriads of sea-birds that
build there and haunt it in all seasons are a sight in themselves;
especially the quaint little puffins, funniest of all British birds,
whether on the wing, the water, or the rocks.   It is worth
while taking a gun or something that will make a noise to scare
the incredible swarms that come circling out from the cliffs. A
native of Dunfanaghy used to spend days on these rocks with a
long pole knocking down sea-birds as they flew over him, that
their feathers might go to decorate pretty women.   Whether
his trade still exists I cannot tell, but his by-name, " Jimmy the
Wallopper," is not forgotten in Dunfanaghy.   Off the eastward
point of Horn Head is a salmon net, fixed a couple of hundred
yards from the cliffs, and stretching perhaps another two
hundred.   It seems a futile trap in a place where the bay opens
eight miles ; but the fish have their known tracks in the sea,
and that net two hundred yards further in or further out would,

they say, never kill a fish. At the base of the cliffs, close to the end of it, is a shelter—half hut, half cave—where a watcher lives to protect the net, not so much from land thieves as those sea-robbers the seals. They follow the salmon right into the meshes, and rip and tear the net with their strong teeth : so if a seal's head is seen bobbing on top of the water—and a queer uncanny object it is—a bullet goes after it. Once there came near to be a tragedy in this shelter. The watcher took out a

Dunfanaghy.

child of his there for company : rough weather came on, when no boats could get near his landing place, and his supply of food ran out, nor could he communicate with the town. The cliff above him was not impracticable to a good cragsman, though few have ever climbed it ; but on that wild day of storm he lashed the boy on his back, and fought up from ledge to ledge to the cliff top, three hundred feet above him. Strangely enough, violent death overtook both the man and boy within a few years. The boy fell over the same cliff when he was trying

to take a cormorant's nest; the man, going home across the
headland, made to jump a small ditch, caught his foot, fell on
his head, and was found there with his neck broken.

On a still day you can approach in the boat and get into the
huge caves, which a blue light--if you have one—will show
you opening up mysterious arches higher than a cathedral
roof. But it is not by any means all days that tempt the
average person to boat round that grim headland, and there
are points in favour of taking your walk round the cliffs. The
road on to the Horn leads over a bridge, across the arm of tideway, where it narrows and passes Horn Head House, a property
that has been in the present family's possession since a
Stewart raised men to fight for King James against the
O'Neills.

The road winds up, through a numberless colony of rabbits,
and finally leaves you in the centre of the headland. Hence
you make your way to the cliff, on top of which stands the
ruins of a signal station. Keeping on to the north you
ultimately reach the Horn, a highest point of the cliff, two
jutting crags of rock ; from which you can drop a pebble to the
water 626 feet below. You will see, probably, two or three
black specks like water-spiders below you ; these are curraghs,
the native type of boat, which consist of hide or, more often, of
tarred canvas stretched over a frame of wicker-work. They are
buoyant as corks, but easily upset ; and if you wear boots—the
people who use them are generally barefoot—nothing is simpler
than to put your heel or toe through the canvas.

The cliff front to the north is somewhat bow-shaped and
almost overhanging—but it is possible, by scrambling between
the two Horns, to get down some way ; and an old gentleman,
whom I know well, has been up and down it in his youth ; not
that I recommend it as a promenade. There is a very curious
result of this concavity of the cliff. As you walk up, if the
wind is blowing off the sea, you will find yourself in one of the
breeziest places imaginable, and may have a hard fight to get

up. Then suddenly as you walk out on this projecting plateau, making a long narrow strip of twenty yards by five or so there is a dead calm a stillness, as if enchanted, about you. Up in mid air there above the Atlantic, between you and the gale there is a wall of wind. If you take up a light sod of earth and fling it straight out it goes a few yards easily, then is suddenly caught up, whirled high, and driven back over your head. The wind striking the cliff face is driven up, and the curve takes it, as it were, back upon itself, so that this strong current makes a few feet of shelter—higher than a man's head -above the cliff top. It sounds incredible, but with a wind blowing at all fair on to the face of the Horn, you have only to test it for yourself.

Further round to the west the ring of cliffs gets a little lower till they gradually sink to a mere hundred feet. But at a point where they are still of a very respectable grandeur there is MacSwiney's Gun. A cave runs in from the sea level, and from the end of the cave a blow-hole rises to the top. On a stormy day a wave is driven into the opening and shot out through this narrow funnel in a straight jet—an immense body of water, carrying with it large stones—while there is an explosion like that of a cannon. Tradition lies in saying it can be heard in Derry; but I have heard it myself at Ards House, on Sheephaven bay, seven or eight miles off as the crow flies; firing shot after shot at regular intervals. MacSwiney, the owner, was the chief whose headquarters were in Doe Castle; a little beyond the Gun there is a circular keep on the Head, which no doubt also belonged to him. In Elizabethan maps three great figures with battle axes are depicted on the waste that stood for Northern Donegal—MacSwiney Doe, the head of the clan, himself a vassal or urraght of the O'Donnells; MacSwiney Banat, whose territory lay westward from the Rosses to Killybegs; and MacSwiney Fanad, who owned the headland that divides Mulroy from Lough Swilly and had his castle in Rathmullen. Of this I shall have more to say, and also Doe Castle you will meet on

your road to Rosapenna.   But the fortress that will be always
present before you as you walk round Horn Head is the
natural stronghold of Tory Island, which lies seven miles out
to the north-west, looking for all the world like some great
towered and battlemented castle.   Its name "Torach" means
in Irish "towery"—*tor* is a tower—and much legend and many
stories hang about it.   It was owned, the legends say, by the
Fomorians, a race of giants who lived in Ireland when Paris
loved Helen and Troy was being sacked.   There is on it a part
of a ruined tower, built of undressed boulders of red granite,
which Conaing, one of the Fomorians, built.   The chief of
the island was Balor of the Mighty Blows, and he, they say,
carried off from the mainland, Glasgavlen, a famous cow that
gave milk enough for a whole barony ; and when her owner, the
chief MacKineely, plotted revenge, Balor crossed again, seized
him and cut his head off on a stone which keeps the red marks
to this day, and is treasured in the grounds of Ballyconnell,
Mr. Olphert's place, near Falcarragh.   It is a large block of
white quartz placed on a raised platform ascended by steps.
But in the *Annals of the Four Masters* a more romantic story
is told. Balor was not only a giant but a monster with an eye
in the back of his head ; and he had a daughter who, according
to the prophecy, would bear a son that would be the death
of him.   So Balor kept his daughter shut up like Danae, but
the chief Kineely made his way over in woman's dress, was
taken in as one of her attendants, and in due time made love
to the giant's daughter.   The end was that a child was born,
whom Balor threw into the sea ; Kineely he pursued and cut
his head off on Clogh-i-neely stone.   But the child floated
and was picked up on the coast by a smith, who reared the
boy and bred him to his trade ; till one day, after many years,
Balor came into the forge, and the boy seizing a red hot iron
ran it into Balor's eye and so avenged his father.

A step nearer to history is marked by the ruins of churches
on Tory, where Columbkill founded a monastery.

Carrying Peat.

In short, Tory is a place with no want of picturesque legend about it, but the few people who have been there are more struck with its present than its past. The islanders live almost entirely by fishing, and the whole soil is covered, one hears, with the fish heads. Tory is now in the highway of the world, compared with what it was; a telegraph wire connects it with Pollaguill Bay on the west of the Horn; there is a signal station of Lloyd's shipping agency there, and a lighthouse. Steamers call there weekly for the take of fish and lobsters, and there are few of the people who have not been on the mainland, and probably also one or two who have been in England, Scotland, or America. They fish, too, in yawls nowadays, which are weatherly boats, though no boat that sails will take you to and from Tory in all weathers, and if you go there you risk having to stay a fortnight. But in the old days the islanders owned just their curraghs, and fished for their living. Curing was unknown to them (now the Congested Districts Board has established a small station there), but they used to try and keep alive not only crabs and lobsters, but also the choicest of their fish, such as turbot, which they tethered by the tail and kept in pools of the rocks. Tory was a lonely place in those days. There was a king in the island who adjudicated; the office, which was hereditary, has, I believe, lapsed. No priest lived there, and it was said that sometimes when a marriage was to take place, rough weather would keep the ministrant from crossing, it might be for a month or two, so there was a system of signals in force. The priest went out on to Horn Head and read the service: at a certain point one fire was lighted, then another, and so on, in order that the happy couple standing devout on the landward shore of Tory, might know exactly to what point in the service his reverence had got, and when they were finally accepted before the Church as man and wife.[1]

[1] Told, I believe truly, of the priest of Tamney when hindered from crossing Kowros ferry. The story is transferred to Tory.

To this day, perhaps, Tory is hardly over civilised; yet by its very door passes a great highway of the nations. All the northern line of transatlantic steamers call at Moville in Lough Foyle, and put out from thence for Canada and the States with hundreds of poor folk turning their backs on the country whence they cannot be rooted up without anguish. Many a man from Gweedore or Dunfanaghy has stood, with straining eyes, on the deck as the big ship, steering her way between

Horn Head from Rosapenna.

Tory and the land, headed straight out for the open Atlantic, nothing any longer interposing between her and the other side. "The sentinel of the Atlantic," a poetic engineer called Tory when he put up the signal station there; but Tory kept ill guard one day of September, 1884, when the unfortunate *Wasp* gunboat ran against its reefs, and all hands but six were lost.

There is a very beautiful story told by Dr. Macdevitt in his

Donegal Highlands, which I have heard from no other source.
Long ago, after a terrible storm, the body of a nun was washed
up on Tory. The islanders had never seen the religious habit
before, but the leathern girdle and beads made them think
that surely a blessing was on the body, and " they prayed
earnestly for light what to do." In response, they thought
they heard a voice telling them that the body was that of a
holy nun, and bidding them bury it under the sod, where it was
laid in the dress that was on it. This they did as lovingly as
they could, "and from that time the ' Nun's Grave ' is usually
graced with the presence of some poor islander, prostrated
before it in humble petition to God, through favour of her
whose bones are interred therein." And not a boat ever puts
out to fish without a handful of earth from the Nun's Grave
carefully deposited in the stern. No one may take more than
a pinch of the clay, " and no wonder, for many a father of a
family, many a poor widow's son has it rescued from
drowning."

Within sight of Tory Island was fought one of the many
lesser actions of the great Napoleonic Wars; but it gains a
certain importance from the fact that it ended the career of the
Irish rebel who did most to endanger England's supremacy in
his country. Theobald Wolfe Tone, a young man of great
talent and good education, was the agent of the United Irishmen in France, where he arrived in February, 1796. Within a
few weeks he had entirely gained the ear of Hoche, then at the
height of his reputation and burning with ambition. The result
was first the expedition of December, 1796, when a fleet of forty-
three sail got clear out of Brest with 15,000 men on board,
Hoche commanding; they were scattered by weather, but
thirty sail reached Cape Clear on December 21st. Hoche's
vessel was missing, and Grouchy, his second in command,
waited for him; but finally resolved to land, and was instantly prevented by weather from entering Bantry Bay, and at last driven
off the coast by a tremendous storm. Tone came back disap-

pointed but indefatigable ; and in June of the next year, when
the Nore mutiny paralysed the British navy, a Dutch fleet was
preparing in the Texel. Again luck stood to the British, and
for almost a month it blew dead into the harbour, while slowly
the English fleet collected : and when Duncan sailed in October
it was only to be defeated. But even before that Tone's
sheet-anchor was gone ; Hoche had died of consumption, and
Buonaparte, now left without a rival, was hostile to the Irish
plan, if only because it had been identified with Hoche.

Yet though fortune had thus twice prevented him at the last
moment, when it seemed absolutely certain that a large force
would be landed to form a spear-head for the revolutionary forces
which then existed through Ireland, from Belfast to Cork, Tone
still persevered. In 1798 came the outbreak, which, disorganised
and unsupported as it was, England had no easy task in crushing.
Buonaparte was in Egypt ; but the Directory called on Tone
to organise a new expedition. In mid-August, when the revolt
was already quelled, Humbert, without waiting for instructions,
set out from La Rochelle on his foolhardy venture, and landed
his thousand men in Connaught, who after a brilliant struggle
were surrounded and taken at Ballinamuck. Matthew Tone,
Wolfe Tone's brother, was with him. Before the news of
their defeat came, another expedition—one sail of the line
with eight frigates—was sent out to support the wild stroke.
Admiral Bompart took them far out west, and then came down
from the north-west, making a course for Lough Swilly. But
he had been dogged all the way from Brest by two English
frigates, and they had sent word to Sir John Borlase Warren,
who lay cruising with his main body off Malinmore Head, near
Slieve League, while frigates scouted up as far as Tory. Bompart
with his squadron was sighted on October 11th, running south-
east with a wind out of the north-west, and the signal for a
general chase was made. The French altered their course due
east, hoping to get clear round the north of Ireland. It was
blowing a gale with a hollow sea, and in the night the *Hoche*,

M

Bompart's ship, carried away her main topmast, which in falling did further damage ; and as a forlorn hope they tried to escape by shifting their course and making to the south-west. Dawn found them virtually surrounded by the English fleet, and Bompart ordered his frigates and the *Biche* schooner to hold on and attempt escaping ; he himself had no chance to do so. The French officers begged Tone to transfer himself to the *Biche*, which had the best chance to escape—as she actually did—because his fate, if taken, would be certain execution. But Tone refused to fly while the French fought for his country, and commanded a battery in the action which followed. At seven o'clock, the Rosses bearing five leagues S.S.-W., firing began. The *Hoche* fought against four English vessels of her own size till reduced to a complete wreck. She struck at 11.20 A.M., and was taken into Lough Swilly. The prisoners were landed, according to one account at Rathmullen, according to others at Buncrana. Tone, in his French uniform, passed with the rest, till recognised at Letterkenny by a man who had been at college with him. He was taken to Dublin, tried by court-martial, defended himself with dignity and courage, and when sentenced to be hanged, only pleaded the right due to the uniform he wore as a general in the French army. But the Court, with needless severity, refused to treat him as an honourable enemy, and shoot him. Tone anticipated his fate by cutting his throat in prison with a pen-knife. Life was not extinct when he was found, and, incredible as it sounds, the authorities having caused the wound to be tied up so as to prolong life a few hours, proposed to proceed to hang him. This odious step was prevented by the energy of Curran, who obtained a writ of *habeas corpus* from the Lord Chief Justice, Lord Kilwarden, on the ground that if Tone was held to be a British subject, holding no military commission, a court-martial had no jurisdiction over him. Such was the lamentable but not ignominious end of a formidable enemy to the English rule in Ireland ; and since the *Hoche* struck her colours, no shot fired in anger has been heard off the shores of Ireland.

Like most things in the country, however, the story had its humorous appendix. An old lady of a well-known family in Inishowen sat at dinner while the action was going on and the guns boomed across the water. She faced the soup cheerfully, the fish with unabated appetite, the mutton with contentment, and the pudding with satisfaction. "Will I bring in the cheese, ma'am?" said the butler. "Cheese, John!" said the dame, in righteous indignation. "Would you expect me to be eating cheese with the French bombarding Lough Swilly?" Her family thought the patriotism came three courses too late, and preserved the story.

Doe Castle from Lackagh Bridge.

CHAPTER XII

A REALLY energetic person, having seen Horn Head—perhaps having walked round in the afternoon and boated round next morning—would certainly climb Muckish. It is a mountain on which you can break your neck, though no one would think so to look at it, and I fancy you have to try and get down the west gable of the peat stack to accomplish this. For another unlikely circumstance, Muckish is abundant in that pretty little plant, London Pride, otherwise "St. Patrick's Cabbage." For my own part, I have been content to look at Muckish from the level; and my advice to you would be to start and take an easy day just going from Dunfanaghy to Rosapenna, skirting Sheep-haven the whole way. Between the post road and the bay lies Ards, the estate of Mr. Stewart, with rich wooding that covers all the irregular hills, and runs down in some places to the very water's edge. The avenue through it is over five miles from gate to gate, and tourists are permitted to go through what is the most beautiful private demesne I have seen.[1] Mr. Stewart, the owner, does not live as a rule in his huge house, and if a company could get the use of it as a hotel, it would be the most fascinating place in Ireland. If it were in Scotland it would, of course, be actively competed for by millionaires ; there would be a yacht in the bay, a boat to row you across to the Lackagh, which is only a mile or two by water but six or seven by land, big

Creeslough with Muckish.

house-parties for the cock-shooting, and the moors would hold a deal more grouse than they do at present.

When you have ridden through the delightful winding

[1] Since writing the above, I have heard that the present tenant has withdrawn the privilege which the courtesy of the owner, and of all previous occupants, had permitted to such strangers as visited the neighbourhood. This prohibition, however, may have been withdrawn ; and any visitor to Dunfanaghy ought at least to enquire.

avenue, sometimes under trees, sometimes with glimpses peering out of the lesser bays, each beautiful, into which the shores of Sheephaven are curved and cut, and further along through green sloping pastures, where rabbits play and scuttle in droves to cover in front of you, you will get back into the road and cross a little river—the Faymore—that comes down from Muckish.   There is a salmon-leap here, artistically built, but it is only a spawning river ; the fish come into the Lackagh —whose estuary meets it near Doe Castle—as early as March, but up here they never go till September ; why, is one of the many mysteries connected with that unaccountable fish. Pushing on another two miles you will reach the little town of Creeslough.

Here you turn sharp to the left, passing a pretty little lake, then ride on over rather a rough road with one very bad little hill on it, until after about three miles you come to a bridge over the Lackagh river.   If it is a fine day and bright, you can get off your bicycle and look into the pool under the bridge. It is odds but you will see salmon lying there in packs with their sides touching one another ; at all events you will have a lovely view of the river, coming down through a heathy valley, with a little wooding on the left bank, and away behind it the intricate foldings of Lough Salt, Barnes Mountain, and the Glen Veagh hills.   On the left bank, by the way, there is a curious thing to be seen if you can find any one to show it you, just above the first pool on the river.   It is a hiding hole under a rock with a tiny aperture scarcely bigger than a rabbit burrow. Into this you can creep, and find yourself in a space large enough to move a little about in.   The place has been partly made up with masonry, and they say that within living memory a "boy who had done a bad turn" of some sort, hid himself there for two or three nights while the police were on his track, and eventually escaped.   About two miles up the course of the Lackagh—its whole course—lies Glen Lough, and into the top of Glen Lough flows the Owen Harrow, which you will remember to have seen coming down from Glen Veagh. But the view from the Lackagh Bridge seawards is incomparably more beautiful even than the beautiful landward one. You look down the length of Sheephaven to its opening ; quite near you on the left is the wooded point of Doe Castle, which, when the

The Lackagh Bridge.

MacSwineys ruled there, was the strongest place in Tyrconnell : further down on the left are the woods of Ards, and along the right, in a continuous curve, are the sands of Downing's Bay, with their sandhills glistening white behind them. The road to Rosapenna turns sharply to the left when you cross the bridge. You follow along it for rather a hilly four miles, but with

beautiful views on every side of you until you come to a chapel
(Roman Catholic Church). Beyond the chapel, as a little girl
explained to us, you will see "a big city, and that's Carrigart,"
and nearly a mile beyond the "city," away out on the sandhills
on the left, "you will see a town, and that's the hotel." You
ride the level mile or so that brings you up the sandy approach
to the hotel, and pull up in front of the pleasant verandah
which runs along the front of the house. The hotel is a large
structure, all constructed of Norwegian pine, which the late
Lord Leitrim caused to be brought to the quay near his own
house about two miles off. The result is a charming building ;
hall, drawing-room, billiard-room, and dining-room are all one
could desire, and the bedrooms perfectly delightful with the
fresh scent of the fir-panels. Out of doors on a fine day the
situation is delightful. Off the sandhills which are all about
the hotel, there is a continual sparkle in the air, and you have
only to climb a grassy knoll behind the hotel in order to see
Downing's Bay below you, and the rest of Sheephaven stretching
away out to the great mass of Horn Head. A sunset here is
wonderful, for the sun sinks, in June, so far to the north as to
clear the Head, and spreads along the horizon a luminous
gold against which the huge black cliff defines itself. Golf
links start from the hotel door, and there is good fishing
to be had. But the most remarkable thing about the
establishment and Rossgull generally is that where you
have now habitable land, was once a place almost as
wild as the Sahara. In the last century Lord Boyne built
himself a great house opposite the village of Carrigart, of
which the ruins can be traced perhaps half a mile from the
hotel. Gardens were laid out, and the old Rosapenna was
much talked of for its beauty. Then the sand began to drift.
It drifted against the house, it drifted in at the windows, it
drifted over the garden beds. Workmen fought it for long,
but at the last the struggle had to be given up and the house
abandoned. This grew worse and worse, and several small

farmers on the Carrigart side of the neck saw their holdings
smothered; till in 1843 the estate was bought by the then
Lord Leitrim, and he fell resolutely to the only means of check-
ing the evil, and planted bent—the coarse grass that grows on
the hills—laying out much money. The roots spread and
matted themselves together; then came a few scanty flowers,
pansies, and sandroses, and last of all the beautiful crisp turf

Downing's Bay, Sheephaven.

which delights the golfer. Nowadays the bent is not only a
protection but a resource, for it affords thatch for cottages.
But the planting has still to be renewed and watched on the
seaward side, and the late Earl spent large sums on this good
work.

At the end of the Rossgull peninsula, between Sheephaven
and Mulroy, on which the hotel stands, is the hill of Ganiamore.

It is an easy climb to the top of this. The view is one of the most beautiful in Ireland. You have under you Sheephaven, lying like a map, with the huge gable end of Muckish rising up beyond it. To the west is Horn Head and the battlemented outline of Tory, while on the other side of the Rossgull peninsula you are able to track out all the devious mazes and windings of that extraordinary piece of water, Mulroy Bay, which enters by a narrow inlet and spreads out like a fan, and not content with that sends out a great backwater up towards Fanad through another narrow gut, and to finish everything sprinkles the whole of its surface with rocks and islands, so that to know and navigate its tides and channels is a proof of very exceptional seamanship. But you will see Mulroy in all its extent when you start on your next stage to Portsalon. The shortest way, if you like to take it, involves two ferries across two channels of this bewildering lough, but I would certainly have you ride down to Bunlinn Glen at the very foot of Mulroy. It is about ten miles to the lower end of Mulroy from the hotel. The road takes you straight out over the hill past Lady Leitrim's house until you strike the side of the main body of the lake. Thence it winds along, prettily enough, a long heathery slope with steep hills to the right and the lough and its islands lying on the left, and beyond the water the Knockalla mountains rising jagged and fantastic. Presently you come in sight of the first fringe of Cratlagh wood, which runs mostly between the road and the lake for about three miles from Bunlinn, and you are in sight of the scene of a very tragic and bloody episode in which wood and lough had to play their part. About 200 yards from you is the place where the third Lord Leitrim was murdered in 1878.

The third Earl of Leitrim had served in the army, rising to be a colonel, before he succeeded his father in the title. He was a man by no means wholly bad and possessed qualities which might, under happier circumstances, have made him famous—absolute courage and a perfectly indomitable will. Nothing could be less like the careless, absentee landlord who has been the real curse of Ireland. He was solitary by nature, and built himself his great house of Manor Vaughan away in a dreary situation, neglecting numberless beautiful prospects in less remote parts of his

Muckish as seen from Rosapenna.

estate. The occupation of his life was the care of his property, and litigation was his hobby—a favourite one in Ireland. On his Leitrim property he was once fired at from a house and immediately rushed in and arrested the offender. On his Donegal estate his life was never safe and he always travelled armed; yet he lived to make old bones. He did his property the immense service of abolishing the old system of rundale, which less energetic landlords allowed to flourish in all its weediness. But the whole trend of modern legislation, which since the Act of 1870, aims at giving the tenant an interest in his holding, ran counter to his seigneurial ideal. No sort of opposition was allowed to stand in his way; if one man sold tenant-right to another his method was simple, to evict both. His violence of temper was such that he had been struck off the Magistracy as totally unfit to administer justice; and to his tenants he was, in plain English, a tyrant. He was not an avaricious tyrant; he did not want to extort unusually exorbitant rents; but he insisted that every man on his estate should hold his land absolutely at his landlord's pleasure. The very idea of a tenant having a right in improvements made at the tenant's own cost infuriated him, and in such cases he either raised the rent immediately, or ejected the man, to establish his supremacy. Nothing could be more characteristic of his tyranny, even in beneficence, than the step he took to improve the breed of sheep and cattle. He imported bulls and rams of choice breeds from Scotland, but he simultaneously, to enforce the improvement, made away with all the existing sires. Naturally he compensated their owners, but no one likes to be done good to by compulsion. Add to this imperious and arbitrary disposition a capricious temper with violent prejudices, and it is easy to see how horrible injustices were perpetrated. Eviction in that county meant often denial of the only means of livelihood. One family which had been turned out were starving and the clergyman of the parish went to intercede for help. "Sir," he said, "I would not give you a blanket to cover their bones." And thus, in April, 1878, when the news of his death came, it brought that surprise which is always occasioned when a thing long expected happens at the very last. Lord Leitrim was seventy-three when he was killed. What the immediate cause was, and whether it was a public or private feud, no one knows;

but it is said that he had eighty processes of ejectment pending
when he died, and, be it remembered, there was then no
question of a combination against rent.

He had set out to drive from Manor Vaughan to Milford on
a hired car. With him, besides the driver, was his clerk, a youth of
twenty-five, who had only just entered his service. Following
was another hired car, on which was Lord Leitrim's confidential

Mulroy Bay.

servant; but the horse in this car was lame, and fell about a
mile behind. The second car had almost reached the first point
where Cratlagh wood divides the road from Mulroy, when the
men on it heard two shots fired. In a moment or two they
came over the brow of the hill, and saw in front of them, at
some distance, the car with only Lord Leitrim on it. Then
they saw him struggling with two men; but the account is by no

means clear, though it is sufficiently apparent that they made no great haste to come up. First they met the clerk running towards them, and saying he was shot ; then the horse shied at a black mass in the road, and refused to pass it ; it was the driver of the front car. Then they came to Lord Leitrim, lying in a pool of water, with his brains beaten out ; and, looking to the lough below, saw a boat with two men rowing away, who in a minute were lost behind one of Mulroy's innumerable islets.

The clerk died in their hands, though the only wound on him was the scar, made by a slug, above his ear ; suffusion of blood on the brain was apparently more the result of a violent shock than of the wound. The driver's heart was riddled with shot. Lord Leitrim had no fatal shot-wound on him ; gun butts had done the work.

The plan was boldly and cunningly laid ; yet its success is surprising, for there was a patrol of two police on the road, within half a mile, who met the frightened horse galloping down to Milford by itself. The two assailants lay in wait at a point where the road comes within fifty yards of the water. The slope is covered with dense wooding down to its rocky edge, and the boat was easily hidden under it. They fired first with charges of heavy shot ; the second time possibly with pistols. The driver was killed at the first fire, and the clerk dropped off ; the car went a little further, but presumably was stopped as Lord Leitrim jumped off to struggle with the two. He was found with his teeth hard set ; he had died fighting ; and at least in this respect he died the death he merited.

The boat was discovered on the far side of Mulroy, with the oars in her ; a rough gun butt broken, a pistol, and a gun were picked up on the scene of the struggle. Why Lord Leitrim had not his revolvers that day, but left them in the second car unloaded, no one knows—or rather, very likely every one in the countryside is well aware. Four men were tried for the murder on circumstantial evidence ; the torn piece of a copybook, which had been used for a wad, was fitted to a torn page in a

book in one of their houses.   One died in jail before the trial ;
the remaining three were acquitted, but died within a year or two.
It is said in the countryside that the chief man in the affair is living
there yet.   But one thing is certain : every Irish-speaking person
within five miles of Milford, and many others, could, and would
not, tell you exactly who it was that killed Lord Leitrim.

The actual scene of the murder was just beyond a black gate
in the wood, about 200 yards from its northern end ; thirty or
forty yards beyond that, you will notice where the whinbushes
have been tracked and padded, and you will see how quick and
easy a way of escape was afforded by the shelter of the wood
and the screen of the islands in the lake.

The Leitrim name has a very different repute in the county nowadays.   The old Earl's nephew and successor was then an officer in
the navy.   He inherited nothing that his predecessor could leave
away from him ; but he came down at once to the scene of the
murder, and while making himself conspicuous by his attempts
to bring the criminals to justice, rode about the country un-
attended.   The tenants, however, soon found that there was to
be a new order.   All the victims of arbitrary ejectment, so far
as was possible, were reinstated.   A very heavy outlay was made
on works of drainage and reclamation.   But a still greater boon
to the countryside was the establishment of a line of steamers
to bring the produce of the farms to Glasgow, and, conversely,
to bring articles in demand to Milford : thus saving a transport
of—in many cases—fifteen miles, and enabling the local shop-
keepers to take nearly a pound per ton off their charges.   The
result of these and other beneficent measures has been a great
improvement in the condition of the people : and Milford, from
being a miserable village, has become one of the most thriving
petty towns in the county.   When you have ridden a mile or two
along the beautiful road by Cratlagh wood, under the oak and
hazel which shadow it, you will get a glimpse across the water of a
trim-looking pier and store.   The building is a mill for grinding
Indian corn, which has kept life in the people in times of hard

pressure from failing crops; and the pier is the *Melmore's*
place of call. Knowing the reputation of Mulroy for rocks and
tide-races, when she was started everybody prophesied that
the steamer would knock herself to pieces in a month, but the
Melmore is still plying without an accident, and passengers
can get themselves shipped in great comfort from Glasgow

Mulroy Bay, looking Seaward.

or Derry to the Rosapenna Hotel, disembarking at the pier
outside Mulroy House.

At the end of the Lough the road turns to the left, and
emerges on a beautiful open glen. If you have time, it is a
delightful walk up the stream to a water-fall about two miles
up; but if, as is probable, you prefer to press on, you will at
least have a pleasant view of all this beautiful greenery. The
road rises now, serpentining uphill for a matter of a mile, and

you pass the farmhouse where the once celebrated Miss Pater
son, Jerome Bonaparte's first wife, is said to have first seen
the light.   Continue until you come to a point where the telegraph wires diverge, and then, unless you want to go to Milford,
turn to the left, and the road will take you past Lord Leitrim's
store and mill, along a level eight miles down the Fanad shore
of Mulroy ; so that you will see the lough in all its aspects, and,
it is to be hoped, in all its beauty.   The road to Portsalon
turns off to the right, before you reach the village of Tamney.
At Kerrykeel, which you pass on the way, is a cromlech.   The
Portsalon road is hilly, but direct, and soon brings you in sight
of the waters of Lough Swilly.   The whole ride from Rosapenna may be put at twenty-three miles.

Colonel Barton's hotel at Portsalon is, perhaps, the best
known of all these Donegal hotels at present, owing to the
fortunate circumstance that he has discovered at his door one
of the three best golf links in Ireland ; but the hotel was started
before golf came to give an impetus to tourist traffic in Donegal,
and its owner deserves the credit of a pioneer.   The history of
it is roughly this : the Government built a pier in Ballymastocker
Bay, and Colonel Barton perceived the possibility of working
in conjunction with the steamer that should bring excursionists
down from Derry.   Naturally he applied for a spirit license as
hotel-keeper, and this brought about a violent opposition from
the neighbouring publican.   The opposition was overruled by
the Licensing Bench, and Colonel Barker got his license.   The
defeated rival, who was a Catholic and Nationalist, went away,
cursing by all his gods against the "bloody Orange majority."
"Ah well," he said to a knot of his sympathisers, "let him
alone, boys ; wait till he gets to hell.   He'll find no Orange
majority there."

The most delightful part about this story is that it was preserved and published by the publican's attorney, who happened
to overhear it, and could not let a good joke perish even when it

N

told against his own side, so he repeated it to the Protestant
lawyer.

The hotel has grown and prospered mightily since those
days, and if you should end your tour there you could end it
in no pleasanter place. It stands looking south across Lough
Swilly; on its right is the broad sweep of Ballymastocker with
its lovely clean sand ; inside of that the sandhills, and behind
them the smooth green of the links ; facing you is Dunree
Head, now become a powerful fort. For Lough Swilly is a
magnificent harbour, where many fleets could ride without
jostling. It slants in somewhat to the eastward, then turns to
the south, so that from about ten or fifteen miles inside the
mouth one has to get far to the Inishowen side to see the open
water. It is defended now by a series of four forts, one at
Leenan just inside Dunaff Head, commanding the opening ;
one at Dunree, which could shell practically the whole Lough
north and south ; one quite near Buncrana, and one on Inch
Island, facing up the Lough.

To the left of the hotel a line of cliffs runs for about six
miles out to Fanad Head, reaching their highest point in a
square-cut precipice that is called the Bin of Fanad. It has a
fall of about 300 feet. Just off the Bin is the one obstacle to
navigation, the Swilly Rock, where, early in the century, the
Saldanha frigate was lost with all hands, the only thing that
came alive ashore being a grey parrot. A strange story is told
in the Napier memoirs of Captain Pakenham who commanded
this unlucky vessel. He was in the Peninsula when a command reached him to join his ship and sail with sealed orders.
He confided to Napier that for the first time he was uneasy
about his safety. It was borne in upon him, he said, that he
would lose his life on this voyage, and that the place where he
would lose it would be Lough Swilly in the North of Ireland.
The forewarning was of no more use than one of Cassandra's
predictions.

There is any amount of sight-seeing to be done from the
Portsalon hotel, besides any amount of golf and very passable
fishing in Kindrum Lough, and when you have exhausted the
resources of Portsalon there is a very pleasant means of getting
away. A steamer runs twice daily to and from Fahan pier,
and the trip up the Lough is as pretty as anything that can
be imagined, especially if you get a fine day. Lough Swilly

Portsalon.

can look grey, and bleak, and windy enough, but under a
bright blue sky there is no more beautiful lough in Ireland. It
is beautiful as you look at it straight up from the direction of
Rathmelton, with the exquisite curves of Slieve Snacht falling
away from its great height right and left. It is beautiful as
you see it from Rathmullen, with the island mountain of Inch
standing full against you ; perhaps prettiest of all from Fahan,

where the purple heather-covered hills rise gently behind you,
and the houses are all set in trees and flowers, and the sands
are golden orange in the sunlight, and over on the far shore
you see the soft green of the Rathmullen woods giving an air
of gentleness and civilisation that is in strange contrast with
the jagged outlines of the Knockalla hills. One of these
ranges behind Rathmullen is quite unmistakable in its contorted
ridginess, and the Irish name for it is Cruiv Drim a Dhiaoul,
which is, being interpreted, the Devil's Backbone. I take
peril upon my head to write this down ; for I asked a man on
the quay at Portsalon, who, they told me, knew Irish, to write
down the correct spelling, and just as he was about to do so a
woman interfered. " No," she said, " you'll write none of that.
That's no good name to be writing." The steamer was just
starting, and I had to jump on board while the altercation
proceeded, and the next thing I saw was the pencil being
tossed over the quayhead, which settled the matter for
the moment. But it is a very harmless Devil's Backbone so
far as I know, and a striking feature in a landscape whose
charm was described long ago by a great master of language in
the days when the present Primate of All Ireland was rector of
Fahan.

A FINE DAY BY LOUGH SWILLY

Soft slept the beautiful Autumn
In the heart, on the face of the Lough—
Its heart, whose pulses were hushed,
Till you knew the life of the tide
But by a wash on the shore,
A whisper, like whispering leaves
In green abysses of forest—
Its face, whose violet melted,
Melted in roseate gold—
Roses and violets dying
Into a silver mystery
Of soft impalpable haze.

Calm lay the woodlands of Fahan :
The summer was gone, yet it lay
On the gently yellowing leaves
   Like a beautiful poem, whose tones
   Are mute, whose words are forgot,
But its music sleepeth for ever
Within the music of thought.
The robin sang from the ash,
The sunset's pencils of gold
No longer wrote their great lines
On the boles of the odorous limes,
   Or bathed the tree-tops in glory :
But a soft strange radiance there hung
In splinters of tenderest light.
And those who looked from Glengollen
   Saw the purple wall of the Scalp,
As if through an old church window
Stained with a marvellous blue.
From the snow-white shell-strand of Inch
You could not behold the white horses
   Lifting their glittering backs,
   Tossing their manes on Dunree,
And the battle boom of Macammish
Was lulled in the delicate air.
As in old pictures the smoke
Goes up from Abraham's pyre,
So the smoke went up from Rathmullen ;
   And beyond the trail of the smoke
   Was a great deep fiery abyss
     Of molten gold in the sky,
And it set a far tract up the waters
   Ablaze with gold like its own.
Over the fire of the sea,
Over the chasm in the sky,
My spirit, as by a bridge
Of wonder, went wandering on,
And lost its way in the Heaven

Rain at Rathmullen.

CHAPTER XIII

ALL around the central—almost circular—reach of Lough Swilly, which lies between Macammish and Buncrana, Fahan and Rathmullen, are evident traces of the past. At Buncrana is an old castle of the O'Dohertys; another stands on Inch Island: and further up, overlooking the arm of the lough that runs up to Letterkenny, stands on the bare top of a hill Birt Castle, where Sir Cahir O'Doherty withdrew in his fury after Paulet struck him, and plotted that final and fatal rising which earned for his fosterers, the McDevitts, the nickname which they are said still to keep, of the Burn-Derrys.

But from the lough itself, or from Fahan pier, you will see
the monument of a far older past than these petty castles point
to.   On the highest summit of the range that divides the
eastern arm of Lough Swilly from the valley of the Foyle and
the town of Derry—on the top of Elagh mountain—stands
conspicuous a circular fort of stonework.   That is the Grianan,
or summer palace of Aileach, and well worthy a visit.   Three con-
centric ramparts of earth and stone enclose a fort or cashel
a ring of cyclopean masonry some five-and-twenty yards in
diameter; the walls are eighteen feet high, and over twelve feet
thick at the base.   Inside this huge wall, from each side of the
entrance gate galleries run, with exits on to the enclosure.
This was the stronghold where the sons of Nial of the Nine
Hostages established themselves.   But according to the legend
in the Four Masters, the place took its name from a princess
of Scotland, Aileach, "modest and blooming in Alba, till the
loss of the Gael disturbed her," and she followed Eoghad of
the Hy-Nial over seas, and from the pair sprang sons, who
founded Dalriada, the kingdom of the Isles and the Antrim
Coast.   Here in later days Patrick came, and converted the
chiefs, and there was no palace in Ireland more famous, till
1101, when Murtagh O'Brien, King of Munster, made a
great raid into the North, and demolished the home of
the O'Neills.

The fort as it stands has been restored by a zealous antiquary, Dr. Bernard of Derry: marks made with tar show the
point up to which the wall was intact, before he and his
helpers gathered together the wreckage and piled it into its
old place.

But this remote and legendary past cannot be so real for us
as the vivid historic associations that centre round the town
of Rathmullen, which certainly should not be left unvisited.
A steamer will take you across to it from Fahan.

This pretty little harbour is, perhaps, the spot in all Tyrconnell

which has the most interesting story. The old Abbey, whose
ruins still show something of the Norman-Irish architecture, was
built for a monastery of the Carmelites by the MacSwineys in
the 15th century; though Knox, the Bishop of Raphoe, rebuilt
it largely when he got the manor of Rathmullen from Turlough
Oge MacSwiney in 1618. To the west of the Abbey once stood
the Castle of the MacSwineys of Fanad, easternmost of the three
divisions of the clan. Now, in 1587, when England was full of
apprehension, for the Armada was preparing, Sir John Perrott,
bastard son of Henry VIII., ruled as Lord Deputy in Ireland,
and it was essential for him to secure peace in that troubled
kingdom at such a time. Sir Hugh O'Donnell, the chieftain
of Tyrconnell, who had been knighted by Sir Henry Sidney, was
paramount in the country; but Sir Hugh was ruled by his wife
—Ineen Dhu Macdonald, a Scotchwoman, daughter of the Lord
of the Isles. Her eldest son was Hugh O'Donnell, famous in
later life as Red Hugh, and even then celebrated by the bards
as a boy of rare promise. Sir John Perrott's main object
was to secure Hugh, and, holding him for a hostage, to control
O'Donnell and the North. But Ineen Dhu—"The Dark
Daughter"—had no thought of letting him go out of safe
keeping; for her heart was set upon this boy, and to ensure his
succession to the chieftaincy in those days, when the custom of
tanistry had come to mean the succession of whatever claimant
for election by the clan could show most backing, she maintained in her own right an army of Scotch mercenaries—"red
shanks" as they were called. Further, to make assurance
stronger, she had linked the boy by the tie of fosterage—
then counted more sacred than blood-relationship—to the
greatest of O'Donnell's dependant chiefs, Owen Oge Mac-
Swiney—surnamed "Of the Battle-axes," and chief of all the
MacSwineys. She sent Hugh to be guarded by his foster-
father in Doe Castle—to this day not an easy place to reach,
and then perhaps the least accessible in Elizabeth's dominions.

How was Perrott to come by his pledge? The story is told
in the beginning of Mr. Standish O'Grady's vivid narrative
The Flight of the Eagle, a book which brings Elizabethan
Ireland really to life again ; and from it I must condense my
narrative.   On May 2nd, 1587, Perrott wrote to Elizabeth and
her Council : " For O'Donnell, if it would please her Majesty
to appoint me to go thither, I will make him and his Mac-
Sweenies deliver in what pledges I list.   Otherwise, if it please
her Majesty, I could take himself, his wife, who is a great
bringer-in of Scots, and perhaps his son Hugh Roe (Red Hugh)
by sending them a boat with wines." In plain English, Perrott
proposed sending an army to coerce O'Donnell, or as an
alternative, a kidnapping expedition : and Elizabeth promptly
decided for the kidnapping.   It was found presumably that
Hugh Roe was the easier object, and accordingly in September,
1587, a big merchantman sailed up Lough Swilly, and cast
anchor opposite Rathmullen.   Her master was George Dudall,
but the gentleman who appeared as her owner and announced
that he came with a cargo of choice wines, was in reality
Captain Birmingham of her Majesty's forces.   And the reason
why he sailed into Rathmullen was that he had heard of a visit
purposed by Owen Oge of the Battle-axes to MacSwiney
of Fanad, on whom the head of the MacSwineys came to
"cosher" or demand free quarters for a period, according to his
right.   Birmingham had been trading freely and generously for
some days, when in came Owen of the Battle-axes at the head
of a great retinue.   " Harpers rode there, their sheathed instru-
ments of harmony slung behind their backs, or borne by attendants ; story-tellers to beguile the intervals of feasting and
music with fragments of ancient epic, and shed a glamour of
the romance of old over the tame familiar facts of the present.
There rode Owen Oge's bard, who composed poems in his
praise, and the professional rhapsodists who recited them, for
the bard proper was a silent man ; he composed, but sung not.

There rode his huntsmen, coercing the hounds with voice and leather; his hawkers with their hooded birds. Sleek racers were led along there beside the more ponderous war-horses. Horse-racing was a great pastime of the age. A king of this region was once pitched from his horse and killed while he rode in a race."

"In the midst of this equestrian and pedestrian retinue rode the chieftain, surrounded by claymores and battle-axes. . . . He wore the broad-brimmed Spanish hat of the period, and a strong buff coat of gilded leather, as did all his attendant gentlemen. . . . The very garb of the Elizabethan-Irish gentlemen seemed to announce, 'Lo! it is peace; but over my buff coat I can slip on my shirt of mail, and over it my hauberk, in a trice. Therefore, beware.'" Red Hugh, then in his fifteenth year, would be the foremost figure in the feudal school who accompanied the chief: boys committed to his tutelage that they might learn the arts of war, and get book schooling as well, for the chiefs' sons in those days were taught—as Cuellar found—to write and speak Latin. Of the party was also at least one knight, Sir Owen O'Gallagher, a great chief in Southern Tyrconnell; and welcome was surely given them with whatever pomp the MacSwiney of Fanad could compass.

But when the cavalcade entered the town, Birmingham shut up his mart, and brought his men back to the vessel. His wines were sold, he said; but if the chiefs and their attendants of highest rank would be his guests on the vessel, they should try his own store. There was no thought of treachery, and naturally enough the young O'Donnell was as eager to see the inside of this great vessel as any boy of his age would be nowadays to board the man-of-war that comes into Lough Swilly from time to time. So MacSwiny Doe and MacSwiny Fanad, with Sir Owen O'Gallagher, Red Hugh, and others rowed out to the ship, and they were set down in the cabin to be merry over the wine, when suddenly the door was bolted on them ; the anchor was weighed, the deck filled with soldiers who had been concealed under hatches ; and Birmingham came in, bidding the chiefs give hostages for themselves if they would, but for Red Hugh no hostage could be taken. The Irish were trapped treacherously ; there was nothing for it but submission. Sons and nephews had to be sent aboard hastily for pledges ; the

Rathmullen.

chieftains were put on shore, sad and angry, and the ship sailed down Lough Swilly in a fair wind, free from all chance of pursuit, for the Irish lords, strong as they were on land, never took to seafaring or owned a war galley ; and Birmingham might sail in safety under the very loopholes of Dunluce, though Sorley Boy, Hugh's uncle, was master there.

Hugh was taken to Dublin Castle ; the unlucky Dudall who

lent his ship for this creditable venture was made a scapegoat
by Perrott, and imprisoned for his treachery to a guest. But
Hugh lay in strong ward for many a year, while his warlike
mother from Donegal keep battled against all pretenders to his
place in the succession. Of Hugh's escape and recapture, of
his second flight, his wanderings in the Wicklow mountains,
and his final dash across the Liffey under the very walls of
Dublin Castle, while Fitzwilliam and his Council reckoned that
all ways were shut that might lead him to the North—of these
things, if you be wise, you will read in Mr. O'Grady's stirring
narrative. But of his subsequent career as the firebrand of
Ulster and scourge of the English, some outline must be given,
for it leads up to the other and still more dramatic pageant that
was played out at Rathmullen—the " Flight of the Earls."

When Hugh Roe was captured in 1587, he was already
married, by agreement of parents, to the daughter of Hugh
O'Neill, the Earl of Tyrone, then a great noble at the court of
Elizabeth. Thus early was cemented a famous alliance. He
escaped at Christmas time in 1591 and reached Ballyshannon in
February. During his imprisonment Government had named
Calvagh O'Donnell's illegitimate son—" Hugh the Son of the
Deacon "—Sheriff of Donegal, but Ineen Dhu, Hugh's fierce
mother, had caused him to be shot by her archers. There was
also a company of English devastating the country; only Donegal
Castle held out, and in it were Sir Hugh and Ineen Dhu shut up.
Hugh—aged twenty—put himself at the head of a force and
expelled the English into Connaught, but the nights of snow and
hunger on the Wicklow mountains had left him with frostbitten
feet, and he was obliged, after his first display of energy, to lie
by at Ballyshannon, and finally have his great toes amputated
before he could accept the chieftaincy which his father then
willingly surrendered, and be proclaimed O'Donnell at the
rock of Doon, according to the formula, " by the successors of
Columbkille with the permission and by the advice of the

nobles of Tyrconnell, both lay and ecclesiastical." Had
descent, not election, decided these matters, after the English
law, the chief of the O'Donnells would have been Neil Garv
O'Donnell (Neil the Fierce), son of Con O'Donnell, who was
son of Calvagh.   As it was, Neil counted that he was the better
man, and made no secret of his spleen.   But, at first, he fought
right well under his cousin, and his cousin was the very man to
keep him busy.   Hugh Roe's first act was to raid the territories of
Turlough Lynach O'Neill, the man who claimed to succeed to
Shane's position, and lived at Strabane.   There Red Hugh made
--by Tyrone's advice---formal submission to Government.   But
he and Tyrone were already plotting to obtain Spanish aid and
revolt from England.   By O'Donnell's repeated attacks, Turlough
Lynach was obliged to resign his title of the O'Neill, which was
then assumed by the Earl of Tyrone : a first sign of disaffection,
as Tyrone had pledged himself not to bear it.   The O'Donnell and
the O'Neill were now virtually lords of all Ulster.   In 1594, Enniskillen was reduced by Hugh Maguire, chief of Fermanagh, acting
under O'Donnell's orders.   In 1595, Red Hugh attempted to drive
the English out of Connaught, but their occupation of that
province had been for a long time effective, and they held
fortresses all through it.   He raided the country, however, unopposed, and when his enemies waited for him in the passes
from Connaught into Tyrconnell, turned to the east, and carried
fire and sword into the Pale.   War was now definitely levied
against the Earls ; and by way of reprisal, George Bingham, son
of Sir Richard Bingham, Governor of Connaught, sailed round
the Swilly, and plundered the Carmelite Abbey at Rathmullen.
It seemed to them worth while even to make a descent upon
Tory—not for any riches of the inhabitants, but for the spoils
of Columbkille's church there, and there "they preyed and
plundered everything they found on the island."   Meanwhile,
however, O'Neill and O'Donnell had driven back Sir John
Norris's army, O'Neill, it is said, killing in single combat a
huge soldier, Segrave of Meath ; and George Bingham, say the

Four Masters, soon paid the penalty of his sacrilege at Rathmullen and Tory, for he was slain on his return to Connaught
by Ulick Burke, who thereupon delivered up the town of Sligo
to Red Hugh.   O'Donnell immediately reinstated in their lands
all those chiefs whom Bingham had expelled in his very oppressive government.   It was a demonstration to the world that
the lords of Ulster meant no ordinary rising, but a systematic
sweeping away of the English from Celtic Ireland.   By the end
of the year, O'Donnell had broken down near a score of the
castles in Connaught ; he had named new chiefs of the great
clans, Burkes, O'Dowds, Macdonaghs and Macdermots ; he held
hostages from them all ; and he was a greater power in Connaught than Elizabeth's Governor.   It was time for the English
to take thought : and they sent the Earl of Ormond and the
Archbishop of Cashel to make terms.   They offered to the
Earls the entire " province of Conchobar," that is, Ulster except
the tract between Dundalk and the Boyne ; Carrickfergus, Carlingford and Newry were to remain trading outposts ; all sheriffs were
to be withdrawn, except in the towns named, and Connaught was
to have similar privileges.   But Tyrone, Red Hugh, and their council "having reflected, for a long time, upon the many that had been
ruined by the English since their arrival in Ireland, by specious
promises, which they had not performed, and the number of
Irish high-born princes, gentlemen, and chieftains who came to
premature deaths without any reason at all, except to rob them
of their patrimonies," decided to reject the peace.   Elizabeth
then sent 20,000 men into Ireland, and Sir John Norris marched
into Connaught at the head of a great hosting.   O'Donnell
marched out too, but the armies only watched each other.   The
English took the wise step of recalling Sir Richard Bingham
and his relatives, and substituting Sir Conyers Clifford " a far
better man than he."   Nevertheless, in 1597, Red Hugh
carried his men to the very gates of Galway and returned across
the Erne, routing on his way the O'Conor of Sligo, who attacked
him with a body of English and Irish troops.   But, in the same

year, an attempt was made to reduce the Earls separately.
The Lord Justice himself moved on O'Neill, while the Governor
of Connaught invaded O'Donnell's country, fought his way
across the Erne and then, after laying strong siege to Ballyshannon Castle, was driven to the forced retreat over the ford
above Assaroe, of which a description by the Four Masters has
been quoted.

In 1598, after negotiations for peace had failed—for Tyrone was
by no means so resolute in his policy as Red Hugh, and still tem-
porised—the O'Neill army laid siege to an English fort on the
Blackwater, near Armagh. A strong army, 4,000 foot and 600
horse, was sent under Sir Henry Bagenal to relieve it. O'Neill
summoned O'Donnell, and the forces met at Ballinabuie, or the
Yellow Ford, on the Blackwater. The result was the greatest
defeat inflicted upon the English at any time in Ireland—by a contemporary English account "thirteen valiant captains and 1,500
common soldiers—many of them veterans—were slain on the
field." Bagenal himself perished, and the fort on the Blackwater was surrendered. Tyrone with energy might have swept
every Englishman from the country: but he had not Red Hugh's
fiery temper, and though Munster and Connaught only wanted
a signal to burst in open rebellion, for three months he stirred
no further. In autumn, however, the clans rose, and the whole
country along the left bank of the Shannon was plundered by
the Irish party ; but O'Donnell confined himself to raiding the
Clanricarde territory in Connaught, and O'Neill appears to have
lain totally inactive awaiting reinforcements from Spain. Elizabeth
meanwhile sent in great forces under Essex, who landed in April,
1559—nine months after Bagenal's defeat. In that time Hugh
O'Neill might have made himself King of Ireland ; but he lacked
nerve, and did not see that the chance of Spanish help was
slight in comparison with the certainty that the English would
reinforce their armies. Twenty thousand foot and two thousand
horse came with Essex ; yet, even so, he felt it needful to pro-
claim that any of the Irish, who had been wrongfully deprived

of patrimony by an Englishman, should be reinstated. Essex marched first into Munster, but returned unsuccessful; and meanwhile O'Conor of Sligo was closely beleaguered in his one remaining castle of Coloony by Red Hugh. Essex ordered Clifford to relieve him : and Red Hugh, having completed his blockade of the castle, cheerfully posted himself on the Curlew Hills to wait for the English ; the fight took place on August 15th, and ended with the hopeless rout of the English. Sir Conyers Clifford was slain, with many other leaders. O'Conor submitted to Red Hugh on the sight of Clifford's head, shown as a lamentable proof of the truth. And on the top of this further blow to the English ascendency, came a new failure of Essex, who, after an abortive expedition into Ulster, patched up a truce with O'Neill and hastened back to his ruin in England.

It was by this time definitely understood that O'Neill stood not only for the Irish against the English, but for the freedom of his faith : and Elizabeth would grant no indulgence to the Catholics. Yet he still made the fatal error of delaying and diplomatising, while Elizabeth poured into the country yet another great army, under Mountjoy and Sir George Carew. At last, however, in 1600, he called a hosting, and marched southwards through Meath, Westmeath, and King's County. But Hugh Maguire, his right hand man, was cut off by Sir Warham St. Leger in a plundering expedition near Cork, where the leaders fell by each other's hand. Except this, little came of the hosting ; O'Neill returned to Tyrone no stronger than he left it, and Carew began steadily to reduce Munster to subjection. Also an attack was made on Ulster from a new quarter. The Irish had no ships ; Elizabeth could strike where she pleased, and in April a fleet under Sir Henry Docwra put into Lough Foyle. They erected three forts : one at Dunnalong on the east or Derry shore in Tyrone's country ; and two in O'Donnell's country, at Culmore in Inishowen, and at Derry, which was then the seat of the great monastery, Columb-

kille's first foundation. Sir Henry Docwra "tore down the monastery and cathedral, and destroyed all the ecclesiastical edifices in the town and erected houses and apartments of them."

Fear of attack confined Docwra to his entrenchments; he had 4,000 men, but sickness spread among them; and Red Hugh left the O'Doherty of Inishowen to watch Culmore, and Neil Garv, his cousin, to blockade Derry, while he himself marched through Connaught and levied war on Thomond, the home of the O'Briens in Clare. But meanwhile Neil Garv was in correspondence with Docwra, who promised him that lordship of Tyrconnell which he held should have been his—not Red Hugh's: and, finally, he went over with about 100 men and, what was more valuable, minute knowledge of O'Donnell's forces. Within a week, under his guidance, Docwra surprised the castle at Lifford, though a trusty soldier set fire to it before it could be taken. In two day's fighting against Red Hugh which followed, Neil did excellent service, by Docwra's own account, and the most Hugh Roe could effect was to keep in check the English forces at Lifford. Docwra explicitly states his obligation to the help of Neil, "without whose intelligence and guidance little or nothing could have been done of ourselves." But, for all that, little good came to Neil of his desertion or of the valour that he showed against his own people; and contentions soon set in between him and Docwra. In 1601, John O'Doherty died, and, as I have told before, Red Hugh—who held his son Cahir as a hostage—preferred that Phelim, brother of John, should succeed. But Cahir O'Doherty was a fosterer of the Macdevitts, a strong clan on the eastern shore of Lough Swilly, and they bitterly resented this slight to him. Hatred of the English was a light thing compared with this strange tie, far stronger among Celts than blood kinship, and they went to Docwra and begged him take up the cause of Cahir ; which he, naturally desirous to split a hostile clan, did : and so it came to pass that Cahir had Inishowen, and the O'Dohertys came over to the English.

But Neil Garv said that Tyrconnell had been promised him, and that Inishowen was part of his claim as overlord. Docwra however, declared that Cahir O'Doherty now held immediately from the Crown, so that there was an end of the O'Donnell's rent in Inishowen.

Rathmullen comes again into the story now, for in this year the English made a descent upon MacSwiney of Fanad, and seized a thousand of his cattle : whereupon the chief submitted, and a garrison of 150 men was put in Rathmullen Abbey. MacSwiney revolted ; but his hostages were hanged, his lands plundered, and he was forced to give new pledges. So strong was Docwra growing, as the English had always done, by using dissensions among the native Irish.

Yet hitherto nothing had been accomplished of any great moment. But in the summer of 1601, while Red Hugh was on a march into Connaught against an Anglo-Irish force, Neil Garv crossed Tyrconnell, marched through Barnes Gap and encamped at Donegal. Red Hugh hastened back to reclaim his own, and beleaguered his cousin in the monastery. The siege lasted till a store of powder in the monastery blew up, and the place was carried by assault : Neil Garv escaped, and brought up a relief force under cover of the fire of a ship, and he and his men resisted inside the walls of the monastery till, in October, word came to Red Hugh that a Spanish fleet had landed at Kinsale under Don Juan de Aquila. Hugh at once set out, marched through Roscommon and Galway, crossed the Shannon, and waited for O'Neill near Roscrea. Carew was sent to block his way towards Kinsale; but a heavy frost set in, and Red Hugh made good use of it, for he crossed the boggy mountain of Slieve Phelim in the night and covered thirty-two Irish miles on the march, "the greatest," wrote Carew, "with carriage that hath been heard of"; and finally effected his junction with O'Neill on the Bandon river. Mountjoy was already besieging the Spaniards in Kinsale : O'Neill and Red Hugh came down to blockade Mountjoy, and cut off his supplies. And now came the critical mistake. O'Neill was for playing a waiting game. Fynes Morison, who was present, says that if this had been done, "all our horse must have been sent away or starved." But the Spaniards also were hard set and sent messages to the Irish chieftains accusing them of cowardice, which infuriated Red Hugh; and in council he overbore O'Neill's better judgment. A night attack in three divisions was planned: but the guides missed the way, the English had warning, and at daybreak the Irish, in disorder, found the English ready for them. Mountjoy vigorously attacked ONeill's body and put overwhelming numbers to a complete rout. The Irish, who had for years been gaining confidence, now went to pieces, as Highland armies have always done after defeat. Red Hugh," say the Four Masters, "was seized with great fury, rage, and anxiety of mind, so that he did not sleep or rest soundly for the space of three days and three nights afterwards." At the end of that time it was decided that he should go in person to Spain to request further help from Philip; and he entrusted the charge of his people to Rory, his brother. Great was the wailing in the camp of Kinel Conaill, says the history, when this resolution was heard. On January 6th, 1602, Red Hugh set sail from Castlehaven, and saw Ireland for the last time, being then in his twenty-ninth year. His party landed at Corunna and saw with joy, for a good omen, the tower of Breogan—Braganza—whence the Milesians, in far-off ages, had come to subdue the Folk of the Danaans. O'Donnell was received with the highest marks of respect by the grandees of Spain and had audience of the King. Philip gave him promises and sent him back to Corunna to await an armament. Months passed, and he was again summoned to Court. But he got no further on his journey than Simancas. Carew, who was busy with his "pacifying of Ireland,"—such a pacification as the Latin spoke of when he said, "they make a wilderness and they call it peace"—had his spies in Corunna, and he knew that his peace would not be lasting if Red Hugh, whether alone or supported, got back to Ulster. So

he dealt with one James Blake, of Galway, and Hugh came by the
sickness that he died of at Simancas in the September of the
same year. It was a black business, yet scarcely worse than the
kidnapping by Perrott; for the Tudors would hardly have troubled
to disavow the act of poisoning, and at least Red Hugh was at
open war with England, when he was poisoned. Englishmen
will reflect that if it was a disagreeable expedient, at least it
secured to Ireland the advantage of English rule. No reasonable man will assert that it would have been an unmixed blessing
for Ireland had Hugh O'Neill succeeded in driving the English
out. But no man who knows the facts will deny that it is hard
to imagine how a worse thing could have befallen any country
than Carew's Pacification or the Plantation of Ulster : from which
sprang the internecine massacres in 1641 — a natural consequence
—Cromwell's heavy-handed repression, and a whole progeny of
cruel and disastrous consequences which endure to this day.

The fate of Celtic Ireland was decided at the battle of
Kinsale. Its fortunes fell with the fall of Red Hugh, who was
the spirit of the whole resistance, as they had risen with his rise.
His people neglected his advice, which was to keep their forces
together, broke up into detachments, each of which was severely
attacked on the homeward way. Ballyshannon, as well as
Donegal, was taken by Neil Garv, who had as usual distinguished himself at Kinsale. Shortly after he captured
Enniskillen. Yet Rory held out in Sligo till word came of Red
Hugh's death, and a message from Mountjoy offering peace for
submission. This did not please Neil Garv, who accounted
himself now lord, both *de jure* and *de facto*, of Tyrconnell, and
as soon as Red Hugh's death was announced, assembled the clan
at Kilmacrenan and caused himself to be proclaimed the
O'Donnell. Meanwhile Rory was with Mountjoy, and Neil, in
despite of orders, seized Rory's cattle. Docwra, who seemed
inclined to fulfil his pledge, reasoned with Neil and endeavoured
to bring him to a more submissive mood, and it would seem
had succeeded, when word came from Mountjoy that he would

bear with Neil no longer; and so he commanded Docwra
to arrest the chief, on the ground that he had committed
treason in taking the style of O'Donnell. Docwra did not
like the commission, as appears from his account—indeed,
he seems to have been much too honest a man for this
employ—but the most he could do was to spare Neil the
indignity of fetters. Neil "seemed wonderful thankful for it,"

Doe Castle.

but to Docwra's disgust seized an early occasion to escape.
Docwra, however, was too quick for him, and cut off his escape
to the North-West. Neil's troop was scattered and he himself
sought refuge with the McSwiney's, in Doe Castle. But Owen
Oge, the lord of Doe, was then in Docwra's hands and was
obliged to take an English garrison into his fortress; so Neil
had no choice but to submit. The unlucky man, through

whom, more than through any other, the English had now got a
hold on Tyrconnell that could never be shaken off, went to
London to plead his services, but James and his Council
distrusted so good a soldier. They accepted Rory's submission,
and gave him the earldom of Tyrconnell, a title which had been
offered in 1541 by Henry to Manus, Rory's grandfather, the
biographer of Columbkille. Rory was put in possession of all
the O'Donnell rights, except a thousand acres about Ballyshannon, and the fishery, which the Crown reserved. Neil was
confined to his estate running from near Raphoe eastward to
the Tyrone border.

The Earl of Tyrone had submitted on the same terms as Rory,
and was graciously received at Court by James, to the vast
indignation of men who had laboured for years to get his head,
and now rubbed shoulders with the arch rebel. But the conquest of Ulster was complete. Mountjoy and Carew had done
their work thoroughly. On September 12th, 1602, the Lord
Deputy wrote to the Lords that he had brought Tyrone to such
a pass of famine "that between Tulloghogue and Toome there
lay a thousand dead, and that since our first drawing this year
to Blackwater, there were above three thousand starved in
Tyrone." Any one who likes to reflect for a moment can picture what that means ; or can read in the horrible account of
an eye-witness what Fynes Morison saw there—knots of
people gathered eagerly round any patch of watercress, and
corpses lying in the ditches, their lips green with half chewed
grass.

In Tyrconnell, happily, the English armies were not seen :
the country was too remote and untraversable to know this
fearful vengeance. Yet even so, the English were not content.
The parable of the poppies held good in their eyes ; and
Tyrone was soon made to feel his altered position. O'Kane,
his chief urraght or vassal, refused him rent : but Tyrone insisted, and Mountjoy supported the claim. Then came Sir
Arthur Chichester, as Lord Deputy, whose policy was to deal

direct with the urraghts and induce them "to depend wholly
and immediately upon the Crown." O'Kane was prompted by
Montgomery, Bishop of Derry, a leading politician and helper
in the good work of pacification, to revive the case. Tyrone
was summoned to Dublin, and the matter was referred thence
to the King's decision. Tyrone was led to believe that his
arrest was intended—and he was probably right ; so hearing that
one of the Maguires had provided a vessel for him, he made a hasty
flight to the North. Meanwhile Rory O'Donnell had not been
happier in his relations with Government. There were perpetual quarrels with Neil Garv, though it seems that Chichester
did that warrior very scant justice. Rory plotted a *coup de
main* on Dublin Castle, and hoped for Tyrone's support—
whether with or without ground no one knows. The whole
circumstances that led up to the " Flight of the Earls " are mysterious. At all events, when the Earl of Tyrone reached Lough
Swilly, the Earl of Tyrconnell was waiting for him at Rathmullen on a great and lamentable day in the history of that
little town. Tyrone, after his hurried journey from Slane, met
Donnell O'Donnell at Raphoe ; they travelled all night, and
dawn was rising on them as they went through Rathmelton—a
company of fifty or sixty persons. Off Rathmullen lay the ship
of eighty tons that Maguire had chartered. On her embarked,
on September 14th, 1607, the great Earl of Tyrone, his Countess,
and his three sons by her ; the son of their eldest son ; and
several other O'Neills of the great house, and their attendants.
With them went the Earl of Tyrconnell : his brother Caffar
O'Donnell, and his sister Nuala, wife of Neil Garv, who had
abandoned her husband when Neil abandoned his chief ;
Tyrconnell's son Hugh, afterwards page to the Infanta of Spain ;
Caffar's wife, and many others.

"This was a distinguished crew for one ship," says the Four
Masters ; "for indeed it is certain that the sea had not supported and the winds had not wafted from Ireland in modern
times a party of one ship who would have been more illustrious

or noble, in point of genealogy, or more renowned for deeds
of valour and prowess, or high achievements than they, if
God had permitted them to remain in their patrimonies until
their children should have reached the age of manhood. Woe
to the heart that meditated, woe to the mind that conceived,
woe to the Council that decided on the project of their setting
out on this voyage, without knowing whether they should ever
return to their native principalities or patrimonies to the end
of the world."

Such was not the comment of Sir John Davies.

".As for us that are here, we are glad to see the day wherein
the countenance and majesty of the law and civil government
hath banished Tyrone out of Ireland, which the best army in
Europe and the expense of two millions of sterling pounds had
not been able to bring to pass."

Ulster was now not only pacified, it was ripe for the reaping.
Tyrone and Tyrconnell were declared tratiors ; their estates
were confiscated, their lands divided up and sold at a nominal
price to English adventurers of every class, from whom most of
the flourishing families in the North of Ireland have their origin.

The story of the Flight was written in Irish by Teague
O'Keernan, a hereditary bard of the Maguires. The original,
written at Rome, is preserved in a Franciscan convent at
Dublin. The Earls meant to reach Spain but were driven by
stress of weather to Rouen. The English ambassador demanded their surrender, but it was refused by Henry IV.
They were, however, requested to withdraw into the Spanish
Netherlands, where, at Brussels, they were entertained by no
less a man than Spinola. No shelter was open to them in
Spain, now at peace with England, and Paul V. offered an
asylum in Rome. Thither they went from Louvain, and were
treated as great princes. But the climate was fatal to
Tyrconnell, who died of fever in 1608, and Tyrone, eight years
later, was laid by him in the church of S. Pietro in Montorio
where already Tyrone's eldest son and Tyrconnell's brother had

found their place. Two of Tyrone's sons entered foreign armies ; a third was murdered at Brussels in 1617. Tyrconnell's son found a post at the Spanish court and died in 1642.

Neil Garv, now admittedly the head of the clan, was not more fortunate. In 1608 he was charged with complicity in the treason of Sir Cahir O'Doherty, who, in revenge for an insult, sacked Culmore and Derry. Among the accusers was Ineen Dhu, Red Hugh's fierce mother, whose resentment neither time nor infirmity could abate. He surrendered, being promised a protection by the Treasurer Ridgeway. Sir John Davies, the Attorney-General, had no difficulty in proving complicity to the satisfaction of his employers, but could not be sure whether the protection had any binding force on the Government which issued it. While the Government were endeavouring to find an excuse for going back on their pledged word, Neil was kept in prison. He was tried in June, 1609, and by a device henceforward familiar, the Crown tried to drive the jury to convict. They were kept three days without food, but as they expressed their determination to starve rather than condemn, they were dismissed without giving a verdict. Neil was, therefore, neither innocent nor guilty, and was sent to the Tower till the matter should be decided. His son, Naghtan, who had been a student of St. John's College, Oxford, and afterwards of Trinity College, Dublin, was sent with him. The question of Neil's guilt was still unsettled seventeen years later in 1626, when he died in captivity. Naghtan's fate is not known : it is to be hoped that he did not live so long.

At all events, it is pretty clear that, after 1609, there was no leading O'Donnell left in Tyrconnell. Daniel O'Donnell, a soldier, first of James II., and afterwards of Louis XIV. and Louis XV., had in his possession, as I said above, the *cathach* of Columbkille, and left it, by his will, to whatever person could prove himself to be the head of the O'Donnells. But as succession to the O'Donnellship, and all other chieftaincies in Ireland, went by semi-elective decisions and not by

lineal descent, the problem was practically insoluble. Red
Hugh left no descendant, nor did Neil Garv ; and it is not
recorded that Tyrconnell's son had issue.

Fuerunt. Their day is over. These two great northern clans,
O'Neils and O'Donnells, made the last stand against the
English : it was also the greatest, for only then was it clear that
the Irish, who fought under them, knew that they were
fighting, not for a question of who should be their sovereign,
but for the right to own the lands which their fathers had
possessed. They fought their fight, and they lost it ; the
stronger and more civilised race conquered, because it was
united in a coherent organisation. But these princes of Ulster
were able to maintain for years the struggle against the soldiers
of England in England's greatest age : they defeated the
English, giving them odds, once and again ; and Lough Swilly
will have at least one sad association for any one who can
imagine the terror-stricken crowds on the shore, the shrill
Celtic lamentation of those that went and those that stayed, and
the face of the great Earl as the sails filled, and he felt the ship
taking him from an Ireland that might have been his, and
from an Ulster where, for ten years, his word had been law.

CHAPTER XIV

AFTER leaving Portsalon, you must make up your mind whether or not you want to see the Inishowen peninsula. If you do, take the afternoon boat at Port Salon and sleep at the Lough Swilly Hotel in Buncrana. If you prefer to go straight to Derry, you can either take train from Fahan, where the steamer puts in, or ride—ten miles of good road—with a foot-path all the way, on which it is against the law to ride.

But the natural desire of man is to get to the end of things, and the northernmost point of Ireland is Malin Head, so I take it that the average person will desire to go round Inish-owen. You go out from Buncrana by a bridge which crosses the Owencranagh river, and you are on a road that leads to what is called the Gap of Mamore, and a very hilly road it is for about six miles. Lough Swilly is in view on your left the whole way. Follow your road straight along until after climbing two high hills it descends sharply into a valley, and at the bottom is a bridge where is a crossroad. You have got to turn to the right at the bridge, and then having crossed it turn to the left, up a road or path which leads straight up the side of the mountain. This is the celebrated Gap of Mamore. The whole valley is very characteristic of Inishowen, a waste of brown, barren mountains, singularly waterless for Ireland. The attraction of the Gap, however, lies in the view from the top, but to get to the top you have to push your bicycle up

The Mail Car.

300 feet of a desperately steep incline. When you have done this—and it would be a hard task for a lady—you begin to get the view to the northern side of the ridge. Dunaff Head is in front of you, but your attent on is immediately distracted, for the road begins to descend, more like the bed of a watercourse than any possible or passable highway. Still as you get a little further down, you see to your left, across Lough Swilly, the great range of mountains from Errigal to Muckish. As you descend a little further, laboriously holding back your machine, you see below you, to the left, Leenan Bay and the fort which is being constructed there. The road turns to the right, and gets worse and worse as it goes along, and the whole operation of getting from one side of the pass to the other takes about an hour before you strike a decent road. As you go down you will easily distinguish your way to Carndonagh stretching to the right. It is a good road when you get to it, and the whole distance from the bottom of the Pass to Carndonagh is about thirteen miles. You pick up the telegraph posts in the little town of Clonmany and they will take you straight to your destination. The road skirts first of all Pollan Bay, then crossing the neck of Doagh peninsula you reach Trawbreaga Bay, round which you have to travel to Malin. It should take you not more than four hours to reach Carndonagh this way, but I am seriously inclined to question whether the journey over the Gap of Mamore is worth the trouble for a cyclist, and unless you are very keen about seeing all the sights of Inishowen you should take the shortest road from Buncrana, which saves at least an hour and has a fine course over the shoulder of Slieve Snacht.

You would presumably lunch at Carndonagh, and go on to Malin Head if an extra twenty miles is not too far. The first three miles you follow the telegraph over a level road into the village of Malin. Reaching this little town you turn out of it to the left, passing Malin Hall, the most northerly gentleman's residence in Ireland, and a very pretty well-kept place it looks.

Harvest in the Rosse.

Rhododendrons were in bloom there in quantities, and I
noticed hydrangeas by a roadside cottage a little further on.
The road, a fairly level one, follows the shore of Trawbreaga
Bay, then turns inland, and after a good deal of winding uphill
you see a long flat expanse below you with a low headland at
the extremity, and that is Malin Head. You ride up to the
coastguard station which is on the right of the Head; continue
along the road which skirts the sea on this side, although in
parts you will have to dismount. Very soon you will see
Lloyd's signal station.   Ride as far as the road will
take you, and then leave your bicycle in one of the houses
and walk up to the tower. It stands on the top of a lowish
hill of smooth green turf. The tower itself is one of the old
signal towers erected a hundred years ago in the Napoleonic
times. Its only inhabitants are two boys, who spend their days
there to work the signals. It is a lonely spot in all conscience,
but the slender wire which runs up the hillside and in at the
tower window, keeps it in constant and living intercourse with
the great mart of Liverpool and the ingoing and outgoing
of ships. Outside the tower is the flagstaff flying its signal, a
red flag above a blue one with a white circle on it ' *What ship
is that?* ' And below them is the red and white pennon for
answering signals. Beside that is a tall semaphore for signal-
ling to the coastguard station. The Head proper lies about
half a mile away to the west, and you ought to walk out there
to see the cliff, which though not very high is a striking one,
and the curious gap in the rocks where there is a continual
inflow of water with no apparent outflow, locally called Hell's
Hole. But the great beauty of Malin is the view looking up
the west side of Inishowen and the mouth of Lough Swilly.
Dunaff Head looks extraordinarily fine, and away in the back-
ground are all the Swilly hills on both shores. Looking
westward the view is bounded by Horn Head, and on a clear
day you can see Tory lying off it. Just north-east of Malin
lies Inistrahull, where there is a lighthouse, much needed, for

A Low Back Car.

the whole Sound between it and the mainland is set thick with rocky islets. Away to the east on a very clear day you may get your first glimpse of the Scotch mountains. With that I think you have seen all that is to be seen of Malin Head, and you may ride back to Carndonagh, where there is a decent inn, and sleep there. But I should rather recommend a fairly strong bicyclist to take the shortest possible way from Buncrana to Carndonagh, do Malin Head, taking the same road both ways, have dinner at Carndonagh, and then ride the twelve miles into Moville and stop at the Carnagariffe Hotel, about a mile beyond it. This hotel stands on Lough Foyle, and was until recently the seat of one of the local gentry. The telegraph wires will guide you from Carndonagh to Moville; it is a road which I have never ridden, but it is said to be good.

Moville is, of course, now familiar to every one as the point of call for the great liners bound from Liverpool to Canada and the United States; it is the focus of emigration for the Protestant North as Queenstown is for the Catholic South and West—one of the two great open arteries by which the strength and life of Ireland is continually passing away to be transfused into the veins of other lands.

At Greencastle, three miles off on the coast—only two beyond Carnagariffe—is the ruin of a castle built in 1313 by Richard de Burgo, the Red Earl of Ulster—a trace of that early grip gained on the northern province which in a short time was so completely shaken off.

Lough Foyle cannot contend in beauty with Mulroy, Lough Swilly, or Sheephaven. Above Moville it is rather the estuary of a river than an arm of the sea. The hills that shut it in rise in gentle slopes, except the square mass of Benevenagh, nearly opposite Moville; but they are richly wooded, and on a sunny summer's evening it is beautiful enough. Its most curious feature is the long spit of land called Magilligan Point, which runs out opposite Greencastle, reducing the width of Lough Foyle from eight miles to one.

This raises another question as to route. If you have never seen Derry, undoubtedly you should go there ; there is no other walled town in the United Kingdom so remarkable. You can either ride in the eighteen miles from Moville by a good road along Lough Foyle ; or you can take steamer in the morning and follow the windings of that historic channel.

But supposing that you are already familiar with the town, your best plan is to take the ferry-boat from Greencastle to Magilligan. You should time your start so as to arrive about low tide, as by doing this you get a delightful ride of seven miles along the hard smooth surface of Magilligan strand before you need turn inland by Downhill, a huge house built by the Earl of Bristol, Bishop of Derry, the strange prelate who headed the Irish volunteers in 1782. A small stream crosses the strand in one place about a mile from Downhill, but it can be ridden through. At Downhill there is a station whence you can send your things to Coleraine, about seven miles distant.

But at this point I must interrupt my itinerary to go back to Derry ; merely adding here that from Derry to Coleraine it is best to go by rail.

CHAPTER XV

In the praise of Derry I cannot go quite so far as its local historian, Mr. Hempton, who asserts that, "whether it be regarded in relation to its singular picturesqueness, or to its historical associations, Londonderry is, perhaps, equally superior to any other city in the British Empire." The assertion is characteristic, for the inhabitants of Derry are, to borrow an expressive word from the north of England, "town-proud." And it cannot be denied that they have a right to be. Their walls stand as the monument of a siege, more famous than any other which has been conducted in Great Britain; of a resistance as obdurate as Saragossa's, and more fortunate. Moreover, in peaceful modern times the town has thriven and gained a considerable commercial importance, chiefly from the success of its shirt factories.

As to its picturesqueness, Derry is totally devoid of any architectural beauties, but its situation lends it a certain charm. It stands on the left bank of the Foyle, where the river is tidal, and at all times a noble stream, over 300 yards wide. The ground on which it stands is a sharply rising knoll, in old days practically an island, for the north of the town—still called the Bog Side—was an impassable morass. Both banks of the river are richly wooded and rise into hills; and from whatever point you see the town you will discern its acropolis, the cathedral stretching up to the sky. The cathedral has been altered greatly since

the days when two guns were posted on its roof (then flat), to answer the fire of Hamilton's army ; but, as Macaulay observes, " it is filled with memorials of the siege." Over the altar are draped captured French colours, with their silk indeed renewed, but the poles and tassels were wrested from the hands of besiegers ; in the vestibule is a huge shell that was flung into the town, containing conditions of surrender. But the main feature of the town is its wall, on whose top a walk runs, wide enough in places, the inhabitants will tell you, for a carriage and pair to drive along it. On the wall are still mounted the guns that were fought in the siege ; one of them retains its name to this day, Roaring Meg, given from the loudness of its report. And on the west side of the wall rises a column, ninety feet high, topped by a statue of Walker, to whom history (in the person of Macaulay) has given the chief credit for the famous defence.

Close to the cathedral is the central square of the city, " the Diamond," from which the streets fall sharply away north, east, and south. Here are gathered the principal public buildings, which, however, have little interest for a stranger. In the centre of the Diamond stands the Corporation Hall, now changed to other uses, which replaced the original wooden one knocked to pieces by the bombardment. The street running west leads to Bishopsgate, a triumphal arch erected in 1789 to commemorate the raising of the siege. On the north side of this street is the palace, a huge red-brick building, constructed by the Earl of Bristol, and more suitable for a prelate whose revenues reached £12,000 a year than for the modest salary with which a disestablished church rewards its divines. The cathedral has been modernised, and nothing in the town, except the walls, speaks even of a moderate antiquity, much less of a Celtic origin ; yet Derry, unlike Belfast, has a history stretching far back into the past.

Derry is the Irish Daire, an oak grove, and its oldest name was Daire Calgach, the grove of Calgach. It stood in what was then Tir Ely, or the province of Aileach, and there can be little

doubt that its neighbourhood to the great palace of the Grianan
on Elagh mountain, was the cause that decided Columba to found
there his first monastery.   In the course of centuries it became
associated with his name. Daire Calgach after the year 1000 is
spoken of as Daire Columbkille.   That it was especially dear
to its founder these verses, a poem assigned to him when living
in Iona, may attest.

> Came all Alba's cess to me
> From its centre to its sea,
> I would choose a better part :
> One house set in Derry's heart.
>
> Derry mine ! my small oak grove,
> Little cell, my home, my love !
> O thou Lord of lasting life,
> Woe to him who brings it strife! [1]

But the foundation which Columba set thus to nestle under
the shadow of the Grianan had little peace.   In 783 it was
burned, and in 832 its position on a navigable river exposed
it to a raid from the Norse and Danish pirates. The marauders
were at this time repulsed by the Lord of Aileach, but twenty
years later the *coarb*, or successor of Columbkille in the Abbey,
was martyred by Saxon invaders.   In 937 Aileach itself was
plundered by the Danes, and from that time onward, we read in
the annals of their inroads at brief intervals.   In 1100 the
foreigners came to Derry under the guidance of an Irish chief,
Murtagh O'Brien, who in the next year destroyed Aileach ; but
his venture by sea only brought loss to him and his allies.   It
would seem that Derry must have submitted to Murtagh
O'Brien, for in 1124 "Ardgar, heir to the throne of Aileach,
was killed by the people of Derry in defence of Columbkille,"
that is, presumably, in defence of the Abbey.   In 1135 Derry
Columbkille was burnt once more.   But the ascendency of the
Abbey seems to have grown in spite of burnings, for in 1158 a

[1] From Dr. Sigerson's *Bards of the Gael and Gall.*

general assembly of the clergy of Ireland, held in Meath, decreed that Flaherty Bradley, the *coarb* of St. Columbkille, should be supreme over all the abbots in Ireland, and three years later his chief, O'Loughlin, exacted tribute for him from them. In the next year the king and the abbot built a cashel, or circular wall, round the Abbey and set up the Tempul Mor or Great Church, which gives its name to the parish—for Derry Cathedral is also a parish church. Derry had need for fortifications, since, in 1164, part of the town was again burnt. Three years later came Strongbow's invasion. But the English did not reach Derry till 1195, when they plundered the Abbey but were roughly handled in their retreat. Then came a period of anarchy, for the invasion had shaken the power of the native chiefs, and fire and sword raged everywhere. Six times in the next twenty-seven years Derry was either plundered or burnt ; the only satisfaction for the monkish chroniclers was to chronicle the miraculous fact that the plunderers, as a rule, met a violent death within twelve months. The miracle would have been their escaping it, so common was slaying in those days. Gradually, however, the first and partial conquest of Ulster established some show of order, and in 1311 Derry was granted by Edward II. to Richard de Burgo, the Red Earl of Ulster, whose fortress still stands at Greencastle. The town was happy enough to have dull annals for the next two centuries, till the outbreak of Shane O'Neill. When Sir Henry Sidney marched against that redoubtable warrior, he sent seven companies of foot and a troop of horse by sea to Derry, to establish a fort in the rear of the enemy. The place was held for the English till 1588, when the explosion of a powder magazine shattered the whole fort and reduced the " Black Abbey and Tempul Mor Church " to ruins.

The present cathedral does not occupy the site of either of these churches. They lay outside the walls of the English city, where a large Roman Catholic church now stands, approached by a lane called " Long Town "—a memorial of the Round

Town which formed part of the group. All of these have disappeared. A second lane, on the other side of the church, bears
the name of St. Columb, and leads to St. Columb's Wells, and
St. Columb's stone, on which are to be seen the marks of the
Saint's knees. To these wells the garrison were obliged to have
recourse during the siege—the water of the town being fouled
—but at great risk. "One gentleman" (Walker writes) "had
a bottle broke at his mouth by a shot."

In 1600 another and even more formidable uprising, under
Tyrone, had to be met, and the manœuvre was repeated.
Sir Henry Docwra, with 4,000 foot and 200 horse, sailed into
Lough Foyle, landed at Culmore, on the left bank some three
miles below Derry, and six days later entered Derry without
opposition. The history of his actions there I have already
outlined : but it may be worth while to give his account of
the place as he found it.

"Leaving Captain Atford at Culmore, with 600 men to
make up the works, we went to the Derry, four miles off
upon the river side, a place in manner of an island, compre-
hending within it forty acres of ground, wherein were the ruins
of an old abbey, of a bishop's house, of two churches and, at
one of the ends of it, of an old castle ; the river called Lough
Foyle encompassing it all on one side, and a bog most commonly wet and not easily passable, except in two or three
places, dividing it from the mainland."

In two years a town was there, capable of housing a thousand
men, says Docwra, who prided himself greatly on his work.
How he was succeeded by Paulet in the governorship, and how
Paulet rashly provoked Sir Cahir O'Doherty into revolt, I have
already told. In that revolt, during 1609, Derry was for the
last time burnt. Probably no town in the kingdom has so
often risen from its ashes.

In 1609 begins the modern history of the town which has
been called, and with reason, the acropolis of Protestant Ulster.
The Corporation of London agreed to rebuild Derry, and so

the town acquired its new name, Londonderry. In 1612 the Irish Society was formed for the new Plantation in Ulster. There were granted to them the towns of Derry and Coleraine, with 4,000 acres at Derry, and 3,000 at Coleraine, beside the fisheries of the Foyle and the Bann ; the Society was pledged to maintain a garrison at Culmore, and to enclose Derry with walls—which were laid out and built in 1617, at a cost of £8357. In 1633, the Cathedral was erected. Under the Commonwealth, Non-conformists used it as a place of worship, and during the siege, Episcopalians and Presbyterians held their devotions there alternately. The first spire was of wood, leaded, but the lead disappeared in the siege, when ammunition ran short.

In the rebellion of 1641, Derry was in a state of siege, but the resolution of the local gentry caused speedy and wise preparation to be made. The Irish Society sent over fifteen guns, some of them still to be identified on the ramparts—now obsolete as they : but Derry was forced to clamour loudly for fresh supplies of food, and above all of powder. The three regiments which were raised by Sir William and Sir Robert Stewart had much ado to keep in check a disorderly force under Sir Phelim O'Neill, that lay about Strabane in 1642, till its retirement gave them a chance to recapture Strabane and relieve Limavady. Derry declared for the Covenant, and in 1648, Sir Charles Coote, with a commission from the Parliament, became governor, and remained so till the restoration. It is hopeless to sketch here the inextricable tangle of parties who fought and plotted against one another in Ireland, till its reduction by Cromwell. Derry had taken up arms to defend itself against the native Irish, and Sir Robert Stewart had been a chief director of its preparations. But now King and Parliament were at war, and Derry, full of London citizens, stood for the republican side. Sir Robert Stewart, who held Culmore fort, sided, like the Scotch, with Charles, and, commanding the river, was a thorn in Coote's side. A treacherous stratagem ended this. Stewart entered Derry under a safe escort, and was

seized by Coote, who made himself master of Culmore. Derry
now became the main centre of resistance to the Royalists in
Ulster, and it was besieged by an army consisting partly of
Royalists, partly of Presbyterian Covenanters. Sir Alexander
Stewart commanded the attackers in this, the first siege of Derry,
which appears to have been a singularly ineffectual blockade,
interrupted by skirmishes. Lord Montgomery presently appeared
to take the command, and summoned Coote to surrender, sending him a copy of the King's commission. This copy Coote
caused to be circulated among the besiegers, whereupon the Presbyterian faction among them " no sooner knew of his lordship
having accepted a commision from the King without their kirk
pastors' leave, and that he would no longer admit their ministers
into his councils, than the whole gang or crew of them, deserted
the siege and his lordship, they at once disbanding themselves
with one text of Scripture, 'To your tents, O Israel.'" Nevertheless the siege continued, till, to the surprise of every one,
reinforcements for Derry appeared in the shape of 4,000 foot,
under Owen Roe O'Neill. Coote had succeeded by fair promises in inducing the distinctively Irish party to join the
republicans against the royalists, and thus made himself
master of the whole north-west of Ulster. The siege
was raised, and Owen Roe entered Derry in triumph. A
splendid banquet was given to him and his following, but
during its course, the Irish general was suddenly seized
with illness. Happily there is no reason to believe the story
that he was poisoned : but this seizure was the beginning of
the end for the last of the great O'Neill leaders, and he died in
the following November.

From the Restoration onwards I note nothing of interest in
the history of Derry for twenty-eight years, save the birth there
of George Farquhar the dramatist. In 1688 began signs of
change. James II. displaced the Corporation of the city and
appointed Catholics—this was in the autumn. In November
William landed at Torbay. James thought by his measures,

carried out through his viceroy Tyrconnell, to have secured
Catholic ascendency throughout Ireland. But, as Walker
puts it in his story of the siege, " it pleased God so to infatuate
the councils of my lord Tyrconnell " that he withdrew the
soldiers who were in actual possession of Derry. Lord
Antrim's regiment which was ordered to replace them was
not ready, and did not reach its destination on the east bank
of the Foyle till December 7th. Word had come to the aldermen
of "some damnable design against the British of those parts,"
and the aldermen, after their fashion, deliberated. Two of
Antrim's officers had crossed the Foyle, and were admitted
within the gates to a parley. But in the meanwhile a
company of the regiment had been ferried over and were
marching on Ferryquay Gate (just south of the Diamond).
The town was in a ferment and thirteen apprentice boys "drew
their swords, ran to the main-guard, seized the keys without
any great opposition, and came with them to the Ferry gate drew
the bridge and locked the gate, the Irish soldiers having
advanced within sixty yards of it." They then hastened to
secure the other gates, and this action of theirs undoubtedly
saved Derry to the Protestant cause. Lord Antrim's regiment
drew off. At this time, according to Mackenzie's contemporary
narrative, the whole number of fighting men in the town
amounted to 300. But the next three months were full of
events and the war of religions which spread through Ireland
concentrated the Protestants of the north upon their sole
surviving fortress. From Coleraine to Lifford they flocked in,
until at the beginning of the siege the walls enclosed nearly
30,000 people.

Ten thousand of these availed themselves of the permission
to leave, and of those who remained nearly 8,000 were soldiers ;
men with the virtues and confidence natural, as Macaulay
points out, to a dominant caste. But Macaulay's dramatic story
is apt to give the impression that the defenders of Derry were
merely the citizens, men unused to warfare, stimulated to

preternatural valour by religious zeal. That is not so. "Town companies" existed in December, 1688; many of those who came in had seen fighting about Coleraine; and a great number were enrolled for active service by Colonel Lundy, who was sent down early in 1689 to be Governor of the town. It is true that their experience of service under him was not encouraging. In April the Catholic army, with James in person at their head, marched northwards. Lundy drew out his forces to oppose them at the crossing of the Finn near Lifford, but the affair was so managed that the Protestants had to beat a disorderly retreat and James advanced along the left bank of the Foyle. On April 15th English ships with two regiments under Colonel Cunningham and Colonel Richards had entered the Lough. Lundy had refused to employ these men against the advancing enemy, and on his return he called a Council of War, at which he declared that the town was incapable of defence and unprovided with food ; that to throw two regiments into it would therefore merely be a useless sacrifice of them. The officers, being commissioned to take their orders from Lundy, sailed reluctantly down the river. Naturally the town was full of rumours of treachery, though it was not yet generally known that the regiments had been finally withdrawn. Matters came to a crisis on the 18th. James marched his army to the strand, not far from where the Great Northern Railway station now is ; and while his army was under the walls, the town clerk insisted on publishing the fact that Cunningham and Richards had been ordered to leave the town with their troops. While the Council was still deliberating, those on the walls fired a cannon at the Irish which, it is said, killed an officer near the king's person. Still emissaries went to and fro ; the deciding incident was the arrival of Captain Adam Murray, with a troop of horse, from Culmore. Fifteen hundred foot were at Pennyburn, a little way beyond the present Lough Swilly railway station. Lundy, hearing of Murray's arrival, ordered him back, but he forced an entrance and immediately assumed the direction of affairs. He broke

into the Council-room, faced Lundy, and told him he was either
fool or knave, and then, leaving the Council, put himself at the
head of the soldiery and supervised the guards.   In the following
night Lundy escaped, disguised as a porter with a load on his
back, and so for a second time Derry was saved from a surprise.
James withdrew as soon as it became evident that resistance
would be offered.

On the next day the popular outcry was that Murray should
be made Governor, but he refused it, asking to be allowed to
command in the field. The Council then, after voting, selected
Major Baker ; and he (by Mackenzie's account) asked for
an assistant, and was given leave to appoint one.   He named
the Rev. George Walker, whose name is the best known among
the defenders.

A fierce controversy rages round Walker's share in the
business.   Mackenzie's book, written as a counterblast to
Walker's own *Diary of the Siege*, makes Murray the hero
throughout.   So does a curious contemporary poem, the
Londerias, which, doggerel as it is, gives the clearest account of
the siege that I have read.   But Macaulay convinced himself
that Walker really was Governor and not merely, as Mackenzie
states, a sort of civilian assistant to Baker appointed to super-
vise the stores.   It was certainly he who received the thanks
of Parliament, and it is he whose statue towers over the walls.[1]

No doubt also in a war between faiths one who combined
the power to lead and organise, with spiritual authority to exhort
and console, gained a real ascendancy and very likely animated
the defence more than any soldier.   But it must be remembered that he was a clergyman by profession, and, moreover,
seventy-two years of age when the siege began.   And I cannot
avoid a suspicion that Walker did scant justice to Murray,

---

[1] So *Londerias*, II., 9, " Baker and Walker Governors they chose ; and
Ash's *Journal*, (April 19, 20, 1889). The government of the city was
conferred on two worthy gentlemen, Henry Baker and George Walker."
See also the documents in the pamphlet *Mackenzie's Charges a False Libel.*

whom he scarcely mentions, except to note one occasion
when he himself rallied Murray's horse and saved their
commander.

Be that as it may, there is no doubt about the siege. The
enemy encamped in four divisions about the town commanding
the roads of access. The defenders were divided into eight regiments two to each of the four quarters. The siege was practically
a blockade from the first ; no serious assault was ever made on
the walls : and there was no cannon in the Irish army heavy
enough to batter them. The enemy's headquarters were out towards Culmore; here Maumont, whom James in withdrawing left
in command, was encamped; and the besieged did not leave them
long in idleness. On the 21st a party under Colonel Murray
sallied out, and in the action had the extraordinary good fortune
to kill the enemy's commander-in-chief ; though Maumont fell by
a bullet wound and not, as is related, by Murray's sword. His
command devolved on Richard Hamilton. Meanwhile the
inhabitants from the wall about Shipquay gate watched this first
trial of forces. In the first week of the siege the fighting was
chiefly on the north east side ; cannon were planted outside
the gate which knocked about the houses, exposed by the
rising ground, but did little other damage. On the 5th of May
a more serious attempt was made from the west side upon the
Windmill Hill which is crowned by Bishop's Gate. Hamilton
drew a trench from the bog to the river and established a
battery: but on the night of the 6th a sally was made
simultaneously from Ferryquay Gate and Bishop's Gate, and
the enemy were driven out with loss. It was . in this
engagement that the flags preserved in the cathedral were taken
and an inscription under a window in the south chancel aisle
commemorates it. From this onward the besieged held a
space about 250 yards wide defended by a trench along the
Windmill Hill and outside the walls. On June 4th the whole
line of this entrenchment was assaulted and there ensued what
is called the Battle of the Windmill Hill. The Irish horse

charged the works on the more level ground near the river, headed by a picked body of gentlemen under Captain Butler and Lord Mountgarret, who were sworn to mount the works. But the attack was everywhere repulsed and the assailants lost heavily. Governor Baker appears to have directed the whole defence with admirable skill and courage.

The siege was now turned into a bombardment, and a quantity of heavy shells, weighing 275 pounds, were thrown into the city, causing much loss of life. Food also began to run short, so that there was great joy when, on June 13th, a fleet was seen in the Lough below Culmore. Kirke, a soldier of infamous reputation for cruelty, was in command; and he showed no redeeming qualities on this occasion. According to Mackenzie's account, the boom was constructed only after his appearance in the Lough; and in any case it was his plain duty to risk a ship or two in the effort to break it. But the batteries on Culmore and the difficulties of the channel intimidated him, and he lay in the mouth of Lough Foyle in sight of the walls for full six weeks. Meantime lead was giving out and the guns fired brick with a lead coating : while food grew daily scarcer. James, impatient of the obstacle, sent down Von Rosen, a soldier who had acquired the methods of war by which Louis XIV. subdued the Palatinate. An assault upon the walls at Butcher's Gate, led by Lord Clancarty, was attempted, and repulsed with severe loss. Then Von Rosen resorted to moral suasion. He drove in all the Protestants for ten miles round, mostly women and children, and hunted them at the sword-point under the walls; sending in a message to the town that all the unfortunates should be kept there to die of hunger and cold unless the besieged surrendered. The reply was the erection of a gallows on the walls and a message that all prisoners—of whom several were of rank and position—would be hanged by way of retaliation. Fortunately Hamilton was not a barbarian, like Von Rosen, and matters were not pushed to an extremity; though the unfortunate people, most

of them half naked, were kept for two days and nights in the
open, where many of them died.

Famine was now imminent: horseflesh was barely procur-
able, mice and rats fetched money, salted hides were regularly
issued in provision to the soldiers. Flour ran out, but some
ingenious man bethought him of a store of starch which, mixed
with tallow, made an excellent substitute and prevented
dysentery. But the garrison was reduced from 7,371 to little
over 5,000, and unless help came there was no choice but
starvation or surrender. Negotiations went on continuously:
but also hostilities. On July 16th Murray led a sally in which
he was shot through both thighs. Baker was dead of illness
and had deputed the governorship to Mitchelburne. At last
deliverance came. In the fleet men naturally were chafing at
the inaction, and Captain Browning, of the *Mountjoy*, himself a
Derry man, was eager to risk his vessel and her cargo. Finally
Kirke yielded; and accompanied by the *Phœnix*, of Coleraine,
Browning headed for the boom. The *Dartmouth* frigate
followed, harassing the enemy with her fire and endeavouring
to draw theirs. At the first impact the boom broke, but the
Mountjoy recoiled and stuck in the mud of the narrow channel.
The besieged, watching from the walls, lost sight of the ships
in the smother of smoke. Then they heard loud huzzas from
the Irish and saw them preparing the boats to board; but in a
few moments the vessels were seen emerging from the cloud of
smoke and creeping up under a light wind. The *Phœnix* had
made for the gap, and the *Mountjoy* got herself off by firing a
broadside, when the recoil of the guns lifted her off the bank.
The *Phœnix* was first at the quay laden with meal; the *Mountjoy* came up later, but it came bringing the dead body of its
captain, who was shot while putting his ship at the boom. It
is strange enough that Browning has received no commemoration in a city so jealous of its memories.

Derry was now safe though the siege was not actually raised
till the night of July 31st: and it is August 1st—or by new

style the 12th —that is annually celebrated as the anniversary of
deliverance.   Kirke entered the city and took command;
Walker, I fear, further ingratiated himself with the powers that
be—his narrative certainly has no word of censure for Kirke's
supineness—and he was chosen to carry despatches to London.
William treated him handsomely, rewarded him, and he
received the thanks of Parliament, conveyed to him in person
at the bar of the House by the Speaker.   He looked forward
to a Bishopric with some confidence and published his own
account of the siege, which represents him as the leading
mover in the whole action.   But his martial tastes took the
old man to the Boyne water next July, where he met his death.
Meanwhile Kirke had deposed Murray from the command of
his regiment—which promptly disbanded itself—and confiscated his horse.   Under such circumstances the real preserver
of Derry retired into private life.   A Murray Club, however,
still keeps his name in honour, and does what it can to remedy
this injustice.

The subsequent history of Derry is one of increasing
prosperity, but not of peace.   Annually, two anniversaries are
celebrated: on December 18th, the Closing of the Gates; and on
August 12th, the Raising of the Siege.   At the December festival
it is usual to burn in effigy the treacherous governor Lundy:
and both are attended with processions of the most aggressively
Protestant character.   At least half of the population is Roman
Catholic and Nationalist, so that these occasions are a fruitful
source of street riots.   Law has interfered and prohibited
repeatedly all that might give offence to religious or political
susceptibilities; but the anniversaries are still celebrated, and
even those who are least in love with Orangeism would scarcely
desire to see the historic commemoration of so valiant a feat of
arms omitted.   The police, I believe, still regularly exercise
their faculties to discover beforehand the vile body of Lundy,
stuffed with squibs and crackers; but at the critical moment he
seldom fails to swing out of the window of the Prentice Boys'

Hall.   One of these triumphs was celebrated by a member of
a very distinguished family in a poem beginning :

> " A was the ardour with which we burnt Lundy,
> In spite of the magistrates noses' on Monday.
> B was the Bandroom of Prentice boys bold,
> Where Lundy was burnt and the Bobbies were sold."

It was on that occasion that the figure of Lundy was
popularly supposed to have been concealed under a bed in the
Palace ; but this detail is mythical.

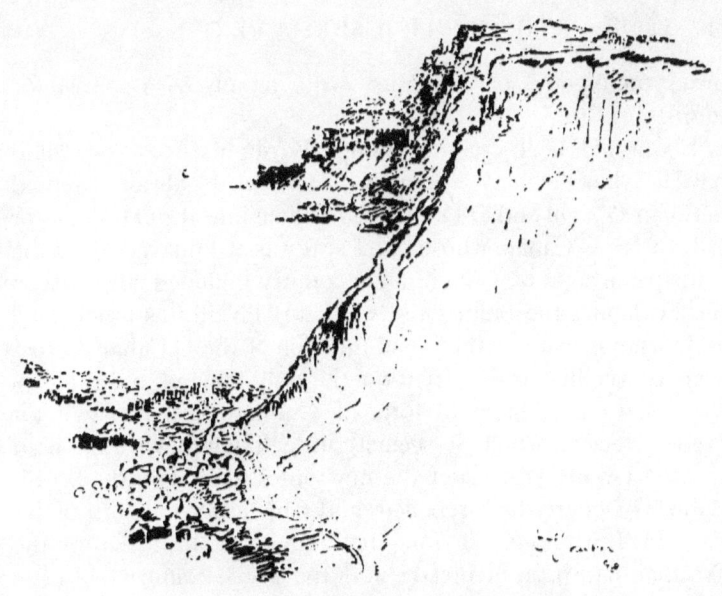

The Causeway and the Giant's Chimney Tops.

CHAPTER XVI

ONCE the tourist is across the Foyle, he lands in a very different country from any that he has travelled in Donegal. All through Tyrconnell, there is no history to write except that of the Gael—a history that stops short with the Flight of the Earls in 1607. But in those days, the history of Eastern Ulster—the Protestant North—was only beginning: and the unhappy religious strife which has played, and has still to play so great a part in the history of this new Ireland of mixed blood always found its main theatre in Derry and Antrim. So, from this point onwards, I can make no attempt to exhaust the historic associations of the route: besides Antrim is not my

own county, and of it I must write merely as a tourist for
tourists.

If you had been crossing Lough Foyle in 1600, you would
have left the O'Doherty's country of Inishowen—always disputed
between O'Neill and O'Donnell—to come into the O'Cahan's or
O'Kane's. O'Cahan, whose chief seat was at Limavady, was the
principal urraght of O'Neill ; his country included all between
the Foyle and the Bann ; and when an O'Neill was proclaimed
at Tullaghogue it was the proud function of the O'Cahan to toss
a shoe over his head. In 1600 the only trace of the English
was the establishment of forts at Culmore and Derry by Sir
Henry Docwra, which it seemed little likely they would hold
good. Twenty years later the new order was established. Sir
Cahir O'Doherty had rebelled and Chichester was lord of his
land in Inishowen. Tyrone had fallen ; in his forfeiture the
O'Cahan had been involved ; and the whole country had been
made over to twelve London companies—a grant of nearly
40,000 acres to 119 families. It was a black day for the native
Irish ; but it must be allowed that the new comers brought
with them the arts of peace ; and the flax industry, which gave
to Ulster what was once its most important crop, and which
is still the predominant industry of its thriving towns, dates
from the English settlement.

East of the Bann begins the great Coast Road, down which
you will travel, and this country of the Glens escaped "plantation" and therefore remains comparatively Celtic in character.
When the O'Donnells and O'Neills went under, the third great
house of Ulster, the Macdonnells, escaped, and were taken into
high favour by James I., thanks to their Scotch blood. Randal
Macdonnell was created Earl of Antrim and received a grant
of the Glens and the Route, from the Curran of Larne to the
Cutts of Coleraine. Yet, although this coastward strip from
the neighbourhood of Coleraine to Larne has never been
violently converted into the home of a Saxon and Protestant

population, and remains largely Gaelic and Catholic, there has
been much infiltration from the planted districts.

The district also has for a long time been well known. Its
natural curiosities in the strange forms of basalt rock, culminating
in the marvel of the Causeway, attracted attention in days when
mere grandeur of cliff scenery was counted repellent. For, bold
as the coast is, it is tame after that of Donegal. Instead of
granite you have chalk, and red sandstone, which give delightful colour, but have not the sombre beauty of Slieve
League and Horn Head, even if they had equal height ; and the
basalt even in the mass of Fair Head inevitably suggests the
hand of some artificer. A more scientific account of the
matter is supplied to me by a friend who writes :

"The surface of Antrim is mostly trap ; this rests on beds of
indurated chalk, below which is a stratum of greenstone. The
next stratum is new red sandstone, and the lowest bed is mica
slate. The trap rises on both sides of the Bann, and the whole
field shows the same scarped features and succession of strata
towards the Roe river in Derry from the Atlantic, North
Channel and Belfast Lough. It is this succession of strata
which gives the peculiar charm to the coast scenery of Antrim. At the Causeway and eastward to Fair Head the trap
assumes a crystalline character, descending to the sea in the
vast masses of basaltic columns for which this part of the coast
is famous."

But the most marked difference in the scenery lies in the
seaward horizon. In Donegal you look out north and west, and
the knowledge that no land lies within a thousand miles either
way adds to your sense of vastness. The Antrim coast depends
for its chief beauty on the fact that it makes one side of a narrow
seaway. The Scotch hills, receding or approaching as the
clouds lift or thicken, sometimes invisible, sometimes flashing
into incredible distinctness, give a fascination to travel
that keeps your attention continually on the stretch. And,

historically, you are forced to see that the essential fact about
Donegal is its remoteness from Great Britain, whereas the whole
history of Antrim has been determined by the easy access from
shore to shore afforded by this narrow and harbourable sea.

Commerce there was from the earliest times, for men were
bold enough to cross the Moyle—as it is called in Antrim—in
curraghs. But it was in the second century after Christ that
Reuda or Riada, with a following of Ulstermen, made a settlement among the Picts, and founded the principality called Dal
Riada, with a share on each shore. The Route, which is the
local name for Antrim, north of the Glens—that is from Ballycastle to the Bann—is called after this Reuda. In 503, a
Christian colony, under the northern branch of the Hy-Niall,
absorbed the older settlement ; Fergus, its chief leader, was
the ancestor of the Kings of Scotland, and in the days
when Columba was Abbot of Iona, the Scotch colony gained
recognition as a separate kingdom. From this branch of the
Hy-Niall descend the Macdonnells, who in the fifteenth century
returned from Alba and gradually conquered for themselves a
holding on the Irish coast.

You will have to go up as far as Coleraine to cross the Bann,
and it is worth going up into the town for a very beautiful view
inland up the course of the river. Coleraine is itself one of the
main centres of what Roman Catholics call the Black North—
a great Presbyterian stronghold. The Scotch element in these
northern places preserves a number of valuable traditions -
one is of skill in baking. Derry, and still more Coleraine,
abound in all sorts of fancy bread, excellent in quality, and far
superior to any that can be got in Dublin. Local usages run
strong in these places, and receipts are handed down in
their integrity from father to son, from mother to daughter. So
by all means stop for lunch in Coleraine and explore the
pastry-cook's in the Diamond. Another famous product of
Coleraine used to be its whisky, and I can well remember in
Donegal to have heard the priest of our parish come up to my

father and express his delight at hearing that there had been a
sermon against the drink. "Sure, I'm for ever at them about
it," he said. "An' it's the bad stuff they take that does the worst
of the mischief," he added. "I told them from the altar that I
never touch a drop myself but the best Coleraine." And a
friend of mine has often told me how in his undergraduate
days, when whisky was still practically unknown across the
water, in what would then have been called genteel circles, he
took with him to Cambridge a gallon jar of Coleraine. The
result was an immediate conversion of the entire college to the
new spirit, and a sudden demand for whisky upon merchants
not a little shocked by such an access of vulgarity.

These are the modern interests of the town; but it has a
history too. St. Patrick having arrived in the neighbourhood,
was offered a site for a church, and he chose a spot overgrown
with ferns which some boys were then clearing. So was founded
the church which came to be known as Coolrathen "the ferny
corner." Columba visited it in 590, and from that date up till
1122, we have records of the names of abbots who ruled the
priory there. In 1213, the English destroyed the monastery.
Later on, in the fifteenth and sixteenth centuries, when the
Scots began to settle on the Antrim coast, Coleraine was the
scene of battles between the Macdonnells and O'Neills. In
1613, the whole of O'Kane's country was granted to London Companies, and from that time dates Coleraine's importance, though
Coleraine itself came within the grant made to the Macdonnells.
The salmon fishing on the Bann was taken away from the Earls
of Antrim, and became a lucrative source of revenue to English
proprietors; though not so valuable as it is in these days of
quick transport. Old men can remember a time when servants
in this neighbourhood used to stipulate that they should not be
asked to eat salmon more than four days a week!

The populous English colony was, of course, an object of
attack in times of rebellion. Coleraine stood a siege in 1641,
and again in 1689; on the latter occasion, the garrison were

driven out and had to throw themselves into Derry. But upon the whole, it is unlikely that any tourist with the Antrim coast before him will care to stop in this prosperous little linen-making town; and I do not care to enlarge upon its history, as it would bring one into a discussion of that modern life of Anglicised Ireland, which has so little affected the wild sea coasts round which the route of our sketching is laid.

Go out from Coleraine then by the road that leads to Portstewart, past Agherton churchyard and rectory—any one will direct you—and you will have a last pleasant glimpse of the Bann running seawards; a little further along, you are across the headland that runs out to the Bann mouth; Portstewart and the sand-hills are close on your left. A road turning to the left, about a quarter of a mile beyond Agherton rectory, will take you into the middle of them. From these sand-hills a road of about a mile long leads into Portstewart, running just inside of a low line of cliffs. Before you reach the town itself, you pass on your left a big modern building, Portstewart Castle; and as you ride along the trim quay, with its row of houses, advertising lodgings to let, you will note one called Lever Cottage. That is where *Harry Lorrequer* was written. Lever was dispensary doctor at Portstewart in 1837, when his first book began to appear in the *Dublin University Magazine*. In these days, W. H. Maxwell, author of *Stories of Waterloo*, and other soldiering books, lived at Portrush: the two men were close friends, and no doubt Maxwell's talk inspired Lever's early tales of Peninsular campaigning. Another man of letters lived at Portstewart in the last century, but born to a very different distinction from Lever's. This was Adam Clarke, who acquired a certain fame as a biblical commentator.

From Portstewart, you have a road of three miles running along the sea to Portrush: and upon a fine day you have continuously a view of the Inishowen headlands across the mouth of Lough Foyle. If the weather is clear, Islay is to be seen on the horizon. On the left of the road, just inside a great stack of rock which rises from the sea, is a fragment of the ruins of Ballyreagh Castle, or, as it was formerly called, Dunferte, a fortress of the O'Kanes which Sir John Perrot took in 1584.

A little rise brings you to the brow above Portrush and you run down into that prosperous little haven on this very harbourless coast. Golf has done Portrush a good turn, for the links there are accounted, on the whole, the best in Ireland, and very pretty links they are, even for a sane man or woman to travel over. For the golfer, it seems, they are a paradise—but a paradise which contains a Purgatory—that is the name they give to one famous bunker which, upon a day of golfing, is full of gnashing of teeth. Outside the links, close in to the pleasant-looking beach, lie the Skerries, a range of rocky islets; and along the road which passes the links runs the electric tramway to the Giant's Causeway, a way paved with contention. The low rail along which runs the electric current—conveyed to the machinery of the cars by a contact with brushes which rub its surface—is exposed by the roadside : and according to the neighbourhood has been the cause of fatal accidents to man and beast. According to the supporters of the company, it was the practice of the natives if they possessed a horse or cow *in articulo mortis*, to take it and place it leaning against the electric rail; not in hope to galvanise the moribund, but in order that it might die there and compensation be exacted from the company. On which side the truth lay I have never discovered, but in the meanwhile it will be just as well not to sit on this rail.

You will follow the line of this tramway from Portrush—and at the time when I travelled the road a very bad line I found it —and sweeping round the point you come in full view of the White Rocks and Dunluce. The White Rocks are a range of chalk cliffs ranging from fifty to a hundred and fifty feet in height in a semicircle around the bay: in front of them is the bright sand with its border of breaking waves, which on most

days come in slowly rolling one after the other in moving curves
cresting higher and higher till they touch the sand, when the
marbled surface begins to show more white, and suddenly they
are shattered and creep up the beach in foam. In the cliffs are
caves, if you like to go down and visit them ; and you will see,
as you ride along, the Giant's Head, a curious face formed by the
jutting angle of one of these cliff fronts. Dunluce stands on a
black projection of basalt beyond the range of the chalk, and
even from that distance you can get a fair idea of its surprising
extent. But you must visit it ; and to that end you ride on till
a narrow cart track—for it is no better—turns up to the left,
while on the right you have the ruins of the old chapel which,
from its peaceful character, did not need to be enclosed in the
ring of fortifications. This castle was the chief fortress of the
Antrim Macdonnells, of whom some brief account must here
be given.

From Eoghad of the Hy Niall and his wife Aileach, daughter
of the King of Alba—the princess for whom was built the
Grianan of Aileach, looking over Lough Swilly—sprang a
numerous family. Two of her sons founded the Dalriadic
kingdom, with a foot on either shore of the Moyle, which early
in the sixth century was consolidated by Fergus Mac Erc—the
prince who on one of his journeys between the shores of Antrim
and Cantire was driven out of his course by wind and lost on
the rock which still keeps his name, Carrickfergus—the Rock
of Fergus. By the end of the sixth century the Scotch kingdom—the Lordship of the Isles—was recognised as distinct and
independent ; and when the Macdonnells came to Ireland, as
they did countless times between the sixth and fourteenth
centuries, they came either as allies or enemies. In 1211, for
instance, they spoiled Derry, but it was as the allies of the
O'Donnells of Tyrconnell. They were not then known as
Macdonnells. Donnell, the chief from whom the Clandonnell
took its name, was Lord of the Isles about 1250. Their step-
ping stone to the Irish coast was Rathlin, which belonged to

them in the days of Robert Bruce, whom Angus Og Macdonnell
sheltered there in 1306. This Angus made a further step into
Ireland, for he married an O'Kane and took for her dowry seven
score men of all the names in O'Kane's country, that he might
settle them on his lands in Cantire. Another marriage alliance
of great moment was contracted by a later Macdonnell with
Marjory Bisset, daughter of a Norman family, who originally
settled in Scotland. But the Bissets being in trouble for slaying the Earl of Galloway, fled across to the Antrim coast, and
there seized and held an estate in the Southern Glens, which
came with Marjory to her husband. But the foundation of the
Macdonnell power in Antrim dates from Alexander or Alastar
Macdonnell, who about 1500 occupied a position on the north of
Ballycastle Bay, and built there his stronghold of Duneynie.
Under it lay Port Brittas, where there was easy landing for his
galleys when they ran across from his lordship in Cantire.
The Lordship of the Isles was now by law a thing of the past,
but the Macdonnells were insubordinate vassals of the Scottish
crown; and as their foothold on the Scotch coast grew less secure
—and indeed from 1500 they were practically outlawed in
Scotland—so they strengthened themselves on the Antrim
shore. Alastar Macdonnell had six sons. James, the eldest
brother, married Lady Agnes Campbell, the daughter of the
third Earl of Argyll, thus for a moment reconciling two bitterly
hostile houses. Moreover, though it was now treason to bear
the title, he was elected Lord of the Isles. His lands in Antrim
centred round Glenarm, which had come to Clandonnell as the
heritage of Marjory Bisset. His brothers set themselves to
extend their power northward into the Route, which was then
defined as what lay between the Bush and the Bann on the shore,
and between the Bann and the Glens inland. Colla Macdonnell,
third of the brothers, built Kenbane Castle, whose ruins may
still be seen about two miles west of Ballycastle. But he did
better than that. The lords of the Route were the MacQuillins,
a Norman family settled in Ireland : whether the name repre-

sents Mac Hugolin or Mac Llewellyn is disputed, but up to
the days of Shane O'Neill it was recognised that the MacQuillin
(it is commonly Anglicised McWilliam) was an "Englishman." MacQuillin was naturally at war with the O'Kane,
for their lands marched at the Bann : and Colla brought his
army of redshanks to help MacQuillin, and was victorious.
Whether by MacQuillin's gratitude, or, as is more likely,

Mouth of the Glen Shesk and Ballycastle.

by his own imperious claim for *bonachta*—free quarters
for his soldiery—he and his men wintered in Dunluce, and he
married Eveleen MacQuillin. But little peace came of the
alliance, and there were pitched battles between the clans. The
final issue began to be fought out at Ballycastle, and was
finished on the second day at Slieve-an-Aura, up in Glen Shesk.
The MacQuillins were totally defeated, and James Macdonnell
made Colla Lord of the Route and Constable of Dunluce.

Colla died in 1558, and was succeeded by the most famous of these Macdonnell fighters, Sorley Boy Macdonnell.

Sorley is, Anglicised, Charles, but in reality it is an old Gaelic name, and was borne by Sorley's ancestor Somhairle or Somerled, who defended his lands in Argyll so strongly against the Danes in the eighth century. But Sorley Boy in Irish state papers is Carolus Flavus—yellow-haired Charles—and there is no want of mention of him. He was born in 1505 and lived till 1590—a warrior till well past eighty. When Sorley became Lord of the Route in 1558, there were hard days for the Macdonnells. The English from 1530 onwards had become anxious to drive out these swarms of Scotch-Irish who poured in year by year; and in Ulster itself there was the redoubtable Shane O'Neill determined to be lord paramount in the north. In 1563 Shane made peace with Elizabeth and turned on the Clandonnell. In 1564 he defeated them in a skirmish at Coleraine, and in 1565 utterly routed them at Ballycastle and took both Sorley and James, head of the clan. Marching northward, he came to Dunluce, which baffled him; but holding Sorley, he held the key of its gates, and swore to starve the chief if he were not given admission. So on that day Dunluce was surrendered. James Macdonnell died in prison and Sorley became head of the Irish branch of the clan. In 1567 he was released from captivity by the bloody death of Shane O'Neill, who, being defeated by O'Donnell and hemmed in, turned to the Scots for help but was hacked to pieces at Cushendun. His death left the Macdonnells directly face to face with the English Nevertheless there were not open hostilities at once. Elizabeth recognised Sorley as Lord of the Route and sent him a patent for his estates. But Sorley, receiving the parchment in Dunluce, swore that what had been won by the sword should never be kept by the sheepskin, and burnt the document before his retainers. In 1571 Walter, Earl of Essex, set out to colonise Ulster, and by way of a lesson in civilisation invited the O'Neill chieftains to a banquet, and treacherously slaughtered them.

What measure he dealt to Sorley Boy's women and children in
Rathlin you shall read elsewhere, but the Macdonnell chief
was no more to be cowed by this butchery than on the day
when they showed him his son's head on the gate of Dublin
castle. " My son," he retorted, " has many heads." In 1584
Sir John Perrot marched into Ulster, and brought cannon

Ballycastle with Knocklayde Mountain.

against Dunluce that shook it sadly till it was forced to surrender.
Sorley was not taken in it, and in the next year he re-captured
it by treachery ; but the triumphant Tudor bastard struck fear
into him, and the old chief, now eighty years old, came to
Dublin and there made his allegiance duly to Queen Elizabeth's
portrait, going on his knees to kiss the embroidered "pantofle"
of her Majesty's royal foot. He died in 1590 at his castle of

Duneynie, and was buried among his kin at Bonamargy Abbey, in Ballycastle. His son, Sir James Macdonnell, succeeded him as Constable of Dunluce, but died in 1601; Sir Randal, another son of Sorley's, fortified Dunluce in defiance of orders, and joined O'Neill and Red Hugh in their rebellion; but after the defeat at Kinsale, seeing the game was up, he made timely profession of loyalty and was taken into favour by James, who granted him formally all the land from the Cutts of Coleraine to the Curran of Larne. Macdonnell remained staunch and was rewarded in 1620 with the earldom of Antrim. He died at Dunluce in 1639. His son, the second earl, had for mother Tyrone's daughter, and so was an object of suspicion, though he lived at Charles I.'s court and married Buckingham's widow. In 1641 came the rebellion, and a Macdonnell—the Earl's cousin—was prominent among the rebel leaders. Antrim seems to have wavered between his loyalty and a natural feeling for those who were fighting to recover the lands from which they or their fathers had been ejected. But he relieved the garrison of Coleraine and gave a hospitable welcome to General Munro in Dunluce. That officer accepted the hospitality, then seized, his host and imprisoned him on suspicion in Carrickfergus. Antrim escaped, and appealed to the King; returned and was again taken by Munro, but again escaped and joined Owen Roe O'Neill, and fought strenuously for the King. Under the Commonwealth he was deprived of his estates, but like the other "innocent Papists" received an allotment in Connaught, whither the Celts, under Cromwell's policy, were being driven as if into a pen. Under the Restoration he obtained, after much difficulty, restitution of his own. But Dunluce by this time had fallen into useless ruins, and the Earl built Ballymagarry House near it as a residence. Earlier than that the castle had begun to crumble, for in 1639, when Antrim's wife, the Marchioness of Buckingham, was entertaining a great party, an outlying piece of the wall overhanging the landward mouth of the cave fell, carrying eight servants in its ruins. It was probably after this that the buildings on the near side of the chasm were erected.

Thus Dunluce has been only a picturesque accessory of the Macdonnell possessions since the Commonwealth, and not a place of strength. The later history of the family may be briefly sketched. The third Earl, like his father, was unable to take a decided part when the troubles came in 1689 : marching to the relief of Derry, he was shut out by its defenders and suffered forfeiture, but regained his estates after much petitioning. The fourth Earl in 1715 was likewise suspected of Jacobite leanings, and threatened with forfeiture. With the death of the sixth Earl in 1791 the male heirs became extinct, and the present holders of the title trace their descent through the female side. The family seat is at Glenarm, which came to the Macdonnells in the inheritance of Marjory Bisset.

I borrow a description of Dunluce Castle, as it is at present, from Mr. Cooke's *Handbook*.

" It is built on a projecting rock, separated from the mainland by a deep chasm about twenty feet wide, which is bridged over by a single arch about two feet broad, the only approach to the castle . . . Its exact date is not known, but it was erected by the McQuillins, probably early in the 16th century. A small enclosed courtyard is first reached, and at the lower end is a square tower, the barbican, in which is the main entrance door. From this a strong wall about seventy feet long runs along the edge of the cliff to McQuillin's Tower, circular, the walls of which are eight feet thick and contain a small staircase reaching to the summit. About twenty yards north is Queen Meave's Tower, and the connection between them has given way. At the northern extremity are the remains of the kitchen which fell, overhanging the mouth of the cave."

The castle has been made by Mr. Frank Mathew the scene of a very picturesque romance of Elizabethan times—*Spanish Wine*—in which, however, he invents passages communicating from above with the sea way into the cave which never have

R

existed—probably because it is only of an odd time that boats
dare enter that perilous passage.

Two other things of interest should be noted about Dunluce.
The wreck of the *Gerona* at Port-na-Spania has been already
recounted. From the wreck Sorley Boy recovered three brass
guns, which were promptly claimed by Government. But Sorley
refused resolutely to give them up—it must have been nearly
his last act—and in 1597, when his son Randal fortified Dunluce
it was on this ordnance that he largely relied. Also in 1584,
when Sir John Perrot took the place, he carried away among
the spoil " Holy Columbkille's cross," a relic which he sent to
Burghley as being " a god of great veneration to Sorley Boy and
all Ulster," though of little price for its jewels—which probably
were only rock-crystals. What became of the cross no one
knows ; it may some day be unearthed in some old house.

The bridge at Dunluce has really no great terrors ; it is fairly
wide and the drop is not big. But it is a convenient test of
your fitness to go over Carrick-a-rede, for if you feel the least
nervousness at Dunluce, the wider a berth you give to Carrick-
a-rede the better. The last thing to be done is either by boat
or land to visit the cave, and indeed it is well worth while to do
both. On the landward side of the round cliff on which stands
the castle, the cave begins in a great hole like the burrow of
some gigantic badger ; you go down a dusty and stony path
into it, and at the bottom, the salt smell of ocean gathered up
in this funnel strikes you suddenly. The cave is a long tunnel
not above ten yards across, and narrowing towards the exit a
hundred yards away. As you stand by the water's edge—or
near it, for this is a thing to be done with discretion, waves
being capricious, incalculable things—looking back you see the
meeting of two lights, the landward, which comes in pinkish
over the stones, and the colder light reflected in from off the
sea face. Overhead is a strangely regular roof with a strong
resemblance to the groining that one sees in Jacobean work :
and on each side springs the arch upon which rock and

castle rest, with its marvellous architecture of buttresses.   It is
indeed a scene that might inspire a master builder.

Leaving Dunluce and getting back on to the road, you
proceed for about three-quarters of a mile round the shoulder
of a hill, then you open the valley of the Bush river, lying
between you and Runkerry Point.   On the other side of
Runkerry is the Causeway.   Your simplest plan is of course to
follow the main road past Bushmills (where is the generating
station of the electric railway), altogether a fairly level run of
four miles.   But this road takes you inland by a considerable
detour, and there is a much prettier way by the sea, which I
recommend if the tide happens to be low.   Just where you
round the hill a steepish road runs to the left to the little
village of Port Ballintrae, a coastguard station and watering
place.   Ride through the town keeping close to the sea, and
the road will take you to the end of a new terrace : beyond
that you have to contend with nature.   Lift your machine over
a stile and you are on a hillside of short grassy turf with a foot-
track well marked across it ; this you can ride for the most
part, and admire on the far side of the bay Lord Macnaghten's
huge house, Runkerry Castle, standing bare and unprotected
on the seaward slope.   But it must not engage your whole
attention or you may break the back of your machine.   After
about a quarter of a mile on the grass you come to another stile,
and beyond it is the river Bush, flowing out into the sandy bay.
About a hundred yards up to your right is a foot-bridge over
the quiet, but pretty river, which winds sluggishly through
sand-hills.   I regret to say that in this river salmon are
generally caught with the worm.   Having got to the far side,
wheel your machine along the river bank to the beach, and at
low tide you will get a mile or more of fine hard sand to ride
over.   At the far side is a cart track, which you must lead over,
and it will take you up to the road near the Causeway station
and hotels.   That was the plan which I had laid out for myself.
but, the tide being in, I was reduced to riding my machine

The Causeway.

through the sand-hills, and it is a practice that I cannot recommend. But, under favourable conditions, it is a sporting way of doing the journey, and should be tried by every lover of leisurely short cuts.

At the Causeway you will find two monstrous, ugly hotels, which, being on the landward slope, do not affect the scenery : and you had best put up at one of these if you have come from Coleraine and seen Dunluce. The Causeway should be seen by boat and by land also ; but especially by boat. A guide is inevitable, and he is also necessary to keep at arm's length the people who want to sell things. The guides are licensed, and have a printed tariff of charges : for a matter of three shillings you can get the most amazing deal of patter. For my own part, I decline to compete with their eloquence. You will have to hear a minute description of the Causeway, so why read one? Even geological theories you can get from them much better than from me. All I have to say is, that if one had discovered the Causeway somewhere in the South Pacific or in the neighbourhood of Iceland, one would have something to talk of for the rest of one's life : but as it is, everybody knows photographs of the place, and it is just like the photo graphs. But, when all is said, it is a very queer freak. From the picturesque point of view the best things are the caves, long tunnels not less beautiful than that under Dunluce, and the great amphitheatre bay, with the basalt columns showing in the face of the cliff like organ pipes. But for picturesqueness the Causeway cannot compare with Dunluce, with its view of the White Rocks, and it is tourist-ridden with a vengeance. Besides, a company has enclosed it with a railing, and makes visitors pay sixpence for admission—an innovation started on Easter Monday of this year, which every good Irishman resents.

If you are staying at the hotel, you should by all means walk round the cliffs which fringe the amphitheatre. Passing Seagull Island you come upon what is called Port-na-Spania (Spaniards' Bay), where the *Gerona* under Don Alonzo de Leyva, was lost, as I have narrated in a note on the Armada. The guides will tell you that this vessel ran in and fired at a castellated projection of the rock called The Chimney—this basalt takes semblance of architecture in the most surprising way—mistaking it for Dunluce Castle. The Spaniards may have fired guns as signals for a pilot or for relief, but they certainly would have no intention of attacking any fort—their one purpose being to get away.

Pleaskin Head, the highest of these points, attains 400 feet, and from it you have the view of the Donegal coast line to the west and the Scotch to the east. Mr. Cooke, in *Murray*, says it is the finest thing in the North of Ireland. I cannot agree with him, but it is a fine view.

The Giant's Chimney Tops

Ballycastle from Golf Links.

CHAPTER XVII

YOUR next stage from the Causeway should be Ballycastle—thirteen miles—easily done before lunch, even if you take Carrick-a-rede on the way. About three miles after you start, the road will take you close to the ruins of Dunseverick Castle, of whose association with the Macdonnell history I have already spoken.

Four miles beyond Dunseverick you reach the village of Ballintoy, where you will see notices posted telling you to " stop here for Carrick-a-rede." Also dirty little boys will rush at you and offer to be your guides. If you like you can trust your machine to one of them and tell him to meet you at the top of the hill, and you can then strike down to the shore and walk along the cliffs until you come to the famous Swinging Bridge, which you cannot miss. But it is a considerable round, and,

what is more important, the infant population of Ballintoy fills
me with no confidence : they would, in my judgment, be
capable of experimenting on the machine. My advice is that
you should laboriously shove your cycle up the appalling hill
which rises for nearly half-a-mile out of the village, until you
come to a cluster of decent-looking farmhouses on the left.
Here you can get a boy to go down with you to the bridge,
and leave your machine in charge of one of the cottagers, who
will also be glad to sell you milk or get you tea, if you desire it,
while you go down the steep hill to this very curious contrivance.

To your left is a small bay with white cliffs, and in it a small
island—Sheep Island it is called. Carrick-a-rede itself is a
gigantic rock, separated from the mainland by a deep channel
sixty feet wide. Carrick-a-rede means the Rock in the Track.
The salmon, with their usual tendency to follow certain tracks
in the sea, come right in here along shore so that there is a
chance to net them, and the nets and boats are kept on the
island rock from which, at certain times of the tide, the net is
shot out. There is no sort of harbour anywhere convenient,
and the boats have to be hoisted on to the rock by a crane
fixed on a platform of rock on the sheltered south-east side,
about twenty feet above the water. During the net-fishing
season, from March to October, fishermen have to go back
and forwards to this island, and a bridge has been constructed
of cables, from the edge of the cliff on the landward side, at a
height of about eighty feet. Two cables are made fast to iron
rings riveted in the rock. These are lashed together by
transverse ropes and on the transverse ropes a boarding of two
planks wide is laid. A single rope fixed to rings a little higher
in the rock serves for a handrail, but is really more to give
confidence than support. The bridge curves sharply with the
weight on it, so that you go down a slope and up one again,
and if there is any wind the whole thing swings sideways as
well as springing under the feet. It can, of course, be crossed
with perfect safety by any one who has a good head, and the

natives carry sheep over it when they want to take them on or off
the island; but a nervous person will find it gives disagreeable
sensations and the prospect of recrossing it is not always
reassuring.   It is a good test to cross the Dunluce entrance
first; if you have any qualms about that, Carrick-a-rede is
a very good place to stay away from.

The view from the island is fine.   Eastward is the line of cliffs

The Bridge over the Margy.

ending in Kenbane Head: north-east the long profile of Rathlin
Island—or Rachray as the natives call it—blocks the horizon.

The road from the hill above Carrick-a-rede is an easy four
miles to Ballycastle.   To your left, though you must make a
special excursion to see it, is Kenbane—the White Head—
where is a great white chalk rock projecting into the sea: and
behind this seaward protection Colla Macdonnell built himself
a castle whose ruins are still there.   Inland of it rises a cliff
only to be descended by a precipitous path.   Colla died there

in 1558 to the great joy of the English, but after his time the castle played no great part in history.

At Ballycastle you leave the Route and reach the Glens, and a prettier preface to them you could not wish for than this clean little town standing at the mouth of a pleasant stream—but, like all the streams in the Glens, of little account for fishing—with plenty of wooding about it. Inland, Knocklayd rises to 1,600 feet at the head of Glen Shesk, whence the river flows, and beyond the bay Fair Head rises, a huge mass ; the shore has the bright clean sand, so delightful a feature of this coast. Inside the beach are golf links, quite good enough for the ordinary performer and on the bay itself is a very comfortable hotel—the Marine Hotel—which I saw at Easter contending feverishly with too much prosperity. However it is presumably not always overfull, and that was the only fault that one could find with it.

The town proper stands about half-a-mile from the sea, and in it is the station of the narrow gauge Railway which runs down Glen Shesk from Ballymoney on the main line between Portrush and Belfast. A fine broad avenue with trees at either side connects the old town with the quarter down by the beach. Broad as this road is, on a fair day a bicyclist will have his work cut out to ride down it ; bolting pigs, jibbing heifers, and anxiously rushing drivers, make a series of hazards that can be dealt with singly, but are very awkward to get by when they happen to concentrate themselves in one spot. It is a thrilling but an amusing experience.

The town of Ballycastle is full of histories, but it has a comparatively modern past. In 1736 a Mr. Hugh Boyd obtained from the Earl of Antrim a lease of all coal and mines from Bonamargy, where the old abbey of Ballycastle stands, to Fair Head. Within twenty years Ballycastle was an industrial centre. Mr. Boyd started work upon the coal-bed which reaches from Murlough Bay to Glen Shesk ; and, oddly enough, his workmen came upon galleries which must have been driven when England was still barbarous, and before Ireland became so. He also built

iron-foundries, saltpans, breweries, tanneries, and what not, till
Ballycastle became a proverb for prosperity.   The Irish Parlia-

A Street in Ballycastle.

ment lent assistance, and spent over £20,000 in constructing a
harbour.   Then Mr Boyd died, and the whole thing fell to the
ground.   Dr. Hamilton, a Fellow of Trinity College, Dublin,

wrote in 1786 a book on County Antrim, the first that drew attention to its scenery and curiosities. Mr. Boyd was then a few years dead : but already "the glass-works were neglected, the breweries and tanneries mismanaged, the harbour became choked up with sand, and even the collieries not wrought with such spirit." The collieries, unhappily, have gone the way of the rest. The coal is at a deep level, and the seams slant downward instead of upward ; and though, even within late years, attempts have been made to reorganise the workings at Murlough Bay—where the output could be shipped from the quarry mouth—they have always failed : and the neighbourhood remains neither enriched nor disfigured by the forces of modern industry.

The great days of Ballycastle, however, were under the Macdonnells. The Franciscan Abbey of Bonamargy was, and still is, their sanctuary and burying place. The ground of the cemetery, as Mr. Hill, their historian, puts it, "literally heaves with Clandonnell dust." Here were buried those who fell in the disastrous overthrow of Clandonnell, at the hands of Shane O'Neill in 1565 : and here, too, were buried those who died in the great fight at Slieve-an-Aura up in Glen Shesk, where the Macdonnells finally put an end to the resistance of the older lords the McQuillans. They tell a story of a clansman who went to the Countess of Antrim asking the lease of a farm.

"Another Macdonnell ? " said the Countess ; " why, you must all be Macdonnells in the Low Glens." " Ay," said the peasant, " too many Macdonnells now ; but not one too many on the day of Aura."

Bon-a-margy, or Bun-na-mairge, means Margyfoot (as Buncrana means Cranagh Foot, Bundoran, Drowes Foot, and so on). The Margy has only a course of half-a-mile up to the point at which the Shesk and Carey rivers join by Dun-na-Mallaght Bridge.

But the Ballycastle shore leads one far back into memories of an older time, long before the Clandonnell came into being.

Into the river Margy there often sailed four white swans that were the children of Lir, king of the Isle of Man. For Lir's wife died, and he married her sister, who looked unkindly on the children of the first wedlock, and by a magical wand changed them to four swans, doomed to live in that transformation till nine hundred years should pass over them—for three hundred of which they were to toss on the stormy Moyle—or till the sound of Christian bells should be heard in Ireland. So it was

Fair Head from the Ballycastle Golf Links.

until Columbkille came, and with a holier magic released them. But however it ended, the Fate of the children of Lir is the second of Erin's Three Sorrows of Story. The third and greatest of the Sorrows of Story is the Fate of the Sons of Usnach; and it was at Carrig-Usnach, the sloping rock on the north side of Fair Head, that the three sons of Usnach landed when they returned to Eire with Deirdre, beautiful as Helen and gifted like Cassandra with unavailing prophecy. It may be

worth while for those who do not know the Celtic legends to
hear the story.

In the days when Conor was king of Uladh or Ulster, Conor
feasted at the house of Phelim, the king's story-teller; and
while they feasted word came to Phelim that his wife had
borne him a daughter. Caffa, the Druid, was of the company,
and he rose up and said: "Let her name be Deirdre (that is
Dread), for by reason of her beauty many sorrows shall fall upon
Uladh." Then the nobles were for putting her to death at
once, but Conor said, "No, but I will take her and she shall be
reared to be my wife." Conor put her away in a lonely castle
with his own conversation-dame Lavarcam for a nurse, to watch
over her. And Deirdre grew up and fulfilled the promise of
her beauty; but she was lonely for want of love and one day she
saw blood spilt in the snow and a raven drinking it. "I
would," she said, "I had a youth of those three colours; his
hair black as the raven, his cheek red as the bloodstain, and his
skin white as the snow." Then Lavarcam said to her, "Naisi,
son of Usnach, of Conor's household, is such a one." And so
the dame brought the two together, for she loved Deirdre
more than she feared the king, and it was agreed between them
that they should fly. Naisi took with him his two brothers, Ainli
and Ardan, and a company of soldiers, and they crossed the
sea to Alba, where the prince of that country made them soldiers
and leaders of his own. But word came to him of Deirdre's
beauty, and he was for seizing her by force; but the sons of
Usnach defeated him and fled with Deirdre to a sea-girt islet
on Lough Etive, and there they lived happily by the chase.

Now King Conor assembled his nobles in the great Eman or
Hall of Macha, that is Armagh, and there was eating and
drinking, and harpers, and bards, and all men's hearts were full
of content. Then Conor rose up and said to them, "Saw you
ever a palace fairer and richer than this my house of Eman?"
and they said, "We saw none." Then Conor asked, "Is there
nought lacking?" and they said, "We know of nought." "Ay,"

said Conor, "but there is a want that vexes you, the want of
the three sons of Usnach, that are exiles from Eire, and have
won for themselves a province in Alba." Then they all shouted
applause, "for," said they, "these three alone should suffice to
guard Ulster." Then Conor asked, "Who will go now to
Lough Etive to bring me back the sons of Usnach? for Naisi
is under vow not to return westwards unless it be under the
warranty of one of these three—Conall Carnach, or Fergus, son
of Roy, or Cuchullan—and now I will know which of the
three best loves me."

And with that he took Conall Carnach into a place apart,
and asked him "What would he do if the sons of Usnach
should come over under his warranty and then be slain?" "It is
not one man's life should pay for that," said Conall, "but upon
every Ultonian that had art or part therein I would inflict
death." "I perceive," said Conor, "you are no friend of
mine." Then he took Cuchullan and questioned him in like
manner. "I pledge you my word," said Cuchullan, "that if
this should come to pass I would slay every man of Ulster that
my hands could reach." "You are no friend of mine," said
Conor, and he drew Fergus apart and questioned him. "There
is no man in Ulster should injure them," said Fergus, "but his
life should pay for it, save only yourself." "It is you shall go
for them," said Conor; "and set you forth in the morning and
bring them to the mansion of Barach, on the shore of Moyle,
and pledge me your word that you send the sons of Usnach to
Eman, so soon as ever they shall arrive, be it night or day with
them."

Then Conor went to Barach, and asked had he a feast ready
for his king. "Ay," said Barach, "but I could not bring it to
Eman." "Offer it to Fergus, then," said the king, when he
returns from Alba; for he is under *gesa* never to refuse a
feast."

But Fergus set out for Alba, taking with him no troop but
his two sons, Illan the Fair and Buine the Red Fierce One,

and Callan his shield-bearer. And when he came into the harbour of Lough Etive he sent forth a loud cry.

Naisi and Deirdre were playing at the chess, and Conor's chessboard was between them that they carried off in their flight. Naisi lifted up his face and said, "I hear the call of a man of Erin." "It was not the call of a man of Erin," said Deirdre, "but the call of a man of Alba." Then Fergus shouted again and again. Naisi said, "It is the cry of a man of Erin." "Truly it is not," said Deirdre; "let us play on." Then Fergus shouted a third time, and the sons of Usnach knew his voice, and Naisi said to Ardan, "Go out and meet Fergus, the son of Roy." Then Deirdre said to him, "I knew well it was the voice of a man of Erin." "Why did you hide it, then, my queen?" said Naisi. "I dreamt a dream last night that three birds came to us from Eman of Macha having three sups of honey in their beaks : and they went away taking three sups of our blood with them." "And how read you the vision?" said Naisi. "It is this," said Deirdre. "Fergus comes to me with a message of peace from Conor; for honey is not sweeter than a message of peace from a false heart." "Let that be," said Naisi. "Fergus stays long in the port."

Meanwhile Fergus and his sons were greeting Ardan, and they came to where Naisi and Deirdre and Ainli were. So the exiles asked for tales of Erin. "The best tales I have," said Fergus, "are that Conor has sent us hither to bring you back under my warranty." "Let us not go," said Deirdre, "for our lordship in Alba is greater than the sway of Conor in Erin." "Birthright is first," said Fergus, "for ill it goes with a man, although he be great and prosperous, if he does not see daily his native earth." "It is a true word," said Naisi, "for dearer to me is Eire than Alba, though I should win more gain in Alba than in Erin." But it was against the will of Deirdre that they departed, though Fergus pledged them his word, and said, "If all the men of Eire were against you, little it would avail them while we and you stood by one another."   "True it is," said Naisi, "and we will go with you into Eire."

So they sailed away over the sea, and Deirdre sang this song as she lost the sight of Alba.

"My love to thee, O Land in the East, and 'tis ill for me to leave thee, for delightful are thy coves and havens, thy kind soft flowery fields, thy pleasant green-sided hills, and little was our need for departing."

Then in her song she went over the glens of their lordship, naming them all, Glen Lay, Glen Marsin, Glen Archeen, Glen

Fair Head from Ballycastle.

Etty, and Glen da Roe, and calling to mind how here they hunted the stag, here they fished, here they slept with the swaying fern for pillows, and here the cuckoo called to them. And "Never," she sang, "would I quit Alba were it not that Naisi sailed thence in his ship."

They landed under Fairhead at Corrig Usnach, and thence they went to the mansion of Barach.   Then Barach welcomed them, and he said, "For you, Fergus, I have a feast ready, and you must not leave it."   Then Fergus grew red in anger, and said, "Ill done it is of you, Barach, to ask me to a feast, for I

am bound under stern vows to speed the children of Usnach
on to Eman of Macha." Then Barach reminded him of his
gesa, and Fergus appealed to the sons of Usnach for counsel.
" You have your choice," said Deirdre : " will you forsake the
feast or forsake the sons of Usnach ? " " I will not forsake
them," he said, " for I will send my two sons, Illan the Fair
and Buine the Red Fierce One with them to Eman of Macha."
Then Naisi answered in wrath : " We find no fault with the
escort ; it is not any other person that has ever defended us,
but we ourselves." Then the company went on, leaving
Fergus sad and sorrowful. But Deirdre counselled them to
go to Rathlin, and abide there till Fergus should have partaken
of his feast ; " for so," she said, " shall Fergus keep his word,
and your lives shall be lengthened." But the sons of Fergus
said she had but scant confidence in them ; and Naisi refused
her counsel. They rested on the mountain of Fuad, and
Deirdre dreamed a dream, and she tarried behind them.
Naisi came back to seek her, and asked why she tarried. " A
sleep was upon me," said Deirdre, " and I saw a dream in it."
" What was the dream ? " said Naisi. " I saw Illan the Fair,
and his head was struck off him, and I saw Buine the Red, and
his head was on his shoulders ; and the help of Buine the Red
was not with you, and the help of Illan the Fair was with you."

So they journeyed on till they came to the hill of Ardmacha,
and Deirdre said to Naisi, " I see a cloud in the sky, and it is
a cloud of blood ; and I would give you counsel, sons of
Usnach." " What counsel ? " said Naisi. " Go to Dundalgan
where Cuchullan lies, and be under the safeguard of Cuchullan
till Fergus end his feasting, for fear of the treachery of Conor."
" There is no fear upon us, and we will not practise that
counsel," said Naisi.

As they drew near to Eman of Macha, Deirdre spoke a last
warning.

" I have a sign for you, O sons of Usnach," she said, " if
Conor designs to commit treachery on you or no."

" What sign is that ? " said Naisi.

" If Conor summon you into the hall where are the nobles of Ulster with him, he has no mind to treachery ; but if you be sent to the mansion of the Red Branch, there is treachery."

Then they came to the gate, and they struck a loud stroke with the wooden knocker. The doorkeeper asked them " Who was there ? " and they said, " the three sons of Usnach, with Deirdre and the two sons of Fergus." Then Conor bade them be lodged in the mansion of the Red Branch, and Deirdre still pressed them to fly. " That we will not," says Illan, " for no cowardice or unmanliness has been known of us, and we will go to the Red Branch." Meat and wine were set before them, and after they had their fill Naisi said, " Bring now the chessboard that we may play." And Conor in his hall asked, " Whom now shall I find to bring me word if her own shape and features still live on Deirdre ? for if her own form live in her, there is no woman more beautiful in the world." " I will go," said Lavarcam, Deirdre's nurse, "and bring you tidings." Then she came and found Naisi and Deirdre playing at the chess, and she kissed them lovingly ; but, said she, " You do ill to be playing on this chessboard, the thing which Conor most grieves the loss of, save of Deirdre alone ; and it is to inquire after the beauty of Deirdre I am come, if it still live on her ; and an evil deed is to be done this night in Eman, treachery and murder." Then she bade them make fast the doors and windows, and exhorted the sons of Fergus to be faithful to their charge, and she went back to the king.

" What news have you ? " said he.

" Good news and bad," she answered ; " for the sons of Usnach are come back to you, the three first in the world for comeliness and valour, and with them you shall rule all Eire. But the worst news is that Deirdre, the fairest woman of Eire, is bereft of her own shape and colour."

After a while Conor asked again for a messenger who should go and spy upon the beauty of Deirdre ; and none were willing till Conor laid his bidding upon Trendorn, whose father and brothers Naisi slew. Trendorn went to the house of the Red Branch, but he feared to knock at the door lest wrath might be upon the sons of Usnach; so he pried till he found a window that was open. Deirdre saw him as she sat playing at the chess and she told Naisi, and therewith Naisi flung the chessman that was in his hand with so true an aim that it drove the eye out of Trendorn's head. But Trendorn went back to the King and told his story. "The man that threw that throw would be king of the world," said Conor, "if he had not short life. What countenance is upon Deirdre?" And Trendorn said, "Deirdre is the fairest woman in the world." When Conor heard that, he was filled with rage and jealousy, and he called his troops together and they surrounded the House of the Red Branch and set fire about it. Then said the sons of Usnach, "Who are ye about us?" and they shouted back, "Conor and Ulster." Then Illan the Fair asked, "Will you break the warranty of Fergus?" And Conor answered, That the sons of Usnach should rue the day when they took his wife. Then Deirdre said, "Fergus has betrayed us." "If he has betrayed you," said Buine the Red, "we will not betray you." And Buine led a sally and slew thrice fifty. Then Conor asked, "Who is this that makes havoc of my men?" "I am Buine the Red Fierce One, son of Fergus," said he. "A bribe from me to you, O Buine." "What bribe?" "Such and such a district of land," said Conor. "What else?" said Buine. "A seat in my council," said Conor. "I will take it," said Buine; but that same night the district given in the bribe became a barren moor. Then Deirdre said again, "Buine the Red has forsaken us; he is the true son of his father." "It shall not be so with me," said Illan, "while this straight narrow steel lives in my hand I will not forsake the sons of Usnach."

Then Illan went out, and three times he charged round the house, and slew three hundred men. He came back into the house and Naisi and Ainli were still playing at the chess.

And a second time Illan led a sally and routed the Ultonians till Conor said to his son Fiacra, who was born the
same day as Illan, "Take my arms, my shield Ocean and
my two javelins, the Victorious and the Cast, and the Blue
Green Blade, and meet Illan." Then there was a mighty
encounter, but at the last Illan drove Fiacra under the shadow
of the shield, and the magic shield Ocean roared, and the three
waves of Erin roared in answer to it, so that the sound reached
Conall Carnach. Then Conall said, "Conor is in danger and I
must not stay." So he girt on his arms and came to Eman,
where Illan and Fiacra were still fighting and no man dared
to come near them. But Conall came behind Illan and thrust
the sword through his back.

"Who is this that has pierced me from behind?" cried Illan.
"Whoever he be I would not have feared him face to face."
"Who art thou thyself?" said Conall. "I am Illan, son of
Fergus, and art thou Conall?" "It is I," said Conall. "An ill
deed you have done, with the sons of Usnach under my
protection." "Is that so?" said Conall. "So it is," said Illan.
"By my hand of valour," said Conall, "Conor shall not get
back his son this day;" and with that he smote Fiacra's head off
him and left them. But Illan struggled to the Red Branch,
and crying out to the sons of Usnach to defend themselves, he
died.

Then the Ultonians came to burn the house, but Ardan
sallied out and slew many of them : then came Ainli and again
put out the fire, and last of all Naisi. But presently Conor set
his battle in array, and the sons of Usnach gave them the
battle of morning and routed the Ultonians. Then returning
to the house they locked their shields round Deirdre, and
sallying forth, and slaying as they went, the sons of Usnach
leapt over the walls of Eman.

Then Conor called his Druid Cathbad and said, "Look now,
if these men escape they will destroy the Ultonians for ever :
play enchantment now upon them and I give you my pledge

there shall be no danger to them." So Cathbad believed him, and he laid a spell upon them, putting round them a clogging sea of invisible waves overwhelming them ; so that the sons of Usnach were as though swimming, while they walked. But no man dared to approach till their arms fell from their hands. Then they were taken and Conor commanded them to be put to death. But there was no man among the Ultonians who would do his bidding, till at last he came upon a Norse captive whose folk Naisi had slain. Then Ardan and Ainli contended which should die first, each desiring that he might not see his brother slain. But Naisi gave to the Norseman his magic sword, which could cleave all before it, and they knelt down together, and with one blow the Norseman struck off the three heads.

But Deirdre flung herself sorrowing on the bodies and tore her hair ; then she chanted over them her lament : calling shame upon their murderers, and praising their valour, their beauty, and their sweet converse. " Life," she sang, " has no cheering for me, sleep, nor feast, nor wine now I hear no more the step and voice of Naisi." And when she had finished singing she threw herself on Naisi and died ; and a great cairn was piled over them, and an inscription in Ogham set upon it.

But Cathbad, the Druid, laid a curse upon Eman by reason of the slaying of the sons of Usnach, and from that day to this no son of Conor sat on the throne of Macha.

Rathlin Island from near Dunseverisk Castle.

CHAPTER XVIII

FROM Ballycastle you may be tempted to cross in a boat to Rathlin, if the weather be fine. But if it is rough no worse sea exists than this narrow sound, where the two tides, that rounding the north coast and that which sweeps up the Moyle, meet in a boiling race whose swirl even on a smooth sea you can trace plainly from Fair Head. The Irish call it *Sloch-na-marra*, "the swallow of the sea," which is descriptive enough ; and it has another name, Coire-Brecain, "Brecain's Cauldron," since the day when Brecain, grandson of Niall of the Nine Hostages, was engulfed there with his fleet of fifty curraghs.

This name has been stolen from it for another not less famous race between Jura and

> "Scarba's isle whose tortured shore
> Still rings to Corrievreckan's roar."

Rathlin is old in history. Pliny and Ptolemy mention it as Ricnia or Ricina. A monastery was founded there in Columb-kille's day, but the exposed situation of the place made it a prey to Northmen, who sacked and burnt the monastery in 790 ; and after the battle of Clontarf, the Danes, repulsed by Brian Boru, made a descent on this outlying spot as they sailed north. In 1216 King John came as far north as Carrickfergus, and granted Rathlin and the Route to the Earl of Galloway. From his heirs it was seized by the Bissetts, who settled in Glenarm. But in 1306 the Macdonnells were lords there, for Angus Og Macdonnell carried Robert Bruce there after his defeat at Perth, and it was in the castle that stood on the east end of Rachray that Bruce, according to tradition, learnt his lesson from the six times baffled spider. Later it would seem to have been lost to the Macquillins, but was retaken from them by Sorley Boy : the first of his conquests. In 1551 the English attempted a landing there, but were repulsed with disaster. But in 1575 Walter, Earl of Essex, was busy with his great scheme of colonising and civilising Ulster. The Irish seemed to him folk so barbarous and despicable that no man could be bound to keep faith with them, or observe towards them any duty save that of extirpation, and he began, though unsuccessfully, the bad work that was finished by Mountjoy and Chichester. One thing, however, he did successfully. Sorley Boy, who defied his forces from fastnesses in the Glens, had sent his women and children and valuables to Rathlin for security. Word came of this to Essex at Carrick-fergus, and he sent off an expedition under Norris with three frigates—one commanded by Francis Drake—and a strong force of soldiers. They landed on Rathlin, and besieged the castle, which surrendered after three days. "There have been slain," says Sir Henry Sidney's *Brief Relation*, "that came out of the castle of all sorts two hundred. They be occupied still in the killing, and have slain all that they have found hidden in caves and in the cliffs of the sea to the number of 300 or 400 more." Sorley Boy, then close on sixty, but with life to last for another quarter of a century, ran up and down on Fair Head, seeing the butchery of his wife and children, and of the wives and children of all his gentlemen, and, a spy reported, "was like to run mad, turning and tormenting himself, saying that he there lost all he ever had."

Essex penned an enthusiastic description of the raid which reached Elizabeth amid the famous revels of Kenilworth ; and from Kenilworth she added in her own hand to the despatch of reply this postscript of congratulation in the euphuistic style of the period : —

" If lines could value life or thanks could answer praise, I should deem my pen's labour the best employed time that many years hath lent. . . . Deem, therefore, cousin mine, that the search of your honour and the danger of your health hath not been bestowed on so ungrateful a prince that will not both consider the one and reward the other."

Is it not odd to see this mincing minuet of phrases called out by such a tale of bloody devastation ? Yet the combination of the two make up Tudor England, as Ireland learnt to her cost.

In 1588 the island was again attacked by the English under Sussex, so that when a question was raised whether Rachray belonged rightfully to England or to Scotland, having been part of the old sovereignty of the Isles, Elizabeth's counsellors advised that it should be claimed for English, seeing that they had often burnt and wasted it, and James might be disposed to claim compensation. With the recognition of the Macdonnell as Earl of Antrim, Rathlin's troubles ceased for a little. But in 1641, when the Irish rebellion broke out, Charles gave a commission to Argyll to levy war upon the rebels. The Campbells were the bitter hereditary foes of Clandonnell, and Argyll was a butcher by disposition. Twelve hundred Campbells landed on Rathlin in 1642, and swept it clear so far as they were able of every living thing. Women and children they threw over the cliffs; and there is a tale told that one Campbell, softer-hearted than the rest, found among the heap a young woman who by some miracle had life left in her, and took her back with him to Isla. She had seen her husband butchered, and had only time to hide away her child, and knew nothing of its fate. But years after, when she had become the Campbell's wife, some hunger of the heart drew her to Rathlin, and she found there her son grown to manhood, and tilling the farm that had been his father's.

Rathlin since that black day has lived quiet enough, though perhaps peace is not the chief character of its inhabitants. The lady who is known to her readers as Moira O'Neill—a good Glenswoman if ever there was one—has this sketch of Rachray people as they look to the outside world.

RACHRAY

Och, what was it got me at all that time
To promise I'd marry a Rachray man?
An' now he'll not listen to rason or rhyme,
He's strivin' to hurry me all that he can.
    Come on, an' ye *be* to come, says he,
    Ye're bound for the Island, to live wi' me.

See Rachray Island beyont in the bay
    The dear knows what they be doin' out there
But fishin' and fightin' an' tearin' away,
An' who's to hindher an' what do they care?
    The goodness can tell what 'ud happen to me
    When Rachray would have me, anee, anee.

I might have took Pether from over the hill
  A dacent poacher, the kind, poor boy ;
Could I keep the ould places about me still
  I'd never set foot out o' sweet Ballyvoy.
    My sorra on Rachray, the could sea caves
    An' blackneck divers, an' weary ould waves.

I'll never win back now whatever may fall,
  Oh give me good luck for you'll see me no more,
Sure an Island man is the mischief an' all—
  And me that never was married before.
Oh, think o' my fate when ye dance at a fair ;
In Rachray thare's no Christianity there.

Going on from Ballycastle, your next day is plainly mapped
out ; you must see Fair Head and reach Cushendal, unless
indeed you prefer to go in a boat round the head to Murlough
Bay and walk back, an excellent suggestion which I find in
Murray. But suppose you keep to dry land. You have about
two miles of somewhat hilly road till you reach the little village
of Ballyvoy, where there is a post office. Keep straight on up
the hill, avoiding the road which runs inland to the right : and a
little higher up you will find a path running to the left up to
some houses where you can leave your machine while you walk
round the Head. It is an enormous round promontory, at the
highest point 639 feet above the sea, and all of it basalt rock at
top. As you look at it from the sea the likeness to a castle
is extraordinary, for you have first a steep slope of shale, and
then about halfway up the basalt springs from these lower strata
in enormous upright columns, silhouetting against the sky the
profile of buttresses, battlements, and towers. To get down to
the sea you must follow the edge of the cliff till you reach
a huge fissure where a slip seems to have occurred, and a
great pillar, one solid stone, has fallen transversely over the
chasm. Under this runs the Grey Man's Path, haunted by
the spirit of the Head. The path itself is easy for any
moderately active person, and it is well worth going down

it, partly to find the yellow horn poppy, a rare flower in Ireland, but chiefly for the upward view of the cliffs. But a warning is necessary to any climber. It looks as if one could scale the cliff by any of the innumerable shallow clefts

The Grey Man's Path, Thir Leith.

with which its face is grooved; the basalt offers steps and handhold ready made. Unfortunately these seemingly solid projections detach themselves with the greatest ease, for the rock is a mass of crystals lying side by side or superposed;

and the result is a miniature landslip, which might have
unpleasant consequences.

The head presents a semi-circular front of about two miles
of cliffs. On top, in the space enclosed, are three lakes,
one of which, Lough Dhu, has an outlet by a waterfall over
the cliff; of the other two, one has a crannog or dwelling
built on piles in it. This lake drains into a stream which falls
over the eastward side of the Head into Murlough Bay; a
beautiful spot, where the shelter given by the Head has
enabled a tasteful proprietor to form plantations about his
house; and a streak of red sandstone which crops out here
gives a note of unfamiliar colour to the view. The whole
place is open ground, so that detailed directions are almost
an impertinence; when you have explored the Head and bay
to your pleasure, you can get back to your machine; but you
should have two or three hours to do the excursion in, and
take your lunch with you.

From Fair Head there is a choice of routes, and any one who
does not care about walking had better get back to Ballyvoy
and follow the post road to Cushendun, which runs inland
through a district mostly of heathery mountain for about ten
miles. But if you want scenery you should go over the shoulder
of Fair Head—following the telegraph wire: only, beware of
the road. It is very hilly—mostly against you till you round a
corner which is Torr Head and see the wire going straight
down an awful hill to the coastguard station, where it ends.
You can, if you like, go down there too, and at the bottom of
the hill turn to your right, where there is probably a level stretch.
Anyhow, nothing can be worse than the alternative, which is to
go straight along at the high level, where you get perhaps half-
a-mile of a gentle slope; then the road disappears round a
sharp corner, and if you round that corner with feet up or
without a brake, heaven help you! A little stream runs down
into Portaleen Bay, and this road falls towards the bridge over it,
steep as the roof of a house but by no means so smooth. The

road winds a good deal and the water takes short cuts when the rain falls, so that deep trenches occur every few yards, and if you do not run into the ditch you will probably break the back of your machine. Once you are over the bridge you have to push up the counterpart of this, and the remaining six miles to Cushendun, though better, are not much better. It is known in the country side as "the road Lady Londonderry was

Murlough Bay.

wrecked on." Frances Anne, the "old Lady Londonderry," who seems to have been a great personage in her day, once set out, with a coach and four and a new English coachman, to drive this road. He got past Cushendun and the road gradually became more and more impossible, until Lady Londonderry said she would turn; but seeing that the road was a narrow track where two carts can just pass, turning was not so easy. The

horses had to be taken out and an army of labourers summoned
to the rescue before the coach could be got facing the way it
was wanted, and gently wheeled back into Cushendun.

I say all this that no one may have reason to reproach me,
but I recommend the road nevertheless : for it was the most
charming piece of scenery I saw on the Antrim coast. On such
a day as is very common in Ireland—a bright flashing day with
great clouds bowling along before the wind, radiant mists of
sunshine and travelling showers, visible sometimes over you,
sometimes ten miles off—it would be hard to imagine anything
more lovely than the Moyle. The coast you are on is beautiful:
you have the sea sometimes right below, sometimes half-a-mile
off : but across the sea is Scotland with its exquisite outline.
The Mull of Cantire runs out, a great mass projecting : you
see the white line of waves breaking on it beyond the blue
water : you see trim white houses on its coast : south of it, and
to your right, Ailsa Craig lifts its extraordinary bee-skep outline
from the sea : and beyond and behind that again is the low dim
Ayrshire coast. But to your left, north of the Mull, the eye loses
itself in a bewildering panorama of blue mountains : a semi-circle
of them, receding into mysterious distance somewhere in the
highlands of Argyle : then further north, advancing somewhat
towards you and defining its shape clear against the sky is the
lovely and unmistakable moulding of the Paps of Jura : while
still further east and south Islay runs out, making a pendant, as
it were, in the picture, to the Mull of Cantire. Fling over that
beautiful tracery of line the mystery and fascination of Irish
air, which lends to every landscape something of the hues of
pearl, something even of the opal, make the scene change and
shift its prominence and its values, at the will of cloud and sun ;
send blue-green showers travelling over the Sound between you
and your vision of the hills ; suppose a sea, blue, but curled
into white horses by a fresh breeze from the north-west, flashing and leaping in the sunshine ; and you will be glad, if you
are of my mind, to be walking, even toiling, up hills, rather

than on a bicycle, with your eyes on the road before you, picking out the way among ruts and pebbles.

Cushendun, as its name signifies (Foot of the Dun), lies at the point where the Dun river flows into the sea. Glen Dun is not the least beautiful of Antrim's glens, and so you will think as you round Tornamoney Point and see Cushendun Bay under you, with its cliffs rising on the far side; beyond them is Garron Point, running out a matter of eight miles off, while far

Lough na Cranagh (Lake of the Isles).

away beyond you can see now the end of your journey—Island Magee, the peninsula that projects a little east of Larne. Inland, too, the scene is beautiful; the glen runs green and wooded up between its enclosing hills, and at the west it is blocked by a beautiful peak conspicuous for its shape among the rounded summits about it.

On the sharp hill that runs down to the first trees, which make the limit of Glen Dun, there are two spots of a special interest. One is at the crest of the slope, on the right as you go down. Nothing marks it except a few almost imperceptible mounds in the green turf among the whins; but on Sundays you will always see folk sitting there and chatting as they look out over the bay. It is a strange place to forgather in, for that is where they bring children who have died before they were christened; the Roman church, with its terrible logic, allows them no room in consecrated ground. A little further down, perhaps fifty yards before you reach the end of the plantation, stands a single thorn tree in the hedge on the right of the road. That is a fairy thorn, and there is probably not a man in Cushendun who would lay axe to it. Some years ago a great branch broke off it in a storm and lay across the road; and it was hard to find hands in the parish who would consent to remove the wreck of it. There was ill luck for any one that so much as moved a twig of the good people's thorn tree.

A few yards lower again you see too, a pretty, square, low built house standing almost on the water's edge. In the lawn between it and the road stands a fragment of some old building, now a mass of ivy. Quiet and peaceable as the place looks now, there was wild work done there. Donnell Gorme Macdonnell was besieged there by the English in 1585, when his father Sorley, then close on eighty, landed in the bay with his following of redshanks and drove off the besiegers. But Sorley Boy had seen a fiercer fight twenty years before that, when Shane O'Neill defeated the Clandonnell forces at Bally-castle. That was in 1565. Three years earlier the English government knew no worse enemy than Shane O'Neill, and was disposed to favour the Macdonnells in the hope to be rid of him. But in 1563 Shane came to terms, went boldly over to London, and there so impressed Elizabeth with his fierce presence, his following of wild Gallowglasses and his masterful demeanour, that she was ready to concede him all he demanded; he might be the O'Neill and welcome, and Earl of Tyrone to that. Shane came back to Ulster prouder than ever, and set to work to show his zeal, as he said, for the Queen's cause; and how better could he do that than by driving out the

T

interloping Scots, who were settled in such swarms along the
Antrim.   Accordingly, in 1565 he marched north and into the
Glens.

Signal fires blazed on Torr Head, and James Macdonnell,
head of the clan, hastened over from Cantire ; but by the time he
landed in Red Bay, just south of Cushendun, Shane had taken his
castle in the red sandstone cliff and was on his way towards Ballycastle and the Macdonnell sanctuary at Bonamargy.   By the
Margy river the whole force of Clandonnell arrayed itself against
him.   Three Macdonnell brothers went into the fight ; one was
slain, but James, lord of Cantire and Antrim, and Sorley, lord of
the Route, were taken.   Shane continued his progress along the
coast, took Dunseverick, but Dunluce was too hard for him.
Still he had in his hands the master of Dunluce, and for three days
Sorley Boy was kept without food till the garrison surrendered
sooner than let the chief die of starvation.   Shane wrote to the
Lord Deputy a glowing eulogy of his own zeal in the Queen's
service, which had made him lord absolute in the north-east
of Ulster.   The Lord Deputy commended him and asked for
James and Sorley Macdonnell, but Shane declared that he could
not consent to let so precious hostages out of his sight till he
knew the Queen's own pleasure concerning them.   So James and
his wife and Sorley were shut up in a strong castle near Strabane,
where neither Queen nor Deputy could reach them ; and there
after a few months James Macdonnell came obscurely by his
end.   Even after death he remained a captive ; Shane buried him
with much pomp and circumstance in the O'Neills' own ground
at Armagh.   But Sorley was proof against sickness—or it may
be against poison—and two years later, when Shane made his
fatal hosting into Tyrconnell, Sorley was still a prisoner.   So
after the day when Hugh O'Donnell met the O'Neills at the
fords of Swilly and smote them hip and thigh, Shane, hardly
escaping with his life, did not know which way to turn.   On the
north and north-west were the O'Donnells ; on the south the
English ; and on the east the Macdonnells, now leagued with the

English for his overthrow. He had thoughts at first of going to
the Lord Deputy at Dundalk with a halter round his neck :
but he bethought him of Sorley Boy and offered freedom
and friendship to the chief of the Ulster Scots. At
Sorley's advice, as it would seem, he arranged to meet Alexander Og Macdonnell, a surviving brother, who with his lev-
ies was encamped on the hill slope north-west of Cushendun.
Here Shane came bringing Sorley with him, and whether the
Macdonnells meant fairly by him or no it would be hard to say.
There were two days' banqueting, and in the revels Shane's
secretary made a rash speech.   Shane, he said, was of a mind
to marry James Macdonnell's wife, whom he still kept in his
power, and the lady was willing.   The Macdonnells swore it was
a foul lie that their chief's wife would match with the man who
had done to death her husband.   The secretary, in Shane's own
temper, said that the O'Neill was a match good enough for the
Queen of Scots herself ; and Shane, on hearing the debate,
struck in and spoke to the same purpose with such arrogance that
in a minute dirks were out, and, once the work begun, the Scotch
hacked to pieces this scourge of their clan.   His mangled body
was flung into a pit, but a certain wise Englishman of the
nearest garrison, hearing of the result, sent to have the head cut
off, pickled it, and sent it to the Lord Deputy with a claim for
the thousand pounds that had been set upon it.   Fitzwilliam
wrote, exulting in the consummation, but wishing to God that
the traitor's end had been more in accordance with his desert.
The daggers, to his thinking, had done their work too quickly ;
and all he could do was to hoist the great Shane's head and leave
it to blacken—where so many Irish heads had blackened and
were still to blacken—over the gate of Dublin Castle.   The
Macdonnells were more civilised than this English noble in
their vengeance.   Shane's body, wrapped, "for lack of a better
shroud, in a keene's old shirt," was miserably interred at
Glenarm, the home of the Macdonnell chief.   The O'Neills
sent to beg that this great shaker of Ulster might rest with his
own kin.   But the abbot of the monastery answered, " Have

you not in your church James Macdonnell, lord of Antrim and Cantire, who was buried among strangers at Armagh ? Then, whilst you continue to tread on the grave of James, lord of

Glenarm from Coast Road.

Antrim and Cantire, know ye that we in Glenarm will trample on the dust of your great O'Neill."

Yet, after Shane's death, the O'Neills and Macdonnells contracted an alliance. James Macdonnell's wife—the mother

of Ineen Dhu, Red Hugh's fierce mother--was then well
advanced in years, but she could bring with her in dowry
a great army of redshanks. So Turlough Luineach, who
succeeded Shane as the O'Neill, wrote to express his willing-
ness to wed with either mother or daughter. But the Lady
Agnes Campbell, of whom Sir Henry Sidney wrote that she
was "a grave, wise, well-spoken lady, both in Scotch, English,
and French, and very well-mannered," preferred to give her
daughter to Shane's vanquisher, the O'Donnell, and she herself
married Turlough, at a great feast held in Rathlin, when there
was a whole fortnight of banqueting.

Such was the end of Shane the Proud; such the tragedy
enacted somewhere by this still standing fragment of wall.

There are other things, too, to see in Glendun if you care to
give the time. As you enter the village you will find a road
going to the right which follows at some distance the course of
the river ; and up this you ought certainly to go. After about
a mile you will pass on the left a chapel which is obviously
new, in a burying ground where many of the tombstones have
dates going far back, and some of them queer carvings of ships
for the graves of seamen. A little further on the right you reach
a wood, mostly of oak, nestling close to the hillside, and a
cottage by the road. Ask your way there, and they will show
where the altar with the "good stone" is. Here, in this corner
of the wood, the Roman Catholics used to hold their service, at
the foot of an old oak tree. But the people thought it hard
there should be no mark of the sacredness of the place ; and
talk came that there was a "good stone" in one of the Scotch
islands—Staffa or Iona, I know not which. Accordingly some
"boys" of the neighbourhood went over one day in a boat,
and it was a dangerous journey they were on ; for the people
of the island would have had their lives if it were known that
they meant to lay a finger on this treasure ; and besides, who
could say but if they touched a holy thing the power that
guarded it might rise up and drown them for their boldness in the

crossing—as the O'Neills' boat was swamped in Lough Swilly, with the bell of Killydonnell on board of her. With what piety they undertook it, and with what terror they accomplished the task, should one day be written by some one who knows the heart of this glenfolk · but the stone is there now for

Cushendun and Mouth of the Cushendun River.

tourists to see and journalists to write about. It is sculptured and inscribed, with some skill, it seems, but wind and weather have worn it to the stage in which the rudest sculpture is beautiful and the baldest inscription mysterious. Before it people came from miles off to pray, with no shelter but the oak

trees ; till, they say, an Englishman staying in the village was
touched with their devotion and poverty and sent as much
money as sufficed to build them the chapel where now the
congregation assembles.

Leaving this "altar in the wood" you follow the river inland
for about a mile and reach a surprising viaduct which spans
the whole width of the glen, here much contracted   a fine work
but eloquent of a wretched past, for it is one of the many
great undertakings set on foot in Ireland to grapple with famine.
The road that crosses it will take you, after a run of four miles,
tolerably level, into Cushendal, where the Glens of Antrim
Hotel is one of the best country inns to be met with anywhere
in Ireland.

It is, of course, a little shorter to cross the Glendun river at
Cushendun, where it flows into the sea, and so follow the post
route.   But I advise the other way, for it gives you a pleasant
glimpse of Glendun.   And if you have prudently decided to
avoid the coast road round Torr Head, even so I would have
you run into Cushendun, partly to see the "good stone," partly
for the sake of a very pretty village, but chiefly for its associations, as it will one day have a name in literature.   "Moira
O'Neill," of whom I spoke before, lived for many years and
wrote there her first songs and tales of the Glenfolk, than
which nothing more admirable has been written by any of the
several lady writers who have done their best to redeem English-
speaking Ireland from the reproach of lacking a literature.

I am permitted to quote one of her songs :—

"SEA WRACK."

The wrack was dark an' shiny where it floated in the sea,
There was no one in the brown boat but only him an' me ;
Him to cut the sea wrack—me to mind the boat,
An' not a word between us the hours we were afloat.
   The wet wrack,
   The sea-wrack,
   The wrack was strong to cut.

We laid it on the gray rocks to wither in the sun ;
An' what should call my lad then to sail from Cushendun ?
Wi' a low moon, a full tide, a swell upon the deep,
Him to sail the old boat—me to fall asleep.

> *The dry wrack*
> *The sea-wrack*
> *The wrack was dead so soon.*

Thare's a fire low upon the rocks to burn the wrack to kelp :
Thare's a boat gone down upon the Moyle, an' sorra one to help.
Him beneath the salt sea—me upon the shore,—
By sunlight or moonlight we'll lift the wrack no more.

> *The dark wrack,*
> *The sea wrack,*
> *The wrack may drift ashore.*

Lurigethan Hill from above Cushendal.

CHAPTER XIX

Cushendal—Dalfoot—is another of these pretty little villages nestling among trees at the foot of a glen down which runs a river to a sandy beach. The hill Lurigethan which overshadows the town, is strongly marked in outline and more imposing than it is given to many higher mountains to be. Here certainly you will repose comfortably for a night, and what remains of the way to Larne—twenty-five miles—can be done in a single day. It is only twenty-five miles of an excellent and level road, which in itself is worth going to see as a triumph of engineering for it has been formed by blasting a way through the seaward face of the cliffs and using the *débris* as a sea wall.

The road runs inland for about a mile from Cushendal, then you strike the shore of what is called Red Bay, and see Garron

Head on the far side of it. Just before you reach the bay, a spur of the hill runs down towards the road, presenting a fine cliff of red sandstone. In it you can trace the remains of an old castle of the Macdonnells. A hundred yards further on, an

Lurigethan Hill from Cushendal.

arch of the sandstone spans the road, and passing through this you see the little village of Waterfoot. Just at the end of the cliff to the right is a cave which was inhabited till a few years ago by an old woman. From this there is about three miles of road on the south side of the bay to Garron Tower, Lord Londonderry's

great house, which stands on the sheltered side of the head.
This house is soon to be an hotel, and if it has arrived at that
distinction when you get there I would certainly counsel you to
stop there, for the grounds are beautiful.   The rose garden alone
is worth going a long journey to see, and there is a delightful
summer house built on a point overlooking the sea, with a fragrant wood of fir trees behind it. The house was built in 1848 by
Frances Anne, Marchioness of Londonderry, daughter of the
Countess of Antrim, a lady of strongly marked character, which
may be readily traced in several inscriptions that she has set
up along the road and in the grounds.   Beyond Garron I may
frankly say that I have no pretensions to guide you.   You have
still eighteen miles to cover before you reach Larne, and you will
hardly wish to pass Glenarm Castle without seeing it, for it is the
historic seat of the Earls of Antrim.   The original castle which
came to the Macdonnells with Marjory Bisset, and had been
built by her Norman forbears, was pulled down in 1597 when the
Macdonnells withdrew to Dunluce and fortified themselves
there.   When Sir Randal made his peace with James and got
his grant of the Glens and Route, he built the original portion
of the existing castle and enlarged it in 1636.   Since then there
has been much doing and undoing, but Sir Randal's name
stands over the doorway.

"With the leave of God this castle was built by Sir
Randalle McDonnel, Knight, Erle of Antrim, having to wife
Dame Aellis O'Neill, in the year of our Lord God, 1636. Deus
est adjutor meus." And in the churchyard you can still trace the
remains of the Franciscan monastery founded by the Bissets
where the brethren were so proud to "trample on the dust of
your great O'Neill."

But the day from Cushendal will be considerably lengthened
if you decide to see Glen Ariff, and it is one of the prettiest
bits of what one may call artificial scenery in the kingdom.   So
that for your last day on this coast, if you are very energetic,
you may ride from Cushendal, see Glen Ariff, which will take you

three good hours, lunch in the glen, go on to Garron Tower and have tea there, and ride in the cool of the evening the remaining eighteen miles to Larne. But that leaves out Glenarm, so you will be best advised to stop at Garron Tower for the night and

Cushendall.

spend an easy day in exploring Glen Ariff and counting its innumerable waterfalls.

Your best way to get there is to cross the bridge at Water-foot, bicycle along to the far side of the bay, and take the road which leads to the right up the south side of the glen. Go on

up this, keeping the river on your right : you will notice on your
left the track of an old railway cutting, which has not been used
since they gave up working the iron ore on this mountain side.
The nearest rail in use is at Parkmore at the head of the glen,
which it connects by a narrow gauge line with Ballymena. After
about two miles the road turns to the right and crosses a bridge, on
your left you will see a gate lodge. The owner of this place kindly
permits tourists to pass through his grounds, and your best plan
is to keep up the avenue, still having the stream on your right,
and you will begin to see that close before you the wide valley
divides into two, each arm having its separate stream. That
running to the left as you face inland is private property ; and
you must cross its stream by a wooden bridge about a mile from
the avenue gate to enter the system of paths which the Belfast
and Northern Counties Railway has laid out. A few yards
below this wooden bridge is a great fall, forty feet in height,
called Ess-na-Crubh—the Horseshoe Fall.

One thing to lay to heart is this. If by any chance it should
be a day of pelting rain when you think of going to see Glen
Ariff, why then, go all the more. These mountain torrents fill
with extraordinary rapidity and a finer sight than Ess-na-Crubh,
and indeed the whole watercourse, as it was on the day when I
saw it, no one need wish for.

Having crossed the bridge there are paths to right and left.
That to the right leads down stream to the point where the
waters meet, and here are two attractions. One is the great fall
Ess-na-Craoibhe, where the stream from the northern glen
tumbles over a rock ninety feet high. The other is a neat
pavilion where you can be provided with tea. It is well to
remember that by following either of the two streams downward
you will come to refreshment.

But unless you are faint with the way, when you have
crossed the bridge, take up stream to the left—the path leaves
the stream and winds up hill through woods which at the right
season must be a perfect heaven of bluebells, and when I saw

them were starry with wood anemones and primroses. Finally
you emerge on a point whence there is a clear view of the
southern valley running inward, and Glen Ariff in all its widen-
ing expanse, spreading towards the sea ; below you is a great
forest of larch and hazel, hiding somewhere in their recesses

Cushendal.

the tumultuous Watersmeet. For the loveliness that man can
add to the face of mountain landscape without robbing it of
its own wild beauty, it would be hard to match this scene.
Forty years ago a traveller wrote that it was pitiable to see Glen
Ariff left as barren as the other valleys ; now the whole recesses

of these upper glens are deep in larch and hazel. And the
country deserves such embellishment, no less than Killarney or
the Wicklow Dargle: better indeed historically, for only a few
miles inland from the head of this glen is Slemish, the mountain on whose slopes Patrick, as a captive, fed the pigs and
sheep of the master whom he returned to convert ; and on the
hills of the glen lies buried, so they say, the bard Ossian, last
survivor of the Sons of Finn, whom Celtic legend and Celtic
poetry loved to represent as surviving his kinsmen and lingering
latest of the Fionna, till the days of Patrick. Many dialogues
between the pair are told, and the Celtic bards do not give the
worst of the encounter to the old bard-mage, who taunted Patrick
with the unwarlike pursuits of his following and sighed for the
days when men loved the whistle of blackbirds and the cry of
hounds better than the tinkle of bells and the drone of masses.

Leaving your high view-point you must let the path take you
through thick larches till you strike the stream which comes
down from Parkmore, and having struck it you should follow it
to the head. Along both sides paths are cut, and upon any
day, but chiefly on a day of flood, to follow them is a series of
surprises ; fall succeeds fall so quickly and with such infinite
variety of shape and movement. Here, too, you have the work
of man more evidently present ; summer houses are built on
low stages over pools, steps are cut in the rocky sides of the
river, and finally at the very head of the glen a most ingenious
effect is managed. The stream here is strangled between two
walls of rock, a bare five feet apart, and comes down through a
winding cleft. Up this cliff is carried a sort of rustic bridge or
ladder, dexterously placed so as to avoid the rush of water,
though in a flood one crosses it in a shower of spray with a
rushing mass two or three feet off that would carry you a long
way before you could regain your footing—if, indeed, you ever
did. We are all superior people nowadays, and we know that
this kind of manufactured picturesqueness is deplorably obvious
but think, as you are crossing it, how it would have pleased

Walter Scott, and what fair ladies and bewildered heroes would have been romantically led up it, by what formidable caterans and gallowglasses.

Once you have reached this stair you may, with a clear conscience, turn back, unless you wish to walk to the very head of the wooding and look out on the open heather; but in any case be sure to come down the other side of the stream, so as not to miss the Watersmeet, Ess-na-Craoibhe, and your tea.

Waterfoot, looking up the Vale of Glen Ariff.

It is a consideration what to do with your bicycle. On the whole I should advise leaving it at Mr. Dobbs's gate lodge. The alternative is to bring it up across the bridge and take it down at once to the tea house. But in any case be sure you ride back from Glen Ariff down the north side of the glen, for along it there are no less than four waterfalls from the top of the hillside; none of them is great in volume, but they have an enormous drop, and even when they are only a trickle they make beautiful silvery streaks down the hillside.

At the foot of Glen Ariff then this guide ceases to be a guide
to the road, and I have only to wish you a safe and speedy
journey to Larne.   There you will see the curious curving
headland that protects the harbour, whose name, the Curran or
Sickle, recalls the Sicilian Drepanum.   At the end of the Curran
stands a fragment of Olderfleet Castle, built originally by the
Bissets, who held under a grant from Henry III.   It was here
that Edward Bruce landed in 1315, with his army of 6,000, when
he undertook his ill-fated expedition into Ireland.   Olderfleet
was his first capture, and he marched thence to Carrickfergus,
and was there crowned King of Ireland.   Just off the point of
the Curran lies Island Magee, a place of considerable historic
interest.   The Bissets held it as part of their grant, but paid to
the crown as yearly rent—a cast of goshawks from its cliffs.   It
became famous, or infamous, in 1642, by one of the worst
acts in the terrible war of reprisals.   Soldiers from Carrickfergus
attacked the inhabitants and threw numbers of them over the
cliffs.   The details of this story have been questioned, but
Elizabethan methods were not likely to be soon forgotten.

Larne is a convenient place for English tourists to end their
tour, as the mail steamers to Stranraer gives them a short and
pretty crossing, with very few miles of open sea.   But if you
are not tired of your machine you may take another day to ride
the remaining twenty-four miles along the coast road to Belfast.
The road passes, at Ballycarry, near the foot of Larne Lough,
the parish of Kilroot, Swift's first prebend, where that formidable
genius first experienced the bondage of his cloth.   The solitudes
of Antrim had little charm for him after his life in Temple's
household, where famous men came and went, but he attempted
to console himself with women's society.   Perhaps the strangest
of all the strange things he left behind him are his letters to
Varina, as he called Miss Waring, the daughter of a neighbouring gentleman—the only woman who could boast of having
refused Swift.

Your halfway stage is Carrickfergus, a place well worth

U

seeing. It takes its name from the fact that the body of Fergus, one of the early Dalriadic kings, drowned in crossing the Moyle

The Coast Road between Cushendal and Glenarm.

was washed up there. But its interest centres on the castle, built so far back as 1178 by Sir John de Courcy. It stands on a rock about thirty feet high projecting into Belfast Lough, and

the work of the Norman builder still defies time. The walls of
the keep, which is ninety feet high, are nine feet thick, and the
ancient portcullis exists ; and upon the whole there are few better
examples of the Anglo-Norman fortress.   For three centuries it
was the only English stronghold north of the Pale that is
north of Dundalk.   It is now occupied as an ordnance depot.
Prince John landed here in 1210 during the reign of his father
Henry II.   In 1315 Edward Bruce with his Scots occupied the
town and besieged the garrison, who were starved into surrender,
but not before they had eaten thirty Scotch prisoners, taken in
a sortie. Bruce was crowned king of Ireland there and Carrickfergus remained his capital till 1318, when he was defeated and
slain by the English colonists at Dundalk.   It was at Carrickfergus that William landed in 1690 on his way to the Boyne,
and a stone upon the quay is shown as the first stone in Ireland
that the monarch "of glorious, pious and immortal memory"
set foot on.   In 1760 a French expedition under Thurot took the
town, but were soon afterwards routed by an English squadron
under Elliott , and a famous action was fought in the bay by the
great Paul Jones against the *Drake* frigate.

Lovers of Sir Samuel Ferguson's poetry will remember
Carrickfergus as the scene of his spirited ballad *Willy
Gilliland*, which tells the story of an outlawed Covenanter's
revenge.

From Carrickfergus it is a short ten miles into Belfast.   I
have no intention of describing the numerous public buildings,
which are such as are generally called " handsome," and lack all
artistic and historic interest.   But it may be worth while to
attempt some sketch of the history of this remarkable town which
has advanced in population and importance during this century at
least as rapidly as any town in the United Kingdom, while
every other town in Ireland with the single exception of Derry,
has been either stationary or retrograde.   At the beginning of
this century it numbered under 20,000 inhabitants, by 1900 its
population will be little short of 300,000.

Belfast stands on the Lagan river, where, flowing into the lough, it separates Antrim from Down. There was no Celtic town

Ess-na-Larach Vale of Glen Ariff.

here, but the ford at the tideway was of strategic importance, and in the reign of Edward III., an Anglo-Norman castle was built

there. It was destroyed by Bruce during his period of kingship
at Carrickfergus, and after his defeat probably fell into Irish
hands. With the beginning of the sixteenth century began the
systematic attempt of the English to reconquer Ulster, where
they held nothing except the castle of Carrickfergus. The
Earl of Kildare as Lord Deputy made inroads into the province

Ballygally Castle.

in 1503 and 1512, and on each occasion he burnt Belfast. In
1552 the castle was repaired and garrisoned and granted to
Hugh MacNeil. Hugh was slain by the Scots and the castle
fell into the hands of the redoubtable Shane O'Neill. But it
was never of any importance to the Irish chiefs, who were not
seafaring folk, and Sir John Perrot in 1582 probably foresaw little

difficulty in securing the port when he advised the establishment of shipwrights there—a far-sighted policy, but not followed, as the growing strength of Tyrone made it impossible for the English to venture beyond the Pale.   Tyrone and his party fell, and in 1612 the castle, town, and manor of Belfast were granted

Garron Tower.

to Sir Arthur Chichester. From that year dates the town's history as a town, not merely as an outlying fortress. A corporation was appointed, two members were to be sent to Parliament, and the town was allowed to erect a wharf, although Carrickfergus as a rival port looked jealously at this privilege.

The new settlers in Down and Antrim were mostly Scots, and Belfast became a centre of Presbyterianism. The members of the Presbytery protested against the execution of Charles I. and provoked an angry reply from Milton, who declared that "the blockish presbyters of Clandeboy" were "egregious liars and impostors" who meant to stir up

Carnlough, between Glenarm and Cushendal.

rebellion "from their unchristian synagogue at Belfast in a barbarous nook of Ireland."

But the town's history is essentially commercial. In 1637 Strafford laid the foundation of its prosperity by buying out certain monopolies possessed by Carrickfergus, thus practically opening trade in the new port. Belfast became a centre for the exportation of linen, which had always been woven in Ireland. After the Revocation of the Edict of Nantes Huguenots settled there, bringing with them skill in the making of damasks and cambrics. But the special impetus to prosperity in Belfast was given by the iniquitous measures passed under William III., which killed the woollen manufactures in Ireland, then competing successfully with those of England. England was not interested in the linen trade, so William could afford to encourage it, and by way of compensation he did so, patronising especially the chief Huguenot manufacturers. The town grew steadily during the eighteenth century, more than doubling its population.

It is curious now to reflect that Belfast was one of the great centres of disaffection and opposition to the union a century ago. Its population, mainly Presbyterian, was strongly touched with democratic views. The French Revolution appealed to them and they were in close sympathy with the American States. The famous Society of United Irishmen was organised in Belfast; but that town has always had a genius for keeping out of harm's way. Neither in 1642 nor in 1689 did it emulate the heroism of Derry or share its sacrifices; and in 1798 the rebellion that broke out in consequence of the United Irishmen's conspiracy did not affect the place where the plot was hatched.

Since 1800 Belfast has been a stronghold of the Protestant ascendency; the gulf which separated Nonconformists from Churchmen in political sympathies has been bridged over. And Belfast certainly has reason to bless the union, for she is the one Irish town which has won a share in the great access of industrial wealth produced by Free Trade. Between 1861 and 1871 the population rose from 119,242 to 207,671. Since then the great shipbuilding industry has developed at an extraordinary pace. The Victoria Channel from the quays direct to the sea has been cut at great cost, and there

is no better example of a great port that has been created in
spite of natural difficulties.

As for the general appearance of the place, it is one of the
cleanest among manufacturing towns.   Its situation, too, on
Belfast Lough is picturesque, and there are fine views of the
Great Cave Hill, which overhangs the town and silhouettes
against the sky a strange likeness of Napoleon's profile.

Still it is not a town which will commend itself much to

Larne.

the pleasure seeker, and except for the interest of Carrickfergus
I would recommend you to end your tour at Larne.

But whether you stop at Larne or Belfast, you will have
come a far way from the wild places of the West, where the
few human habitations are the tiny scattered white-washed
cottages with a row of projecting stones back and front let
into the walls to moor the thatch against the storm winds of
the Atlantic.   Each is different ; East and West, Celt and
Saxon or Scot, Catholic and Presbyterian, have not harmonised
too well at times ; but the union in disunion of the two

makes up modern Ireland, a country which is young yet : which, as Curran said, will never be rotten till it is ripe. And whether in West or East the tourist will, I hope, find besides much natural beauty, a common element of Irish character in a ready and kindly welcome.

Glenarm.

CHAPTER XX

SALMON fishing in England, and in most parts of Scotland, has become almost exclusively a rich man's amusement. In Donegal it is still within the reach of everybody who can afford to pay five or ten shillings a day for his pleasure. Of course, to get the pick of it, you must pay more than that : but it is a great point that you can get it by paying for a single day or a week. The best known of the Donegal fisheries is that at Ballyshannon, where the river being of large volume is more or less continuously fishable, but the charges are naturally high.

Next to that comes, I should say, the Gweedore fishing, which has many points to recommend it. There is a good hotel to stay at, where things are arranged for the convenience of anglers, and the river is the ideal thing of its kind : about five miles of water from lake to sea, and no still water in the whole of it. Runs succeed each other with the infinite and beautiful variety that makes it a pleasure merely to put a fly over the waters of a mountain stream. The whole river can be fished from either bank, and there is no tree along the course of it. Down near the sea it flows through a cliffy gorge, and one is often fishing a deep swirling pool, pent in between rock sides fifteen or twenty feet high ; and though the fish run small, as indeed they all do in these small rivers, the strength of the water and the broken ground along the banks must make playing them an exciting business. Over twenty have been killed by one rod in a single day, and I should say that in most seasons some lucky man gets a bag of ten. But of course this sort of thing has to be paid for. Ten shillings a day is the charge for the river, and in addition to that there is your gillie. You are entitled to keep one fish for a day, but not more than two in the same week. In the months of April and May the river is free to any guest at the hotel. I could not advise any one to count on the April fishing. Last April up to the 5th only one fish had been killed in the river, and that was in the lowest hole where the fish come up with the tide, and if they do not find sufficient water, the spring fish go back again and hang about in the estuary. But a fresh would have brought up some, and in May I see no reason why there should not be excellent sport. June and July, however, are the best months. The lakes are free at all times to guests, and in August they should be as good a chance as the river. The first thing, however, to remember, is that you must take out your salmon license —which costs £1—in the district, and a salmon license is necessary for white trout fishing. A license can be had at the Gweedore Hotel or at Rosapenna ; in fact at any fishing centre. The second thing to impress upon your mind is that salmon fishing is a delusion. There is no better sport, but none more annoying; and on these small rivers the conditions are particularly aggravating. Where there are trout, you can generally induce them to take at some time in the day or night, unless the water is muddy—and then you can get them with a worm, if you stoop to that branch of the art. But a river may be cram full of salmon and for days together, even with cloudy skies, they will never really rise if there has been a long spell of low water. I have seen the long pool at the Lackagh broken every minute

Without a License

with rising fish and not been able to stir one, day after day. It was then that Neddy Gallagher used to sit down and tell us about an Englishman that once took the river for two months and paid a hundred pounds for it. "The first month he fished it up and he fished it down and niver turned a tail ; and the second month he sat down on a rock in the river and he to the cursing. That was the sorest time ever I put in. But the only thing he hooked in the two months was a heifer."

Still, that was exceptional, and there is always this about a salmon, that he does not know his own mind. You may fish over him twenty times and the twenty-first he may take you. The odds are that he won't, but there is no certainty against it as there would be with a trout. I saw a salmon killed this year on the Lennan in dead still water, without the ghost of a ripple on it. He had risen some time in the afternoon, but refused to come back in spite of many offers. Just before dark my friend went out again on to the pool. Four times we drifted the boat up and down past that fish, and four times the flies were put into the exact spot—a little creek by the bank about a yard square—where he was lying. Then we tried the head of the pool, and coming down the cast was made again, and he sucked down the fly somewhere deep below the surface. In the same way, at the Lackagh, I have seen the eel-weir fished for twelve hours on end by a keeper. Within one half-hour in the day he killed two fish, but he had fished the same spot for hours before and hours after without a rise.

It is a great point in the Gweedore river that there is no long pool of this sort above the tideway, with a weir above it for the fish to gather in. The salmon leap is a good half-mile up, and below that there is a series of rapids and holes, in any one of which a fish may lie, so that there is always broken water to fish in. On the Lackagh and the Lennan the fish gather in a long stretch of smooth water, and without wind fishing is hopeless. The Lackagh, flowing from Glen Lough to Sheephaven, is barely two miles long. There is one throw called

The Throat, where it leaves the lake ; then comes about a mile of continuous fall, too shallow to fish except actually in a flood. Then you come to a hole called the Grass Garden, about fifty yards long, with a run at the head of it ; immediately below that is the pool of two hundred yards or so, and at the head a stream is made by an old eel-weir which is probably the best salmon throw in the county. The Lackagh is free to guests at the Rosapenna Hotel up to the end of July : it is an early river and quite worth fishing in March and April. After July it is reserved by Lady Leitrim. At all seasons the Leitrim fishing is only one side, but there is always plenty of water in the pool, when two rods can fish facing each other. Glen Lough is also a capital chance for salmon, and the white trout-fishing in both river and lough may be excellent in August and September. Indeed, a wise man would let the salmon alone most days and fish for white trout and also for brown, which are plentiful of the herring size—the same flies do for both —but the worst of salmon fishing is that one is always tempted to give up the certainty of amusement with trout for the chance of the stronger excitement—which is worth the sacrifice, *if you get it ;* but woe is me for the blank days I have spent!

I cannot recommend Rosapenna as a fishing centre in August, for the place is demoralised by golf, the river is not available, and they do not let you keep your fish. Still, the passing angler might do worse than try a day on Lough Kiel. He will see one of the wildest places in Donegal, and will have a chance of getting really large trout. One weighing 12½ pounds was caught there a few years ago. It is one of the few places in Donegal where the minnow is of any use.

One of the best spots in the county for an angler to pitch his headquarters is Ramelton, a village of some 1,500 people, situated in the valley of the Lennan, at the point where it flows into Lough Swilly. There is a hotel there—The Stewart Arms —which needs only good management to make it comfortable enough, but I cannot speak of it from experience, and the

reports I have are not encouraging. Of the fishing I can.
Nearly all the river is free to everybody, though in certain parts
the riparian owners will not allow trespass; but a civil request
would probably get over any difficulty of this sort where it
exists. The part which is preserved is the stretch from the
tideway up to the weir at Drummonaghan bridge—about half-
a-mile in all—and this is incomparably the best of the fishing.
The Lennan is, I should imagine, the earliest river in Ireland,
and in the old days, before the close season was instituted, it
used to be a custom for the squire of the parish, who owns the
weir boxes, to present his friends with fresh-run salmon at
Christmas. The fishing now opens on the first of February,
and efforts are being made to shift the date to January 1st—
beginning the close season at October 1st. This early fishing
is the best, so much so that in February, March and April, each
rod pays £1 a day, but after the 1st of May only ten shillings.
This sounds pretty stiff, but only two rods are allowed on the
water and there are no supplementary expenses. Moreover, the
angler is entitled to keep one fish, and if he chooses to do so he
can cede this to the fishery at the London market rate, which
at that season of the year averages close on two shillings a pound.
This year out of the first forty sovereigns paid, only five or six
represented blank days; the most successful fisherman killed
forty fish in his first ten days; nine being the best day and none
blank. The same gentleman, made a record two years ago for
the river, killing eleven fish which weighed 125 pounds. It
sounds as if there should be good fishing all through the
river while men are killing three or four fish in the day commonly in one part of it; but I am told that the spring fish do
not, as a rule, go up above the first hole till March. This year,
however, there were plenty right up to Gartan by St. Patrick's
Day.

The pool at Ramelton is an awkward place to fish, being a
long stretch of flat water so much sheltered that few winds
strike it; but the fish at this early season appears to take so

freely that they can be got even in bright weather and smooth
water. Later in the year from April onwards, however many
there may be in it, it is much harder to stir them. August,
and especially September, generally bring some good sport,
and a day's white trout fishing in the shallow water just
about Ramelton bridge is one of the red-letter days in my
recollection.

But the angler staying at Ramelton would, of course, be
very foolish—except it may be in February—to limit his
fishing to the pool. At any time when there is plenty of
water the upper river is a good chance, and after a fresh
probably a better chance than the stretch below Drummonaghan waterfall. Suppose then you go up it. The
waterfall is made by a mill carry some fifteen feet high,
with a boarded passage for the salmon to get up by ; and
there is no finer sight than to see this on a day of flood
when the water comes roaring over the stones, brown and
frothy, and every now and then you see a flash of purple, a
black back shows itself, scarring the smooth rush up the
salmon gap. If the fish keeps perfectly straight he gets over,
but let him slew the least to one side, and he is swung broadside on ; then comes a second or two of frantic struggling till
he gives up the battle and rolls down on his side, showing silver
at every turn. Sometimes the whole place is alive with them,
and you see the fish endeavouring to scramble their way by
side nooks and corners in the carry, often almost on the very
bank. It is these wild rushes that make salmon the easiest
fish in the world to capture, if they are not protected ; you
can shoot them, you can gaff them, you could frequently even
take them out with your hands. After a long drought, when
the first drops of a fresh come down to the lower holes—
especially in autumn—the fish go simply wild with desire for
the upper waters and the spawning grounds. I have seen
them on the Lackagh, when a hundred or so were lying
under the bridge in the tideway, on the evening before a

X

fresh, move up on the first of the tide. Between this point and the pool lies a long shallow stretch full of great rocks; and into this the fish hurried, not waiting for the tide to cover it, but scuttering through little runs of water, often with their backs clean out.

From above the Drummonaghan carry there is a very long stretch—about a mile and a half of deep smooth water. Indeed, Drummonaghan bridge is one of the prettiest spots in the country, with the river racing and tearing over the fall, under the bridge and down through a shaded gorge where trees almost meet above it; while above the carry it stretches smooth past a green slope on its right bank and on its left a fringe of snipe-haunted bog, inside of which lies the road and inside that again Drummonaghan wood, full of bilberries in summer and woodcock in winter—a place of pleasant recollections. If you follow the stream on its right bank, you pass along a range of "holms" or water meadows, largely filled with rushes and cut by drains not easy to cross. This part of the river is little fished, and it is much hampered by trees, but there are good throws for salmon in it, and it is certainly full of trout. Probably, on a good day, if one could get a wind on it, it would be the best chance of all for a full basket, and the fish would run heavier. But in that country people turn up their noses at trout fishing, and in point of fact, when the good day comes, one is off after the delusive salmon. But I should very much like to see what a skilful dry fly fisher could do there on a calm evening in summer, dodging in and out between the trees. The ordinary Lennan trout is almost herring size—three or four to the pound. I have killed hundreds of them and not one in the hundred over a pound weight. But I have twice killed four dozen to my own rod, and that is a good day anywhere. Also I have known of big trout—2lbs. and upwards—being got in the evenings about Claragh by dapping under the trees. However, this water between Claragh bridge and Drummonaghan

is to me comparatively unexplored. Just above Claragh
the dead water ends and for a mile or so there is beautiful
fishing : swift runs alternating with pools, and at the bend of
the river one great hole, Lagmore, which is generally full of
salmon. Above Tully bridge there is another few hundred yards
of rapids—with one excellent salmon throw : then come two low

Donegal.

carries and then begins a stretch of still water up to
Drummon bridge, where there is one of the best spots for both
salmon and trout. From Drummon the river has a course
of, it may be, a mile and a half, through flat bogs on either
hand, until you get to Lough Fern. Lough Fern is a large
shallow sheet of water about two miles by one, and it is

probably as good a piece of free fishing as exists.
From April to October it is a good chance for salmon
—though I have never known of anything startling done
in it: five salmon to two rods is the best. But this
year before June several rods had got two fish in the day :
and on any sort of fishing day you can get a dozen of trout,
while three or four dozen to two rods is very ordinary fishing.
Boats are kept on it, which cost five shillings a day, by
Margaret Boyle, who also puts up anglers in a cottage, so
clean and comfortable that it is a much needed example to
the country side. If you stay with Margaret you can fish the
lake or the lower river or the upper—for the Lennan just
comes into Lough Fern and out again within a matter of
three hundred yards—and you will have pleasant scenery all
round you. To the south of the lake is Moyle Hill and
Moyagh, Mr. Swiney's house—which is generally to be let in
summer—to the east the view is blocked by the Fanad Hills
above Mulroy—to the north is Lough Salt immediately above
you—and to the west you look up the river valley to Kilmacrenan, and away back to the Glen Veagh mountains and
the sharp crest of Errigal.

If you are at Ramelton, Lough Fern is four miles out along
a level road—but I must say a very ill-kept one—about half an
hour on a cycle. But this lake and the river are by no means
your only resources. If you get on the top of Moyle Hill—
about five hundred feet—you see eleven lakes within a radius
of five miles. Lough Keel is visible on the southern slope of
Lough Salt, and this can only be fished with Lady Leitrim's
permission. There is no restriction on any of the others.
Lough Fern is below you to the north. East, away above
Milford, is Lough Columb, but you had better let that alone.
It is a big lake, over a mile in circumference, and the trout
there are like salmon, short, thick and red-fleshed, running
over two pounds. But the story is that no man can get more
than two in the day, and the only acquaintance of mine who beat

the record got a third actually into the boat, when it made a
jump and a wriggle and got over the side. There is generally
no boat there and the place is little fished—unless it is poached
with the otter ; so an enterprising person might destroy the
tradition and win glory by dry-fly fishing, or possibly by the
minnow. The minnow is absolutely useless on Lough Fern
and the Lennan, but on Lough Keel it succeeds, and Lough
Columb, like Lough Keel, is very deep. Besides this there are a
host of smaller lakes in the bog-land that lies between Ramelton
and Milford, varying from a mile to three or four hundred yards
round, all of them with trout, and all of them, I suspect, with
big trout. It would be easy to hire a flat-bottomed punt in
Ramelton and get her put on any of these places. I fished
one some years ago, with a friend, in summer when the water
was dead low and the salmon fishing hopeless. It was a tiny
lake, a couple of stone-throws across, but surrounded by a belt
of shaking bog and bulrushes so that the otter could not be
worked, and probably no fly had been on it for ten years.
In two hours we got about a dozen, and each of us got a big
one—as big fish go in Donegal. The fish were keenest on the
Alexandra fly with its silver body, from which I infer that they
would have accepted a minnow. Remembering how rare it is
on Lough Fern to see a fish over a pound, it would not surprise
me to see a fish of four or five pounds in one of these bog
holes, as in a dozen we got two weighing about three pounds
between them, and I lost another, which jumped ; it looked
much bigger and was certainly not less big than the best we
got.

   There is to me a certain charm about fishing places that are
not like the river in Galway, where you stand on a quay with a
dry goods store behind you and thrash water that has been
thrashed every fishing day for a generation, and I have often
thought I should like to take a Berthon boat or canoe and
thoroughly investigate these little loughs. But there would
always be the temptation to go and risk your sovereign or half-

sovereign on the pool, or pursue the unappreciative salmon
from Lagmore up to Tully, from Tully to Drummon, and from
Drummon past the "thorn-hole" to Lough Fern and the
throws above it. Anyhow, I think any one who goes to
Ramelton with reasonable expectations will have no cause to
find fault with my suggestion.

There is one other hint which I throw out to the enterprising.
At a certain place in the narrows of Mulroy the tide runs like
a mill-race, and then, if you get the right time of tide when
the white trout are running up, you will get in the salt water
such fly-fishing as people only dream of—a school of white
trout all mad for the fly ; or you can meet them in a boat. But
they pass and are gone, and after a wild ecstasy of half an hour
or so you are left lamenting. I know nothing about this fishing—
or about trolling for white trout with a sand eel, which is also said
to give wonderful sport : but I have heard people speak of it
almost with tears in their eyes, and they were truthful for
fishermen.

A few hints as to tackle may follow this disjointed list of
recommendations. Bring your own gaff and landing net, and
get a gaff that is easy to carry, for you will have to get through
a good many hedges. A fourteen foot rod is amply big enough
for all you will want : on the pool at Ramelton they use a
sixteen foot, but nowhere else to my knowledge. Of course, if
you are going regularly to camp in one place, there is no
reason against bringing the contents of a tackle-maker's shop,
but mind you bring a fourteen foot rod. Also, do not be
deluded into buying large flies. What tackle-makers sell as
medium should be the largest and have plenty of small ones.
In summer you will often be reduced to fishing with stout trout
tackle and white trout flies. Patterns vary, but generally speaking the very bright ones do not answer. At Gweedore they swear
by the Jock Scott, and won't use the Butcher. At Ramelton it
is just the opposite. For the spring fishing at Ramelton blue
flies—the Blue Doctor and Greenwell—are said to answer, but

salmon are unaccountable. My friend on the pool killed his
eleven fish one day on a small Blue Doctor used as a bob ; next
day with the same cast he got five or six, but not one rose to the
same fly.   It is essential to have a good many patterns—
ranging from lake trout size upwards—of clarets, fiery browns
and hare's ear, with olive hackle through it. The orange grouse
also—the best trout fly in this county—is said to do well for
salmon. As to white trout, the same applies, though nearly all
I have killed myself were on a common blue fly, dark wing,
blue silk body with tinsel : one of the regular stock patterns.
The Alexandra also is a good fly. For brown trout nothing
looks nearly so killing as the wonderful confections of English
makers, with cork bodies, tails that stick up, and a regular ento-
mological classification; but for practical purposes I had rather
fish with a hare's ear, black and orange, orange grouse, or the
other conventional arrangements. It is my belief that Donegal
trout are accustomed to them and prefer them.   In any case I
believe in a fly with a good fuzzy body, though not tied—as
Irish makers, and particularly the local sweep or other expert,
generally tie them—on coarse gut. The local tied flies are
excellent things to send as patterns to be copied, with trustworthy hooks and gut that has some delicacy about it.

To give an appearance of system to this chapter I will
append a detailed list of Donegal fishing possibilities ; omitting
the Erne, of which I know nothing.

The first place is Carrick, where you are offered two salmon
rivers and several lakes absolutely free of charge, and are
allowed to keep your fish—only, you must take out a salmon
license in the hotel even if you already have one. I have not
tried the fishing, but mean to do so before long, for it is a
tempting offer. Next comes Ardara, where the Ardara river
is free, so are several brown trout loughs, but the Ownea is
preserved, and Mr. McNelis, the hotel proprietor, rents about
two miles of it above the tideway—beautiful fishing water
where I lost a fine salmon. They say that in August the tide-

way which runs down through sands affords excellent white
trout fishing. The conditions are a payment of 5s. a day, only
exacted on condition that you kill fish. Next I may mention
Dungloe, where there is a large number of lakes, some good
for white trout; the charge is 15s. a week for a fishing ticket.
At Gartan you have Lough Akibbon and Gartan Lough; in
the latter trout are abundant, but small, in Lough Akibbon
they run larger. There is a trifling charge of 1s. 6d. a day.
The Lennan, in its upper waters, is as good as in any other
part from June onward, and it is charming water. It has,
moreover, the great advantage of being deep and not a flood
river.

Of Gweedore, of Rosapenna and Ramelton I have already
spoken. These three rivers are the only ones of any use for
salmon before June.

The cyclist can, of course, carry the whole paraphernalia of
two rods, gaff, and landing net on his machine. But my
advice, on the whole, if you really mean fishing, is to settle at
some place like Carrick. If you merely want an odd day take
a trout rod and net which are no great encumbrance. Have a
good stiff rod of twelve feet with a spare top; take out your
salmon license and fish for white trout when you get half a
chance. Keep thirty or thirty-five yards on your reel and a
salmon cast in your fly book, and then if you meet a good day
you need not be a bit afraid to fish for grilse in any of these
small rivers.

As to golf, I must rely on the testimony of an expert. The
first links you meet is at Rosapenna, an 18-hole course, part of
which is not up to the best standard. Next comes Port Salon,
absolutely first-class. On Lough Swilly there are two other
links, one at Mackamish three miles from Rathmullen, a pretty
9-hole course but too small. The other is Lisfannon, half-
way between Fahan and Buncrana, a very good 9-hole course.
That exhausts Donegal. In Antrim, Portrush is classic, and
at Ballycastle and Larne there are decent little links.

Every August a series of golfing competitions is organised, beginning at Lisfannon and ending at Rosapenna, and it is a pleasant way of making a tour through this part of the county even if you go no further. Colonel Barton, of the Port Salon Hotel, will no doubt always be glad to give information as to dates and arrangements for this outing.

It remains to say a word as to the hotels. I have stayed at nearly all in the county. On the Antrim coast they are fully civilised, and I need not particularise. But in Donegal, though I have always had a clean bedroom and civility, I have sometimes found things rough and untidy. All the decent hotels in the county—with the exception of the Lough Swilly Hotel at Buncrana—have been started by gentlefolks, and mostly not as a business speculation. The best of them all is Rosapenna, which is as good as you would expect to find at an English watering place. Port Salon should rank next, then Carrick and Gweedore ; and I would make a special class for Mrs. Johnson's St. Columb's Hotel at Gartan, which is so small as hardly to be fairly compared with the others, but is perhaps the best appointed and served of them all.

The race of professional hotel-keepers in all the outlying parts of Ireland will have to move with the times. It would pay any one of them well to send a son to serve an apprenticeship in some good English hotel and see how things are done. The average Englishman expects to have hot water brought to him and not to ring for it, however willingly it may be brought. Still there is a certain advance in this respect, and, at least, if you ask for it the request will be understood. Twenty years ago a gentleman I knew of went to stay at an inn to fish. At eight next morning he began to clamour for hot water. He was surprised to see a look of surprise on the servant's face, and still more surprised at the long delay. Ultimately he heard steps approaching, and with them the clink of glasses. The door opened and in came the hot water on a tray accompanied by lemon, sugar, and a lavish measure of whisky. That was how they understood hot water in Crees-lough.

However, the English are a great race, and if they take to going to Ireland they will undoubtedly reform the hotels there as they have reformed over Switzerland and half the Continent ; indeed the thing is largely done already, and my earnest and final recommendation is that they should go and complete the good work and make friends with their fellow subjects over the Channel.

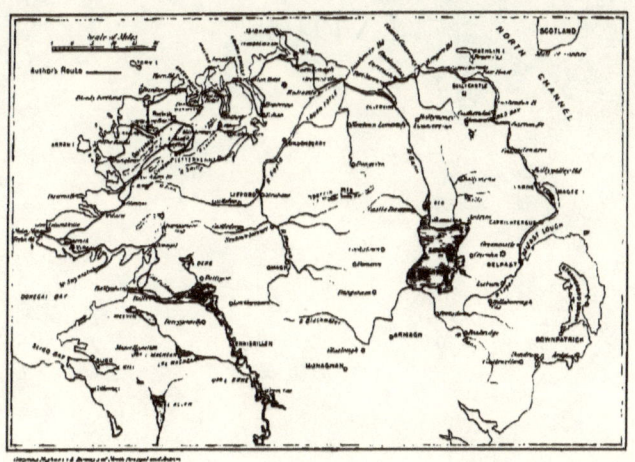

Chapman-Mytton's Map of North Donegal and Antrim

INDEX

INDEX

THE END

RICHARD CLAY AND SONS, LIMITED, LONDON AND BUNGAY.

THE
HIGHWAYS & BYWAYS
SERIES.

Extra crown 8vo. cloth elegant, gilt tops, 6s. each.

Highways and Byways in Donegal and
ANTRIM. By STEPHEN GWYNN. With Illustrations by HUGH THOMSON.

DAILY CHRONICLE.—"Charming . . . Mr. Gwynn makes some of the old legends live again for us, he brings the peasants before us as they are, his descriptions have the 'tear and the smile' that so well suit the country, and with scarcely an exception he has brought his facts and his figures up to date . . . Above all, he shows that he knows the people; he enters into their minds in a way no Englishman could . . . Most entertaining and admirably illustrated."

Highways and Byways in North Wales.
By A. G. BRADLEY. With Illustrations by HUGH THOMSON and JOSEPH PENNELL.

PALL MALL GAZETTE. — "The book is crammed, surfeited, with picturesque detail, every natural and historical feature is dwelt upon with affectionate interest and consummate skill of description, and the drawings are more than adequate. To read this fine book makes us eager to visit every hill and every valley that Mr. Bradley describes with such tantalising enthusiasm. It is a work of inspiration, vivid, sparkling, and eloquent—a deep well of pleasure to every lover of Wales."

ACADEMY.—" May be regarded as a standard work for all visitors to North Wales."

ST. JAMES'S GAZETTE.—"A worthy successor to Mr. A. H. Norway's *Highways and Byways in Devon and Cornwall*, and like that delightful book, has the inestimable advantage of illustration by Mr. Joseph Pennell, and Mr. Hugh Thomson—an ideal partnership."

DAILY CHRONICLE.—"The illustrations are supplied by Mr. Joseph Pennell and Mr. Hugh Thomson, and it would be very difficult to see how Messrs. Macmillan could improve so strong a combination of artistic talent. . . . This book will be invaluable to many a wanderer through the plains and mountains of North Wales."

STANDARD.—" Written with knowledge and humour. . . . Nothing but praise is due to the pictures of places, and humorous incidents of olden times, with which Mr. Joseph

Pennell and Mr. Hugh Thomson have enlivened a welcome and artistic book."

GLOBE.—" Must be acceptable to all lovers of the beautiful in art and nature."

Highways and Byways in Devon and CORNWALL. By ARTHUR H. NORWAY. With Illustrations by J. PENNELL and H. THOMSON.

SPEAKER.—" Mr. Pennell's exquisite drawings re-create for us our country, not indeed more beautiful than it really is, but more beautiful than ninety-nine in a hundred would ever discover without the artist's eye to help them. . . . Many have written books of their itineraries in the West of England, but Mr. Norway's is the most delectable."

DAILY CHRONICLE.—" So delightful that we would gladly fill columns with extracts were space as elastic as imagination. . . . The text is excellent ; the illustrations of it are even better."

PALL MALL GAZETTE.—"As refreshing and exhilarating as a breeze from the moors in a man-stifled town."

WESTMINSTER GAZETTE. — " Will be read with intense interest by every west-countryman, from Axminster to the Land's End, and from Land's End to Lynton, for within this triangle lie the counties of Devon and Cornwall."

ACADEMY.—" Mr. Norway has made a book that is pleasant to read, and the illustrations are—Mr. Pennell's."

DAILY NEWS.—" It may be truly said that every landscape gains in beauty, that each old story finds new pathos under his skilful hands, and that he has touched nothing that he has not adorned."

TIMES.—"A happy mixture of description, gossip, and history, and an agreeable style, would make the book welcome to all lovers of that exquisite region, even without the help of the illustrations by Mr. Joseph Pennell and Mr. Hugh Thomson, with which the book is so well furnished. These artists' names and styles are so familiar that we need say no more than that they have given their best work to the book."

To be Published Shortly.

Highways and Byways in the County of York. By ARTHUR H. NORWAY. With Illustrations by JOSEPH PENNELL and HUGH THOMSON.

Highways and Byways in Normandy. By PERCY DEARMER, M.A. With Illustrations by JOSEPH PENNELL.

MACMILLAN AND CO., LTD., LONDON

10.4.99.

www.ingramcontent.com/pod-product-compliance
Lightning Source LLC
Chambersburg PA
CBHW031338070726
47496CB00017B/1203